SOLE SURVIVOR

WILLIAM ODAY

Cover by Christian Bentulan

Edited by Walt Hunt

WANT BOOKS FOR FREE?

Join the Readers Group to get a free copy of The Last Day, Sole Prey, and Saint John. One novel, one novella and one short story, all for free. You'll also receive exclusive discounts on new releases, other freebies, and lots more.

Go to WWW.WILLIAMODAY.COM to find out more.

READERS ARE SAYING

"This story is simply amazing! I could not put it down!"

"This was a fun fun ride!"

"Exciting and full of adventure!"

"Kept me up at night reading."

"Action packed story!!"

"Another great read from Oday!"

"A page-turning thrill ride."

"You gotta read this!"

"This story has it all.....mystery, action, romance and humor."

"A must read!"

"I love this author and this series!"

EXTINCTION CRISIS SERIES

Any man whose errors take ten years to correct is quite a man.

— *J. Robert Oppenheimer*

1

DR. HARI GANESH hated that mankind's survival hung by the ragged thread of petty politics and budget subcommittees. That the future of humanity might depend upon available, and yet unallocated, resources made his jaws clench and stomach burn.

Such infuriating ignorance!

And he had another call later that day in which he would be required to grovel and beg and assure. All for a cause that should've required no persuasion.

The thought turned his stomach and left him feeling agitated. He would need to remain calm to effectively do the job. And so he'd decided to go for a walk in the garden to settle his mind.

But this was no ordinary garden.

He exited the elevator and approached the soldier standing guard at the security door that led to the subterranean gardens level. The football field sized cavern was his favorite location in the vast underground complex that was Project Hermes. It was one of the few places where he could temporarily escape the burden of being the director.

All of the expectations.

All of the achievements and disappointments.

All his responsibility.

And he felt the weight of the upcoming collider test more keenly than anyone could ever understand.

Out of long familiarity, the soldier nodded as Hari swiped his key card over the reader. It blinked green and the door silently slid open revealing a narrow corridor beyond.

He followed the winding hall carved out of solid rock. He trailed a finger over the dark surface, feeling the sharp ridges and cavities where a chisel or hammer had long ago left its mark. The upper offices level had been finished with sheetrock walls and ceilings, low pile carpet, ninety degree corners and all the small things that made a space feel normal.

The lower levels, on the other hand, had been finished to a functional state. Further improvements had been deemed too costly and unnecessary.

It hadn't been Hari's decision as most of the complex had been finished when he first arrived so long ago, but he approved nonetheless.

The undulating rock surface gave one a sense of place. Aside from the lack of windows, the upper offices felt like they could be in any skyscraper or office building in the world. And it made the transition to the other levels that much more jarring.

Thick cables ran overhead along the center of the corridor. A glowing yellow light every dozen feet kept most of the shadows at bay. The hue of the lights had been carefully selected to match the wavelength of sunlight.

Humans evolved up on the surface and so the project had made many accommodations to make life hundreds of feet below healthier, more pleasant and sustainable.

But there was only so much that could be done.

The constant hum of the air exchangers and the ever-present odor of mildew mixed with the harsh cleaners that fought to control it were subtle reminders of the limits of human ingenuity.

Hari rarely noticed them anymore.

Their ubiquity made them fade into the background.

He arrived at the final security door and again swiped his card. The reader flashed green and the magnetic locks disengaged. The door slid open and the lush scent of thriving vegetation enveloped him.

Entering the gardens was always literally a breath of fresh air.

After another turn, the corridor opened into an expansive cavern that seemed to stretch on forever. The roof high above had ordered arrays of massive grow lights that cast warm light down on field after field of crops.

Everything required to meet the nutritional needs of everyone at the project.

Monthly shipments arrived with all of the luxury goods that gave life variety, but all of the essentials were here.

Beans, corn, broccoli, lettuce, carrots, onions, and more filled the space. Each crop was grown in precise fifty by fifty foot production grids that were internally organized into tidy rows. Each grid was tended by its own farmbot.

Spiders, as they'd quickly been nicknamed.

And for good reason.

Each bot dangled from a string of bundled cables attached to overhead trusses that allowed it to cover every square inch of the grid as well as move up and down. Extending from a spherical torso the size of a human head were articulated arms ending in claws, shovels, water nozzles, nutrient solution nozzles, and other more mysterious implements that Hari had never bothered to ask about.

There was no dirt.

That would've required too much water and also would've invited too many pests.

The spiders, along with the agricultural hardware techs that kept them going, operated the largest aquaponics system in the world.

All of the crops were only part of the system.

The far end of the cavern housed massive tanks filled with Blue Tilapia. That specific species was chosen as it had a high tolerance for brackish water and could thrive in water as cold as forty-seven degrees.

Neither was an issue so long as the system had power, but it was one detail among many that increased the facility's self-reliance in the event of catastrophe.

The fish waste fed the plants and the plants cleaned the water that recirculated back into the fish tanks. The tilapia were grown to full size and then harvested and served in the cafeteria to meet daily protein requirements.

The kitchen staff had long ago exhausted every possible way of preparing the fish.

Hari appreciated that they still tried to be creative after so many years, but he still would've preferred more regular deliveries of beef, chicken, turkey, or really any protein that wasn't tilapia.

The project's extreme self-sufficiency was an integral part of maintaining a low profile on the island. Of course, being several hundred feet underground helped, too.

But that was as much a requirement for minimizing external influences on the particle collision tests as it was for safeguarding secrecy. As deep as the gardens level was, the collider ring itself was deeper yet at an average of six hundred feet underground.

Accurate study of the quantum signatures of particle collisions required an absolutely sterile vacuum. Any spare neutrinos or electrons passing through would instantly invalidate the results.

The extreme depth along with the hardened electrical infrastructure meant that the entire complex was well protected from damaging solar radiation or any other electromagnetic radiation that might occur.

It wasn't explicitly designed to withstand a direct nuclear strike, but it could probably survive one with minimal damage.

Hari zigzagged through the aisles, breathing in the vibrant air, letting it soothe his jangled nerves. He hated the weekly report sessions with Mr. Hill. A walk through the gardens was often required before and after to keep his irritation in check. He inhaled another sweet breath and felt the muscles in his legs begin to loosen as he walked.

Industrial air exchangers sucked out the oxygen-rich air at one end of the cavern and piped back in the carbon dioxide rich air from the rest of the complex at the other end. Safety sensors on every level ensured that the air was always safe to breathe.

Even so, it was never as full and alive as here in the gardens.

He finally made it to his destination which was a small section of a grid reserved for the personal use of the upper level management. Other than the techs that kept the operation running and the custodians that kept it clean, there were very few personnel allowed access to this level.

Food was security and so it was secured.

But the weight of leadership had its perks and this was

perhaps the one he appreciated most. Hari knelt down on aching knees and touched the plant he'd come to see.

A clone of the famous Shenzen Nongke Orchid. The mother plant had sold for over two hundred thousand dollars at auction.

He stroked the pale green leaves and wondered for the thousandth time if it would ever bloom again. It was supposed to every four to five years. But this one hadn't in ten.

Not since his assistant Zhang had disappeared.

Not since Hari had killed him.

Killed the man that had been like a son to him.

The orchid had been Zhang's. He had cared for it every day, always taking a few minutes out of his busy schedule to tend to the plant.

Hari knew it wasn't possible, but he almost believed that it somehow knew its true owner was gone and so refused to show its beauty.

A hollow clanging noise drew his attention away. Everything sounded vaguely hollow in the gardens due to the hard surfaces of the distant roof and walls.

He looked up and saw a bald man from the custodial staff cleaning up a mess several grids over. The spider must've blown a circuit because it looked like it had taken a chainsaw to the vegetation in that grid. Hari had seen the man countless times emptying a trashcan, mopping up a mess, and all the other usual cleaning activities.

His phone buzzed in his pocket. He pulled it out and answered. "Yes?"

"The video call you were expecting is on hold in conference room two."

"It wasn't supposed to be for another forty minutes."

"He's on the line now."

Feeling every minute of his sixty-seven years, Hari stood up and started back toward the elevators. "On my way."

As much as he despised reporting in like a child to a parent, it was never wise to ruffle the feathers of the man who controlled the project's annual budget.

2

Hari was no stranger to achieving the seemingly impossible. After all, the project had done just that ten years ago. However, the following decade of research and collider tests had achieved nothing of note. Refinements to the existing technology had proven frustratingly elusive. So much so that some at the project had begun to believe that any further progress was likely impossible.

But it wasn't.

Not theoretically.

He drew in measured breaths to ease the tension in his chest. He drummed the conference table with long skeletal fingers, noting the jolting ache of every impact. Each contact sent a low-powered electrical signal racing through his nervous system. At the end of that path, his brain fulfilled its primary function of interpreting stimulus in an effort to avoid pain and to seek pleasure.

When stripped down to the bare essentials, survival was nothing more than following those two simple dictates. First, to avoid pain. And second, to seek pleasure.

But the complexity of the human psyche could subvert those directives, such that pain became pleasure.

So Hari continued the sequential tapping, the four fingers of his right hand rising and falling in cyclic waves of deserved discomfort. He looked around the spartan conference room, the door shut and the blinds drawn. Some might've thought it sterile, but he approved.

He took another slow breath, still trying to ease the anxiety constricting his chest. After ten long years of searching, the answer was finally within reach.

If it didn't turn out to be yet another failure.

He stared at the large monitor covering one wall, waiting for it to blink to life. Despite dehumidifiers running twenty-four hours a day, the air always felt damp between his fingertips. And it was always a little cooler than his thin frame preferred. The first eight years of his life on the streets in the unrelenting heat of Kolkata had set a permanent preference for heat.

He often hoped that when his day finally came, he would pass in a warm place like Florida or Southern California. A place that would warm his old bones and failing brain.

Hari pinched at the sharp ache in his right hand. Medication would help but it had side effects, both obvious and subtle. And he eschewed anything that might affect his long term mental acuity. Especially any medication that required daily doses and became a crutch with a catch.

So many people in the modern day used so-called life-style drugs that altered their brain and body chemistry to be happier, or calmer, or thinner, or to have erections that lasted longer. Every ailment addressed by the promise of a pill.

They all required a compromise that he was unwilling to make.

He winced as an especially sharp twinge pulsed up through his wrist. He accepted the sensation as a reminder that he was still alive and that the wrong he'd done might yet be remedied.

He'd killed a man.

A man that was the son he'd never had.

All for an idealistic truth that no longer mattered.

The dark screen blinked on and a featureless head spoke. "Dr. Ganesh, I presume."

He'd never clearly seen the man that was his boss since joining the project, but the silhouette on the screen was not the same as before. This one had a narrower head and a thinner neck. And the voice sounded younger.

A squirm of doubt twisted in Hari's stomach. "Where is Mr. Hill?"

"You report to me now."

"Why? What happened to Mr. Hill?"

"I ask the questions, Dr. Ganesh. Not you."

"What might I have the pleasure of calling you? Or will you not answer that either?"

"Call me Mr. Hill."

"How original."

"Originality isn't my concern. An update on your lack of progress is. There is a growing opinion that the extravagant sums being spent on this project could be utilized better elsewhere."

Hari's gut twisted with worry. They couldn't shut him down now. Not before the upcoming collider test. "The previous Mr. Hill understood the value of what we are doing here."

"Dr. Ganesh, I am here to determine whether your

project merits the funding it receives. Let me say from the outset that I have grave doubts on the matter. But I'm granting you the opportunity to change my mind."

What a pompous mental midget!

Hari tried to hide the disgust on his face, and didn't succeed. The Hermes Project had fundamentally altered humanity's understanding of reality. Not publicly. But to the scientists inside the project for now and to the wider public some day.

That this simpleton would show up out of nowhere and question the measly amount dedicated to such an important project was a slap in the face. A slap in the face to everyone who had worked so hard for so long.

And especially to himself.

But he swallowed his anger and resigned himself to selling what had already been bought. "As you are new here, please indulge me while I relate a brief history of our past efforts. That will more suitably frame how far we've come." Hari had no idea how informed this new Mr. Hill was and he didn't want any decisions about the project's future made without the context of the problem and their progress to this point.

"Proceed."

"In 2003, the NEC Earth Simulator supercomputer in Yokohama, Japan finished seventeen months of calculations building the most comprehensive climate model known.

The age of Big Data had arrived with a big conclusion— the extinction of the human race.

Subsequent simulations on newer and faster supercomputers have refined that result, but the basic premise hasn't changed. Humanity has around one hundred years left on this planet."

"Continue."

"It was the simple understanding of exponential growth, specifically that of the global population, that made the result inescapable. Too many humans have created inescapable problems. Climate change. Resource depletion. Decreased biodiversity. Acidification of the oceans. We are entering the final phase of the Holocene extinction event that humanity started some eleven thousand years ago."

"So I've been told."

The tone of his voice made his skepticism abundantly clear.

"And so we looked to escape doom by leaving the planet and finding a new home. Of the two final options considered, pursuing faster than light travel was decided upon over generational ships. Unknown to the general public, CERN began directing most of its resources toward this end. And unknown to all but those employed here, Project Hermes was founded to beat them to it. We thought we'd discovered the key ten years ago. But that key unlocked a different door. One that for a decade we've not been able to take more than a step through."

"Yes, I'm fully aware of the project's shortcomings."

Hari gritted his teeth. He'd led the project to the most important scientific discovery of all time. Beyond the atom. Beyond relativity. Beyond quantum mechanics.

Who was this man to question him?

Yes, there had been stuttering progress since the initial discovery, but unraveling the mysteries of the universe wasn't like manufacturing smaller transistors. It didn't follow a predictable curve like Moore's Law.

Scientific advancement came in leaps and starts, as it always had.

"Research into the fundamental nature of reality is not like plugging numbers into a spreadsheet, Mr. Hill." The new Mr. Hill seemed to lack even the limited vision of the previous Mr. Hill. This one felt more like a spreadsheet, bean-counter type.

"While that may be true, annual budgets are precisely like that. And the funds allocated to your project have been called into question. So if you'd prefer to retain that funding, I'd suggest you get to the point."

Yes, the new Mr. Hill was a definite downgrade on the only marginally acceptable original.

"Mr. Hill, I have good news and bad news."

"Do you think this is a children's game, Doctor? Because I will shut you down the instant that I feel that is the case."

Hari bit back a scathing reply. "I assure you, Mr. Hill, I do not. I simply state the truth."

"Tell me the bad news."

"The bad news is that the last two years of research have confirmed the conclusion that faster-than-light travel is not possible. Or, if it is, it is so far beyond our current or near future capabilities that it is effectively impossible within the given timeframe. As such, it is not a solution to our extinction predicament."

"That doesn't bode well for your continued funding. What's the good news?"

Hari tried to keep the childish excitement from his voice. But even with his advanced years, a tone of youthful exuberance seeped in. "Our other avenue of inquiry has progressed to a point of possible revelation."

"Could you stop speaking like a philosopher and start speaking like someone who wants to keep his job?"

"Mr. Hill, I think we have it this time."

"My predecessor heard that a number of times before. All of which turned out to be untrue."

Hari nodded.

"What makes this time different?"

"Because this time, I feel it."

He could almost see the movement of arched eyebrows on the shadowed face.

"You *feel* it? I find that wholly unconvincing."

"I could go into the relevant quantum equations and groundbreaking mathematics that my team has developed over the—"

"Spare me the technobabble."

"Precisely. So, you'll have to trust me when I say that we've made a monumental breakthrough. And I believe the upcoming test will confirm it."

"Why is this so-called breakthrough not related to faster-than-light travel? Because that's what we need if we're going to have any hope of survival."

"As I stated, that possibility is in the past, Mr. Hill. And so we effectively have one last hope. A critical refinement to our existing methodology. One that—"

"It better be a real solution this time, Doctor. The future of your project depends on it."

"No, Mr. Hill. That is incorrect."

"What? Why?"

"Because the future of the human race depends on it."

3

BOB RANDY took a sip of hot latte and savored the earthy, rich flavor. His assistant had made it for him just like she did every weekday morning. And it was perfect. Its perfection was half of the reason he'd hired her.

A knock at his office door and it swept open.

A woman half his age, with looks like one of those pin up calendar girls his father used to ogle, strolled in like she owned the place. Over the past seven years, Veronica had become his indispensable right hand. She'd proven her worth far beyond her gorgeous butt and impossibly long legs.

The fact that she wasn't opposed to showing them off wasn't lost on him during her employment interview all those years ago. She reminded him that he was a man, with lust throbbing in his loins and visions of bending her over a desk in his mind.

That had been the other half of the reason for hiring her.

That she'd become so much more only affirmed his belief in his own good judgment of character. He knew talent when he saw it. How else could he have pulled off a decades long career in the cutthroat world of Hollywood producing?

Seriously. Producing in Hollywood was like a rare earth magnet that drew in sociopaths like metal shavings. If there was a stronger magnet for damaged egos in the world, he was unaware of it.

Corporate finance, maybe.

And producing reality TV was like a distilled version of the general disease that afflicted the entertainment field. It was like that rare earth magnet with a billion coils of bare wire wrapped around it and plugged into the sun.

Everyone was a shark.

And if you didn't get that, you were the food.

Bob knew it all too well because he was having a bad run. And sharks smelled weakness like blood chumming the water. The fact that his last series, *Hot Hobos - From Railcars to Runways*, had been cancelled after only half a season dumped a lot of chum in the water.

Veronica kicked the door shut taking care to stabilize the two items she escorted to his desk. A tight black skirt hugged her round hips and clung to the valley between her legs. She had curves in all the right places, not like the anorexic waifs that the fashion industry tried to brainwash women into being these days. No, here was a woman that could drain you dry and then keep you warm all night.

Sweet Jesus.

For years now, she'd provided vivid material for his daily? ...weekly? ...monthly now? masturbation sessions. God, he was old. It wasn't that he was no longer capable of a good session. He was. It was just that he didn't care as much as he used to. There were times when he had every intention of taking a few moments for himself, but then other things superseded the desire. Like his favorite James Bond film, *From Russia with Love*, was coming on. Or the afternoon nap that had become a daily habit in recent years would edge out the victory.

"My eyes are up here, Bob."

Bob kept his eyes on her legs. "What are you doing?"

"Celebrating your birthday," she replied as she set a cupcake with, presumably, sixty candles poking out of the top on his desk

"That thing looks like a porcupine's butt on fire. It's a fire hazard!"

Veronica rolled her eyes and shook her head. "You'd have more friends if you weren't such a jerk."

"I don't want more friends."

"Well, I'm sure it would be nice to receive a birthday gift from someone other than your assistant for once."

"I'm too old for birthdays. Once you turn fifty, birthdays suck. The last thing you want to do is celebrate the passing of another year. Another year closer to being worm food."

"Happy Birthday to—"

"No thanks on the birthday song! Isn't it illegal to sing anyway? I think somebody got sued for that at some restaurant chain."

She shook her head in resigned disgust. She did that a lot. "Make a wish and blow out your stupid candles."

Bob's eyes traced down below the skirt to the smooth skin of her legs. He grinned.

"Don't waste it, Bob. You might not have many left."

"You should've been the reason my wife divorced me."

"Bob, you're sixty. I'm twenty-nine."

"I know. Perfect, right?"

"You're not rich enough and I'm not desperate enough."

"How rich would I have to be?"

"Multi-trillionaire level."

"So you're saying there's a chance?"

"There is no chance. I'm engaged, in case you forgot," she said as she proudly showed the ring on her finger.

"Don't do it. There's still time to save yourself. You think you're happy and that you're the luckiest girl in the world. But you're not. Wait until he screws your best friend and says, 'It's your fault for not giving him the attention he needed.'"

Veronica frowned. "Speaking of your ex-wife, she sent me a card for you."

"Why'd she send it to you?"

"I don't know. Why does everything she sends you come to me?"

"Because she's always loved a dramatic gesture. Like sleeping with the traitor that used to be my best friend!"

"Do you still want it?"

"Her body? I'll admit it crosses my mind every now and then. She did tons of yoga. She was so flexible she could—"

"I'm talking about the card. Do you still want the card?"

"Oh, sure."

Veronica handed him her phone and tapped a link in an email entitled To Your Pathetic Boss.

Bob slipped on his bifocal glasses and stared at the small screen. A gilt-edged envelope rotated into view. An embossed sticker with his name on it floated away and the envelope opened. A flock of tiny birds flew out toward the screen.

Wait.

Those weren't birds.

They were hands flapping like birds. The hands closest to the screen curled into fists with extended middle fingers before flying off the screen. A swarm zipped by until one landed right in the middle of the screen. A huge middle finger with the other fingers tucked into a fist.

A message appeared over the top in fancy red cursive. It appeared a little bit at a time like it was being written in real time.

I wish you'd never been born!

Bob stared at it. He looked up at Veronica who had a nervous grin on her face. "That's seriously creative. I knew I married her for something more than her deviant sexual appetites."

He hit the *REPLY* button and typed a response.

Tell Roger I hope you both go to hell.

And hit *SEND*.

It had been less than ten months since he came home after a flight got cancelled and discovered his best friend and his wife together. Doing things she hadn't wanted him to do in years.

And she was the one that filed for divorce!

It still made his stomach burn if he thought about it too much. And the worst part was that he still wasn't over her. Not completely.

"She should get a job with Hallmark. Surely, there are millions of divorcees out there that would love to send cards like this to their exes."

"You've got an eye for talent."

Bob's flippant reply choked in his throat. She hadn't said it sarcastically. She'd meant it. A well of emotion expanded in his chest. The unexpected compliment was the most deadly. Stupid birthdays always made him ridiculously emotional. "You really think so?"

He almost made himself puke it sounded so pathetic.

"You hired me, didn't you?"

Bob nodded. "I hired you because you make a great latte and you wear a skirt that gets my—"

"And look how much more I do now."

Bob shrugged. "You're right. But I'm still glad you're good at the first two."

The landline phone on his desk chirped. A button blinked red.

Without him having to ask, Veronica lifted the phone and punched the button to answer. "Mr. Randy's office. This is Veronica. May I ask who is calling?"

She listened a second and then replied. "Let me see if he's in. Please hold." She hit the hold button and then double-checked to make sure the call actually was on hold.

She was a keeper. He'd seen careers ruined by smaller mistakes.

"It's the big boss. He wants a word. Should I tell him you're out?"

Bob reached for the phone. "Nah. He probably just wants to wish me a happy birthday. After all I've done for him over the years, it's the least he could do. "

He took the call off hold and answered. "Hello Malcolm, what can I do for you?"

"Bob, you're fired."

4

Bob slammed the phone down so hard the plastic neck cracked. A second later, the translucent button flashed red again with an incoming call. His trembling finger hovered over the square knob.

Get a grip on yourself, you pitiful old man.

He'd fired enough people over the years to understand that it wasn't personal. It was just business. Just part of the game. But now that it was his head on the chopping block, it didn't feel so impersonal.

The light blinked on and off, on and off. An ominous, evil red that promised to relegate him to extinction. He'd just be another dinosaur swept off the face of the earth.

He yanked his hand away like the phone was a venomous snake about to strike.

"Want me to tell him you got sick?"

The voice echoed into his ears and through the emptiness where his brain had been seconds ago. He looked up and saw Veronica's lips moving. It was like she was speaking in slow motion. The sounds coming out of her mouth weren't words so much as whale sounds several octaves lower. An electric pain shot up his arm and ignited in his chest. An invisible spear stabbed at his heart.

His muscles seized and he bounced off the chair onto the floor like a fish tossed onto the beach.

The sensation vaulted higher, ripping through his limbs like a lightning bolt.

Bob clutched his chest as an instant of calm realization settled in.

Was this a heart attack?

A flash from his youth showed his father walking through the front door after yet another long, hard day at the steel foundry. Black soot streaked his face and holes dotted his clothes where glowing sparks had landed and burned through. A tight frown creased his mouth as he removed his boots in the entry hall.

"Daddy!" Bobby shrieked from across the living room. He scrambled over the couch and sprinted for his father.

His father looked up and the edges of his mouth crept upward.

"Don't touch him, Bobby!" his mother shouted from the kitchen. She appeared carrying a glass mixing bowl filled with a red sauce that smelled like spaghetti was going to be dinner. She wore an apron with a faded sunflowers print. Her naturally wavy brown hair was lashed into a tight bun to keep it under control while she worked. "You just took a bath and I will not have you getting dirty again!"

Bobby skidded to a halt and somehow managed to keep from throwing himself into his father's outstretched and waiting arms.

His father's mouth settled back into a frown as he glanced at his mother. "Helen, my boy wants to give me a hug after a long day at work."

She marched over and screamed in his face. "Go wash

that disgusting dust off of you before it gets all over my house! I swear to God. I vacuum and mop every day and all you do is come home and make everything filthy again. It's more work for me, Robert! More housework when I already have to go out and find more work!"

Dad's mouth twisted into a snarl. "Not now, Helen!"

"Not now? Not now? Then when? Now's as good a time as any! Bobby's going to find out sooner or later."

Bobby turned to his mother. Something wasn't right here. "What do you mean?"

"Tell him, Robert!"

His father opened his mouth and then it clamped shut.

"Your father is getting fired! He's not man enough to hold down a job!"

"Shut up, Helen!" His face flushed and his nostrils flared.

"Bobby, your father is a loser! A good for—"

Her words cut short as his father spasmed and clutched his chest. He fell like a stone to the floor, gritting his teeth in agony.

And he never walked through their front door again.

Bobby always regretted denying his father that last hug. He would've dug through a mountain of black soot to have another chance at one last hug.

"Bob? Bob? Are you okay?"

Bob blinked hard and looked up, trying to focus on the face above him.

Veronica. His assistant. Kneeling beside him with one hand supporting his head. Her full lips trembled and her deep blue eyes were wide with concern.

She was an absolute stunner. If only he was thirty years younger. She would've been his next ex-wife.

A familiar acrid taste filled his mouth. He felt the

tingling burn under his tongue. A nitroglycerine pill. Veronica must have stuffed one into his mouth. The pressure in his chest slowly dissipated and the pain subsided to a dull throbbing ache.

"Bob? Hello?"

"I'm fine," he said. The words croaked out like he had a toad lodged in his mouth. "Fine." He glanced to the side and caught a wide open view of baby blue, lace panties. The barest hint of a shadowed cleft showed through the gossamer fabric.

There were worse ways to die than staring at something so beautiful.

"I'm fine," he said again, not pulling his eyes away.

"Are you staring at my crotch?"

"What if I was?"

The hand supporting his head vanished and his skull smacked the polished wood floor. "Ow! Why'd you do that?"

Veronica stood up and tugged her skirt down. "Why do you have to be like that?"

"Honey, I had to nearly die to get a good look between your legs. Can I get another peek?"

"Don't be disgusting."

Bob took a deep breath and looked up at the off-white acoustic ceiling tiles. Tiny holes dotted the area above his desk, evidence of the thousands of pencils that he'd stuck up there over the years. He ran his fingers through his hair and couldn't help but notice how little resistance the thin limp strands of gray presented.

Sixty years old. What a birthday this was turning out to be. First fired and then nearly killed by a heart attack, just like his old man.

There was irony or poetic justice or something in it, for those who cared enough to figure it out.

"Want a piece of gum?" Veronica asked, holding out an unwrapped stick.

"Are your hands clean?"

"Yes or no?"

"Sure," he said. "And thanks." He popped it into his mouth and chewed to get rid of the bitter taste of the pill. "Can you help me up?"

"Are you going to try to look up my skirt?"

"If I say yes, will you still help me?"

She rolled her eyes and helped him into his seat anyway.

"Thanks."

"Don't mention it."

The phone that had gone dead blinked to life again.

Bob punched the button to answer it on speaker. "What?"

"Don't hang up on me when I'm firing you! Do you think this is easy for me?"

"Yes, Malcolm. I do think it's easy for you because it's not you getting tossed out onto the street."

"Don't you think that's being overly dramatic?"

"Are you seriously firing me? After what I've done for this network? I produced *Barflies* in the '80s and *Schwartzfeld* in the '90s. Two of the biggest hits ever on network television!"

"Bob, you know we appreciate all you've done for this network in the ancient past."

Bob snarled at the phone. This latest in a long line of network presidents was the youngest yet. The execs were always clamoring for a younger demographic and had put all their chips on Malcom Calhoun to deliver. He couldn't have been more than forty years old. Bob was snorting coke off strippers' tits when this punk was suckling his mother's funbags.

Life had no sense of shame.

"Malcolm, listen to me. I've got a huge hit on my hands here."

"Huge hit, huh? Like *Hot Hobos – From Railcars to Runways*? Need I remind you that the show bombed, Bob? Bombed like a U-boat in World War II."

"A U-boat was a submarine! It didn't drop bombs! Trying to sound smart by using metaphors you don't understand makes you sound like an idiot."

"I'm the president of this network. And you're fired. Who's the idiot now, Bob?"

If he could've shoved his hands through the phone line and choked this kid to death, he would've. "This new show is going to be a smash hit, Malcolm. I promise you. Have you read the treatment? I sent it over through interoffice mail weeks ago."

"You sent paper? Bob, why can't you send email like a normal person? I don't *do* paper. Can I look at paper on my phone while I'm lunching at Serenity Tao's?"

Bob's fingers squeezed the chair's armrests and his jaw tightened.

Veronica tapped his shoulder and he glanced up. She shook her head and waved a finger at him. She touched her heart and mimed breathing slowly and deeply.

Bob rolled his eyes. "Listen, Malcolm. It's called *Sole Survivor*. It's going to be the next big thing. Guaranteed."

"You've got thirty seconds to save your job. Speak."

Speak? Like a dog.

What a schmuck.

Bob drew in a deep breath and swung for the fences. He rattled off the overview, coming in at thirty seconds on the dot.

There was silence on the other end.

That was good.

Maybe.

"I've got it all set up, Malcom. I just need the green light from you. Don't let this one slip away."

Another few seconds of silence and then the reply.

"Is anyone going to die? Isn't that place known for having killer bears?"

"The island has the largest bears on the planet. Around thirty-five hundred of them. Point seven bears per square mile. So I'd say it's highly likely that there will be dangerous confrontations. That's part of the allure."

"If someone dies, legal is going to throw a hissy fit. And I don't like hissy fits from legal, Bob."

"I'll get waivers. Legal can draw them up. Iron-clad waivers that'll keep this network out of any unpleasant entanglements."

"I want them on my desk by tomorrow morning. Everything better be tighter than a gnat's cornhole. Capiche, Bob?"

Malcolm Calhoun was no more Italian than the Spaghetti Warehouse. Hearing him pretend to be some kind of Godfather almost made Bob want to get whacked.

"I understand."

"You've got your green light."

"Yes!" Bob's death grip on the phone relaxed. A flood of relief washed over him. The pressure in his chest subsided. He took a deep breath and smiled. The release lasted half a second.

"With one condition."

"What condition?"

"I want you on site to ensure everything goes according to plan."

"What? Why? It's ten million miles away. It's a frigid wasteland of eskimos and ice. I'm not going there."

"You're going there or you're fired. Your choice."

Wasn't much of a choice.

"Fine."

"This is your last chance, Bob. Screw it up and your career is FUBER."

With that, the line went dead.

Veronica giggled. "Did he mean *FUBAR* or *UBER* or both? Like you're screwed and will end up as a personal taxi driver?"

Bob would've laughed if it wasn't his neck on the chopping block.

5

EMILY WILDER stared at the leaning tower of medical bills with a hollow feeling in the pit of her stomach. It wasn't just the height of the structure that numbed her brain. It was also that every envelope in the stack contained a bill that individually was more than she and her grandmother could afford. Dealing with disease in America wasn't cheap. In fact, it was a booming multi-billion dollar business established and protected by the lavish donations given to the lawmakers and regulators in Washington.

How could it be otherwise in the kingdom of Crony Capitalism?

Yeah, she was bitter.

Fighting Acute Myeloid Leukemia had taken her grandmother's savings and, if she couldn't afford to continue treatment, it would take her life too. Before the horror of the last ten months, Emily wouldn't have believed this kind of thing could happen in America.

Sure, she understood the country had glaring faults. Like condemning brutal totalitarian regimes that had oil we wanted while simultaneously embracing the rulers of

Saudi Arabia because they gave us as much as we wanted. She understood that this was a nation founded on lofty ideals but mired in the practical concerns of the modern world.

Understanding and accepting all of that, it still shocked her that anyone in America could wake up one day to an illness, and in short order, dealing with that illness could utterly devastate their financial lives, not to mention their personal lives. Being twenty years old, such belief could've been chalked up to being a naive idiot.

But naiveté wasn't a character trait she could claim. Losing both parents by age ten put that possibility well beyond reach.

No, it hadn't been naiveté. It had simply been ignorance. Ignorance of the reality of being very sick in America.

She plucked the envelope from the top of the stack and ripped it open. She traced her finger down to the bottom line.

$31,078.

Thirty-one grand!

In one envelope.

Emily shook her head and hurled the folded paper at nothing in particular.

Something smashed into the shared wall between their apartment and the one next door. The Huertas were at it again. Mrs. Huerta screamed and her husband responded in kind. Unfortunately, the thin wall that separated the two units made every word as clear as if the two were arguing in her living room.

But at least she wasn't hearing their second most favorite shared activity. Ear plugs and a pillow over her head weren't enough to drown out Mrs. Huerta's moaning and Mr. Huerta's groaning.

Emily looked around the cramped apartment that she and her grandmother shared and sighed.

Less than a year ago, they lived in a spacious condo in Berkeley. One her grandmother had owned for several decades. Long before the wild appreciation of the past twenty years. But paying to treat the illness had swallowed that life in no time.

And now they lived in a tiny one bedroom apartment in Oakland. Not a good part of Oakland. A part they could afford. Between what Grammy got from the government and what Emily made at her job waiting tables at Mantas on the Bay, they managed to put food on the table and avoid getting evicted.

But that was about it.

She pushed away from the desk in frustration and nearly tipped over backward as the leg of the chair hit the couch behind. She silently cursed because she didn't want to upset her grandmother watching TV behind her.

Emily pinched her eyes shut and rubbed them until stars twinkled across her darkened lids. She opened them and glanced at the black solar G-Shock watch on her wrist.

10:28 AM.

She was going to be late for the lunch shift at work. Fancy restaurants weren't her thing, but it was money and something to do while she figured out what to do with her life.

Another loud scream from the apartment next door startled her. She glanced back and saw that Grammy hadn't noticed. Lucky her that she was hard of hearing.

It spared her all the sounds of shouting and screwing.

The bright TV bathed the room in flickering illumination. Dim light leaked in through the single window. They kept it shut with the blinds drawn most of the time because you could only hear police sirens for so long before they made you want to kill someone.

This room was smaller than her bedroom in Berkeley. And this was technically the living room slash dining room slash her bedroom. The utility room, as Grammy euphemistically called it. The single actual bedroom held her grandmother's bed. The rest of the apartment consisted of a small shared bathroom and a tiny kitchen that was basically an attached closet to the utility room.

Anytime Emily grumbled about their situation, Grammy would use a fake older-than-she-was voice and talk about how in her day things were so much worse. She'd keep doing it until Emily couldn't help but laugh. She may have been old and dying, but she still had a sense of humor—one occasionally more wicked than the worst witch in Oz.

Scooter must've heard her chair squeak when it moved because he waddled over and smacked his head into her leg. Despite having arthritis in his knees and barely being able to see, he still enjoyed life. The rhythmic thump of his tail was proof.

"Come here, baby," Emily said as she lifted him onto her lap. She scratched behind his ear because, one, that was his favorite spot and he deserved it, and two, because he'd keep maneuvering his head into position until she finally gave up trying to pet other parts of him.

A white glaze clouded the depths of his twelve-year-old eyes. The cataracts covered most of his vision. On their last checkup at the vet, Dr. Jones had said he would lose the rest soon. They hadn't been able to pay the bill, but he assured them that after so long seeing to Scooter's health, he wasn't about to abandon him now, no matter if payment was possible or not.

Emily had cried that day.

She hadn't cried since the death of her father ten years ago. But she'd cried that day.

Dire need inspired profound gratitude.

Especially in those not used to accepting kindness.

She leaned down and kissed Scooter's head. Most of his sandy-blond, scraggly hair had wide streaks of gray in it. He didn't look like Benji's cousin like he once did. Perhaps he was now the older more distinguished cousin.

A foul stench in the air made her grimace. "Oh, Scooter! Whoa!"

Maybe not so distinguished.

Advanced age had brought with it an unreliable digestive system and a single one of Scooter's farts could stink up the entire apartment for half an hour.

Emily heard her grandmother sniff the air. "Lord Jesus! Take me now! This is more than an old woman can handle!"

"Grammy, don't say that."

"Dear, I'm older than King Tut and in worse shape than his mummy. I'm allowed to make a sick joke now and again." She clicked off the television and levered herself up with her trusty cane. "I'm going to clean up breakfast."

"I can do it before I leave for work." Emily glanced at her watch again. She was so going to hear about it at work. "You should take it easy."

"Dear, taking it too easy isn't much different than being dead. So, let me live a little. Besides, I'm angry at that nitwit on TV for not listening to me. I told him to ask for an L. That would've filled in two spots and surely even he wouldn't have been too stupid to see it spelled HALLOWEEN. He could've won four thousand dollars from that round alone." She shuffled into the kitchen muttering to herself. "Idiot didn't listen and I told him the answer."

Emily was pretty sure Grammy understood that the

game show contestant on TV couldn't actually hear her. She had cancer, not one of the myriad debilitating diseases that affected the mind.

The sound of water running and dishes clinking echoed out of the kitchen.

She shouldn't let Grammy exert herself like this. Less than a week ago, the precarious stasis that had been her health had taken a turn for the worse. She moved with a little less energy each day. She complained of dull pains that weren't going away. But every time Emily tried to convince her to go to the doctor, the stubborn woman waved her off.

"I'm old and I'm dying. Of course, I feel terrible. I don't need to rack up another thousand dollars in debt for a doctor to tell me what I already know."

And so Emily would give in even while the anxiety gnawing in her gut grew.

She ripped open the next envelope from the top of the pile.

A credit card offer.

That was a shocker.

The usual avalanche of credit card offers had mysteriously stopped months ago. As greedy as those companies were, they apparently weren't stupid. They knew a bad bet when they saw one.

She read the interest rate off the folded paper.

Only 29.97%!

And some people wondered how credit cards could destroy people's lives.

Still, it was worth saving. Maybe she could run it up to the limit before defaulting. She was about to tuck it into the *Save* pile when she noticed the name and address at the top.

Mr. Alejandro Huerta.

The male half of the noisy neighbors.

She crumpled it up and tossed it at the trash can next to the desk. It bounced off the small mountain of crumpled paper extending above the rim and rolled under the couch.

It was technically a felony to mess with someone else's mail, but in this case, she considered it a public service. Though she did make a mental note to retrieve and destroy the evidence later.

A dish crashed to the floor in the kitchen followed by a dull thump.

Emily jumped out of the chair and raced to check on Grammy, already knowing the horror of what she'd find before the worse reality of seeing it.

6

The frail cold hand in hers belonged to the last living person in the world that loved her. Emily sat beside the hospital bed gritting her teeth and fighting the rising panic in her belly. Losing both parents at such a young age had hardened her beyond her years. Had made her wary of getting attached and becoming vulnerable.

She hadn't been on more than a handful of dates throughout high school, and the one year she'd spent in college hadn't added more than a handful more.

She'd had enough experience with boys to conclude that the cost wasn't worth the benefit. Surprisingly, sex with no strings attached wasn't something they were generally capable of, no matter how much the stereotype indicated otherwise.

It didn't take more than a couple of dates and rolls in the hay for the guy to ruin it with talk of something more. And she was a strictly no strings, no chance type of girl.

Her last date had been more than six months ago. She'd sworn off boys for the time being. Not worth the aggravation. Not when so many heavy things weighed on her heart.

Emily placed her other hand over Grammy's hand to warm it. The crinkled, paper-thin skin felt ice cold in hers.

A lump lodged in her throat as the unwelcome thought of losing Grammy again battered its way into her consciousness. She bit her lip and tasted the sharp tang of blood.

Emily prided herself on being tough. As hard as a rock. Hard enough to weather the storm. Hard enough to push through whatever life threw at her.

It was how she'd survived this far.

There were probably people in the world who had lost both parents in their youth and yet had somehow turned out to be perfectly open and unguarded individuals.

She wasn't one of them.

And the thought of losing Grammy felt like the final blow that would knock her down and shatter her into a million pieces.

She blinked through burning eyes at the bony body tucked under thin hospital sheets.

The hollow, sunken eye sockets. Closed and unmoving as if she were already gone. The pallor of her sagging skin. The ever-present purple scarf that covered her naked scalp. Her protruding nose reminded Emily of her father. The two had once shared more physical traits, but the wasting disease had left only a prominent nose for resemblance.

In the silent moments before dawn, Emily would sometimes lie in bed wondering where her parents were. Wondering if she'd ever see them again. She prayed she would, even though she didn't strictly believe in heaven and hell and all that went with it.

Which was manifestly ironic, she accepted. But the complex affairs of the heart weren't constrained by the simple truths of reason.

Emily leaned forward and tucked a corner of the scarf

behind Grammy's ear. The room and everything in it blurred as the dam behind her eyes started to collapse. She tucked her face into the crook of her elbow while still holding Grammy's frail hand between hers.

"I can't lose you. I can't," she whispered to a universe that didn't care about what she could or could not do.

"I'm still here," a whispered voice replied.

Emily lifted her head and a twisted smile contorted her face. All the happiness and sadness in her heart stretched her mouth into an odd shape that was both full of joy and empty of hope.

"Chickpea, don't worry about me. I'm not going anywhere yet." She reached a shaky hand out and touched the small silver heart pendant hanging around Emily's neck. A fleeting sadness colored her face.

The curtain that separated her bed from the others in the shared room swept open. The scrape of the metal rings on the metal bar set Emily's nerves on edge.

A doctor she didn't recognize nodded solemnly at both of them. "Hello, I'm Dr. Farthing. I know you were expecting Dr. Bertone, but she had to leave unexpectedly. Some political admin fire that needed to be put out. Anyway, I'll be your attending for the rest of the day."

Emily glanced at her watch.

5:28 PM.

After they'd stabilized Grammy in the ER, she'd been wheeled into this room where they'd spent the last several hours waiting for another update.

The first doctor, Dr. Bertone, couldn't have been sweeter and more caring. But that hadn't made the news she'd delivered any better. The insurance company had given her grandmother a single night to recover in the hospital. After that, the full cost for another night's stay would be her responsibility. And as they couldn't afford the copays for the care already received, another night was out of the question.

Emily supposed Dr. Farthing was there to deliver more bad news.

"Can I speak with you for a moment, Emily?"

Emily's brows raised in equal parts concern and confusion. "Sure." She turned to her grandmother. "Is that okay, Grammy?"

Grammy didn't respond. She was staring at the muted television attached high up on the opposite wall. Her lips moved quietly as she directed the contestant on TV to choose the right letter to solve the puzzle.

"I'll be right back." Emily and Dr. Farthing took a few steps away from the bed and stopped.

His lips compressed together into a flat line as he flipped through the chart in his hands. "I'm sorry to say I've got bad news."

It looked like he really was sorry. Some doctors behaved like people's lives were nothing more than the numbers and notes attached to the clipboard. But while only a few were monsters like that, they all sometimes had to do monstrous things. This one had a pained expression as he continued.

"Your grandmother's disease isn't responding to the medication any longer. We've seen this before with AML and it was always a risk."

Emily's heart sank into her feet, leaving her chest hollow. "What do you mean? How can it not be working anymore? It was going well for months. Well enough, at least."

Dr. Farthing frowned and nodded. "It was. We don't understand all the factors involved yet, but it sometimes stops working in some people. In simple terms, the disease figures out a way around the treatment. It's done that with your grandmother."

Panic filled the empty space in Emily's chest. "Well, maybe it will start working again. Right? That could happen. Couldn't it?"

Dr. Farthing's mouth twisted to the side. "I suppose anything is possible. But I have to be honest with you, we've never seen the efficacy improve after a downturn like this."

Emily's hands balled into fists. "I knew I should've brought her in days ago. It's my fault."

Dr. Farthing squeezed her shoulder. "It's not your fault. This isn't the kind of thing that can be prevented. The treatment simply stops working. We don't know why yet. As it stands, she likely has no more than a few months left."

A few months?

7

Something pinched tight in Emily's gut. "So she's going to die? That's it? There's nothing we can do?"

Dr. Farthing handed her a brochure. "I'm not sure this is the right thing to do, but I felt compelled to mention it. Here's information on a new stem cell treatment that has just cleared the European Union's Medical Association. It hasn't been accepted here in America yet, so we can't prescribe it. That said, clinical trials in Europe have shown it can help with situations like your grandmother's."

"Okay. So how do we get it?"

Dr. Farthing sighed. "As I said, that's the hard part. It's not available here and insurance companies don't cover it."

"What are you saying then?"

"I'm saying you'd have to obtain it abroad."

"Okay. We'll do that. What? Why do you still look like that?"

"I'm sorry to say it's one of the most expensive treatments available, at least at this early stage in its development."

"How much?"

"The first course of therapy lasts six months and it costs in the ballpark of sixty thousand dollars."

"*Sixty thousand dollars*?"

Dr. Farthing nodded. "I'm afraid so."

They already owed more than three times that and there was no way they'd be able to come up with another sixty. Not in a million years.

Emily squeezed her eyes shut and swallowed hard.

So, this was it?

Her grandmother was sentenced to death because they couldn't pay enough money to fatten the bank account of some medical millionaire somewhere?

The muted television on the far wall suddenly chattered to life.

Emily glanced at the screen and saw a somber looking news reporter standing in front of the black security fence surrounding the White House. His perfectly manicured hair shined like a plastic helmet.

An old man behind him held up a homemade sign so the camera could see it.

∼

COMMIES GONNA BURN!

∼

"…WHILE the Secretary of State has warned China that such actions are a destabilizing influence in global markets and politics."

Emily marched over and jabbed the power button to turn it off. The last thing in the world she cared about just then was the perpetual sword-rattling of the two most powerful nations on the planet. She turned back to continue her conversation with the doctor when the TV blinked back on.

Emily spun around and saw Grammy holding the remote.

"What? I can't watch the news while you two discuss my future without me?"

The reporter continued. "...started months ago as minor disagreements over the tariffs imposed on imports to the United States from China have continued to—"

Emily turned it off again. "Would you mind leaving it off for a few minutes?"

It blinked on again.

"Would you mind including me in a discussion about my own health?" Grammy raised her eyebrows and tilted her head to the side.

Emily jabbed the power button.

Off.

On.

Off.

On.

Off.

"Grammy! He said the treatment isn't working any more."

Her grandmother set the remote down on the bed sheet. "Yeah. I could've told you that."

Emily's growing frustration melted away as she sensed the acceptance in her reply. The resignation.

The phone attached to Dr. Farthing's hip buzzed and he answered it. He listened for a second and then nodded. "I'll be right there. Get the OR ready." He ended the call and frowned. "I'm sorry, but I have to attend to another patient right now. I'll be back as soon as I can to answer any questions you may have." He nodded again as if affirming that was all he could do and then hurried out the door.

Emily approached the bedside and slipped her hand into her grandmother's. She swallowed hard and fought back tears. Letting a few break loose would mean losing her tenuous grip completely. She wasn't going to fall apart and wail uncontrollably if she could help it.

Her grandmother patted her arm. "Chickpea, I'm old. So very old."

"Don't say that."

"I say it because it's true. I'm lucky to have made it this long. Without you, I would've given up when we lost your father." Her eyes stared into the distance. "My beautiful boy. It's been so long since I've seen his smile."

A sharp spasm in Emily's chest nearly made her cry out. Over ten years without her father. Lost and presumed dead on Kodiak Island. His body was never found and, somehow, that made it worse. It withheld a sense of closure. Of reality.

The funeral had felt fake because of it.

Her grandmother pulled Emily closer and combed the bangs out of her face. "Chickpea, you're the strongest person I've ever met. You've had to be to survive."

She didn't feel strong. Not when her mother died. Not when her father died. And not now, when her grandmother had so little time left. "I don't want to have to be strong. I don't want to lose you. I'll be all alone."

Grammy sighed and the pain that was always behind her good humor came to the front. "If I was God, I wouldn't make you do it. I know how hard it's been."

"Grammy, the doctor said there's a new treatment available, only in Europe. But it's helping people in your situation." Emily dropped her gaze and stared at the cold hands in hers.

So cold and so frail.

"It's our last hope."

"What's the catch?"

"We have to pay for it ourselves. And the first course of therapy is sixty thousand dollars." Her voice cracked into a hushed whisper as she said the number out loud.

Her grandmother snorted a forced laugh. "Only sixty thousand? We should be able to dig that out of the couch cushions."

"Don't joke about it. We'll find a way to pay for it."

"Chickpea, we can't afford it. We can't afford all the bills we already have much less another like that."

"I don't care what we owe. I'm not going to lose you. I can't."

Emily's phone buzzed in her jeans front pocket. She gripped it through the denim and forced it to voicemail. A few seconds later, it buzzed again.

"Go ahead and get it. We'll have plenty of time to be wildly emotional."

Despite the weight pushing her down, Emily smiled. "Maybe it's someone over in Europe who wants to give us the therapy for free."

"Never know until you answer."

Emily fished the phone out of her pocket and glanced at the number. Nobody she recognized. She answered it. "Hello?"

"Is this Emily Wilder? Daughter of the late Charles Wilder?"

"Who wants to know?"

"My name is Bob Randy and I want to offer you the chance to win a million dollars."

Emily hung up.

She didn't know the name, and the chance to win a

million dollars screamed scam like that email she'd gotten from the guy in Zimbabwe that needed her to forward her bank info so he could get his inheritance out of the country before the corrupt government seized it. He, of course, offered to cut her in on a large chunk of it if she agreed.

She'd laughed as she sent that one to SPAM, but those emails wouldn't get sent if nobody ever fell for them. Which meant that somebody did.

Poor fools.

They must've been utterly desperate.

Emily sighed. Just like she was now. Desperation could make a person do things they wouldn't normally do. Believe things they wouldn't normally believe.

"Who was it?"

"Somebody offering me a chance to win a million dollars."

"Why'd you hang up?"

"Because calls like that are never legit."

Her phone buzzed again and the same number showed on the screen. A boiling anger in her chest erupted. She answered the call. "Stop calling me! I won't fall for your scam. I'm not an idiot!"

"I know you're not an idiot. But, I wonder if you're a survivor. Because if you can outlast nine other contestants in surviving alone on Kodiak Island, you'll win a million dollars."

Emily's mouth snapped shut cutting off the stream of curse words about to fly out.

That wasn't the inheritance in Africa ploy she was expecting. It wasn't like any scheme she'd ever heard of. And Kodiak Island? The place that had swallowed her father ten years ago?

The voice on the other end continued.

"Do I have your attention now? Because I assure you this is very real."

Emily stared at the wasting form that was her grandmother. There was a ninety-nine percent chance that this guy was talking nonsense.

But what if he wasn't?

Wasn't her grandmother's life worth that one percent chance?

"I'm listening," she said.

8

MARCO MORALES swatted at the stinging bite on his calf, but the horsefly that caused it buzzed away to safety before his palm connected. As idealistic as he was, he'd long ago found peace with killing the little buggers. Yeah, they were part of the web of life and other parts of the web depended upon them for food, blah, blah, blah. He understood all that more than most, and he respected it, also more than most.

But whatever, the cursed things spread disease and their bites hurt like crazy. The female of the species anyway. Just like mosquitoes, it was the females of the species that caused so much misery.

Not so different from his ex, Justine.

She'd been gone two weeks and that wasn't nearly enough time to forget their previous three years together. She was the one.

Until she wasn't.

He'd laid it all out there, put his heart on the line, and she'd shoved a dagger in and bled him dry. And all because he wouldn't leave the land his family had owned for generations and move with her to Los Angeles. So they could have a fresh start. A new beginning.

She'd called it a lost cause.

Wrong. A cause was only lost when everyone gave up fighting for it.

He hadn't given up. So many others had, but not him.

"Umm, Mr. Morales, the children are ready to continue when you are."

Marco flinched at the unexpected voice. His mind had taken to filling every available moment with remembering her. Like scratching at a new scab until the tender skin peeled away and the blood leaked out. He rubbed his chest and the hollow ache inside, and then stuttered back into his role as nature guide to the two dozen sixth graders squeezed into the shade of a large boulder. He took a sip from his Camelbak and nodded. "Okay then. Everyone hydrate?"

"I drank ten gallons!" a kid with a bright green mohawk said. "And now I have to pee like a race horse!"

The other children burst out laughing as Ms. Cooper scolded the boy and tried to regain control.

"You'd die if you drank ten gallons at once," Marco said. "Anyone know why?"

A girl standing so close to him she continually bumped his elbow shot her hand up. Her hand had been more up than down since the walk began. He liked a teacher's pet as much as anyone did that was on the teaching side of learning. "Lauryn."

She beamed when he said her name. "It's because it throws off your homeostatic balance. The balance between saline and freshwater in your system. One lady who did a contest in California ended up dying because she drank too much water too fast. She didn't win the prize."

"No duh, she was dead," the mohawk kid said to the amusement of the rest of the class.

Lauryn turned to him and flashed a snarl before her angelic aspect returned.

"Enough about that," their teacher said as she lifted a brow at Marco. "Shall we get back on the path?"

Marco nodded and turned to the swarm of wiggling children. "Right. Get with your partner! Before they dump you and move on." He turned back to the teacher and winced at the alarmed looked on her face.

"Is everything okay, Mr. Morales? Should we cut this field trip short?"

Marco squeezed his eyes shut and shook his head. "Sorry, I'm fine. Let's move out!" He turned toward the trail and bumped into Lauryn. "Where is your partner?"

She leaned toward him and whispered. "Can I be your partner? I'd really rather depend on someone who knows what they're doing out here."

"Lauryn," the teacher said with the barest hint of exasperation coloring her voice. She pointed at the ground next to her expectantly. Even the teacher's pet could get annoying at times.

Marco lowered the wide brim of his hat to keep the blazing afternoon sun out of his eyes. He started back on the narrow path, sinking into the forward momentum. His long, muscled legs stretched with every stride. Small puffs of dust billowed into the air with every impact of his sandals. It was the middle of May and the land was already parched and brown. It was going to be yet another record-breaking hot summer.

How many years in a row did we have to endure these perpetually climbing temperatures before folks accepted that things were changing?

And not for the better.

Sporadic tufts of brittle grass crunched underfoot as they continued on.

"This is boring!" a voice shouted from behind.

He didn't have to turn around to know it was Mohawk. He shouted over his shoulder, so even the kids in the back could hear. "We're almost there. Trust me. You're going to love it."

"Yeah, right," Mohawk said. "More dirt is all I see."

A warm breeze caressed Marco's toes as he crested a ridge, and the land opened below for miles into the distance. Low hills carpeted in grass bleached by the blazing sun. The wind painted ever-changing patterns in the long blades of grass. He'd spent countless hours sitting on this ridge, spotting the shapes of animals in the shifting patterns of grass as other kids might look at clouds.

From this vantage point, the land looked alive. And not in the fancy metaphorical literary sense that might be taught in a college creative writing class. The kind of class that his ex would've loved and he would've hated. It literally looked alive. A broad wind flattened a large patch of grass one way, and then a swirled breeze swept through, ruffling a trail through the smooth surface. Something like he'd seen Bugs Bunny do in the cartoons of his youth. A leading edge that left behind a trail of piled dirt.

It was a beautiful spot. Magical. And utterly horrible. Fifteen days ago, he'd asked Justine to marry him on this ridge. And she'd left the next day. Needless to say, it wasn't the response he'd expected.

Marco glanced over his shoulder, and the class followed in a line like ducklings after their mother.

Mother.

Justine had said again and again that she wanted to be a

mother someday. The disconnect was that she'd apparently meant with someone else.

A sharp chirp pulled him out of the cesspool of his thoughts. A wry smile crept across his face. Several high-pitched shrieks behind him indicated the children had spotted the animal perched on a rock less than twenty feet off the trail.

Marco slowly turned around and held his finger to his lips. "Keep your voices down and gather around me. Slowly, so we don't scare him away." He waited while the children circled round, their tittering voices barely controlled.

The ferret perched up on its hind legs, staring at them and sniffing the air. The white fur of its underbelly contrasted with the black fur covering its legs. The white fur on its face accentuated the black fur surrounding its eyes and connecting over the bridge of its nose. It looked like a mask. Like something a superhero or a fast food burglar might wear.

"O-M-G. It's the cutest thing I've ever seen," a whispered voice at his shoulder said.

He didn't have to turn to know Lauryn was back in her preferred position.

"*It* is a male Black-Footed Ferret. And he's the patriarch of an extended family."

"What's a patriarch?" Mohawk asked.

Marco was about to answer when Lauryn butted in. "A patriarch is the male head of a tribe or family. As opposed to a matriarch, which is—"

"So, he's the big boss? I could beat that dumb ferret with my pinkie finger."

The ferret's nose twitched and his whiskers trembled as he sniffed the air, keeping a careful watch on the intruders.

Marco rolled his eyes. "He's actually very smart. The

Black-Footed Ferret nearly went extinct a few times over the past fifty years. There are only four surviving populations in the world. This is one of them."

Mohawk shouldered his way to the front. He pointed at the ferret with an incredulous look. "I thought you said we were going to do something cool. Something better than looking at a dumb ferret."

Marco sighed. He'd been doing these nature walks with elementary school kids for over a year as a way to educate them and hopefully get them to connect with a world that didn't involve an illuminated screen.

But there was always one kid like this. Always at least one.

He had a sudden urge to flick Mohawk on the head, and then do the same to his parents when they showed up to confront him about such abusive treatment. "Well, we'll be working on some bushcraft skills later. You look like the type that would particularly enjoy basket-weaving."

It was a mild insult. A barb leveled at a kid hardly half his age. He should've taken the high road, but the high road didn't always get you to your desired destination. Sometimes, the low road was the better option.

"That's sissy stuff!" Mohawk shouted so loud that the ferret dropped to all fours and darted into a nearby hole in the ground. "I want to make that thing you're carrying. What'd you call it? An atlas? Now, that could kill a ferret, for sure!"

Marco pulled the two sticks out of the wool sheath slung behind his shoulder. The short stick had a carved cup at one end. The six-foot long stick was blunt on one end and sharpened to a point at the other. He pointed to the short stick. "This is an atlatl," he pointed to the long one, "and this is the dart that it throws. Ancient man used it to hunt animals far larger than ferrets."

"How large?" Mohawk said, now fully engaged and interested.

"The biggest animals alive at the time. Woolly mammoths. They were like elephants with dreadlocks and thirteen-foot tusks."

Mohawk's eyes went wide. "Cool," he said in a whisper.

There was hope for this kid yet.

Marco notched the blunt end of the dart into the cup of the atlatl, and then held them both cocked behind his head in one hand. "It was invented around thirty thousand years ago. The dart can travel a hundred miles per hour and deliver two hundred times more force than a thrown spear."

"Whoa," Mohawk whispered in awe. "Can you throw it at something?"

Marco was about to answer when he noticed two people on a ridge in the distance. What they were doing wasn't obvious from this distance, but that didn't matter.

He already knew what they were doing.

On *his* land.

Twenty minutes later, Marco arrived at the ridge with the two men at work. He noted their beat-up white truck had no company emblem or name on the side. He approached them unnoticed from behind.

A squat bald man with an expansive beer belly peered through a bright yellow scope perched on top of a tripod of metal legs that put the scope at eye level. The man adjusted the two dials on top of the scope as his taller coworker pointed into the distance, scratched at a thick bristly beard, and said something that the wind carried away.

Marco waited until he was right behind them before speaking, and then he shouted. "Hey! What are you doing here?"

The bald man flinched so hard he knocked the tripod over and it crashed to the ground.

Of course, Marco already knew what they were doing. These two, or others just like them, had been scurrying over his neighbors' lands over the past six months. And every time they left a particular parcel, the land was purchased by an undisclosed party a short time later. The old timers that owned the adjacent properties had been longtime friends of his family. Generations of mutual respect and support.

And one by one, they had all sold and moved on.

None of them ever spoke of the sale, whether from the shame of surrender or from a non-disclosure agreement that would've clawed back every dime if they let a word slip about the transaction.

Whatever the case, someone was buying up all the land for miles around and, it appeared, that someone was now interested in his land, too.

"Come on, son," the bearded man said while the other picked up the tripod. "Why'd you do that?"

The bald one righted the tripod and blew dust off the mounted scope. "Now I gotta get it lined back up just right."

Marco couldn't have cared less. "You didn't answer my question," he said in an icy tone.

The taller man stroked his full beard and looked Marco over, likely deciding if he was the type that could be bullied or not. The bald one stood there looking uncomfortable in the extended silence.

"Look here, son," the tall one began in an imperious tone.

"I'm not your son," Marco said as he took a step closer. "And I'm considering breaking your jaw for insulting the memory of my father."

The bearded man slowly nodded. He held up his hands. "I didn't mean no disrespect. We're just here to do a job. That's all."

Marco stepped forward again, purposefully moving into the man's personal space and claiming it. At six-foot-four inches, Marco stared straight into the watery blue eyes of a man twice his age and looking like his height was the only thing that kept him from having a belly like his buddy.

Uncertainty filled those tired eyes. He was probably used to literally and figuratively looking down on those around him.

But Marco stood level with him. That combined with the rippling muscles in his lean arms and legs communicated a message the bearded man probably wasn't used to hearing.

Submit.

Or else.

As advanced as modern humans were, we hadn't evolved so far beyond our bestial selves that we'd moved beyond the simple dynamics of dominance.

Marco leaned forward until their eyes were inches apart. "This is my land. Leave. Now." His jaw clenched tight as he longed to swing the two atlatl sticks at this idiot's head.

The bearded man tripped over himself backing up. "Listen friend, we're not here to cause trouble. Just trying to earn a dollar, you know?"

"I didn't hire you. Who did?"

The sound of children's shrieking voices filled the air as the leading edge of the school group arrived. The stern voice of their teacher kept them corralled away from what was clearly a brewing conflict.

The bearded man shifted his gaze and looked over Marco's shoulder. "You can meet him yourself," he said as he nodded into the distance.

Marco turned and saw a black Cadillac Escalade roaring up the hill in their direction. A plume of dust billowed out from behind leaving a trail that the wind shifted and curled into a dissipating cloud.

So this was it?

He was finally going to get to meet the man. The Big Boss. The man who had broken apart a community that had stood together for hundreds of years.

He couldn't wait to give the guy a piece of his mind.

The shiny SUV powered up the final hill and skidded to a stop twenty feet away. Blacked out windows made it impossible to see inside. The driver's door opened and a man in a dark suit jumped out and opened the rear door.

A shiny white cowboy boot extended below the opened door, and then a large man in a pristine white suit stepped out. He stood up to equal Marco's height and tucked in his shirt as if to advertise that he was a middle-aged man that took care of himself. He adjusted a huge gold belt buckle that had a rippling flag frozen on the front. A single red and white stripe next to a single star.

The flag of the Lone Star state, Texas.

He looked like a Dallas Cowboy.

And not the NFL football type.

10

This idiot was clearly the city cowboy type. The kind that had a Hummer with oversized tires that had never left the pavement. The kind who rarely had dirt lodged under his fingernails. He wore *white* cowboy boots, for crying out loud.

Enough said.

The man adjusted the oversized cowboy hat on his head, tugging it down a little in front like he was moving into business mode. At a similar height, his eyes leveled on Marco's and didn't blink as he strode over like he already owned the place. He stopped just short, well inside the usual sphere of expected social space, but not so close that an immediate physical response was required.

In other words, he'd just peed on the ground in Marco's territory, modern-style.

He broke the staredown with Marco and turned to the two workers. "Hey boys, you run into a problem here?"

The two men glanced back and forth between Marco and their boss like they were about to make a run for it.

"Yeah, there's a problem," Marco said. "They, like you, are on my land. And I didn't give you permission to—"

"Now, son, we don't need to get—"

What was it with these types? Did they all have daddy issues or something?

"I am not your son. And you are breaking the law by being here."

"You own this land?"

Marco nodded. "I do."

"Where are your parents?"

Marco knew at twenty-four, he didn't fit the typical mold of the wrinkled old rancher, but it wasn't his fault his parents had died in a plane accident just before he turned eighteen. Most kids couldn't wait for the imagined independence of turning eighteen. Marco wished he could've waited forever.

"I own the land. That's all you need to know."

A wide smile broke out across the man's meticulously tanned face. His bleach-white teeth sparkled like a commercial. "Then you're just the man I've been meaning to talk to." He extended his hand into the narrow gap between them. "They call me Big Tex, good to meet you."

Marco's lip curled up as the urge to hammer his fist through this idiot's face surged in his chest. He didn't reciprocate the hand shake. "Get off my land."

Sucked in breaths and ooh's sounded from the gathered school group off to the side.

"Awesome," one said in a whisper. Probably Mohawk.

Big Tex held his hand out an instant longer, then let it drop. He held Marco's gaze for a silent stretch while both men gazed evenly into the other's eyes.

Measuring.

Silently squaring off.

Big Tex nodded and turned away. He walked a few paces and stopped, staring out across the endless grass-covered hills. He swept an arm across the landscape. "Look at this. All of this." He turned back around. "Everything you can see out there is mine. All of it. In a matter of months, there will be an oil pipeline running through it. The LockRock XL is going to bring shale oil from Canada down to refineries in this great country. It couldn't be more important. It's a matter of national security."

A matter of personal enrichment, more like.

"It's not running through here," Marco said.

Big Tex removed his hat and dabbed a handkerchief at the sweat beading on his forehead. "You don't want to do this. I'll make you rich. I'm talking generational wealth. Your grandkids' grandkids will be set."

"I don't want your blood money, and I'm getting tired of asking you to get off my land."

Big Tex pointed his ten gallon hat at Marco. "Don't be stupid, kid. You wouldn't be the first stubborn fool I've had to run over to get where I am today." He flashed a shark's smile.

Talking with this guy wasn't achieving anything, so Marco decided upon another course of action.

The low road.

He pulled the atlatl and dart from the wool sling at his back. He notched the dart and raised them so they were parallel to the ground.

The confident smirk on Big Tex's face evaporated like an ice cube dropped into the sun.

"Easy there, friend," he said as his arm raised with that enormous, ridiculous white hat out in front.

"You're trespassing and reasonable requests don't seem to motivate you."

Big Tex spread his arms wide in a conciliatory gesture. "I'm just trying to talk some sense into you. You don't wanna go to war with me. I promise you that."

Marco's upper lip lifted revealing clenched teeth. He took aim and whipped his arm forward and down. The dart rocketed forward with the compressed force warping the long shaft.

It shot through the white hat, ripping it out of the man's hand, and punched into the SUV's front tire. A loud hiss accompanied the sinking of the front corner of the vehicle. The chromed wheel touched the ground.

The brown skin of Big Tex's face had gone paler, like he'd missed a few tanning sessions mid-winter. A spot of gray appeared in the crotch of his white pants. It spread down his leg and wicked outward as it went.

"He peed himself!" Mohawk screamed from a safe distance away. A chorus of shrieking laughter erupted, competing with the teacher's loud instructions to follow her. That they were leaving.

It wasn't how Marco had planned for the morning to go, but it wasn't a bad result. All in all.

Big Tex sprinted for the SUV and dove into the already opened door. The driver slammed the door shut and jumped into the front seat. A second later, four tires shot up fountains of dirt as the SUV lurched forward and carved an arc, heading back in the direction from which it had come. The dart snapped, a foot-long section with the pinned hat still protruding from the ruined tire. The vehicle roared forward, leaning forward on the corner like a bull with a bum knee.

"That was awesome!" Mohawk shrieked from a distance.

Marco turned around and saw the teacher herding the

children back toward the trailhead and the safety of their school bus.

He'd lose that school, no doubt. And when word got around to the other schools about what he'd done, he'd probably lose them too. And for someone who didn't have much cash flow and was trying to keep his family's lands out of foreclosure, that wasn't a good development.

Even so, he couldn't help but smile.

11

A long dark thread hung from the armpit of Marco's sport coat. He tucked it up under his arm rather than chance pulling at it and having the whole sleeve fall off. Twenty dollars at the local Goodwill had bought him slacks and a sport coat. The slacks were fine, but the coat had seen better days.

Like a thousand of them.

"Marco, you know your father and I went way back. He did more than a few favors for me over the years. I'd do anything possible to help you."

Marco lifted his eyes off the shabby coat that represented his best effort at appearing respectable. He uncrossed his legs and scooted forward in the chair. "I know that, Mr. Crawford. And I appreciate it." He saw the kindness in the old man's eyes. And also the sadness.

"Call me Ken. I've known you since you were shorter than a weed. Listen, if it was up to me, a handshake would do it. Your father was always good for it and I know you would be, too." He exhaled and the air rattled in his chest. "But, it's not up to me anymore."

Marco understood. The blowout when Ken's only son had refused to take on the family business hadn't been front page news, but everybody in town knew about it anyway. Ken Junior had ended up in Seattle or somewhere trying to make it big in a rock band. Shortly after his departure, Ken Senior had sold the bank.

Ken removed his thick glasses and rubbed the sunken skin on each side of his nose. "You're going to have to put your land up as collateral to get the loan. I know you don't like it, but the new management won't make the loan without an asset to cover it. And your land is the only asset you have."

Marco bit his lip and squeezed his clasped hands so tight the fingers went white from lack of blood. He'd seen too many people lose their land in exactly this situation.

Not from this bank. But from so many others just like it. First Bank was the first bank established in Baker, Montana, back in 1826 and had faithfully served the community for nearly two hundred years. Ken's family had supported the town from its earliest days and had become prosperous for the support. The business had been passed down through the generations.

Until last year when Ken had sold it to one of those big multinational banks. Marco couldn't remember for sure which one. Chase, Morgan Stanley, whatever. They were all the same.

Raving bloodsuckers forever in search of the next victim to drain so that their stock price grew a fraction of a percent. One-tenth of one percent meant something when you were dealing with trillions of dollars of phony money.

One of those bloodsuckers had purchased First Bank, but they had done everything possible to maintain the veneer of a local business. They'd even kept Ken on, though he'd been reassigned (demoted was more accurate) to Vice-President of Operations.

Ken single finger-typed a bit more into the computer on his desk, staring at the monitor like the answer was hidden in code. "Been a while since I've run through a loan myself. "

"I know you don't have to do this. Thank you for dealing with it personally."

"Wouldn't have it any other way." His furry white brows lifted. "There it is." He punched another key and his eyes scanned some text. The etched corners of his wrinkled mouth turned down. "It's saying you'll have to put up eighty percent of your land for collateral."

"Eighty!" Marco said a whole lot louder than he'd intended.

Ken's frown inched lower. "Yep. It's a software program now. You enter the numbers and it lays it all out for you. Completely automated so you can't get around it. The new bosses don't understand the human element."

"Do it," Marco said before he could stop himself.

What choice did he have? He'd been swimming as hard as he could to keep his head above a growing pile of debt, and all his efforts had done nothing more than delay the inevitable. He either had to pay the liens or the government would take his land. The loan was a lifeline.

And he had to take it.

Even if it meant risking the very thing he was trying to save.

"Do it," he repeated.

Ken nodded. "Okay," he said as he returned the glasses to their customary perch. "Alright. Let me finish this and I'll get the papers printed out. A few signatures and you'll be set."

The bell on the string attached to the front door jingled

as it swept open.

Marco looked over his shoulder through the glass of Ken's small office. Big Tex strode in, again, like he owned the place. Maybe he did this time. He marched in and stopped on the other side of the glass with a wicked grin plastered across his face.

Ken walked around his desk and opened the door to his office. "Can I help you? I'm busy with a client here."

"Call your boss, old man."

Ken's stooped form straightened and he replied in clipped tones. "I'll do what I want, when I want." He moved to close the door but Big Tex stepped forward blocking the way.

Marco jumped up, ready to mangle him.

Big Tex looked him up and down and laughed. "The next time you need to beg for a loan, at least be smart enough not to wear a cheap suit."

Marco noticed the idiot's white pants didn't have a stain in the crotch. "New pants, huh?"

Big Tex scowled and his nose flared.

The phone on Ken's desk rang, pulling all of their attention to the sudden interruption.

Ken shuffled over and answered it. The voice on the other end didn't wait for him to speak. It jumped in loud enough to hear but not make out. After a minute of listening, Ken shook his head. "But, I—"

The voice interrupted and Ken went silent again. Another minute passed and he set the phone back down on the receiver.

Big Tex laughed. "Let me guess. That was Mr. Joseph Dixon, the president of the corporation that owns this bank."

Ken nodded. "It was."

"And let me further guess that any loan you were about to offer Mr. Morales is now withdrawn and no more assistance will be forthcoming."

Ken's eyes misted over as the saggy skin hanging to his jaws quivered. He turned to Marco and nodded. "I'm sorry, Marco. But he's right. There's nothing I can do."

Marco's knees went weak. Gravity seemed to wobble through a wave of uncertainty. He swallowed hard and concentrated on keeping his legs from giving out.

No loan meant no way to pay off the liens.

And that meant ninety days from now, his land would be sold at auction to the highest bidder.

He turned to Big Tex and those gleaming white teeth made his stomach turn. His hand clenched into a fist and shot out before he could stop it.

Not that he would've tried.

Red blood spurted out of the mess that was his broken nose. "You'll go to jail for this!" Tex screamed with gurgling words. "I'll take your land and your freedom!"

Marco raised his fist again and Big Tex winced and pulled away. He shouldered by, knocking the idiot against the door and stormed out through the small lobby and out into the warm evening air.

He made it around the corner before the weakness in his legs sent him to his knees. He covered his face, shaking his head in disbelief.

It was over.

Land that his family had owned for generations upon generations would now be stolen away. Sold to the highest bidder.

Bought by Big Tex.

Marco dropped his arms and stared up into the deeper blues above the ring of pale orange sky. He wanted to scream, or cry, or both. But the tears wouldn't come. In their place seethed something colder.

Rage.

Worse, impotent rage.

The kind that festered and ate a person from the inside out. The kind that reared its insidious head thirty years later when a terminal case of cancer appeared.

The phone in his pocket buzzed.

He snatched it out and answered in a frenzy, hoping beyond hope that Ken was calling to tell him it was all a mistake.

"Ken?" Marco said.

"Who?"

"Is this Ken?"

"Ken who?"

The fragile hope that had taken wing in Marco's heart crashed to the ground, the feathers burned and bones broken.

"What do you want?"

"Is this Marco Morales?"

"Who's asking?"

"My name is Bob Randy. I'm the executive producer for a reality TV show called *Sole Survivor*."

"What?"

"You sent us a video several months ago talking about why you should be selected for the show."

Through the impenetrable fog of the last few minutes, a ray of memory speared through. He had done that. Never figured he would hear anything about a long shot, pie-in-the-sky thing like being on a reality TV show. "I remember. What do you want?"

"I want you, Marco Morales, to have a chance at winning one million dollars."

12

SUYIN LI missed spending time in the great outdoors, but she missed her mother more. Free camping in the state park forests near Baltimore was the only vacation her parents had ever been able to afford. Free meant you didn't get anything fancy like toilets and showers. But she'd always thought the trade-off for not having someone's station wagon blasting music next to their two thousand square foot tent was worth it.

They stopped going camping when mother left.

Su had been sixteen at the time. Just getting into boys and dating and becoming an adult. But all that took a backseat as she witnessed the final stage of her parents' self-destruction.

Her neighborhood didn't offer many open spaces where a person could enjoy some peace and quiet. Central Park Heights was better known for gang shootings and police sirens going off at three in the morning. But just because they weren't as numerous as in a rich neighborhood didn't mean they didn't exist.

They did, if you knew where to look.

Someone yelled from the hallway outside her apartment door. Su glanced at the locked door in agitation and then back at the open book on the kitchen table in front of her. *Emergency Medicine - A Comprehensive Study Guide*. Comprehensive was right. Clocking in at over two thousand pages, it was heavy enough to cause a medical emergency if you dropped it on your foot.

She scanned the page, trying to find where'd she left off. The tiny text was hard enough to follow without the constant distraction of noisy neighbors shouting in the hallway, especially because the front door was about as solid as balsa wood.

For the millionth time since her mother had left and her father had let his addiction destroy their lives, she felt it in the depths of her soul.

A sucking emptiness.

An aching desire for something better that was always just out of reach.

There was a famous quote from somebody she couldn't remember about being rich and being poor, and that being rich was better.

Su didn't know anything about being rich or even middle-class, but she knew all about being poor.

And it sucked.

It sucked the life out of you.

She slammed the book shut and shoved the yellow notepad filled with scribbled notes away. Every other fourth year student at Johns Hopkins Medical school had a laptop and did all of their work on it. As part of her full scholarship, she'd gotten one and used it until she had to sell it to bail her dad out of trouble last month.

It was back to pen and paper until she could scrounge up enough to buy another laptop. And that wasn't going to be any time soon. At least she was nearly finished with school and would be starting her first year residency later this summer.

All the hard work. All the heartache she'd endured. Finally, a glimmer of hope. The promise of a better life.

If her dad didn't somehow ruin it all.

She checked her phone and sighed. Not because it was four years old and required restarting twenty times a day to get it to work, which it did, but because it was ten at night and her dad still wasn't home. With him, that wasn't a good sign. With normal people, maybe that meant they had a late night at work or that they had to make an unexpected stop for groceries.

Getting home late could mean any number of things that weren't a big deal for normal people.

Her father wasn't a normal person.

He was an addict.

She squeezed her eyes shut and took a chug of Red Bull. There were too many distractions and she had to get this procedure down cold. Emergency Medicine was the last rotation of her medical school career and she'd been looking forward to it forever. Until, that was, she'd met her attending doctor. He was the hardest nutjob to have ever strutted in a white coat.

He took great pleasure in belittling and humiliating the residents and interns in his charge. The slightest error would send him into a frenzy. He claimed it was his holy mission to "transform dimwits into doctors."

She looked at her phone again.

Ten o'clock.

She didn't need another thing to worry about.

He should've been home hours ago.

Su pounded her fist on the closed book. "I need some

air." She gathered the book, the notepad, and various supplies and threw them into a black backpack. She needed some space and knew just the place.

She marched into the bathroom, threw open the cracked window, and stepped out onto the fire escape stairwell. Ten stories below, cars roared by. Drivers probably trying to get out of the neighborhood before they got jacked.

She grabbed the pipe running up the wall and pulled herself up, levering a foot on each side. Hand over hand, one step at time, and a minute later she pulled herself over the ledge onto the roof of the apartment building. She got to her feet and followed the well-used path to the corner of the building.

While most of the flat roof was dotted with large air conditioners, thick pipes and the pumps that pushed the water through them, there was a space at the front corner that opened up and offered a perfect spot for someone intrepid enough to discover it.

Which she had, on the first day she and her father had moved there. A downgrade from a bad neighborhood to a downright dangerous one. They'd moved after mother left because father couldn't afford the bad neighborhood.

Su still didn't understand how it all fell apart so fast.

First his addiction. Then the fighting. Then her addiction. Then she left. They'd never had enough money, but her parents had somehow always made it work. For sixteen years. And then in less than a year, he'd destroyed it all. Not that mother was an angel.

She wasn't. She'd fallen into her own addiction and eventually abandoned them both for whatever life she thought she needed.

That was the one single thing Su had to credit her father for.

He never left.

To be fair, she also had to give him credit for what he'd done for almost a year now. He'd gone to support groups. Gone to rehab. A year of trying to get better and repeatedly falling down. It was almost like he couldn't stand on his own anymore. But he was trying and that had to count for something.

If she could just get through the last rotation, finish med school, and make it to the start of her residency. Fifty grand the first year.

That was the pay.

It would change *everything*.

Well, maybe not her father. Only he could do that.

Suyin dropped into her favorite corner spot. With equipment boxing it in on the backside, it afforded an expansive view of the sky beyond the ledge. The soft hum of the machines muffled most of the sounds of the city below. She dropped her backpack and lay down with it under her head. Below the level of the ledge, the sour smell of the neighborhood faded a little.

The dark sky had the familiar orange glow that large cities always had. Like a computer monitor that couldn't achieve true black. It was a faded black.

But at least she could see stars.

A few of them.

They twinkled through the layer of pollution blanketing the city.

Still, she felt happiest while outside under the sky and stars. They brought back so many warm memories of her life before everything fell apart. Her mother had loved being surrounded by trees. By nature. She loved anything that took them out of the city and into the wild.

She always said that cities were necessary for humans to

evolve, but that nature was necessary for us to remain that way.

The early memories helped her remember her mother wasn't a total monster for leaving. For quitting.

As unappealing as it sounded, she had a lot of work to do. And she needed at least a few hours of sleep not to be a zombie at work tomorrow. Dr. Holier-Than-Thou would rip her apart if she yawned while he was explaining something.

Su sat up and unpacked her bag. She pulled out her phone and flipped on the LED light. A few minutes later she had all her study materials fanned out in front of her.

The city faded away as her attention focused.

Time stood still when she was deep in the concepts. Rather, it didn't stand still, but she didn't notice its passing.

It could've been minutes later when a loud screeching of tires on pavement snapped her awake.

She checked the time. Midnight and still no text or call from her father.

Su jerked as a gunshot ripped through the dull hum of the surrounding machines. It had come from below. And nearby.

She shoved the books aside and scrambled over to the edge of the roof, pulling herself up to peek over the ledge.

Ten floors below in the shadow of the building, a man lay face down on the sidewalk next to a gray car with both doors open. Another man in a dark suit knelt next to the still form.

The man in the suit rolled the other over and stood, partially blocking her view. He pointed a gun at the other's head. He shifted it slightly and fired. He yelled something, slammed the back door shut, and then jumped into the passenger's seat. Tires squealed and the car took off as the door slammed shut.

Lights flicked on all along the front of the building as people awoke to investigate. Light flooded the sidewalk.

A cold panic gripped Su's chest. Its icy touch left her breathless and frozen.

Even from ten stories up, she recognized the man's face.

Her father's face.

Bloody and mutilated.

Baba.

Daddy.

13

Books forgotten, Suyin raced back to the pipe leading to their apartment, shimmied down, leap-falling the last six feet. The race to the street below blurred until she skidded to a halt and dropped to her knees beside her father.

Long, ragged lacerations on his face and arms.

Contusions covering more skin than not.

She searched his body, lifting his shirt and feeling everywhere. No bullet holes. She measured his pulse and studied his eyes and breathing. Someone had beaten him half to death, but he would live.

"Baba, we need to get you to an emergency room."

A weak hand lifted to touch her cheek. Sad eyes regarded her. "No, Su. Upstairs. I'm... It's nothing."

Anger welled in her chest. The sorrow hardened. "Nothing? Nothing? They almost killed you!"

"Please, Su," he said as he tried to sit up and groaned. "Upstairs."

Su bit down, cutting off the sharp reply about to come out. Now wasn't the time.

"Fine," she said and she helped him to his feet. She draped a bloodied arm over her shoulder and carried as much as supported him inside.

The small crowd of gathered neighbors at the front door parted. Whispers followed as the two lumbered toward the only functioning elevator in the cramped lobby.

Minutes later, she helped her father into a kitchen chair.

"Need a drink," he said.

What was new? His second favorite addiction was drinking. Probably to try to forget how badly the first had ruined their lives.

Su shook her head. "You know we don't have any alcohol here."

He gestured toward the fridge. "Inside the ice maker."

Her jaw dropped. She spun on her heel and threw open the freezer door hard enough to dent it on the corner of the kitchen cabinet. She yanked open the ice maker cover and found it.

A half-empty bottle of gin.

"How could you? Do you want to die?"

"Just give it to me."

Swallowing the acid burning in the back of her throat, she grabbed the bottle and took it to the table. She slammed it down, half-hoping the glass would shatter and the clear poison would spill out onto the floor.

Her father tried to open the lid, but his fingers were too mangled to do the job.

She yanked the bottle away and spun the metal cap off. It dropped to the peeling linoleum floor and rolled away. She wet a kitchen towel and began cleaning his face as he took a drink. Then another drink. She went back and forth cleaning his wounds and rinsing the scarlet blood from the towel in the sink. The water diluted it pale pink before washing it down the drain. "You're going to need stitches. More than a few of them."

Another gulp was the only reply.

Su gathered the necessary items out of the medical supply cabinet above the fridge. She laid them out on the table in what had by now become an all too familiar routine. She used iodine to disinfect her hands and then irrigate the largest laceration. A gaping cut that ran down the left side of his face, from the temple to the jaw. She chose an eyeless needle with attached number ten suture thread, she met his gaze. "This is going to hurt."

"I know."

She pressed the sharp point into the skin next to the injury. She pressed harder and the tip pierced the surface. Red welled up as she squeezed the sides together with her other hand.

Her father winced as she turned the curved needle into the wound and pushed it through to the other side.

Two sides of her mind pulled on her focus like the center of the rope in a tug-of-war. The doctor in her remained calm and detached while it assessed injuries and worked to heal them. However, the daughter that loved her only remaining parent was apoplectic with fear and anger.

She hooked the curved needle back up through the skin on the other side and then pulled it all the way through. A solid knot and she started another stitch. "Baba, why did they do this to you?"

She knew the answer, but didn't want to believe it.

Maybe it would be different this time. Maybe he'd shown up on the front sidewalk, half-beaten to death for an innocent reason.

Yeah, maybe.

Her father winced as the needle carved a narrow channel through his flesh. "I had a bad turn of luck."

The doctor didn't falter, but the daughter sure did.

"You were gambling! I knew it!"

"Su, please. Let me explain. I had it all going—"

"How many times have I heard that before? A thousand? More?"

"I nearly fixed it all. Nearly. It was just at the end that it all fell apart."

Su tied off another stitch and continued to the next. She huffed. "It never ends well. Never! How much do you owe this time?"

She paused.

His swollen shut eye opened a crack.

And stared in silence.

"How much?"

"Two hundred thousand."

"Two hundred thousand? Two hundred thousand?"

The doctor lost ground.

Her hand jerked the stitch closed, harder than was strictly necessary.

"Owww!" Baba said with a groan.

"We can't possibly pay that back. We couldn't pay back a tenth of that! Not even a tenth of tenth!"

Baba slowly shook his head. "No."

"What happens if we can't pay?"

Baba's eyes grew still, unblinking. "They'll kill me."

The needle dropped out of the doctor's hand and hung from the thread embedded in Baba's cheek.

A raw animal scream clawed up her throat. It crouched, ready to leap out into the world.

And her phone rang.

Who would call at this hour?

Confused.

Concerned.

Worried.

And rapidly edging toward terrified, she answered it.

14

Su thumbed on the call, already worrying over who was behind the No Caller ID on the screen. "Hello?"

"Is this Suyin Li?"

"Yes."

"You don't know me, but I know you. And I know your father. The promising young doctor is fixing up her father, yes?"

Terror morphed into rage.

The two emotions held such close kinship.

"You're the one who hurt my father! Don't lay another—"

"Your father owes me two hundred thousand dollars. And if I don't get it in forty-eight hours, I'll kill him."

She hung up.

It was a reaction more than anything.

The phone rang again.

No Caller ID.

Hanging up wasn't going to change anything. Not answering wasn't going to either.

She thumbed on the call and started yelling. "I want you

to leave us alone! We can't do that!"

"But I haven't even extended the offer yet."

The offer?

If *the offer* included anything about paying back any portion of two hundred thousand dollars, talking about it was pointless.

"It's impossible! And threatening to kill my father won't change that!"

"Kill your father? I've been called a lot of names over the years, more than a few of them deserved, but murderer? I protest innocence on that count."

The voice didn't sound right.

"Who is this?"

"My name is Bob Randy. Am I speaking to Suyin Li?"

Bob Randy?

The name didn't ring a bell.

"What do you want, Mr. Randy?"

"Please, call me Bob. Only my shrink calls me Mr. Randy. And only after she said no to the tenth time I asked her out on a date. I mean, think of it. On a hot date with a hot shrink. Twice the fun at half the cost! What's not to like?"

What was this idiot talking about?

"Goodbye, Mr. Randy."

"Wait! Hold on a second. I need you, Suyin Li."

Su tapped her finger to end the call.

What was with tonight? It was supposed to be a boring night of studying. It was supposed to be easy in that tediously difficult kind of way that she'd mastered by high school.

The phone rang again.

No Caller ID.

The first one or the second one?

Baba stared at her in confusion. He nodded at the phone. "Aren't you going to answer it?"

Su tapped on the call and listened.

"I apologize for oversharing. Just call me Bob."

"Do I know you, Bob?"

"Not yet, but I'm hoping to change that. I'm the executive producer of a reality TV show called *Sole Survivor*."

Sole Survivor?

A faint tickle in the back of her mind. Baba had mentioned it a long time ago, asked if she wanted to apply to be on it. Some kind of survival type show. She'd asked him if he was crazy. Johns Hopkins Medical School didn't smile on months long absences. Especially those not involving your own death. "*Sole Survivor*?"

The voice on the other end continued. "You applied to be on the show six months ago. It's taken longer than we wanted to get rolling, but we're finally there. The question now is, 'Will you be joining us?'"

"I applied to your show?" she asked before her eyes opened wide. She looked down at her father.

His gaze stayed locked to the ground.

"Baba, did you sign me up for—"

"Yes. Is that the show?"

She nodded. She didn't have words.

"It's a million dollars, Su. A million! Think of what it could do. Especially now."

Her thumb hovered over the red button on the screen. The muscle twitched to hang up, but then froze in motion.

She never would've agreed, on a normal day, in a normal life. She would've finished her EM rotation and then started her residency. And then she would've finally made it to the next phase of her life. One where she was helping people. And one where she was getting paid decent money to do it.

It was a dream almost come true.

But what kind of dream would it be if it killed her father?

"If I accepted, when would it start and how long would it last?"

"You'd leave in a few days. As for how long? That depends on you and the other nine contestants. Whichever of you lasts the longest alone in the wilds on Kodiak Island will take home the money."

Wilds of Kodiak Island?

As in Kodiak Island, Alaska?

As in the home of the Kodiak bear, the largest brown bear species in the world?

Su traced the lacerations still unattended on her father's arms. They needed attention.

And if they didn't figure out a way to pay off a two hundred thousand dollar gambling debt, there would be more of them. Too many to fix.

Baba would die.

A bitter seed of resentment planted itself in her heart. She wouldn't be able to finish the rotation. She'd have to do it again and maybe redo the entire year, and that was assuming they didn't kick her out of the program in the first place. And forget about the residency. That would be given to another graduate.

The dream she'd clung to for years, the one that had been the only thing keeping her sane, fissured into a web of cracks.

And then shattered completely.

But she didn't have a choice.

Her father hadn't given her one.

"I'll do it."

15

EMILY sipped a cup of coffee that tasted like it had been brewed years ago. For a place called Queen's Diner, this wasn't exactly the royal treatment. She took another sip. Stale and bitter. Not altogether unlike her soul.

When you had a bad day, people would say it just wasn't your day.

Well, this just wasn't her life.

They also said you won some and you lost some, but her life seemed to only deal in the losing.

Losing her mother and father long ago.

Close to losing her grandmother now.

Definitely losing her if she tapped out and so didn't win the million dollars.

She cut off a portion of pancake and reindeer sausage and decided to try them together. Each was tasty on its own. So why not? She crammed the overloaded fork into her mouth.

And they were more than twice as good together.

A server wearing a faded, pink smock with a pen stuck

behind her ear glided over and tapped the table. "Need anything, hon?"

It was the kind of question that Emily couldn't answer with any sincerity.

Yeah, she needed a lot of things.

The emptiness that had become a permanent part of her life since her father disappeared was another reason she was here.

She needed closure.

Maybe this experience on this same land where he had disappeared would bring it?

How exactly that might happen, she had no idea.

But being a server herself until very recently, she knew what it was like having to deal with crazy customers. So, she made it easy.

She shook her head and lied, "No, I'm fine. Thanks."

"Well, you let Flo know the second that changes," the woman said with a genuine smile and then drifted over to the next booth to check on a couple of old guys. The one facing Emily had eyebrows that looked alive. Like furry, wriggling caterpillars.

She expected them to sprout wings and flutter off any second.

If only transformation was that easy.

But it never was.

Maybe butterflies just made it look that way.

She turned to look out a large window at the long, narrow lake across the street.

At the near end, a seaplane lifted off with water trailing behind like anchor lines. It climbed into the air and veered off and beyond the frame of the glass window.

Her father would've taken a plane just like that.

The last time anyone had seen him and his guide was

when they were walking out of Port Bailey to, presumably, check out the tracks that had been found.

And that was it.

Radio silence.

He never came back.

It was like he'd vanished off the face of the earth.

There was something about the uncertainty of it that made it so much worse. Losing her mother had been devastating, but there was a shape to it.

A way to handle it.

Her father's death had left a gaping hole in her heart. One that had molded her passions and interests for years.

She checked the time on her black G-Shock Solar watch. It was just about the only solid thing in her life. Given to her by her father on the night he left. It matched an identical one he wore. It was supposed to keep them connected.

It didn't.

But it rarely left her wrist even so. She'd replaced the band once in the ten years since she'd had it, but that was it. The rechargeable battery was still going strong and everything worked perfectly.

Except the connection part.

Emily stared at it wondering if it was the same time wherever her father had gone.

If heaven or the afterlife or wherever had time.

Time for what, was the real question.

What would the afterlife need time for?

It had forever.

Watches would lose their purpose in a time that stretched into infinity.

But she was in Kodiak. And here it was 6:37 AM.

Time meant something here. And the people she was

meeting were seven minutes late. That, or she was at the wrong diner. That was a possibility.

The old man with the crazy eyebrows said something that caught her attention.

"That's what I heard. Some reality TV show called *Sole Survivor*. Ten people from the Outside trying to survive on their own in the wilderness. Last one to call for rescue gets a million dollars! You believe that?"

"Believe anything these days," the one facing away from her said. "Mark my words, one of 'ems gonna get theirselves killed."

Never one to be quiet in the interests of just getting along, Emily got up and circled around to their booth. "Have any advice so I don't get myself killed?"

Both men looked at her like she was a lunatic.

They weren't wrong.

The man who'd been facing away had deep lines etched into his scowling face. Like maybe his face never stopped scowling. "You one of 'em that's doing it?"

"I am. I've been training for this kind of thing for a long time."

"Training and Kodiak are two very different things."

"I'm about to find out. So? Any advice?"

The etched-faced man took a drink of hot coffee and sucked in air to cool it.

Bugbrows leaned over. "Stay away from bears."

Etched-Face burst out laughing, spewing coffee onto the table. He wiped his mouth and grinned. "Yep, watch out for Hannibal."

Flo's voice replied from behind her. "You two, hush. Hannibal's been gone for a decade. It was a regular bear that got that hiker last week. Probably old and starving. Don't listen to them, dear. They've got too much time and not enough sense."

"Not as much time as I'd like," Etched-Face muttered as his gnarled finger tapped his cup.

Flo leaned over and refilled the two half-empty cups on the table. "Anyway, if that bear ever was real, it's dead or moved on long ago."

Bugbrows looked at Emily. He squinted and the fuzz clinging to his forehead dropped, obscuring his eyes. He blinked as he added his two cents...

"Maybe."

16

A short time later, the small silver bell that hung on the front glass door tinkled as it opened. A slender girl shorter than Emily walked in. Her long, straight black hair shone in the golden morning light. She carried a backpack that went a foot above her head. She had the Sole Survivor show badge pinned to her chest with her name in the white space below.

Suyin.

The same badge they'd all worn for the last three days while doing twelve hour days training on the various things they'd need to know out in the field. How to operate the cameras was apparently the most important thing because that had taken up the largest chunk.

"Su, over here!" Emily called out.

Su turned and a glowing grin lit up her face. She waved and the backpack teetered dangerously on her back. She froze to stabilize it, succeeded, then grinned again. She wobbled over and slumped into the opposite seat in the booth. "Good morning!"

"It's morning, at least," Emily said with a twisted smile. "So this is the day, huh?"

Su swallowed hard and nodded. "I guess so. Are you scared?"

Emily bit her lower lip and shrugged. "A little. You?"

Su nodded. "More than a little. A lot. Way more."

The two had bonded over the last three days in a way that shouldn't have been possible in such a short time. Especially for someone like Emily.

Emily reached over and took both of Su's hands in hers. "You're going to be fine."

"We don't even know where we're going."

Emily shrugged. "Each of us gets our own remote location on the island. I'm hoping for a beach next to water filled with fish."

"I'm hoping for anywhere where bears don't go."

"Don't worry. It'll take a while for each of us to adjust and get our systems going, but we'll make it."

There was something about Su that drew a person in. It shouldn't have been possible, but they got along like old friends. They just clicked.

They'd even shared with each other the reason for their being on the show. Each had shared the hurt and worry, and been comforted by the other.

Su smirked. "I worry a lot. It's a problem."

"Sister, you're not alone."

The bell tinkled again.

They both turned to see who had arrived.

Su's brow raised. "And now, *we're* not alone." She waved her hand in the air. "Marco! Over here!"

A flutter in Emily's chest annoyed her to no end. She wasn't here for that. Despite being the definition of tall, dark, and handsome, Marco was her opponent in this game.

And a few days of knowing someone didn't remotely change that.

Maybe in another life, a better one, maybe something could've developed.

He was definitely her type.

Black wavy hair. Lean and muscled. Loved the outdoors. Gray-blue eyes that could make a girl forget her name. Walking around with a chip on his shoulder like he was about to put his fist through the first idiot's face that got too close.

There was anger there, always bubbling just below the surface.

Just like her.

Marco strolled over to the table, shrugged off his pack and slung it to the floor in one graceful movement. His arms bulged in angled planes. Prisms of flesh that separated light and shadow in ways that brought color to her cheeks.

Emily took a quick sip of cold coffee to give her brain something else to focus on.

Marco caught her eyes before they could escape.

"Is that coffee?" he asked.

"Not good coffee."

"Don't care."

Emily snorted. "Exactly."

Flo appeared at their table as if by magic. Despite the crisply ironed crease down the middle of her pink smock, the darker hues of old stains that didn't come out revealed that it wasn't always so neat. "I know. I know. The coffee's terrible. I've told Ed not to keep yesterday's brew countless times. He won't listen."

She threw her hands up and lowered her voice to imitate him. "How do you think I keep these lights on?" She gestured at the door. "Keep that door open? I do it by not throwing out perfectly good coffee."

Emily took another sip. "It's not perfectly good."

Her voice returned to its normal pitch. "Don't I know it. Tell the boss. Better yet, leave an online review saying it. That's the only way to get him to pay attention."

Flo turned to Marco. "Good morning, handsome. Anything I can do for you? Anything at all?"

Marco's eyes widened as a smirk crept onto his face. "I'd love some of that terrible coffee, to start."

"Coming right up." She winked. "And you let Flo know if you think of anything else."

"Will do," Marco said as he moved to sit next to Su.

Su scooted closer to the open end of the booth's seat to block him off. "There's room on Em's side."

Marco's brow lifted. "Em, huh? You two besties now? How's that gonna work out?"

Emily scooted over to make room, not sure if she was mad or thrilled at Su's actions. They'd trained with seven other contestants over the last three days, but they'd ended up hanging out together. They were the youngest three of the group with Emily the youngest by far. All of the others were older. Several were ex-military. Several others were survival instructors. One guy was famous in the prepper community.

But Marco was hard to read. It wasn't that he clicked with them so much as he totally didn't click with all the others.

"Sisters stick together," Su said as she grabbed a menu. She grimaced. "They serve reindeer sausage? Isn't that like sacrilegious to Christmas or something?"

Emily stabbed another bite, slid it through an amber

puddle of syrup, and popped it in her mouth. "I never knew Rudolph tasted so good."

Marco reached for the last bite and, like a snake strike, Emily jabbed his hand with her fork. "Mine."

His eyes burned for an instant as he pulled his hand away. "Selfish much?"

Emily shrugged her shoulders. "Gotta get the easy calories while I can."

Marco's eyes narrowed and he nodded in agreement.

She was already playing the game. It wasn't that she was normally so competitive. Okay, she was. But this contest and the one million dollar prize money was about way more than simply wanting to win.

It was about keeping her grandmother alive.

And so she'd give herself every advantage she could.

Su's phone rang and she fished it out of the baggy front pocket of her cargo pants. She glanced at the screen and her jaw tightened. "My dad. One sec." She thumbed on the call. "Hey. Yes. I'm fine."

Emily jabbed the last bite of Rudolph and coated it in syrup.

Marco mouthed the word *coffee* and jumped up to track down Flo. He moved like a panther. Easy grace and coiled power. He projected a predator's confidence.

"Yes. We go out this morning. Don't worry. I'll be fine." She listened and then continued. "I know. We're lucky they agreed to wait." She listened again. "I know what's at stake." She looked up at Emily and frowned. "I'm not the only one who needs to win."

Emily cut off another square of pancake and used it as a sponge to soak up syrup and get into her belly. She'd done her best in the last week to pile on the calories, but she'd only managed to add a thin layer of padding over her normally athletic frame.

"I love you, Baba. Stay safe. And please, don't do anything stupid while I'm gone."

Her dad said something, presumably reassuring his daughter.

Emily reflected on the reason Su had shared for being in the competition. Her dad was circling around the drain, a few orbits away from getting sucked under. If Grammy's health wasn't at stake, she would've done everything she could've to help Su win.

"Okay. Goodbye." Su tapped off the call and exhaled. "I wish I could believe him. But without me there, he'll probably get in trouble in a matter of days."

Moisture welled up in the corners of her eyes.

Emily reached across and interlaced her fingers with Su's. "This isn't going to be easy for any of us. But the only way to win is to keep your head in the game. Besides, Providence Medical Center is right around the corner in case any of us get hurt."

Su frowned. "Yeah, and a lot of good that will do us out in the bush."

Emily's attempt at levity fell flatter than a sheet of sandpaper. She just wanted to help, even if she didn't know the best way to do it. At twenty, she was five years younger than Su but still felt like an older sister. But then, Emily wasn't a typical twenty-year-old. Pain did that to a person. It burdened you with perspective and maturity beyond your years. Su understood that, but not to the degree Emily did.

Emily squeezed so their palms connected. "You have to forget about what's going on back home. Just while you're here. Dwelling on it too much will only make you weaker."

Su nodded, blinking away the gathering tears. "You're right. You're right. I know you're right."

Emily noticed Flo returning with Marco in tow. "Get a big breakfast. It'll be the last one like it for a while."

Marco swung in next to her, balancing a white porcelain cup of coffee in each hand. His broad shoulders bumped her over a little as he landed, but the black liquid filling each cup didn't so much as ripple.

"Excuse me," she said.

"You're excused." He pushed one of the cups across to Su. "For you."

She shook her head. "Thanks, but no. I don't do caffeine unless it's the night before an exam. And then I do a lot of it."

"Suit yourself," he said as he pulled it back to his side of the table.

Flo tugged the pencil from out of the gray hair tucked behind her ear. "What can I get you two? See anything you like?" Her eyes never left Marco.

Something burned in Emily's gut. A territorial urge that had no right being there.

Marco wagged a finger in Emily's direction. "I'd like some of that."

"Well, honey. She's not on the menu. However—"

Marco's face reddened. "I meant what she ordered."

"Tall stack of buttermilk pancakes and an order of reindeer sausage?"

"Yep, two orders, please."

"My, aren't you a big eater? What about you?" Flo asked while her eyes remained locked on Marco.

"The same, please. One order, I mean."

"Coming right up," Flo said as she scribbled on a ticket and then twirled away from the table.

Su leaned forward over the table with a conspiratorial look bouncing between Emily and Marco. "So Marco, what did you really mean by that?"

Marco glanced at Emily and then back at his coffee. "I didn't mean anything by it. So don't put words into my mouth."

Maybe in another time and place, she and Marco could've given it a shot. But not here. And not now.

Emily turned to face him and waited in silence until he looked up and met her gaze. The warmth drained out of her face and a hard chill settled in her eyes. "Good. Because I'm not here for the sausage. I'm here to win."

17

Frothy white spray blasted upwards on each side of the ancient fishing boat every time the bow crashed into another wave. Icy droplets curled inward and stung Emily's face like tiny needle pricks. The sharp scent of brine filled her lungs.

"Port Bailey's coming up," the captain said, standing at the helm of the center console. His legs absorbed the shifting energies battering the boat's hull while Emily lurched to the side now and again when an unexpected wave hit.

Another hit and Emily grabbed a rail to steady herself. But the action of the waves wasn't the only thing threatening to knock her over.

The boat carved around an outcropping and squat buildings appeared in the distance. It was the first sign of civilization they'd seen in hours. A sea plane would've been faster, but the battered fishing boat she was on wasn't the first hint that the show's producer, Bob Randy, was pinching pennies everywhere possible. He'd probably rented this floating heap at a huge discount.

"We've got a strange connection, you and I," the captain said to himself as much as to her or the show's camera operator who currently had his equipment aimed at the distant port.

Emily looked at him with equal parts confusion and suspicion. It was an odd thing to hear from someone she'd just met. Especially one that in no way appeared to be trying to hit on her. "We do?"

"Yep," he said with a nod. "Bob Randy told me you're Emily Wilder. Your father disappeared on this island ten years ago."

"He did."

"The man that disappeared with him was my best friend, Kagan."

Kagan?

Kagan!

That was the name of the guide that had taken her father out to Port Bailey. Emily pulled her rubber hood open a little as she turned toward the captain. "Do you know what happened to them?"

The captain scratched a thick, more salt-than-pepper beard. "Nope. Just vanished one day. Not like Kagan at all. He was as wily and tough as they come. Survived things that'd kill any normal man ten times over. He once walked twenty miles out of the bush with a branch the size of your arm through his gut."

Of course, he didn't know what happened. No one did. That was the infuriating incompleteness of it. Her father had been taken from her, and she'd never know why.

Life abided by its own rules and equations. And some problems simply didn't have solutions.

Emily watched the captain. Noticed how his eyes stared

back through the years to the last time he'd seen his friend alive.

"I'm sorry you lost him," she said.

The captain frowned and the bushy beard hid his cracked lips. "I'm sorry you lost your father. I guarantee you Kagan did whatever he could've to keep them both alive."

The captain slowed the boat as they neared Port Bailey.

The squat structures turned out to be shipping containers surrounding a couple of taller, central buildings.

The whistling wind quieted as they coasted closer.

A phone rang and the camera operator lowered his gear to dig it out of his jacket pocket. He clicked on the speaker and a familiar voice boomed.

"Are you there yet?"

"We're pulling up now."

"Good! Get that camera on her. Right up in her face. Port Bailey was the last place anyone saw her father alive. If she starts crying, I want it on tape!"

"Uhh, Mr. Randy—"

"It's the human drama! Viewers eat it up!"

"Umm, she's—"

"What? Is she losing it completely? Tell me you're recording!"

"Mr. Randy, sir?"

"What? What? What?"

"She's listening to you right now."

"What?"

"You're on speaker phone."

The stream of obscenities cut off as the camera guy tapped the phone and held it to his ear. He winced a few times as Bob continued screaming and then finally nodded. "Yes, sir."

The captain shut down the engine as they glided toward the dock.

The camera guy secured his phone and then brought the large camera back up to his shoulder. He looked through the eyepiece as a tiny red light on the front blinked on and off.

She didn't blame the jerks for wanting to milk her emotion like a cow at a dairy farm. A father who mysteriously died. A daughter returning to the scene, putting her own life on the line to win a million dollars.

Will the island take them both?

Is her family cursed to extinction?

It was a compelling story. Like a sick fabrication from a twisted author's mind. Something gripping that would tug on a viewer's heart strings.

She knew all that.

And it didn't tick her off so much as it repulsed her.

It was disgusting.

Callous exploitation for commercial gain.

Emily turned away from the lens two feet in front of her face. She stared out over the dark blue water and white waves out beyond the point.

The camera came around to her side, a foot from her face.

Okay, it ticked her off, too.

"Leave me alone!"

"It's my job."

She knew what she'd signed up for. And that it was a means to an end. Still, that didn't mean she had to just sit there and take it. She grabbed the lens and shoved, nearly sending the cameraman into a hard landing on his butt.

"Hey! Come on! I'm just doing my job!"

The captain pointed to the cameraman and then at the

back of the boat. "You! Get to the stern and grab the line. Be ready to jump on the dock when I say."

"Stern?"

"The back! Go to the back!"

"Jeez. Okay, man," he said as he carefully set his camera on the seat. He stumbled to the back and looked around in confusion. "What line?"

The captain shook his head in disgust. He pointed. "The rope! Grab the rope and be ready to jump."

"Seriously?"

"I'm the captain of this vessel. You are under my command. Do it before I chop you up and use you for bait."

The cameraman climbed up on the side to gather up the dock line.

The boat's engine roared and it lurched forward.

"Noooo!" the camera guy shrieked as the boat was suddenly no longer under his feet and his face hit the water. He popped his head up a second later, spewing water and screaming through chattering teeth.

"How cold is that water?" Emily asked.

"Unfortunately, not cold enough. The suit and life jacket will keep him alive until rescue arrives."

The radio on the central console crackled to life. "Mack, did you drop that kid in the water on purpose?"

The captain picked up the transmitter and squeezed the button to speak. His beard parted and he grinned wide enough to show a few missing front teeth. "Barb, honey. I didn't know you were already back. You gonna keep the bed warm for me tonight?"

"In your dreams, ya crusty old salt!"

Emily stared in confusion.

The captain shrugged his wide shoulders and his belly bounced as he laughed. "My girlfriend. Some of the time."

The radio crackled again. "Care to answer the question?"

"Oh. Yeah, I did it on purpose. Can you fish him out for me?"

"How many times am I supposed to clean up your mess?"

"Honey, I just want you to be ready for when I'm too old to wipe my own butt."

"That's disgusting! You're sleeping on the floor until I can forget that image."

"Sounds fair. I'll be back later to pick up Captain Nemo."

"Yeah, okay. What should we do with him in the meantime?"

"I don't know, Barb. Read him nursery rhymes. Breast-feed him. Whatever!"

"Is he cute? I'm all of a sudden in the market for a better boyfriend."

"Don't break my heart, honey. You know it's the only part of me still working."

A lip smacking sound came through the radio. "Be safe out there. Chop's picking up."

"You know me," Mack responded.

"Yeah, that's not reassuring. I'll babysit for you but you owe me."

"Deal."

He reattached the transmitter to the radio and powered up the boat. "I'll take you to your drop off point."

"It's not here?" Emily asked.

"Nope, they apparently wanted to parade you around the base first hoping you'd fall apart for the camera."

Emily gritted her teeth. Heartless worms. She hopped over to the camera on the seat across the boat, hefted it over head, and then tossed it into the expanding wake behind the boat.

It felt good.

But it was pointless.

She'd be aiming a camera at her own face for the next however many weeks or months.

Still, it felt good. And that was something.

The boat continued forward, picking up speed. Emily lost herself in the whistling wind and the endless water.

Some time later, the slowing of the engine snapped her out of the reverie. Had it been ten minutes? Twenty? She glanced at her watch.

Way longer.

The boat cut right and angled toward a small cove in a vast stretch of beach. The chop eased as they left the open ocean behind. They coasted in and the bow channeled into soft sand. "This is your stop."

Emily flung her backpack up above the waterline and then jumped off.

The captain hefted the case filled with camera gear to the edge and lowered it until she had it with both hands.

She staggered up the beach and let it drop to the sand. It must've weighed fifty pounds. Hauling it around was going to be a serious pain.

She returned to the waterline for her backpack.

The captain stared at her in silence.

"Thanks for the ride, Captain."

"Call me Mack."

"Thanks, Mack, for everything."

"Least I could do. You stay safe."

"I'll do my best."

That was all anyone could do.

Mack nodded and then glanced over his shoulder as a larger swell rolled in. It lifted his boat and the engine sputtered on. The boat pulled back and, minutes later, disappeared around a bend.

Emily realized she hadn't moved a muscle since it pulled away. She took a deep breath and turned to face her future.

Thirty feet away, a wall of towering Spruce trees cut the beach short and kept everything beyond hidden in dim light and deeper shadow.

Something twisted in her gut.

Excitement.

The thrill of starting a big adventure.

Fear.

The anxiety of knowing it might not end well.

18

Emily hit record on the camera and then flipped the screen around so she could see herself while recording. The small screen had a red dot blinking in the upper right corner. The rest of the screen showed a close-up of the inside of her nostril.

Tiny hairs and a glob of pale green snot clinging to the side.

She dug it out and checked again, flaring each nostril in turn to get a good view.

And then remembered she was recording.

"Oh. Sorry about that. Not a good angle."

She secured the camera to the selfie stick, extended and twisted the pole to rotate the now attached camera into position. Once she was more or less framed up, she figured she should say something.

Something smart or insightful about beginning this adventure.

After a minute, she decided anything would work.

Anything at all.

But still nothing came.

Her mind was blank.

"Uh, sorry. I was supposed to be recording when I got dropped off, but... uh, I forgot. Anyway, this is my new home."

She sounded like a complete idiot.

And didn't look much better.

It was like being one of those tourists that ended up staring at the camera rather than the scene they'd travelled so far to see.

The small screen showed her upper half and a thick green mass of towering trees in the background.

She rotated around and backed up, trying to get a better shot for the people that would someday be watching her first few minutes in the competition.

Something caught her boot and she fell backwards into the sand. Her left wrist slammed into a partially submerged boulder. The selfie stick jumped out of her hand and plonked down beside her. The camera lay sideways in the sand, but still had her partially in frame.

It showed her flat on her back in the sand.

Real graceful.

Emily ground her teeth while staring up at a bright blue sky filled with enormous perfectly defined white clouds. She shook her head in disgust.

Not at the sky.

At herself.

She'd forgotten one of the simplest rules of survival. Watch where you step. Because if you don't, you might trip over something and fall on your face.

It was a stupid mistake that hadn't caused any lasting harm. But the margin for error was shrinking fast and another mistake like that could just as easily cause a sprained or broken ankle.

And then it would be over.

Just like that. One brainless instant and BAM!

Done.

She turned and stared into the lens—the little black eye that would be watching her for as long as she was here. "Well, that wasn't a promising start."

Thankfully, she was on sand so nothing was bruised beyond her ego. She looked at herself on screen, half her face coated with sand, thinking about the people who would someday watch this. "I know what you're thinking right now. That bet you made on me in the office pool isn't going to pay out. Right?"

The camera didn't respond.

It wasn't much for conversation.

Emily sat up and the G-Shock watch on her wrist fell off onto the sand. That never happened. She grabbed it and noticed the metal clasp was cracked and bent open.

"Unbelievable. In the first minute? Really?" she muttered.

Bending the clasp back into shape might've worked but it wouldn't have been secure. And there was no way she was going to chance it.

She tucked it into her pocket and then wiped her face off. The tiny grains scrubbed her skin like the loofah her grandmother always kept in the shower.

Foul thing.

Her grandmother swore by it.

Emily wasn't worried about soft skin. And even if she was, the whole concept of the loofah was revolting. It was a scrubbie thing filled with dead skin and the resultant bacteria that fed on dead skin.

Revolting.

She retrieved the selfie stick and framed herself on

screen. "Don't write me off yet. I'm just getting started. Speaking of which, what's next?"

She waited as if there was someone on the other end pondering the question. "Well, there's something called the rule of threes in survival. It's a general guideline but helpful all the same. It goes like this." She held up three fingers. "You can survive three minutes without air, three hours without shelter in a harsh environment, three days without water, and three weeks without food."

She stood up, dusted off, and framed herself looking at the wall of green further up the beach. "The numbers are dependent on the circumstances and the individual, but they're helpful in establishing priorities." She took a big breath and tasted as much as smelled the ocean air. "I can breathe. So first priority is covered. Next up, I need to find a place to make camp." She turned back and forth showing the expanse of the beach in both directions. "This beach is too exposed." She pointed at the seemingly impenetrable wall of green. "I'll need to look in there for a better option. Preferably something with a fresh water supply nearby."

Emily stared at the camera, aware again of how ridiculous she felt talking to it which was basically the same as talking to herself.

"Well, bye for now."

She clicked it off and turned in a circle as she scanned her surroundings. This time making sure to avoid the stick that had dropped her a minute ago.

Pale yellow beach as far as the eye could see.

Deep blue ocean for miles.

Vivid green trees like a wall to keep out invaders.

And she in the middle of it.

She was alone.

Truly alone.

19

She was physically separated from the entirety of the human race. Port Bailey was the closest blip of civilization and it was too far away to offer any reassurance. She glanced at the neon yellow device attached to her backpack that doubled as both a SAT phone and also as a Personal Locator Beacon, or PLB. Amazing that it was so small. Like a cordless phone back when people still had land lines.

That was her only link to the outside world. The world of cars and computers. The land of lattes and social networks.

One call would reconnect her and also end her chance at the one million dollar prize.

The show called it tapping out, like surrendering in a fight which was right on the money.

This was going to be a fight like she'd never known. And she'd known more than her fair share.

A fight with the elements.

A battle with the mind.

A war of endurance until only one of them remained.

She was young, but she wasn't naive. This wasn't going

to be a blissful return to the welcoming arms of mother nature. Not that nature was evil or had it out for her.

It simply was.

Both beautiful and brutal.

The comforts and amenities of the modern world dulled that reality. But being out here alone in a vast wilderness brought the intrinsic character back into sharp focus.

Emily slung her pack on and dragged the heavy gear trunk higher up the beach, well above the high-tide line where logs, seaweed, and other debris had been stranded by the last outgoing tide.

She dropped the trunk at the base of a tree and did the same with her pack. No sense carrying them around while she scouted a good spot to make camp.

Survival out here was going to be a calories game as much as anything.

She had to start thinking in terms of calories acquired versus calories spent.

Emily detached the daypack and verified its contents. PLB, canister of bear spray, head lamp, and the other essential gear for any trip that took her out of sight of her main gear cache. She grabbed the selfie-stick with attached camera and decided she'd record again when she found a suitable camp spot.

She passed under a thick canopy of stretching branches and entered the forest. The scent in the air changed. The briny bite of the sea gave way to a thick odor that was equal parts damp decay and crisp evergreen. The heavy scent settled on her tongue like a mouthful of wet leaves. The air smelled alive.

The density of the foliage above was matched by the tangle of brush, branches, exposed roots, and decomposing debris below. Picking through it was a slow and laborious task. It was going to be a long afternoon of bushwhacking.

A branch on the ground a few feet away shifted as something underneath scampered away.

Emily slipped out the kukri knife secured in a sheath at her hip. She scooted the branches and leaves around, listening, but whatever it was had apparently found an escape.

It was a good sign.

Smaller animals meant that the larger animals that fed on them were probably in the area. Maybe something big enough to offer substantial calories. Getting higher up the food chain was great for additional calories, to a point. The peak of the pyramid was normally occupied by humans. But on Kodiak Island, that spot was shared with the largest brown bear species on the planet.

One that could grow to over two thousand pounds and stand ten feet tall on its hind legs.

In other words, not anything she wanted to meet in a dark alley. Or anywhere for that matter.

She glanced at the swooping lines of the kukri's blade. The wide, curved carbon steel was great for the usual camp chores like chopping wood, making kindling, and such. And the tapered point did well with finer tasks like skinning game, carving tools, and the like.

No blade was perfect for every task, but this one did well enough at them all. Plus, it was her dad's favorite field tool. He'd bought it long ago during a dig in Nepal. The combination of practical utility and sentimental attachment made it one of her most prized possessions.

She slipped it back into its ornamented leather sheath and continued on, picking her way through the forest.

Hours had passed when the criss-crossing branches and

ever-present brush started to thin out. Another few dozen feet and she stepped into a small clearing.

Clearing wasn't exactly right because there were branches high above. But at least they weren't thatched together so tightly that they choked out the blue sky like everywhere else she'd been in the forest.

Emily noticed a new sound.

Like wind rushing through the trees.

She listened, turning her head back and forth to localize the source.

No, not wind.

Water. Moving water. A stream, maybe.

Her dry throat ached. She had a canteen in her daypack. An empty canteen. They were allowed to bring the container but not the water. Her mouth was dry from dehydration while her clothes were wet from sweat. She swallowed, but the insides of her throat were like sheets of sandpaper rubbing together.

She continued on, angling right a little in the direction of the sound. A few minutes later and she discovered a small stream running through a dug out channel in the terrain. A relatively open area twenty yards down promised easy access for filling her canteen.

Emily plowed through the remaining obstacles and dropped to her knees. She scooped up a handful of freezing cold water and studied it.

Her body practically pulled it into her mouth, but she resisted. The last thing she needed was to pick up a stomach bug. Vomiting and diarrhea were quick trips to serious dehydration out here. Like every other contestant, she was one sickness away from tapping out.

The water was mostly clear, with a slight amber tint to it. No dangerous organisms could be seen wiggling around. It smelled fresh, with none of the fetid stink that warned of dangerous organisms too small to be seen. She looked upstream and saw that it flowed through patches of thick moss and banks of pebbles here and there.

It was a risk.

But survival was always a risk.

She drank deeply, scooping up more as the first swallow coated her throat with an icy chill. She gulped down several handfuls before her hand suddenly froze in front of her face.

A rivulet leaked out from between her fingers.

Her eyes focused on the dark mud on the opposite side of the stream, a few feet away.

A wide oval depression with five smaller depressions adjacent. Five thin lines extending beyond those.

A bear print.

A *huge* bear print.

Easily three times the size of her hand.

20

MARCO woke up having the distinct impression that something was touching his neck. Something furry with four tiny paws. He snapped a sleep-slowed hand at the intruder, but it darted away to safety.

He sat up and brushed off the skin that probably had Hantavirus or something on it. His brimmed hat moved on the ground next to him. He lifted it and another Tundra Vole shot away before he could smash it.

The size of your average gerbil, they wouldn't be much of a meal, but anything was better than the wild greens and dandelions he'd been munching on for the last three days.

The voles were getting braver each night. Brave enough to crawl over his body while he slept. He grimaced, not because he was disgusted but because he was disappointed at not taking advantage of the opportunity for calories.

He made a mental note to set up a couple of deadfall traps around the camp later that day. He stretched his shoulders and neck, feeling the deep ache resulting from all the hard labor.

But the effort was worth it. He was making progress on phase one of the homestead plan. He had a lean-to built against the broad side of an enormous fallen tree. It had stripped poles wedged tightly together on each side for walls and a roof of similar construction. The back wall was the fallen tree and the entrance was open to the circle of stones from which hot embers smoked. He'd eventually need to enclose it for better insulation and protection, but there were ten thousand things to do and only one of him to do them.

Marco twisted his head to the side and felt the satisfying pop and release. He repeated the reward on the other side. He stared out into the trees.

A haze of predawn light painted everything in subdued hues of gray. Birds chattered in the branches nearby.

Today, he would continue working on the shelter. There were about a million cracks that needed chinking. Fortunately, there was an endless supply of mud, moss, and duff to do the job.

His stomach gurgled in protest.

It apparently didn't like the idea of burning another giant load of calories before having a few to digest first.

He agreed completely.

All the work had taken a toll. He got tired way too fast. And then required way too much rest before he could get back to work.

He needed food. Something more substantial than what he'd managed to forage thus far. A fish or a bird or something. Even one of those voles would do. More than one of them would do better.

Yep, he needed to build a couple of deadfall traps today. But, first things first. He'd check the snare he'd built and baited yesterday. He'd seen a few ptarmigan in the area and so had landed on the Hopi bird snare in an attempt to get one.

He could almost smell the delicate meat cooking in a stew. His stomach pinched again and he winced. His mouth watered, ready to do its part in consuming the imaginary meal.

Marco hustled through getting ready for the ten minute walk to the clearing where he'd set the trap. He grabbed the atlatl and dart he'd made yesterday and took another look over the camp to ensure everything was sorted. It was, so he headed out thinking about how amazing it would be to find a trapped bird.

After walking a few minutes, ducking under tangles of branches, stepping over rotting logs, he found the game path that led the way to the trap.

Walking on a game trail was always a risk, but bush-whacking the entire distance was also a risk because it burned ten times more calories than using the trail.

It was a game. A deadly serious one.

Always weighing risk versus reward.

Something buzzed and blurred across his vision and landed on a branch near his right arm.

A grasshopper clung to a twig. Bright green with dark stripes down its body. Two eyes that looked like droplets of ink shined in the morning light.

Sucker was big. Three inches.

It was calories. Not enough for him, but easily enough to interest a ptarmigan.

Marco tucked the atlatl and dart under his arm and slowly dug the camera out of his daypack. He flicked open the screen and started recording. He zoomed in so the grasshopper filled the screen.

It was beautiful.

In a whisper, he spoke to whoever the people were that would be watching this someday. "This thing buzzed by my face and landed right there. Almost like it wanted to get caught. Let's see if I can oblige him."

He zoomed back out and then wedged the camera in the fork of a nearby branch. With it more or less pointed at the grasshopper, he eased his right hand toward the target.

Inches away and he struck.

The grasshopper took flight—right into Marco's open hand.

He snapped his fingers shut and felt the legs scratching and tapping as it tried to jump free. He would've shouted for joy if he wasn't within shouting distance of the trap's location. He carefully opened his day pack and stashed the prize inside an interior pocket. He wanted it alive to better entice the birds. He could probably lash some long grass around its body and rear legs to keep it from triggering the trap while struggling enough to attract attention.

Marco turned toward the camera with a stupid grin on his face. "First catch of the day!" He flashed a thumbs up and then wondered if viewers would think he looked as idiotic as he felt.

Whatever.

"Next stop is the bird snare I built yesterday. Cross your fingers it's got something in it." He slapped the screen shut and tucked it into his pack. He continued on, spirits lifted by the unexpected bounty.

The day was going well.

But he knew better than to put too much stock into that.

A few minutes further and he spotted the snare on the ground through the trees. The pyramid-shaped assembly of horizontal sticks lay flat on the ground.

Flat on the ground!

Rather than tilted up on one edge with the bait stick waiting to be triggered. He'd only managed to bait it with a few berries he'd found, but maybe that had been enough.

He paused and scanned the area. He'd set the trigger stick to release with the lightest of touches. So just because it was down didn't guarantee anything had been caught. Sometimes the wind caught it, or the wood shifted a little, or any one of a hundred variables changed and the trap collapsed with nothing in it.

The sticks that formed the cage were too close together to see anything from this distance. So he tiptoed closer.

At a dozen paces, his boot landed on a twig and snapped it in half.

Something brown and white inside the cage went wild. It ricocheted around chirping like crazy.

Marco sprinted over and dropped a hand on the trap to pin it to the ground. He didn't have much experience with ptarmigans, but the sounds coming from inside the trap weren't what he was expecting. He laid the atlatl and dart on the ground and then knelt down to peer between the slender bars of the trap.

Two shiny black eyes regarded him. Like tiny, polished marbles, they stared in silence.

It wasn't a bird.

It was far cuter.

But was it too cute to eat?

21

A moist, brown nose crinkled and long whiskers on each side lay flat. Its upper lip curled back revealing an impressive, if miniature, set of sharp teeth. Marco recalled seeing a picture of this animal when they'd spent all of a few hours reviewing the local fauna.

A stoat. Also called a short-tailed weasel.

Brown fur on its head and back with white fur on its chest and belly. Though the markings were different, it looked a heck of a lot like the black-footed ferrets back home.

"Why'd you mess with my bird trap? I thought weasels were smarter than birds." He reached a finger near the cage and its occupant hissed like a cat. It was clearly angry and yet it was undeniably adorable at the same time.

Marco chuckled, and then his momentary mirth darkened.

His ex was adorable too when she was angry. The crease between her eyebrows that meant business. The pouty lower lip that turned him on as much as made him cautious. But she was gone. Out of his life, but not yet out of his head.

The woman he was supposed to marry gone forever.

He gritted his teeth and shook his head.

If he didn't get his mind right, his land would be gone forever, too.

Marco regarded the weasel, while the weasel stared back in silence with its mouth open and tiny fangs bared. "It's your lucky day, little guy." He didn't actually know if it was a guy or girl. Weasels didn't wear pink or blue fur to make it obvious.

If it had been another few days subsisting on wild greens, Mr. Weasel would've turned into Mr. Dinner. But Marco's affection for the weasel's endangered cousins back home tipped the scales in favor of freedom.

Like a movie Caesar judging the fate of a gladiator in the arena, Marco extended his fist and then popped his thumb up. "Life."

He lifted the side of the cage facing away from him.

The weasel bolted out but then stopped a dozen feet away. It sat up on its hind legs and watched Marco.

"Don't push your luck. I can change my mind."

The weasel didn't move.

Marco waved his arms in the air. "Go on!" He picked up a nearby twig and flung it.

The weasel watched the poorly aimed projectile fly by and then looked back to Marco with its head tilted to the side. Almost like it was saying *Is that the best you can do?*

Marco threw another twig, this time with more force and precision, trying to score a direct hit.

The weasel dodged to the side and again perched up to observe.

"I should've given you a thumbs down." He ignored the pesky varmint and returned to the task of baiting and resetting the trap.

In minutes, he had the trap reset and the grasshopper tied up. He reached under the trap to secure the lure to the end of the bait stick.

A blur of brown startled him and the grasshopper was gone.

The basket collapsed on his hands.

"You little criminal!" Marco shouted as he pulled back and sat on his heels.

Again a dozen feet away, the weasel stopped and sat up on its haunches. Only this time, it had a juicy grasshopper in its paws.

"Don't you do it!" Marco shouted.

The weasel snapped down and bit off the upper half of the insect. It sounded like crunching potato chips.

"That's my bait!"

The weasel's upper lips curled back and it hissed before continuing to chew its meal.

Marco grabbed a rock and took careful aim. A lucky shot might brain the thief. He whipped his arm forward and the weasel dodged to the side as the pebble shot through the air where its chest had just been.

The evasive maneuver wasn't totally successful though because it dropped the lower half of the now unbound grasshopper.

The surviving half leapt away and disappeared into the grass.

The weasel pounced through the air like a polar bear going after a buried seal. It arced through the air and came down with its front paws extended to catch the escaping half of the meal.

The legs kicked again sending the surviving half another few feet away. The weasel pounced again and missed.

The two continued like this a few more times until the

weasel won out. In a flash, he stuffed it into his mouth until only a twitching rear leg hung out.

As annoyed as he was, Marco couldn't help but smile. "Nice job." The emperor's thumb in his mind was drifting back up toward the undecided middle. He turned back to the unbaited trap. He'd have to find more berries. And if that weasel cleaned it out again, well, he might not get another reprieve.

Marco gathered his pack and got to his feet. He needed to get back to camp to continue work on the shelter. Maybe he'd score a few berries along the way. Maybe another grasshopper if he was lucky. He looked at the weasel before setting off. "You're starting to look like a pork chop, pal."

The weasel swallowed the last of the grasshopper and hissed a reply.

Marco shook his head. "You're an ungrateful little grouch. You know that?"

22

The fading evening light brought with it a chill in the air. Marco laid another log on the fire and surveyed his situation. The chinking had gone well. He scanned the walls and roof and noted with satisfaction that every crack or hole had been packed tight. Tomorrow, he'd gather branches with leaves to add another layer of insulation and rain protection.

Not a bad setup.

Not bad at all.

His stomach grumbled.

He stuffed another wad of foraged greens into his mouth and tried to convince his empty stomach that it was enough.

His belly button felt like it was rubbing against his spine. It had only been a few days, but the combination of minimum calories consumed and maximum calories burned made it feel like weeks.

There hadn't been enough time to work on deadfall traps. The chinking had taken longer than expected.

Everything took longer than expected.

That was part of the struggle of survival.

It was like having a house where everything was broken but he had no tools or materials to make the needed repairs.

Ingenuity and making do with what he had were the orders of the day.

And although the two could usually get him where he needed to go, it always took twice as much time and work as it should have.

Marco picked up his canteen and took another drink of the water he'd boiled that afternoon. He secured the cap and collapsed back onto his sleeping bag. He stared up at the low ceiling and the thin layer of gray smoke wafting in from the fire, swirling around, and then drifting out again.

The hard ground pressed into his upper back. The layer of pine needles below the sleeping bag needed fluffing, but his arms wouldn't move. They felt like the rest of his body did, like he'd been transported to a planet with twice the gravity. It was a physical force pushing him into the ground.

He took a few deep breaths and decided he was done for the day. He needed rest. He needed a lot of things, but rest was one of the more immediately important ones.

Marco closed his eyes, doing his best to focus on the pleasure of being warm and not the pain of being hungry.

It could've been worse.

It could've always been worse.

Like another night of having voles scamper all over him. It was both irritating and frustrating because they made it impossible to get a decent night's sleep and also were a source of calories that he hadn't yet been able to catch.

He'd make the deadfall traps tomorrow. A trap could be a far more efficient hunter than a human because it was always working.

But it was too late and he was too tired to mess with it today. He stared up at the parallel poles of the roof and yawned. He closed his eyes and watched a rotating carousel of all the foods he wished he could eat. It was becoming an undesired nightly meditation.

He didn't realize he'd fallen asleep until something scampered across the roof causing debris to fall down into his mouth. He spit it out, wiping his mouth with his hand.

The last of the daylight had fled some time ago. Only the dull orange glow of the fire offered any illumination.

Marco grabbed his camera and flicked it into night vision mode. He aimed it up at the roof and started recording.

"I think we've got a vole invasion going on."

Then something crossed the roof again and more bits of dirt and leaves tumbled down. It sounded too heavy to be a vole. It moved again and Marco followed the sound with the camera.

Recording in the green and black hues of night vision, the screen showed a bright green head pop out from the edge of the roof and peer down at him upside down. Ink-black eyes studied him.

The weasel thief!

"I should've eaten you!" He threw a piece of kindling at it and the weasel ducked back before it hit.

The little pest poked its head back down and hissed at Marco before disappearing again and scurrying across the roof and jumping to the ground outside. The sounds of its departure faded.

Marco sighed as he turned the camera on himself. "A decent night's sleep would be amazing, but I guess that's too much to ask." He rubbed his eyes and looked back at the camera. "I swear that weasel has a death wish. If something else doesn't kill it, I will."

He shut down the camera and slipped back into the relative warmth of the sleeping bag. Less than a minute passed before he drifted back to sleep.

And it felt like less than another passed before something pulled him back up into the waking world.

Tiny feet scurried up the sleeping bag and stopped on his chest.

Even in the dark, he knew another vole had decided to investigate the shelter to see if there was anything worth nibbling on.

Unfortunately, his arms were inside the bag and getting them out would toss the vole off, letting a tiny bag of calories escape and bother him later in the night.

Marco lay there, stone-still, trying to decide how to get his hands free without scaring it off.

Before he'd decided on a course of action, something heavier landed on his chest.

A whirlwind of shrieking, rolling, diving, contorting movement scared him half to death. He swatted whatever it was away and scrambled for the camera.

He flicked it on and then watched the screen as he aimed it toward the sounds of the struggle.

A high-pitched squeak gurgled to quiet as the weasel came into view. It was on all fours pinning the vole down with its mouth clamped around the smaller animal's neck.

The weasel let go and turned to Marco. It bared its teeth and hissed.

"Hey, mind sharing a bite with me? You owe me that much."

The weasel bared its teeth again and then began tearing into the vole. The gristly sounds of the carnage echoed in the small space. The vole was pretty small, maybe half a bite for him, otherwise he would've pursued more aggressive negotiations.

He settled back down, keeping the camera recording the spectacle. The wet, smacking sounds of a dinner in progress made his stomach pinch tight.

"The least you could do is keep it quiet. I'm trying to sleep over here."

The weasel paused, looked up, and bared its teeth. A scrap of dripping meat dangled out of its mouth.

"Are you always such a grouch?"

The weasel hissed again and then returned to its meal.

"I'll take that as a yes." Marco rotated the camera back to himself, watching the screen until he was in the frame. "It appears I may have a new nocturnal protector. One that eats like a pig at a trough." He directed the last part toward the weasel.

A hiss echoed back in the darkness.

"Oscar. That's your name. Oscar the grouch."

Marco smiled as he shook his head. "Good night, everyone. And good night, Oscar."

Losing the potential calories of the other voles to his new campmate wasn't a welcome development. But if it meant he got a decent night's sleep in return, well, he'd consider it a decent trade. Besides, if he caught any in the deadfall traps before the weasel could wipe out the population, he'd eat those while the grouchy weasel watched.

First come. First served.

He closed his eyes and listened to the wet crunching sounds that confirmed the vole was no more.

Marco wondered if Oscar would stick around. If he'd become a permanent fixture at camp.

He was a cute, if annoyingly grouchy, little guy. And some company wouldn't be the worst thing to happen. It would sure beat the camera that was starting to feel too much like a Wilson volleyball with a handprint for a face.

Still, he wouldn't go so far as to say he'd made a new friend.

Not when he hadn't decided for sure whether Oscar might end up as dinner at some point.

23

BOB forced down another sour gulp of coffee. In a matter of days, he'd gone from enjoying delicious lattes and his assistant's long legs to hanging out in a booth at Queen's Diner in Kodiak, Alaska.

Him. Bob Randy. Producer of two of the most successful TV series ever created. *Barflies* and *Schwartzfeld*. Each alone should've set him up for life with money and a career.

But his ex-wife had spent the money faster than he'd earned it. And a succession of forgettable flops had made him persona non-grata at the network.

At least he didn't have to deal with the rest of the crew. They'd all shacked up in a house rental on the edge of town and he'd just as soon never see any of them. He kept daily tabs on what editorial was doing for trailers and promotional material, but there wasn't much to do until they started cutting together the first episode. And that wouldn't happen until after they collected the first round of tapes from the remaining contestants.

Aside from the lack of urgent work, Bob couldn't stand seeing their groveling and apologetic faces. They knew he'd been banished to the middle of nowhere as some kind of punishment. Producers at his level never had to go out on location. That was low-level work for the kids and the scrappers with something to prove.

He was supposed to be way beyond that.

Bob crammed in another bite of reindeer sausage to get rid of the bitter aftertaste of the stale coffee.

Queen's Diner.

What a joke. The only thing good about this backwater dive was the waitress, Flo. Even though she was mostly gray and a little wrinkled, she still had a look that made him question his rule about screwing anyone less than two decades his junior.

He took another bite of salty sausage dipped in sweet maple syrup.

The breakfast was decent, too.

"Honey, need a fill up?" Flo asked as she silently appeared beside his booth.

"Like I need another ulcer. God, no."

"Well, you let Flo know the second that—"

Bob snatched the buzzing phone off the table and waved her away. "Veronica, tell me you got a reservation somewhere."

"Sorry, boss. I've called every lodging in town, including B&Bs and personal rentals. Everything is booked solid due to the upcoming Crab Festival."

"Sounds like one weekend I spent partying in Tijuana. You wouldn't have known it by the looks of that girl, but—"

"No thanks to that story. Anyway, they have an extra room at the crew's house."

"No!"

"Well, then I don't know what—"

"I'm living in a motel. Motel! With an M!"

"It's the only option right now."

"It's a dilapidated wreck! I thought they'd left a mint on my pillow until it crawled away!"

"Bob, take a deep breath and calm down. Remember your heart."

"It wasn't a heart attack, Veronica. The doctors said so."

"No, but it was an acute stress response exacerbated by coronary artery disease. Are you taking the pills?"

"No, I'm not taking the pills. If it's a choice between having a limp Johnson and cottonmouth all the time versus cleaner arteries, I'd rather die sipping a scotch and banging a hooker for all she's worth."

"You're sick, Bob."

"Hookers need to earn a living, too."

"I'm talking about your physical health. Your mental health is beyond repair. Promise me you'll take the pills."

"I'm not going—"

"Fine. Then you'll be eating roaches off your pillow at The Weary Traveller until the show has a winner. It could be weeks. It could be months."

Weeks?

His chest tightened.

Months?

A heavy blanket of despair settled on his shoulders. "I'll take them."

"Promise me."

"I promise. But I want out of that—"

"Please hold."

Bob ground his teeth as the line went quiet.

She clicked back. "Malcom is on the other line. It's the first time I've been able to get a hold of him in days."

"What are you waiting for? Put him through!"

The line clicked.

"Tell me some good news, Bob."

"We've got a hit, Malcolm. I'm telling you it's gonna be huge."

"You keep saying that."

"We're four days in and five people have already quit. They found the guy that tapped out yesterday naked on the beach. Ex-military something or other and he was screaming like a little girl. Refused to return to camp to get clothes on or get anything."

"All of that recorded?"

"Of course."

"Good. What about the girl?"

"She's still in it."

"Good. When can I see the first episode?"

"We've got the tapes from the ones that quit and we're collecting tapes from the others in a few days."

"They're not tapes, Bob. Welcome to the future."

Bob choked down a biting retort and continued. "I'll get my guys on splicing together a first look a few days after we collect *tapes* from the survivors."

"Good. And don't send it on *tape*. I want a digital download."

"Got it."

"It better be good, Bob. For your sake."

The prepubescent punk thought he could threaten him? Him!

Bob opened his mouth to launch into a tirade detailing everything he'd done for the network over the years.

And the line went dead.

"I'm too old for this," he said to nobody that cared to listen. He glanced up at the muted TV hanging from the wall in the corner of the diner. A banner scrolled across the bottom.

BREAKING NEWS: China recalls diplomats from the United States and closes all embassies.

Bob glanced over his shoulder and saw Flo dropping an armful of dirty plates behind the long counter. "Honey, can you turn that up?"

"Sure thing, sugar," she replied with a wink.

A lock of curled, gray hair slipped down in front of her face and she attempted to blow it back out of the way as she reached for the remote. The smock and apron weren't the most complimentary outfit in the world, but anyone could see she was trim and took care of herself. She was a little flat up top for his tastes, but a nice rack wasn't everything.

He mentally pictured her in nothing but panties. Black lace ones that had a split in the crotch. She had great lips. On her face. Very suckable lips.

The faint beginnings of a hard-on stirred in his pants.

What was wrong with him?

Thinking about her that way, even in the quiet confines of his own mind. It was disgusting, even for a pervert like him.

She was probably fifty years old, for Christ's sake!

The sound on the TV came on, distracting him from further self-abuse.

He turned back to see the news segment interrupted by someone walking into the frame and handing the anchor a paper.

The kid couldn't have been half his age, a freaking baby. His glistening black hair looked like it had been made in a mold and attached to his head. The hard angles of his jaws and high cheekbones guaranteed a successful backup career as a male model.

Bob's lips twisted into an unconscious grimace. He preferred the plain faces and cheap suits of the anchors from his generation. They were the real deal, but they'd all died or retired by now.

Replaced by this new generation where they all looked like models. The men were more suited to wearing a banana hammock on some white sand beach and the women looked like they should've been strutting down Paris runways, dazzling vapid crowds by wearing outlandish hats and little else.

The kid's eyes widened as he read the paper and then glanced back up toward the camera with his mouth hanging open.

He sat there, staring.

Where did they find these gorgeous idiots?

"We're still rolling," an offscreen voice said.

The male bimbo blinked, but not much else.

"Read the update!" the offscreen voice shouted.

The man-barbie looked down and read the paper. "After the alleged currency market manipulations by the Chinese government, the United States congress today passed a controversial measure to enact sweeping trade tariffs and embargoes on Chinese imports. The Chinese have just issued a statement that decries the new measures as illegal under international law and dangerous to global stability. They have furthermore summarily recalled all foreign diplomats and closed all embassies in this country."

An inset video in the upper right corner of the screen appeared. Text at the bottom of the video indicated it was the Chinese embassy in Washington DC. Chinese soldiers shuffled men in dark suits into a long line of black SUVs parked inside the compound. The front gates opened and four SUVs pulled out and disappeared from view. The soldiers slammed the gates shut as more SUVs were filled for departure.

Maybe this was all just the usual chest-thumping and brinksmanship.

Maybe.

The camera angle widened revealing something that made an already uncertain *maybe* a great deal weaker.

More soldiers. American soldiers. At least thirty of them lined up on both sides of the street. They stood in formation facing the embassy. Their black rifles were held in front with the muzzles pointing down.

But that was no guarantee they would stay that way.

One of the two old-timers in the booth next to his spoke. "They're gonna nuke us. Always knew it was gonna happen. Russia or China. Take your pick."

The other replied, "They're gonna hit us with an EMP. Electromagnetic pulse. It'll fry any technology made in the last fifty years. Read all about it in a book a few years back. Laid the whole thing out. They're gonna fry all our technology and turn us into savages."

"Didn't some crook in congress quote that book?"

"Yep."

"Wasn't he that family values guy that ended up marrying three different wives?"

"Yep."

"The same one that wanted a president impeached for getting a blow job?"

"Yep."

"Think he'll ever get what's coming?"

The two old codgers were silent for a second. Then both started shaking and guffawing so hard that they looked like they were about to fall out of the booth and break a hip.

Bob turned back to the TV. Another group of SUVs zipped out of the gate and raced away. The soldiers on each side of the gate stared at each other with grim intent. An odd counterpoint to the bustling activity all around.

The soldiers only had eyes for their adversaries across the great political divide and across the dangerously small physical one.

Things were going downhill fast.

All it would take was one minor miscommunication, one small error in judgement, to spark a conflagration that might end up starting World War III.

24

DR. GANESH opened his desk drawer and pulled out a pile of manuals he hadn't reviewed in decades. He set them aside. There was nothing more to learn there. He reached in again, all the way to the back, and found what he was looking for.

A half-empty bottle of bourbon.

Nothing more to learn there either, but it helped to dull the ache of an old memory. He knew it wasn't good for his brain chemistry, and yet he had a drink from time to time anyway. If only being a hypocrite was the worst thing he'd ever done.

If it were, he wouldn't need the occasional drink in the first place.

Ten long years ago, Zhang Yong had disappeared.

Hari stared at the amber liquid, as if somehow an answer might appear inside. One that had never been there before. It wouldn't. But that hadn't stopped him from looking.

He tapped the space bar on the keyboard in front of him.

The frozen image on the monitor started playing. He'd watched it too many times.

Snow spilling out onto the concrete floor of the collider ring. Zhang stumbling toward the shimmering curtain hanging in mid-air. Disappearing through it. Minutes later, the fractal rainbow curtain fading, leaving nothing but melting snow. Time Gate One, or TG1 as they'd come to call it, had vanished.

Zhang Yong hadn't been seen since.

And it was Hari's fault.

And not in a general way. Like he'd spearheaded the project and an accident had claimed one of his charges. That would've been hard enough to accept. His guilt was far more direct, more deceitful, and more despicable than that.

Hari spun the metal cap off the bottle and clinked the neck on his cup as he poured out a generous portion. He tilted the end up to add a little more.

The memory-fuzzing elixir hit his throat with a familiar, welcome burn.

Zhang had been like a son to him. He was supposed to have gotten out of the tunnel long before the test began. And none of them could've known what was going to happen.

Rather, what did happen.

They'd expected hints, if not outright answers, to the question of faster-than-light travel. What they'd discovered instead was something that still made him uneasy, even now after they'd successfully reproduced the phenomenon half a dozen times since.

Time travel.

They hadn't realized it immediately. Even for cutting-edge work in the field of theoretical quantum physics, it had been a shocking discovery.

More fiction than science one second before it happened.

And so they'd embarked upon a path to understand it, control it, use it.

Ten years ago, Hari was a different man. A far more idealistic one. Now, the agony of Zhang's loss had ground him down into a more practical one. Despite all the facts and figures he fed the powers that be to secure continued funding for the Hermes Project, he had a single goal in mind.

He took another sip, blurring into a drink, blurring into a gulp.

He scrubbed back the video to when Zhang vanished into the time gate.

Hari couldn't imagine the horror of Zhang's last minutes. Lost in time over eleven thousand years ago. Odds were that he died in short order. But what if he didn't? What if he'd survived?

Hari could never decide which would be more horrifying.

But what if it didn't matter what happened when he disappeared? Because what if they could pinpoint that instant and bring him back? If they could control all of the variables to a sufficient degree, it was theoretically possible to reproduce the complete quantum signature of that first collision.

It was possible to go back and save Zhang, wasn't it?

That single question had relentlessly driven the last decade of his life.

A knock outside his office made him jump.

He hurriedly scooted the glass and open bottle behind the stack of manuals, and then closed the window containing the classified video on his screen.

"Just me," the custodian said. He sniffed the air and glanced at his watch. "3:28 PM. I like your style. No reason to wait until the work day is over."

Hari didn't know whether to invite him in or tell him to get out.

The two looked at each other for a silent moment.

"Mind if I join you?"

It was the bald custodian. The one he'd last seen in the gardens.

"Have a seat." Hari glanced at the man's badge to get his first name—pathetic that he'd seen the same face for years and never bothered to attach a name to it—"Alberto. Does bourbon work for you? It's all I have."

"Call me Bert. And it'll do," he said as he settled into the offered chair on the opposite side of the desk.

Hari dug out another cup from a desk drawer and noticed a crusted brown ring on the bottom. "It's not the cleanest."

Bert waved him off. "It's self-sanitizing."

Hari's mouth tried to reflect the levity of the comment, but the tight frown barely uncurled enough to become a straight line. He poured a respectable portion and then tilted the neck up to stop.

"No need to be shy about it. My shift is just about over."

Hari nodded and added another two inches before passing it across the desk.

Bert accepted it and held it raised. "A toast. To those we've loved and lost."

A knot formed in Hari's throat. A cold, hard knot. But nothing the bourbon couldn't burn through. He clinked their glasses together and then took a long, slow drink.

A trail of fire coated his throat on the way down. He

exhaled and the fumes singed the inside of his nose on the way out.

Bert took a sip and nodded in appreciation. "Smooth. This a director level perk?"

"One of a few. In exchange, I get the privilege of never leaving the facility."

Bert's eyes opened wide. "You never leave?"

Hari shook his head.

"Dr. Ganesh, that's not—"

"Call me Hari."

"Hari, you must know that kind of thing will make you crazy."

"If it hasn't already." Hari glanced at Bert's custodial badge again. The red background signified support staff. The picture showed a noticeably younger version of the man. They'd both been with the project a long time.

How many times had he seen him?

And how had he not once noticed the name on the badge?

"So, why Bert and not Alberto?"

The other man laughed. "I know. I used to get teased about it in elementary school. The kids were relentless. 'Where's Ernie? How's Sesame Street?' Hated it growing up, but my mother insisted because she had an unhealthy adoration for Burt Reynolds."

"Burt Reynolds?" Hari asked. "You mean The Bandit in the black Trans-Am with the gold bird on the hood?"

Bert nodded. "That's the one."

"Wasn't his name spelled with a U?"

"I think you'll already agree that it didn't have to make any sense."

Hari nodded.

"Yeah, it was tough growing up. But after making it out

of high school, nobody cared and by then, it just was my name. It stopped being a thing. And then later, after my mother passed, I wouldn't have given it up for the world. I am my mother's son."

In his youth, Hari had always wondered what it would be like to have parents that cared enough to stick around. He would've gladly gone by any name to have a family. But growing up an orphan and bouncing through well-meaning but misguided foster care homes had given him drive, an ambition for something greater.

Life didn't always give you a choice. Sometimes, it made the decision and how you reacted was the choice.

Bert raised his glass again and Hari followed suit. "To one day reuniting with those we've lost."

"I hope that's possible."

"Doc, in this universe, anything is possible."

Hari took another drink and the liquid now warmed instead of burned.

Bert finished a sip and looked up at a framed picture of Hari and Zhang hanging on the wall.

Zhang wore a black robe with the red circlet for finishing his Ph.D. with honors. As his advisor, mentor and friend, it had been one of the proudest days of Hari's life. He'd felt a parent's pride in a child's achievement.

Bert frowned. "I never thanked him enough for what he did for my wife."

"Dr. Yong?"

"Yep."

"What did he do?"

"He pulled some strings at the hospital in Juneau. Got Rose into an experimental treatment that we never would've had a chance at otherwise."

"Is she still being treated?"

"She passed last year."

"I'm sorry."

"Me, too. But that treatment gave her another nine years. Gave us another nine years." Bert looked back to the photo. "Are you going to bring him back?"

Hari's eyes opened wide. Even the numbing blanket of the bourbon didn't dull the shock. "What do you mean?"

"With the upcoming test. Did you figure out how to do it?"

Hari's mouth hung open. How did he know? Had there been a security breach? Was Bert more than he pretended to be?

Bert chuckled. "I'm no spy. But I do read people pretty well. I've worked here a long time and folks reveal a lot when they think you're just another piece of office furniture."

Hari consciously closed his mouth.

"So, are you going to do it?"

Hari set his glass on the desk and willed his hand to remain still instead of clicking open the video of Zhang's disappearance in time. "I hope so."

"Me, too."

25

SUYIN lay in the knee-high grass soaking up the morning sun like a lizard that had spent a lifetime in darkness. The warm, golden light made her skin tingle as it seeped deeper into her bones. She reached down and hiked her cargo pants up around her thighs. Her teeth were still chattering a bit, but it was nothing compared to the continuous earthquake of the night before.

It had been freezing cold and she was only just starting to thaw out.

The thought of tapping out had crossed her mind.

And crossed it again.

And again.

It circled around in her mind like a greyhound chasing the ever-elusive mechanical rabbit.

Hypothermia had been a real concern. But she'd made it to the rising sun.

The problem was that she was a naturally skinny person. That was fine in normal life because she could grab a handful of snacks like salted peanuts or a Pink Lady apple pretty much anytime she wanted. With as little money as they had, she now understood what real food scarcity was like.

It was all relative.

The wilds of Kodiak Island were another world entirely. Nature's grocery store didn't run sales and even when she could see food on the shelves, that in no way meant that she could get to it.

Day six.

Six days into the competition and all she could think about was quitting. Peanuts and apples waited on the other side of pushing the button.

Tapping out, the show called it.

Like they were professional wrestlers and this was all staged.

It wasn't.

The hunger clawing in her belly wasn't a prop or a fabricated conflict to get the crowd going.

It was real.

It was never ending.

It sucked.

Six days in and she hadn't gotten more than a few handful of limpets from the nearby cove and some wild grasses they'd learned about during the ludicrously brief orientation. They'd spent more time learning how to operate the camera gear than actual stuff that might save your life.

Speaking of which, she was obligated to film at least twenty minutes each day. Any day that passed without doing that was an automatic DQ.

Disqualification.

Stupid rules.

Su flopped her arm over and found the handheld camera. She flipped the screen around and starting recording. The face on the screen nearly made her turn away.

Her cheeks were more concave than before. Her cheekbones too pronounced. If she'd had more time, she would've taken a month to fatten herself up before the show began. Her normally shiny black hair lay limp and dull like dried seaweed. Her streaked face gave testament to her general lack of hygiene over the past six days.

Sure, she brushed her teeth with the frayed end of a stick. Sure, she washed her face off with a handful of water each morning. But she had yet to bathe and the morning ritual splash didn't cleanse so much as create more contrast between the dark dirt lines and the finger swipes of clearer skin.

Su shifted her focus to the lens. She'd stared at her face on the screen for half an hour yesterday and the end result had not been positive. Lacking food, her body had turned to breaking down fat and muscle to meet its caloric needs.

And close examination of the process made her already fragile outlook infinitely harder to manage.

With more effort than it should've required, she sat up, hit record, and then shifted the metal pole with the camera at the end into position. She glanced at the screen to verify she was more or less framed, but didn't linger on the view.

She winced as her belly cramped in protest. The hunger pains had been growing in both frequency and intensity over the last few days.

"Well, it's the morning of day six."

The flat, defeated tone of the delivery nearly made her shut the camera off.

"I haven't eaten much since arriving. If I don't find an abundant source of calories soon, I'm not sure how much longer I can stay. I guess I could starve myself for another week or so, but what would be the point?"

She reached into the grass with her other hand and found the long, straight branch she'd cut from a tree yesterday. It was as thick as her wrist and a good blend between durability, strength, and weight.

"So, I'm going to try something new today."

She set the camera on her nearby pack, settling it so that she remained in frame. She showed the length of the eight foot branch. "I got a pretty straight one. Should be good enough."

She pulled her knife from its sheath and started shaving on one end. "First, we need to sharpen one end down to a point."

After a while, her arms started to ache with the effort. Curled shavings fell away as the point appeared.

"Next, we need to make a cut right down the point." She tapped the edge of the knife into the point, then used a small stick to batten the blade deeper into the wood. After splitting it down the middle about six inches, she levered the blade free. "Next, we need to make another cut perpendicular to the first one."

Another few minutes and she'd quartered the pointed end. She studied her work, the depths of the cuts, the flexibility of the quartered points. "That should work."

She retrieved two sticks she'd made earlier. Each was about the length of her middle finger.

How appropriate.

She wedged the first one into the split end of the spear and battened it down into position. Every inch lower on the shaft forced the sharpened end apart in halves. Eight inches down looked right. She twisted the spear ninety degrees and did the same with the second stick into the opposite cut. She pounded it down the shaft until it pushed in tight to the first one.

The end of the spear now had four splayed fingers. She carved the ends, shaping each finger into a sharp point. Not so fine that they would easily snap off, and not so blunt that they poked rather than pierced.

Her shoulders burned with the effort. Her body begged to lie back down and soak up the morning sun. She wiped her sleeve across the sweat gathering on her brow.

A gentle breeze cooled her face. The grass tickled her ankles and calves like a hundred tiny hands.

Laying down and staying that way seemed like the best idea ever conceived. Even this minimal exertion drained her. But that wasn't an option. Lying around all day wouldn't put food in her belly.

Su rolled the spear in her hand, studying the result of her work. She'd need to find some longer grass or strip bark for lashing. Securing the cross sticks in place would ensure the points stayed spread and strong. She touched the four points.

It could work.

It could.

She brought the four points into frame and up close to the lens. "This is my last big idea. It's probably not a good idea, but I don't know what else to try at this point. I have to get food. Something that can keep me going."

The breeze died and her forehead again warmed in the bright sun. The breeze had gone, but the surrounding grass still tickled her legs.

She glanced down and had trouble understanding what she was seeing at first.

Hundreds of black sesame seeds dotted her bare legs.

Sesame seeds with tiny, translucent red, segmented legs.

"Ticks!" she shrieked as she flung the spear away and jumped to her feet. "Ticks!"

The exertion made her head swim. Made her nearly vomit and pass out at the same time. She scraped at her legs, clearing hand-sized swathes of skin with each frantic swipe. After several minutes of chaotic effort followed by double and triple checking to be sure, she was relatively certain she'd removed all the disgusting little bloodsuckers. Less than a dozen of them had already burrowed in and started feeding.

She stood in the center of an imperfect oval of stamped-down grass, like a miniature crop circle created by aliens with no time for the finer details. Her chest heaved and her head swam.

She could quit. Right now. Tap out and be back home in days.

Only she couldn't.

Tapping out would kill her father.

Not for the first time in the last six days, acid burned in her gut. A fury born of resentment and fanned by misery.

She should've been finishing med school.

Not starving and battling ticks out in the middle of nowhere.

Anger flooded into her limbs, bringing cheap energy like a sugar rush without the calories.

It was better than nothing.

26

Suyin heard the river before she saw it. A rushing hum of endless energy. A vein that offered life to those skilled enough to draw it out. She'd discovered it an hour and a half from her campsite on the third day while on a scouting walk. It was too far away to be used as a regular water source and too dangerous to be used as a hunting ground.

Too dangerous because she wasn't the only hunter present.

While still a hundred yards away, looking down a small hill to the river beyond, she'd already spotted three reasons why it was too dangerous.

A sow with two cubs.

Even with female Kodiak bears being smaller than their male counterparts, they were still way bigger than Su. And the mother fishing in the river below was no exception.

Su dropped to the ground to better blend into the background. She watched the short grass between, trying to determine if the wind would carry her scent below.

The sow stood patiently in a small waterfall watching the water and waiting. The two cubs a little distance away bounded through the water, splashing and taking turns bowling each other over. It was the kind of scene that would've been beautiful and heart-warming if she'd seen it on a nature show from the comfort of her couch.

In her current circumstance, it was more terrifying than anything.

She was about to rise into a crouch and move away when movement to the left caught her attention.

A huge brown shape loped out of the trees and toward the river. It moved with a fluid grace that was fast but not rushed. A male Kodiak. A bruin. They averaged over a thousand pounds and stood nine feet tall.

The sow noticed its approach and leapt into action. She called to the cubs with sharp, pleading whines. Their playtime ended at once. They both stood on their hind legs and spotted the danger. Their mother angled toward them and away to the far side of the river.

The bruin crashed through the river, shooting up geysers as it drew nearer.

The shorter legs of the cubs made their escape too slow.

The male would get to them before they could get out of the river. It let out a deep, warbling growl as it closed in. Now twenty feet away.

The cubs squealed in terror, leaping and stumbling toward the far bank.

The huge male splashed to a stop as the mother intersected his path.

She opened her jaws revealing a mouth full of sharp, pale teeth. She tilted her head to the side and roared.

Even at this distance, the sound sent a chill up Su's spine. It was a warning. A warning that any animal that wanted to live would pay attention to.

That is, unless that animal was a bruin nearly twice as large.

The male stood up on its hind legs. A towering brute in the prime of its life. It bellowed a reply that utterly drowned out the sow's sounds. The bruin bellowed again, swiping at the air between them.

The cubs made it to shore and didn't stop. They sprinted away, hooting and yelping.

The sow roared again, risking her own life to buy more time for their escape.

Just as the bruin dropped to all fours and started forward again, the sow spun around and took off.

She got to the muddy shore and then darted toward her cubs in the distance. She joined them, and after a quick look back to verify the pursuit was over, all three loped away to make good their escape.

The male didn't seem to care. He turned back and ambled his way over to the small waterfall. He stopped at the base, where the sow had been moments before. Apparently, that was prime hunting ground and the male hadn't taken kindly to another bear laying claim to it. It moved with an almost lazy grace as it turned its head and clamped down on a salmon arcing through the air.

Su's stomach gurgled in loud protest. There was food over there and her stomach wanted some! It didn't care to consider whether the bear was likely to share or not.

Because there was food!

As much as she wanted a bite of the freshest sushi on the planet, she wanted to live to enjoy it.

She'd have to go further upriver, follow it until she found a stretch unclaimed by the bears. She stood to a crouch and then headed off to the right to stay parallel to the river while heading upstream.

Su walked for another three hours, passing numerous bears getting their fill in the river below. She finally found a section that appeared unoccupied and another few minutes of silent observation confirmed the initial finding.

Her mind warred with itself.

Going to the river was a big risk. A deadly risk. But the potential reward was a massive boost in calories. Something she desperately needed if she had any chance of continuing in this competition.

Su tried to get herself to walk closer.

She couldn't.

The longing and the fear two equal but opposite values in an equation that summed to nothing.

One salmon would completely change her life. Just one. It was the difference between tapping out and not.

She had to try.

Her father's life depended on it. His bruised and lacerated body appeared in her mind. He'd gotten himself into that mess. He should've been the one to get himself out of it. It shouldn't have been her responsibility.

She was the child, not him!

Parents were supposed to be the responsible ones.

But real life relationships didn't necessarily abide by the customary roles of the family dynamic. Her relationship with her father certainly didn't.

And so it was up to her.

Su gritted her teeth and headed down to the river.

Missing the added volume of several sizable tributaries, it was more a large creek here. She scanned the area as she went, expecting the terrifying sight of a brown bear to appear at any minute.

But none did.

Maybe she'd gone far enough to leave their hunting

grounds behind. If so, that would be great, except that it might also mean that there were no salmon to be had in this area.

There was only one way to find out.

27

Lush green grass covered the banks on both sides of the creek. It grew long and thick and seemed to revel in the arrival of spring and the promise of warmth and life. A thick copse of trees bordered the near side a little further upstream, almost like they'd gathered together for protection, as if they knew something she didn't.

Su took in the beauty while at the same time scanning the area for signs of bears. The grass wasn't trampled flat like in the more popular fishing spots. There were no desiccated salmon heads or fins lying around. There were no piles of berry-filled scat in view. There were no tracks, damp or dried, that she could see.

In short, it looked relatively safe.

Relatively safe because while it appeared totally safe, totally safe took on a new meaning when you were surviving alone on an island with nearly one bear per square mile.

A breeze moved through the trees in gentle waves of irregular white noise. Like the kind she often pulled up on her phone to help her sleep at night.

Back when she had a phone in her hand or within reach at all times.

She had a phone of sorts now that was always within reach. The PLB. But using it would mean losing the competition and losing her dad. So using it was out of the question.

Su stepped through the calf-high grass, hoping it wasn't filled with a hidden horde of disgusting bloodsuckers like before. She arrived beside the water and paused to consider her next move.

The glassy surface at her feet reflected the blue sky and crisp white clouds above so perfectly that vertigo momentarily made her wobble as it felt like she was about to fall down into the sky.

As if gravity might suddenly stop working and the invisible strings that tied her feet to the ground might be severed and she would drift away into the endless expanse.

The thought was both comforting and terrifying all at once.

Su dropped her daypack and dug out the camera. The viewers at home would love to see this. They would've loved to see the bear chase earlier, but she hadn't thought to record it. This would have to do.

And it was undeniably beautiful. And probably more easily appreciated from the comfort of a couch when the dangers that accompanied the beauty weren't a concern.

She framed herself like they'd learned in the ridiculously short training program. She lined up on the one-third vertical line, and the creek and field behind occupied the other two thirds.

She nodded in approval. It was very cinematic.

If only they'd promised extra credit for those who went above and beyond on the assignment. They had, of course, promised no such thing, but Su wasn't the type to deliver less than her best no matter the reward.

But rewards were nice.

Med school had been a welcome refuge from her normal life. One that rewarded her innate drive and attention to detail. Surviving in the wilderness of Kodiak Island required the same traits, but it offered no study guide for her to memorize.

And failing a test out here could have more direct and lethal consequences.

For her and her father.

She shrugged off the thought and hit record, trying not to focus on how exhausted and weak she looked.

"So, I've walked a long way up from where I last saw bears fishing." She pointed up over her shoulder at the water behind her. "It's a pretty big river downstream, but just a creek up here. Should be easier to get into without drowning. Haven't seen any salmon yet, but hopefully some will turn up. I need food. Calories. Energy."

She grimaced as her stomach pinched tight in apparent protest at the mention of food when there was none.

She grabbed the fishing spear she'd constructed and held it in frame. "Hope this thing works. I'm running out of ideas here." She set the camera on top of her pack and aimed it out at the creek so it could record her fishing expedition.

She kicked off her boots, and peeled off her socks. A single big toe touching the water sent a sharp shiver up to the crown of her head. She couldn't let her clothes get wet. With only a single backup for each item of clothing, keeping everything dry and in good repair was vital.

Her head swiveled back and forth, as if anyone was

nearby to see. She shrugged out of her coat and clothes, and then paused at her underwear and bra.

The camera was recording.

Surely, they'd blur out the private parts.

Right?

But even if they did, that still meant that everyone that watched the footage before it got blurred would see. She opted for modesty. The cotton underwear and bra would dry quickly in the sun and she could go without them on the walk back to camp if needed.

Su stepped into the water up to her ankles. Her feet sank into the bed of small pebbles that covered the bottom. She sucked in a breath and forced herself to stay put. It was a surprise there weren't ice cubes bobbing along with the gentle current. Goose bumps covered her legs like a dusting of sand.

The water was no more than a dozen feet across here and appeared to be a couple of feet deep. While the sides were mirrors of the sky above, a rippling channel of faster water in the middle glittered like a comet's tail.

She looked over her shoulder at the camera with the blinking red dot. "Wish me luck." She turned back and carefully made her way toward the middle. Her movement sent out slow ripples that distorted the smooth surface and revealed the pebbly bottom below.

A little ways from the center, with the water just below her knees, a flash of movement from below the surface caught her attention.

She nearly shouted with glee as a large salmon, two feet long at least, swam against the current making its way upstream to die.

It wasn't going to have to go any further if she could help it.

Su eased the spear into position as the fish approached.

It swam closer, practically right by her.

The sharpened four prongs hovered just above the surface and the fish below.

She had it dead to rights.

Food.

Finally!

She struck!

28

The water bubbled and churned and she could tell before it cleared that she'd missed and hit the gravel bottom. She caught a glimpse of her prey as it darted to safety further upstream. It was long gone before she could take a single step in pursuit.

She screamed in frustration.

How could she have missed?

It was right there!

Then she remembered.

Too late, but remembered.

Light refracted at the surface boundary going from water to air.

Idiot! She already knew that and they'd even mentioned it during the training.

Stupid mistake!

She had to aim nearer than what appeared correct. She spotted a dark pebble on the bottom, aimed the spear a couple of inches nearer than looked right, and then tried to hit it.

One prong glanced it, but it wasn't a direct hit. She

aimed again, another couple of inches nearer than before. She thrust again and this time hit it dead center. She practiced a few more times until she felt confident in the angle.

Okay. Better.

But still. She'd lost that one.

What if that was it?

What if that was her one chance and it was gone?

Su gritted her teeth and shoved away the clawing despair.

She had to keep going. Giving up meant going home.

"Just one more chance," she said in a whisper. "Please."

An hour passed as she wandered back and forth across the creek, up and down, waiting for another opportunity.

There was none.

The sun had started its descent toward the horizon and the warmth of the afternoon had given way to a chill in the air.

She couldn't risk staying any longer.

It was a long hike back and doing it in the dark was asking for trouble. Demanding it, really.

She started toward her pile of belongings on the far shore. Her shoulders slumped in defeat and she dragged the spear behind.

She could've had food today. A ton of it.

If only she hadn't been a complete idiot.

She passed the middle of the creek, shaking her head in defeat, making her way to the shallower water along the edge.

She almost stepped on the salmon below the surface before she noticed it!

She stuttered to a stop and then slowly brought the spear into position. She aimed a little below and closer than looked visually correct.

And struck!

This time, the spear hit something more forgiving than the gravel bed.

The water churned and splashed, but the pierced fish at the end of spear remained.

She leaned onto the shaft, shoving it down as hard as she could, and then lifted the end up and the flapping fish stuck on the end nearly yanked the spear out of her hand.

"YES! YES! YES!" she shouted in victory. She sprinted for the bank to get her prize to safety. Her mind buzzed and heart raced.

She got far enough onto the bank to ensure the fish didn't somehow break free and flop back into the water.

She knelt down, pinning it to the ground.

It was smaller than the first one, but still more food than she could eat in a week.

Empty eyes stared back as it continued to struggle. A long hooked nose with a speckled green head. A scarlet red body with parts of the skin sloughing off. It was ugly. And stank of the impending death to which it had swum so far to surrender to.

And yet it was also the most amazing thing in the entire universe.

It was life.

Her own and her father's.

It was possibility.

The tall brush upstream to her left rattled and swayed, thirty feet away. Two bear cubs waddled out and froze when they saw her.

Were they alone?

The brush crashed apart and a sow lumbered into view.

A chill colder than the ice-cold water settled in her gut and radiated to her fingertips. Were these the same ones she'd seen earlier? Had they picked up her scent and followed her here?

Su was no expert, but the mother looked skinnier than the one from earlier. Folds of fur hung loose off prominent bones. The sow angled toward her, moving in front of the cubs, before stopping. Its lips curled back to reveal long, sharp teeth.

A deep rumble, almost lower than could be heard, vibrated in the air.

Su slowly rose, holding the speared salmon out in front.

The sow sniffed the air, licked her teeth. Her head tilted to the side and she let out a growling bellow.

Su's legs went weak and she nearly collapsed. Her heart pounded like a fist punching in her chest. Her brain screamed.

RUN! RUN!

But she couldn't. They'd drilled that into them over and over. Don't run from a Kodiak. You'll never make it. And running might incite an attack where none may have occurred otherwise.

Su laid the spear on the ground. A distraction. Like throwing your wallet to the side hoping a thief would go for it instead of you. She slowly crept backward toward her pack, toward the bear spray in one of the exterior mesh pockets.

The sow started toward her. It chewed up the space between them with long loping strides.

Su screamed and dashed for the spray. She snatched at it with shaking hands. She spun around and the can slipped out of her wet hands and fell to the ground.

The mother bear roared and closed the final distance.

Su lunged for the can and squeezed the trigger before it left the ground. A blast hit her in the face, instantly blinding her. Choking and gagging, she managed to turn the can and pull the trigger again in the direction she thought was right.

The hiss of more spray accompanied the sound of a surprised yelp. A rush of air buffeted her face as the bear skidded to a stop.

Su stumbled back, tripped over her pack, and crashed to the ground.

The thumping sound of the retreating mother accompanied her howling voice.

Gagging uncontrollably, Su pushed up and tried to open her eyes. She only managed a squint because the wider they opened, the more they burned. Through a wavering blur, she watched the mother crash into the brush with the two cubs not far behind.

Her eyes pinched shut and she crawled to the water. Her lungs burned. Hacking coughs wracked her chest. She couldn't breathe. The spasms wrenched her so hard it felt like her ribs were cracking.

Her hands splashed cold water and she crawled in. Dunking her face under the surface did little to ease the agony. Her stomach clenched tight and she vomited up bile. She wiped away the clinging tendrils and plunged into the water again.

How long she stayed like that, dunking her face, wondering if any second teeth would tear into her flesh, she didn't know.

The burning fire in her eyes began to fade. Enough so that she could keep her eyes open a sliver. The coughing eased to sputtering.

No teeth had come for her.

When the misery had finally eased enough that she could breathe more or less regularly and keep her eyes open for short periods, she stopped washing and scanned the area.

The bears were gone.

The salmon was, too.

They'd come back for it. Or something else had gotten it.

Su crawled to the bank and flopped onto her back. The adrenaline that had buzzed through her body evaporated leaving an edgy emptiness behind.

Tears streamed down her face.

Real tears now, not the weeping fluid caused by the bear spray.

A suffocating weight settled over her, like the air had thickened into paste.

She was alone.

So alone.

Her chest shuddered, and not from the choking spray.

She just wanted to go home.

To quit and go home.

A vision of her father's beaten face flashed before her eyes.

She couldn't quit.

She couldn't go home.

29

EMILY reached for the can sitting on a flat rock at the edge of the fire. The boiled water should've been cool enough to drink. Water for breakfast. That was it. Nine days of mostly water for breakfast. But she needed it. Her fat tongue scratched the inside of her mouth. She touched the steel can and then yanked her fingers away. "Oww!"

Needed to cool another minute or two.

She stuck them in her mouth and realized there was no saliva to cool them. She pulled them out and blew on them while she took a seat on her bushcraft version of a Tempur-Pedic Comfort Supreme. Poles, pine boughs, and duff weren't what you'd find in a mattress store, but they sure beat freezing to death on the unforgiving ground.

Emily arched a brow at the camera on the makeshift shelf across her small shelter. "Lesson number one thousand nine hundred and forty eight. Don't grab a hot can. Yeah, I know. Big surprise." She reached over and clicked it off. She wasn't in the mood to perform today.

She wasn't in the mood for anything today. Anything that didn't involve eating.

She arched her back to stretch the aching muscles. A part of her wanted to lay back down to rest, and another part of her knew it wouldn't be all that restful so she may as well do something useful.

As if checking fishing lines that continually got stripped of bait could be considered useful. Whether she found she'd been cleaned out again or not, it was more useful than waiting for a cheeseburger to fall out of the sky and land in her lap.

Maybe today would be the day.

Not for the cheeseburger, but for a fish.

You never knew what the day might bring. That's why you had to get off your butt and do something. Today might turn out to be a big win, but she wasn't going to find out by wasting away inside her shelter.

Emily rose from her bunk, stood to full height and commended herself for going the extra mile on the shelter. It wasn't about to appear on an HGTV tiny house episode, but it was solid and comfortable considering the circumstances. She'd burned a ton of calories harvesting and preparing the poles and then constructing the enclosed lean-to shelter. It had started simply enough with two poles supporting a ridgepole and then smaller poles angled off that to the ground. Layers of branches laid across created a simple roof.

But Emily wasn't the type to do a shoddy job on something as critical as a shelter. Less important things, maybe.

So, the last several days had been a slow and exhausting exercise in home improvements. Like that show her grandmother used to watch called *This Old House*. Only there was no behind-the-scenes crew who came in and did everything for you so that you could remodel a whole house in less than a week. That combined with the fact that her toolbox consisted of an axe and a knife made for slow going.

There was still more to do—there was always more to do —but she'd reached a milestone yesterday when she'd finished building the front face and so enclosed the space.

She touched the slanted ceiling an inch above her head. The air near the top was noticeably warmer than below. She glanced at the fire contained by a ring of rocks. It had burned down to coals and was threatening to cool down so much that it would be hard to get going again.

She grabbed her makeshift fire-tending stick and swept the few glowing red coals into a pile in the center. That would keep it hot enough to keep going while she was away. Though it would need attention after she returned from the morning's fishing expedition. She grabbed her daypack. She added the black trash bag she'd found on the beach yesterday to the existing supplies.

The past nine days of surviving on the island had taught her that blue skies could turn to rain in minutes. And the extra layer of rain protection over her jacket was a welcome improvement.

She looked around and saw a dozen things that needed attention today.

But first things first.

More water. Then fish.

Hopefully fish.

Half an hour later, she arrived at the nearby cove and stopped at the tree line a little ways up from the rocks and waterline. She'd seen a bear across the cove yesterday and, while it didn't make a threatening move toward her, it also made her antennae twitch knowing they were in the area.

Of course, she knew they were in the area because they'd been told to watch out for them. But hearing about it and seeing one across a few hundred feet of water was something else entirely.

She scanned up and down the beach and across the cove and didn't see anything. Still, she was going to be quick about it. No use hanging around in an exposed position any longer than necessary.

Four poles sticking up out of the rocks marked and anchored the lines she'd set. She climbed over the slippery moss-covered angles toward the nearest pole.

Something white and red in a crevice in the rocks. She knelt down and dug it out.

One of those little metal boxes that breath mints came in. She popped open the lid and it worked fine. A little bit of rust on the hinges and in the interior corners, but fine other than that.

An idea came to her!

She dug her watch with the broken clasp out of her pocket. With the plastic bands folded underneath, it fit perfectly! She snapped the lid shut with a grin.

After stashing the box in the thigh pocket of her cargo pants, she continued on to the first pole.

It was still wedged tightly between the three rocks that she'd jammed into place. The monofilament line stretched over a few more rocks and dipped down into the water below. She reeled the line in making sure to wrap it around a flat piece of wood that she used to keep the line from tangling.

To mostly keep it from tangling, at least.

She wound the line in and, through the clear water, saw the unwanted result as the flashing silver hook bounced along the sandy bottom. Whatever it was down there was a grade A maximum-security felon as it had cleaned out a handful of limpets so far.

She'd have to go searching for more limpets later when the tide went out. Disheartened by yet another failure, she dropped the hook and moved on to the next pole.

The news there wasn't any better. If she ever did catch whatever was stealing her bait, she was going to eat it as much out of need as out of revenge. She stomped over to the next pole with a tight frown creasing her face.

Bad news was part of life. She knew that more than most. But still, it was hard to keep up a positive mental attitude on an empty stomach.

She started pulling the line in and immediately noticed that it felt different. There was resistance. Maybe it was snagged in some seaweed or something.

Emily steadied her breath and did her best not to get excited. The emotional roller coaster could take you out as fast as anything else. Faster, maybe. If you let yourself get too high, it made the fall hurt that much worse.

Still, a little wiggle of nervous anticipation tickled in her belly as she continued winding in the line.

Yes!

She spotted it fifteen feet away and several feet below the surface.

A fish!

A part of her wanted to dig the camera out of her pack to record this victory, but a larger part didn't want to give the fish a single second longer in the water where it might somehow escape.

She hurriedly reeled it in, half-panicked that it would break free the instant before she got to it. She leaped away from the water's edge, dragging the line and fish with her. She squatted next to it and shouted in triumph.

It was less than a foot long, had dark gray skin, and big

yellow eyes. A rockfish if she remembered right. More head than body and more bone than flesh.

But it was a fish!

The first fish she'd managed to catch in the nine days since arriving.

Nine days.

Felt like a few hours sometimes and like a few years other times.

She grabbed the head and pried the hook out from the thin skin connecting the jaw. With a finger through its gills to guarantee it didn't get away, she raised it above her head in triumph. She jumped up and down, turning in a small circle shouting to the heavens with words that weren't in a dictionary and yet had been spoken since the dawn of mankind.

Primitive sounds.

They were wild, and free, and thankful. They were a prehistoric celebration of the victory of life over death.

More precisely, the victory that the fish's death had brought to her life. She teetered around in a circle on the uneven and slippery rocks until something in the tree line beyond froze her in place.

A column of gray smoke rising into the air above the trees.

A fire.

Coming from the direction of her camp.

The elation of her spirit soaring through the air did an abrupt one-eighty and crashed into the ground.

"Oh God, please don't be my shelter."

30

Emily raced over the rocks, her boots slipping on wet moss, throwing her off balance as she went. She was as much running as falling as she cleared the last rocks and made it to the beach. She paused long enough to stuff the fish in her bag and sling the bag around her back as she continued up the beach. She raced through the trees, ignoring the branches that slapped and cut at her arms and face as she went.

Please don't let it be my shelter. Please.

After another twenty minutes of running as fast as she could with as little energy as she had left, she arrived at the small clearing that held her campsite.

Her heart sank as her chest expanded and contracted violently, trying to suck in more air than her lungs had the capacity to hold.

What had taken many days and countless hours of effort, energy, and calories, was now a blazing, crackling torch. Everything she owned was in the burning pyre that used to be her shelter. She shrugged off her daypack letting it fall to the ground and sprinted to cover the last fifty yards.

Flames reached fifteen feet into the sky with the dark trail of smoke rising higher above. It was an inferno.

And a promise that her time on the island was over.

But Emily was never one to accept defeat, especially one dictated by someone other than herself.

The slanted roof had caved in and all the pine needles, branches and smaller poles were burning fiercely. All that remained was the skeletal outline of the three thicker poles that were the framing structure. Everything that was not in her daypack was likely lost. But there was no way to know until the fire had gone out.

She grabbed a long pole left over from the build and began dragging burning debris out of the center of the fire. The heat from the nearby flames singed her skin and made the air painful to breathe. She continued pulling material out to the edges and stamping it out.

She swung at the side support pole and the fire-weakened wood exploded. The ridgepole collapsed into the center sending up a spinning tornado of flaming embers.

Emily jumped back to safety and waited an instant before diving back in.

The yellow-orange flames licked at her hands and fingers making her want to scream. But she kept at it, pushing and raking the fire across the ground to move it away from what was once the interior of her shelter. The wind changed and a plume of smoke enveloped her just as she took another big breath. It carried the acrid stench of burning plastic and other noxious chemicals.

She doubled over, hacking and coughing and spitting out the choking air. She staggered to the side to get to fresh air and the wind changed again bringing the plume back around her, swallowing her in a cloud of toxic smoke.

She stumbled again to the side, this time going further

in an attempt to lose the mysterious magnetism that always seemed to draw a fire's smoke to wherever you were. She managed to get a small gasp of fresh air which only served to make her cough all the harder.

Her eyes watered, blurring everything. She forced them open enough to continue pushing and raking at the remains of her shelter.

She shoved aside a flaming branch and found the can that was her makeshift kettle. She'd found it on the beach on the first day and taken it as a sign of good luck.

Now it lay blackened and partially melted into a misshapen form.

So much for luck.

After sifting through the ruin for several more minutes, she soon realized there was nothing left to save.

Her stomach grumbled.

Had a more selfish organ ever been created?

Her shelter was gone. Her sleeping bag was gone. Her backpack and everything in it was gone. The case of extra camera gear was a melted lump of plastic, not that she cared about that one. Besides, she still had one in the pack she'd taken fishing.

She'd lost everything that made her stay in the wild marginally tenable, and all her stomach could do was grumble and pinch and complain about how little it had gotten to eat over the last nine days. It seemed like a separate thing.

Like an enemy.

Or the weakest link on the team. The one that would drag her down and make her tap out.

Emily staggered over to her daypack and collapsed. At least she hadn't left it behind. That would've definitely been an endgame scenario. She stared at the fire thinking about everything that had gone up in flames.

Who was she kidding?

The few things she had in her daypack weren't enough to keep her going. The end game had arrived.

Her stomach cramped and she doubled over. The briny smell of the dead fish in her pack filtered into her nose.

Well, her shelter was gone and there was nothing she could do about it. But she did have the promise of a good meal stinking in her daypack. She glanced at the flames and, like it or not, realized she had a good fire going.

One that she could cook a fish on.

As devastated as she was at the loss of her home, it didn't stop her from gutting the fish, spiking it on a sharp stick, and holding it over the fire.

It was a meal. That was something.

She let it cook on each side for several minutes until the skin blistered and peeled apart in places revealing delicate flesh beneath. The rich smell mingled with the sharper scent of smoke in the air.

Her mouth watered.

This wasn't how she pictured her first successful catch going down. But that was life in the wilderness.

Control was a fleeting illusion.

And yet, you had to believe in it to some degree as the alternative was to simply lie down and die.

Emily picked out a chunk of white flaky filet with sore, red fingers. She shoveled the bite into her mouth and ignored the stinging heat as it went down her throat. She tore off another bite and did the same with it.

It was good. Really good.

It would give her a needed injection of calories and energy.

She sat there eating the best meal she'd had in forever, right next to the smoking remains of what was once her home.

This was her life.

The good. The bad. The utterly tragic.

She wolfed down another bite.

It was going to take everything she had to make it through another day.

31

MARCO finished packing his gear for a daylong outing and crawled out of the shelter with a sense of growing anticipation squirming in his gut. After a quick stretch to get blood flowing into his aching back muscles, he grabbed the camera with the attached selfie stick and prepared to record. Recording several times a day for the past eleven days had made it part of the daily routine. It no longer felt like the ordeal it had at first. He wouldn't have gone so far as to say that he looked forward to the required check-ins, but he at least no longer felt awkward, stammered over his words or looked like a bashful virgin on his first date.

A screeching noise from behind brought a smile to his face.

He turned just as a brown and white coated weasel leapt off the low roof of the shelter and landed on his shoulder. Oscar scurried around behind his neck and tucked into the pocket of space created between it and the top of the pack.

Marco chuckled. "I don't recall offering you a ride, buddy."

Oscar hissed in a way that wasn't so different from a furious cat, circled a few times, and then coiled into a little ball and settled in.

His tiny claws tickled Marco's skin and brought goose-bumps up on his arms. The sensation subsided once the stowaway stopped moving. "Someone hasn't had their morning cup of coffee."

Marco could almost smell the phantom rich aroma of a freshly brewed cup. The lack of coffee was probably the thing he missed most. Even a single drink of that swill from Queen's Diner would've been the highlight of his day.

But there was no coffee.

And worse, there wasn't much food.

Hence the reason for the day's expedition.

He moved the selfie stick until he was in frame on the screen and then rotated around so that his back faced to the east. He adjusted the angle until the black dots in the bright blue morning sky came into view. "Well, I woke up this morning and noticed something that could be a big deal."

With his other hand, he pointed up into the air and moved his finger into place so that on screen it looked like he was pointing directly at the black dots. "It's hard to make out at this distance, but those are vultures."

The dots moved in tiny circles as he tried to keep his pointing finger steady in the right place. He only partially succeeded. Hunger had him a little shaky pretty much all the time.

He counted the dots as he spoke the numbers aloud. "One, two, three, four, five. Five scavengers all circling in the same vicinity can mean only one thing. They found a carcass of some kind. It's something big enough to interest several of them. And you've probably noticed that I haven't been having too much luck on the calories front. Either the ptarmigan in this area are smarter than I thought or I'm dumber than I thought because I have yet to take a single one. Whichever the case, the practical result means I gotta find another source of food. And sooner than later."

He took a breath and looked around the campsite to verify everything was in order for his departure. He grabbed the atlatl and dart leaning against the shelter and secured them to his pack. He'd made them over a week ago but still hadn't managed to kill anything. The ptarmigan were small and flighty, so getting close enough for an accurate throw wasn't easy.

But he had plans to fix that.

"I wanted to show you something I've been working on." He picked up the long carved pole leaning against the shelter and rotated it around in front of the camera. "I know it doesn't look like much yet, but this has the makings of a very passable bow. Now I know for the kids these days, it's all about rail guns and super lasers. But a good bow can make for a fine weapon. And more, it can make for an efficient and lethal long distance hunting tool."

He set the half-finished bow stave down and turned back to the camera. "You probably noticed that there is something missing in its current state." He glanced at it again and back to the camera. "And I mean aside from still needing a good deal more refinement and also setting of the curve. Yup, you guessed it. It needs a bowstring. But, it's not like I can run down to the local sporting goods store and buy a sixty pound Dacron recurve bowstring."

He moved his body and the camera so that again the distant vultures were framed over his shoulder on the screen. He pointed them out again.

"And that's another reason for the expedition. It's a gamble going so far, but there's gotta be something big there. And if it isn't too far gone, I may be able to get what I need to turn that pole into a proper bow." He turned in the direction facing the distant vultures and stared at them for a moment.

It was going to be a long, long walk. And it was going to consume a lot of calories. If it didn't pay off, it was going to be a big strike against his continued participation in the contest.

He turned back at the camera. "Well, the next many hours are going to be riveting. It will be me walking in as straight a line as I can manage to the destination. Rather than bore you with the details, I'll check in when we get there."

Marco clicked the button and turned off the recording. He secured it to his pack. The pack's waist belt was cinched several inches tighter than it had been when he arrived eleven days ago. Not a surprise considering his biggest bounties were nothing more than a few voles the size of gerbils and the odd grasshopper when he could eat it before Oscar found out.

In less than a week, he and the little porkchop had somehow become inseparable. Sure, he could've cracked the weasel's skull with a rock and had a great dinner, but then he would've been alone again.

And some things were worth more than simple calories.

Friendship, if you could call it that.

Marco reached behind his head to pet the little furball and Oscar chirped in irritation and nipped at his finger. The tiny needlelike teeth could've drawn blood with minimal effort, but the weasel was careful to bite him just hard enough for it to hurt but nothing more.

"Oww," Marco yanked his hand away. "Hope you enjoy your nap while I do all the work."

Marco oriented to the distant birds circling in the sky and then broke into a long smooth stride. He prayed this journey would turn out to be worth the effort and calories.

If it didn't, he doubted he'd last much longer.

32

He'd perfected the mechanics of moving fast and smooth over the many years of exploring his family's land back in Montana. It required a certain gait, a particular swing of the legs and arms that wasn't too fast or too slow. It was a different kind of walking than one did in the city. It wasn't something that could be figured out academically or by watching someone else do it.

You had to do it, a lot.

There were no shortcuts.

It was the refined product of experiential learning – the single most powerful teacher in life.

Marco let his body drop into the zone, into the flow of continuous movement. He let his mind move into a state of simple awareness. Just the land passing by.

It was a moving meditation.

And it too was something only achieved by countless hours of doing.

His awareness focused on the ever-changing now, observing the sounds of the rustling grass in the breeze, the whispered breathing of the sleeping weasel, the slow drift of the few clouds in the sky to the north, the rhythmic beating of his heart, the uneven ground under each step. An infinite number of inputs that he was aware of on a subconscious level.

While he maintained that continual awareness, his thoughts meandered to home and the situation that had driven him into this contest in the first place. They drifted further and landed on the girl that was supposed to have been his wife.

Justine was the love of his life. Only that wasn't possible because he wasn't the love of hers.

He'd spent the week after she dumped him at his buddy's house wallowing in self-pity, drinking beer in quantities that were normal for his friend and a first for himself.

His buddy had offered all the usual unsolicited advice and counseling best friends typically offered in that situation.

It was a bit of a drunken haze, but one thing came back with clarity.

His buddy had told him that it was actually a blessing in disguise. That getting your heart broken once made you a better companion for the person you were destined to eventually end up with. His take was that anyone who hadn't been through it didn't know how utterly devastating it was, and so wouldn't be able to commit with the depth of someone who had.

At the time, it had sounded like more bottom of the tenth beer type counseling, but the more he'd thought about it in the succeeding weeks, the more he'd started to think that maybe it was true.

As the terrain passed by, Marco let his mind wander deeper into the memories, the many happy years before the unhappy ending. The nights spent sleeping out on a blanket surrounded by nothing but the velvet-black sky and stars that looked close enough to touch. Making love under those same stars. The night he revealed his feelings while her bare breasts pressed against his chest and their hearts thumped in unison.

She'd felt the same way.

They were two bodies joined into one. Him inside her. Her warmth surrounding him. One being, one breath.

It seemed impossible that it could've gone from that night to never seeing each other again.

The stroll down memory lane wasn't necessarily a mentally healthy exercise, but it helped the hours of walking slip by. And remembering the good times helped, in a twisted sort of way.

Besides, it was ten times better than constantly fixating on food and what he could be eating if he tapped that button and called it quits.

The sun had arced through its daily pinnacle and had started its descent when Marco pulled to a stop on a ridge. On the far side of the shallow valley below lay the thing he'd come so far to find. Two vultures spiraled high above its location. Latecomers to the feast.

It was impossible to tell what it was because a swarm of battling birds hopped and shoved and pushed each other around jockeying for a spot at the table. But whatever it was, it was big.

Marco scanned the valley and noticed with concern that the carcass and scavengers were in the middle of a shallow bowl surrounded by higher ground. He wouldn't have much warning if something decided to pay a visit.

He watched as one of the flying vultures spiraled down and landed next to the mob. It hopped over and joined in on the battle to pick it clean.

Marco had used the circling birds to pinpoint the location of the dead animal. If he could do it, he knew other animals could do the same. Predators as diverse as lions on the savanna to the bears on this island were used to following vultures to a kill. The birds were like a giant buzzing neon sign that promised an all-you-can-eat buffet.

Approaching the carcass would be dangerous. If a bear happened to arrive while he was anywhere nearby, he'd probably end up dead. There would be nowhere to run, nowhere to hide.

Marco bit his lip and chewed on the peeling skin while considering what to do.

It was a big risk. A potentially catastrophic risk.

But everything was a risk out here. Going another day without food was a risk. Going to sleep each night with nothing more than a few branches for security was a risk.

The potential for bad outcomes wasn't getting smaller as he dawdled there considering the possibilities.

So he took a step and headed toward what could turn out to be his best day on the island thus far.

It was the uncertainty, and not the walking, that made his pulse quicken.

33

He started down the ridge toward the carcass, hoping there was enough of it left so that he could find what he'd come for. So that taking such a huge risk didn't turn out to be pointless. He untied the atlatl and dart as he went, readying them for a throw when he got close enough.

There might end up being good meat on the body below, but then again there might not be. It could turn out to be too rotten or already picked over. But those vultures looked like great targets. He'd never tried vulture meat, but maybe it tasted like chicken.

And these birds were far larger and slower than ptarmigan. Odds were good he could take one down.

The large black and gray scraggly feathered birds noticed his approach and started squawking and screeching as he got near. Notably, they didn't actually leave their prize, but they didn't like him coming closer. Scavengers were by nature a tough breed. Any animal that made a regular meal out of rotting flesh and all the accompanying putrid sights and smells was a serious survivor.

One of the smaller ones hopped out of the writhing pile

and turned his head to the side peering intently at Marco. The bulging, folded bare skin above the tuft of feathers circling its neck resembled human skin that had been burnt red under a hot sun. Its head and beak were streaked with blood and a pale white translucent cord dangled from its beak.

Intestines probably.

Marco grimaced as he got closer. Scavenging a carcass was nauseating work. The thick stench that coated your tongue was enough by itself to make you want to vomit. He notched the dart in the atlatl and raised both for a throw.

Too late, he realized he should've dropped his pack before getting this close. The weight and straps were going to make for a difficult throw. Still, if he could get close enough.

The stubborn beasts flapped their wings and screeched in alarm. One by one, they hopped around to the far side of the corpse, but were still unwilling to relinquish the resource.

Oscar perched on top of the pack behind Marco's head squeaking and chirping like crazy. Marco considered flicking the little bugger in the head to get him to shut up.

As the birds broke apart, they revealed the carcass of a large male Roosevelt elk. It was hard to tell what condition it was in from this distance. A few of the more stubborn birds ignored him and continued to tear off strips of meat or organs. One perched on top of the point of the antlers that rose three feet above the ground.

Marco sprinted the final stretch with the atlatl raised and ready. He got within range and whipped it forward.

The dart shot toward the large one perched on the antler.

The dart punched it in the chest and knocked it backward several feet onto the ground.

"Yes!" Marco shouted with glee.

Finally, something to eat!

The speared vulture stopped moving in seconds.

He considered retrieving the dart and trying for another before they all flew off but decided to first check if anything on the carcass was usable. Closer now, he saw that it was in decent condition. Maybe a couple of days old. He didn't want to kill anything that he might not end up needing.

The death of their comrade sent them all into a frenzy of flapping and screeching, but the rest backed away until they were all in a semicircle a dozen feet away from the elk.

Stubborn birds. They didn't leave, but they did keep their distance.

Marco slipped out of his pack and set it on the ground. He didn't want it to soak up any of the smells or fluids from the dead elk. He pulled the can of bear spray out of the side webbing and clipped it to his belt.

Oscar perched on top of the pack, hissing at the elk like it was about to get up and charge him.

"Didn't know you were such a chicken," Marco said with a chuckle. "If I did, maybe I'd have eaten you already." He dug out the camera and flipped open the screen. He set it next to Oscar and aimed it so that it had a good view of the proceedings. He hit record and then trotted over to the far side of the elk before turning back to face the camera.

He spread both arms and smiled, even though the corpse at his feet smelled so bad it made his eyes water.

"Well, took a good five hours of walking but we made it. This is the remains of a Roosevelt elk. A big one, too."

A tingle of excitement raced through his limbs and a gurgle in his belly reminded him that he hadn't eaten anything substantial in far too long. He looked at the camera and then decided that entertaining the comfortable folks at home was far less important than harvesting what he could off this amazing find.

And more importantly, doing so as fast as possible and then getting out of the area before one of the countless Kodiaks on the island arrived on the scene to investigate.

Marco pulled out his knife and continued talking as he started slicing away the skin. "Over here we have a good portion of salvageable meat. I don't know if you can see but there are quite a few maggots which I'll definitely harvest and use for fish bait later."

The only problem with talking was that it meant he had to take more breaths, which wasn't a pleasant experience to say the least. The rotten stench had a slightly sweet tinge to it which made it even more sickening.

Oscar apparently decided the animal wasn't a threat because he bounded over and climbed up onto the carcass. He stood up on two legs and swiped at the air while chirping triumphantly.

Like it was his kill.

Marco laughed. "I think there'll be enough for the both of us, little buddy."

Oscar turned to him and hissed.

He was seriously asking for a flick in the head.

Marco pointed up and down the animal's spine. "Here's the prize I was hoping we'd find. It's a sinew that runs along the backstrap and it can be used to make a bowstring. The atlatl is a good tool, but there's a reason humans moved on to the bow."

The smell had his stomach churning. He was done talking.

"Time to get to work."

34

He started at one end of the spine and pulled the sinew out as he cut. Blood and other internal juices made it slippery and hard to hold onto, but he kept at it and soon was making good progress.

The screeching vultures behind started hopping closer now that Marco was a visibly smaller potential predator.

Oscar dropped to his all fours and pounced on an area of meat thick with wriggling maggots. Their milky translucent undulating bodies resembled a mound of wet rice.

Only wiggling.

He shoved his paws straight into the pile of pupae and grabbed a mouthful. He stood up and looked at Marco as he shoved them into his mouth. Several maggots fell out and bounced off the elk's rib cage and rolled down the slope to the ground below. His delicate little jaws worked back and forth as he shoved at the ones spilling out of his mouth.

The vultures hopped closer as their desire for a meal overcame their fear.

Marco was about to jump up and reestablish himself at the top of the predator pyramid when Oscar leaped to the ground and charged them. He chirped and chattered and screeched with wild abandon.

Marco watched over his shoulder wondering if he was going to have to intervene before one of the birds tried to snatch his brave, and ridiculously foolish, little friend.

One of the larger vultures took a few steps toward Oscar.

In a blur, the weasel leapt and latched onto the base of the bird's neck. An instant later, he delivered a piercing bite to the lumpy red skin.

The vulture squawked and flapped its wings sending a buffeting wind at Marco's back as Oscar kept his jaws clenched tight. The other birds backed away giving both the carcass and the bird under attack more space.

Oscar jumped down and spun around to face them. He screeched and lunged forward sending the whole flock stumbling over each other to get away from the little devil. Once they'd retreated far enough for the weasel's satisfaction, he returned to his perch atop the carcass and stuffed in another mouthful of maggots.

Marco chuckled. "Watch out for Mr. Tough Guy." He returned to working on the sinew, tracing the tendon-like tissue with his finger next to the blade to keep from cutting through it. He slowly worked his way through the length of it, already dreaming of turning it into a bowstring and what that would mean for his odds of sticking around.

He finished cutting it away and then wadded it up into a large leaf he'd brought for exactly this purpose.

It wasn't butcher paper, but it was better than nothing.

After it was wrapped, Marco stuffed it into the thigh pocket of his cargo pants. He could probably get two full bowstrings out of it. One for use and one for backup. The thought put a smile on his face almost as much as the thought of finally having a proper meal did.

The idiot birds began to slowly close back in and Oscar drove them back again before returning to another cavity overflowing with maggots.

Marco returned to the section of meat on the hindquarters that was relatively free of pupae and cut into it. Sure, he already had the vulture but he wasn't going to turn down a few extra days worth of food when it was sitting right here in front of him.

He pushed the blade through the skin and the handle slipped in his hand. Fortunately not enough so that the blade sliced through his fingers. Blood and viscera covered his hands which made handling the knife a challenge. He shoved the tip deeper in, hacking as much as cutting through the dense flesh. He carved off chunks and started a pile on the flank.

After a few minutes, his shoulders began to burn with the exertion. Sweat beaded on his forehead and ran down his nose and cheeks. He wiped a bicep across his forehead to keep it out of his eyes.

They were going to have enough meat for weeks. There was more here than they could ever hope to carry all the way back.

The screeching birds started closing in again. They were like the tide going out and in.

Marco paused, but Oscar was already on it. "Thanks, buddy," he said without looking up. He just wanted to knock this out and get going. He worked the knife deeper into the flesh so that his hand disappeared.

Oscar squeaked and chirped like crazy. He was really getting into it. The vultures were going crazy, too. They must've been sick of one little weasel pushing them around.

"Hold them off another minute or two," Marco said as he felt the blade cut through an especially tough tendon that had been keeping a chunk of meat affixed to the body. "There we go."

He had more than he could carry. Maybe he could gut the vulture and stuff some of the elk inside the cavity?

Like turducken, but with a vulture and an elk.

Vultelk?

Or was it the other way around?

Elkture?

He could never remember what the order of the stuffing was for that monstrosity of a dish.

Marco knelt there covered in viscera, smelling like death, and yet couldn't remember ever being happier. He was going to eat tonight.

Eat like a king.

It was shocking how quickly you could go from being a king to being a pauper.

A deep growling sound sent arctic cold splashing down his back. The fine hairs on the back of his neck stood on end and the thicker hairs on his arms and legs did the same.

His eyes inched up from the carcass to the recording camera still sitting on his pack. In the tiny screen with the red blinking light, he saw himself kneeling beside the elk. In the background, he saw the birds flapping and hopping around in distress.

But that wasn't all he saw.

He also saw the hulking mass of an adult male Kodiak bear.

And it was no more than twenty feet behind him.

35

Fear punched him in the gut with a physical force.

The bear opened his mouth wide and roared. The deep baritone echoed in Marco's head and sent a new wave of ice cascading throughout his body.

Oscar darted over and scrambled up onto the elk. He hissed at the bear from his new perch next to Marco. Facing down the vultures might've been brave, but facing down a Kodiak would've been a death wish.

Without moving his head, Marco glanced at the atlatl by his pack and the dart stuck in the dead vulture. He cursed his stupidity for not retrieving them immediately.

Not that they would've helped much.

But he did have the can of bear spray!

If he could get to it in time.

He switched the knife to his left hand and slowly reached down with his right. He watched the tiny screen in horror as the bear took a few steps forward.

His fingers bumped into the can and he traced his fingertips up to the clip. He squeezed it open and eased the can free.

The bear lumbered closer.

Now less than ten feet away.

He wrapped his fingers around the trigger.

And then the Kodiak charged.

He had no time to aim. No time to do anything other than pull the trigger.

A cloud of noxious chemicals blasted out as the bear crashed through him.

The two tumbled over the elk's body and Marco got thrown to the side.

His chest burned from the spray or maybe the impact. It was hard to tell the two apart. He squinted his eyes open and saw the bear stumbling around batting at its nose and eyes.

Marco sat up and groaned.

It felt like he'd been run over by a truck.

He would've preferred that because a truck didn't have giant claws and teeth. He scanned the ground for the spray but didn't see it.

While the bear wobbled around, Marco stood up and teetered away in the opposite direction. Whatever he could do to put distance between them was a good thing.

He considered going back to the carcass to look for the spray, but that was nearer the bear too and so wasn't going to happen.

He crept backward putting more distance between them. He kept moving and yet knowing that at any second, the bear would come to its senses and chase him down to finish the job.

He was right.

The Kodiak stood on its hind legs and towered ten feet high. Its roar shook the air. It dropped forward on all fours and came at him.

It was over.

That much was clear.

He had nothing. No knife. No atlatl. No spray.

No wait, he had a pocket full of raw meat.

Marco crouched and waited for the impact. Yes, he was going to die, but he wasn't going out without a fight. As much as he could give to a thousand pound top of the food chain predator.

The bear closed the distance with terrifying speed.

Marco's body tensed as the crushing impact drew near.

A dark blur to his left.

The blur flew off the ground and hit the bear in the side of the head.

The bear lost its footing and tumbled end over end to a stop. It jumped up to all fours and shook around like a cross between a bucking bull and a dog shaking to get rid of water in its fur.

As it rotated around, Marco spotted a flash of brown and white against the larger mass of fur.

The bear howled and stood up to swat at the unwelcome hitchhiker.

Oscar scurried over its massive body in a blur.

Marco clawed at his burning eyes. The scorching air trickling in and out of his lungs didn't help. He staggered over to the carcass frantically scanning the ground for the can of bear spray.

A glint of red showed in the grass.

There!

He grabbed the can and looked up just as Oscar raced over the grass and zipped through his legs.

Marco raised the can and squeezed.

The long stream nailed the charging Kodiak in the face.

A full frontal hit and Marco tracked down his aim to empty it as the bear continued forward.

Not ten feet away, it stuttered to a stop, shook its head wildly and roared in fury.

"Oscar! Come on!" Marco shouted as he ran for the ridge in the direction of home. He snapped up the camera and his pack on the way and a few seconds later felt the tiny weasel land on his hip and then scurry up to his shoulder.

He kept running until he made it to the ridge above and watched as the bear fell over sideways as it struggled. He wondered how fast the spray wore off.

He didn't stick around to find out. He broke into a fast jog that he thought he could sustain for a while. The adrenaline in his veins warmed his legs and lungs to the task.

Maybe he was going to live.

But all that food was gone. The shot vulture. The scavenged elk. All those calories.

Gone.

His atlatl and dart gone, too.

But he still had the sinew in his thigh pocket. And that meant he'd soon have a bow.

And it would be desperately needed because if that bear didn't end up killing him, this run home might.

36

DR. GANESH hadn't slept in days, and he looked like it. Wavy gray hair sticking out at all angles gave him a vague resemblance to an Indian version of Einstein.

He rubbed his aching hands together, as much from anxiety as to alleviate the pain. He stood at the back of the operations center watching the fourteen scientists seated at control consoles, all busily doing final pre-ignition sequence checks.

This was it.

A particle collider test set to operate at forty-three tera-electron volts using radically improved electromagnetic coils. More power and more precision. It would be the highest powered test to date, if nothing melted down or blew up. Over three times the official world record of the thirteen TeV achieved at CERN. And still far more powerful than the thirty TeV test that Project Hermes had achieved which opened the first time gate.

While that first discovery had been revolutionary, the following tests hadn't resolved the inherent instability in the time gate's quantum signature. None of the seven time gates they'd successfully created over the past decade had lasted longer than a few minutes.

And so getting much more than a scoop of soil for radio-carbon dating had been difficult.

Another critical issue was that they had yet to succeed in controlling the collisions with enough precision to create an identical quantum signature. Theoretically, that would allow them to pinpoint an exact moment in time.

So even if they could never resolve the instability issue, they could at least reliably return to the same time. Without solving either, the phenomenon would remain nothing more than a marvelous curiosity. And that wasn't helpful for either solving humanity's approaching extinction predica-ment or for completing his personal mission to go back and save Zhang.

But this test could change everything. And they had reason to believe it might as the mathematical models suggested as much.

The shadowed outline of the new Mr. Hill watched over them all from a screen on the back wall.

Hari studiously ignored him.

Each station affirmed go status in turn and then they all waited for his confirmation to initiate.

They all waited for him, even the imperious Mr. Hill.

"What are we waiting on?" an impatient voice sounded from the large screen at the back.

The new Mr. Hill wasn't good at waiting.

Hari stopped rubbing his hands together and started a silent prayer to the gods of his ancestors.

Brahma, Vishnu, Shiva. Please bless this endeavor. Help me to bring back the one that I lost.

He hadn't given the gods their due for many years, and

he prayed they wouldn't hold it against him now when he desperately needed their help.

"Dr. Ganesh, is there a point to—" the annoying voice from the screen started.

"Quiet, Mr. Hill!"

"You can't speak to me that way! I've got your project by the balls and I'd be only too happy to get the shears out. If you try—"

"Shut your mouth!"

Hari had no patience for this. Not now.

Mr. Hill raised his voice in protest. "I will not—"

"You will be silent or I will have that monitor torn off the wall and thrown into the garbage."

Some indistinct grumbling quickly faded away.

"Good," Hari said as he scanned the control room and noted with approval that every technician, every process, every parameter was in place.

"Initiate the sequence," he said in clipped tones.

37

SUYIN doubled over in pain and vomited. Nothing more than a few tendrils of thick saliva came out. Her torso cramped so hard it felt like her ribs were about to crack.

She'd made the stupid decision to drink some unboiled water yesterday after a flash storm drenched her campsite and snuffed out the fire. The day and a half of pouring rain that followed had made it impossible to get another one going.

It hadn't been a choice she'd made lightly. But after a full day of feeling light-headed and weak, she'd decided the alternative was worse. So she'd gone to her normal spot at the nearby creek and filled up. The water had been cloudier than usual from the rain. But it was that or let her systems slowly shut down due to lack of water. She'd drunk so much that her stomach ended up feeling like an over-stretched water balloon.

It was empty now.

Puking for two straight hours had a way of doing that.

And the puking wasn't the worst part.

The way she was losing fluids from the other end was worse.

It was probably dysentery picked up by microscopic bacteria in the untreated water. The symptoms matched.

She wiped away a thick rope of spit dangling from her chin. Her throat burned like fire and her ribs ached like she'd been on the losing end of a heavyweight prize fight. The bile that coated her tongue had that unique raw sewage stink that came when you emptied your guts.

People could smell a thousand different ways, but the stuff that came out of their guts always seemed to basically smell exactly one way.

Putrid.

She tried to spit that taste out. It was bad enough to make her stomach cramp and threaten a repeat performance.

And all that was bad enough.

But that still wasn't the worst part.

The ground under her feet seemed to wobble back and forth as if it was the deck of a ship in a storm.

The dizziness hadn't gone away.

Not completely.

It could've been a symptom of any number of things, but lack of calories was high on the list of likely reasons.

She carefully sat down on a fallen tree trunk alongside the steep slope behind. Moss grew on the decomposing bark and it sunk in a little as she tested it with her full weight. It held. She pulled the camera and selfie stick out of the side webbing of her daypack and turned it around to point at her.

Knowing she looked like death warmed over, she opted not to pull out and flip the screen to verify it. Sometimes it was better not to know. She hit record and didn't really care where in the frame she ended up being.

"Quick check-in. I'm not well."

The words came out thick and clumsy.

She winced at another shooting pain and then continued. "So that water I drank yesterday, the water I didn't boil first. That was a mistake."

Performing was too exhausting. So she clicked it off, set it on her pack, and then surveyed the area. Behind the makeshift seat, the grassy slope dropped for sixty yards into a thick bank of fog that obscured wherever the bottom was.

Su braced her hands on the spongy bark to stabilize herself. She didn't want to fall backward and pitch over the edge. It wasn't a cliff exactly, but it was far too steep to safely climb down.

She sighed. Her body felt like a battery with no charge. Every movement was like pushing through tar.

Her body didn't have much left to give.

And so this outing for food was pretty much her last-ditch effort to keep going. Either she'd find a decent stash of calories, maybe salmonberries or mushrooms or something, or she'd have no choice but to tap out.

There were salmon in the river, but after the encounter with the sow and cubs, she couldn't bring herself to go back.

Thirteen days.

It didn't sound like a long time.

But she was at the end of her rope.

Thirteen days with nothing more than foraged greens and a dead vole she'd scavenged a week ago. A vole had two or three bites of meat to it. And that was a week ago.

Sick.

Starving.

Delirious with dysentery.

And yet as she sat on the log looking around, she realized something even worse.

She recognized nothing about this area.

Bubbling fear stirred in her belly.

Or maybe it was the bad microbes.

Either way, she was lost.

Well and truly screwed.

She would've screamed at herself for being such an idiot if she'd had sufficient strength. As it was, the realization just made her already rock-bottom attitude dig another six feet under.

She shouldn't have walked so far, but knowing this was her last move had driven her onward. Searching for something, anything that could give her strength.

And instead she'd ended up sapping her remaining strength and losing her bearings. Maybe the illness had drawn her attention inward, made her less aware of her surroundings. Her brain was processing through a thick soup, but it knew one thing with crystal clarity.

She was done.

She'd have to tap out.

Her eyes went to the neon-yellow PLB clipped to the daypack.

One call. One ticket home.

It was in her hand before she knew it. Her thumb hovered over the call button.

One call.

And her dad would die.

But she couldn't sleep out here overnight with no shelter.

It was wet and cold.

And she was sick and weak.

She'd die.

And it wasn't melodrama or exaggeration. If she didn't tap out, she wouldn't survive the night.

In the ER, she'd learned about triage and focusing limited resources on the patient with the greatest need. If a patient arrived with a broken fibula and another arrived with intestines spilling out of their abdomen, it was simple to decide who got priority.

But what if two patients arrived and both would die without immediate attention?

It wasn't a situation she'd ever faced.

So, what was she supposed to do now when faced with that impossible choice?

Su chewed on the inside of her lip and tried to be rational. It wasn't easy. After a while, she realized there was only one answer.

She had to keep going. It was only late morning and she had several more hours before an absolute decision had to be made.

Her father's life was worth a few more hours of struggle.

One step at a time.

That was the path.

And hopefully, it somehow led to food and back to camp.

She nodded to herself as if agreeing with an idea offered by someone else.

"Get up. Come on."

She took a deep breath, knowing getting back to her feet wasn't going to be easy and staying on her feet even less so. Her joints hurt being still and moving was worse.

She pushed up off the log and got halfway up.

The soft bark shifted.

The part of the log under her hand caved in and her hand punched through. She teetered backward. She stepped back to regain her balance and only succeeded in smacking her heel on the trunk.

She tumbled over backward and hit the steep grassy slope. Two uncontrolled rolls later and any hope of halting her descent was gone.

In a blur of sky, grass, and bone-crunching impacts, she fell.

First down the slope and then into the fog below.

After a time that both seemed like forever and an instant, she crunched to a stop with her face buried in mud.

She managed to turn her head to the side and suck in a breath that brought in as much slime as air.

She coughed and blood splattered out onto the dark ground. She dug the sludge out of her eyes until she could more or less see.

The dagger-like stabbing in her side told her she'd probably severely bruised or fractured a rib. At least one.

She blinked a few times to focus her eyes. The PLB lay on the trail a few feet away. Looking beyond it, she saw that she was sprawled out on a narrow muddy trail.

There were prints in the mud.

Boot prints.

Slowly, gritting her teeth and holding her middle with one arm, she pushed up with the other.

The sharp pain took her breath away until it ebbed to a level where she could take shallow breaths.

She scanned the ground nearby trying to determine if the prints were fresh or otherwise.

The scan revealed something else.

Paw prints.

Big ones.

Lots of them.

This was a game trail.

Probably used by hunters as well.

It disappeared into a thickening forest in the distance.

She crawled over and grabbed the PLB. The digital display showed it was ready to make the call anytime she was.

She turned to see what was in the opposite direction.

Through an opening in the forest, something glinted silver. Something out of place in the darker hues of the surrounding woods.

She clawed at the crud still in her eyes and then took another look.

It was something!

A chain-link fence!

And fences meant people!

With her pack somewhere on the ridge above and effectively in outer space, getting back to camp was no longer an option.

There were two options left.

Tap out or get to the fence and find help.

She was ready to quit, but the fence wasn't that far off.

Could she get there?

Would getting there change anything?

She nodded, again agreeing with the suggestion her own mind offered.

Get to the fence. Try to get help.

If that didn't work, tap out.

38

Getting to the fence took forever because she couldn't move faster than a slow shuffle. Part of the reason was because anything more than a small step ignited breath-stealing agony in her torso. Another part was because the thick mud threatened to pull her boots off with each step. It made a squishing sound every time she planted a step and a slurping sucking sound every time she dragged it out to take another.

The game trail exited the forest and went by a forty by forty foot area surrounded with fencing. And this was no ordinary fence. It was over twice her height and crowned with tight coils of razor wire that leaned out over her head.

Inside the fence was a complex array of what appeared to be measuring gear. Some of it like radio towers stretching up into the sky. A radar that slowly turned in a circle. Several satellite dishes pointed at the sky. Huge pipes snaked over the ground between various bits of gear. It looked like something you'd find sticking off the side of a space station.

She was about to grab hold of the fence for support

when she noticed a yellow sign attached to it a little further down. It had black block letters and a picture but she couldn't make it out from this angle.

She shuffled over and an icy chill squirmed down her spine as she read it.

SHOCK WARNING
ELECTRIFIED FENCE WILL
CAUSE INJURY OR DEATH

A white sign next to it in red block letters completed the warning.

RESTRICTED AREA
AUTHORIZED PERSONNEL ONLY
NO TRESPASSING BEYOND THIS POINT

She stumbled back from the fence nearly tripping in the muck as she went. After managing to stay upright, she took a number of slow breaths, waiting for the pounding in her chest and the echo in her ears to subside.

What was something like this doing in the middle of nowhere? Whoever put it there was serious about keeping people out.

What next?

She could try following the game trail to see where it went. But scanning the length of it in both directions showed no manmade structures and, besides, she couldn't make it much further anyway.

Getting this far had sapped her completely.

The waves of dizziness that had previously been inter-mittent were now a constant companion.

Like she was bobbing around in the open ocean. And

there was an ominous promise that it would soon pull her under.

Just as her thoughts turned to the PLB in her hand, she noticed something she hadn't seen before, at the far corner of the installation.

On top of a twenty foot tall pole were four security cameras angled down and arranged like the cardinal directions on a compass, presumably to give three-hundred-sixty degree coverage.

Someone, somewhere must be monitoring them!

In an unbridled burst of excitement and hope, she ran over to it. The mud sucked off one of her boots as she went.

She stopped below the cameras and raised her arms to wave. Lancing pain immediately choked the breath out of her. She cradled her middle with one hand and waved at the camera with the other.

"I need help! Please! Help me!"

She carried on shouting and waving until a sudden bout of dizzy exhaustion swept over her and knocked her down. She landed hard and the world cut out.

At some point, the world blurred back into focus.

Half her face was stuck in mud. Su blinked until she recognized the PLB laying a few inches away.

It was time.

She had nothing left.

Dying out here wasn't going to save her father.

Tears welled in her eyes and rolled over the bridge of her nose and into the mud.

Her chest shuddered and the promise of further pain in her ribs kept her from completely falling apart.

She reached for the PLB and shifted it around so her thumb could hit the button to make the call.

I'm sorry, Baba.

I'm so sorry.

Her thumb touched the button, but froze before pressing it.

Something.

She listened.

SLURP.

SQUISH.

SLURP.

SQUISH.

Her heart soared. A warm and wild hope glowed in her chest.

Someone was coming!

They must've seen her on the cameras!

She was going to get help, and maybe, just maybe, they'd let her continue with the competition because she hadn't tapped out. Not technically.

Su carefully pushed herself up, her ears attuned to the sucking sounds of the approaching rescuers.

It was getting louder. And the overlap of the sounds suggested there were at least two people coming.

Thank God!

She waited in stupefied disbelief and gratitude.

She'd pushed it too far. She knew that now.

But she'd gotten lucky.

She stared down the trail as the sounds got closer, and then the rescuers appeared.

Her heart sank like a stone.

Ice flooded through her veins.

It wasn't rescuers.

It was a Kodiak bear.

A large male with scars criss-crossing its face and one missing eye.

Su punched the button to make the call.

The bear charged.

In a panic, she reached back for the can of bear spray, but it and her pack were at the top of the ridge.

"Suyin, this is Bob. Did you hear the news? Are you tapping out?"

She was about to scream for help when the bear smashed down on her backside, driving her into the mud.

Something snapped in her pelvis and blinding pain shot through her body.

She screamed in agony.

And that wasn't the worst of it.

The worst happened next.

Searing pain stabbed into her back as the giant bruin bit through her clothes and into her flesh.

39

BOB waited for a refill of donkey urine coffee. That wasn't what it was called on the menu, but that was how it tasted. And that might've been a disparaging comparison to donkey urine.

What he wouldn't give to have his assistant appear in the diner and deliver him an afternoon latte with a smile on her full lips and a sway in her fuller hips. He'd been stranded on this god-forsaken island for over two weeks now. The thirteen days since the competition started and the several days of frantic preparation before that.

And with four contestants still fighting for the prize, it could be weeks, months even, before only one was left and he could finally go home.

He almost wished he'd died back at his office, on the floor staring between Veronica's legs. At least he would've died happy then.

Now he was stuck at his regular booth by the large front window at Queen's Diner in the dump that was Kodiak, Alaska. Watching seaplanes land and take off from the slender Lilly Lake below had gotten old on the first day. He barely registered their comings and goings now.

He would've found a better culinary establishment to spend his days but for two things. One was the reindeer sausage, which was legitimately a delicacy he would miss when it was time to go. And two, there was something about the suggestive swagger of the lady that worked here. Her saucy attitude and friendly banter had occupied more and more of his thoughts as the days dragged by.

The TV hanging in the corner up by the ceiling caught his attention for the first time all day. A woman sat at a news desk with wide eyes reading the paper in her hand. Her hair stuck out on one side like she'd been halfway through hair and makeup before being rushed out to go live.

A banner scrolling along the bottom said Emergency Broadcast Update. The video split in two and, from another location, a short pudgy man in a sloppy suit appeared.

Bob recognized him from a TV show on investing. Crazy Cash with Joe Crammer, or something. It was more about melodramatic rants and red-faced shouting than it was about any meaningful investment advice. There had even been reputable studies showing his investment advice was worse than random guessing. Far worse. To the point that some folks claimed they'd made tons of money by doing the exact opposite of what this financial charlatan recommended.

Anyway, it was all spectacle and no substance, which didn't bother Bob in the least.

Spectacle could be worthwhile for its own sake.

Take his assistant's round backside, for example.

The problem was that many people actually thought the guy knew his bellybutton from an option and so had lost their shirts following his idiotic investment advice.

Idiots.

Both them and him.

Bob was old enough and had been screwed over enough to have honed a hard-earned BS detector. He could spot BS like the Hubble telescope saw infinitely distant stars. Once you knew what to look for, it glowed like a glittering galaxy.

And that Crazy Cash guy shone like Batman's spotlight on a new moon.

Anyway, that idiot was jumping up and down, his face as red as a beet, shouting something at the news anchor.

Thank God the TV was muted.

"Here's your coffee, sugar," Flo said as she magically appeared at his elbow and poured out a steaming cup.

"Do you get CNN or something? I'd even take FOX news over this garbage."

"Sure thing, honey," she said as she dug into the front pocket of her smock and pulled out the remote. She clicked it over to another news channel and this news anchor looked like he'd missed Hair and Makeup completely. She clicked the volume up.

"...of the United States has yet to make an official statement on the situation. However, financial markets around the world have shut down as the dollar continues in free fall. There are reports that China may be selling off its nearly one point five trillion dollars as a pre-emptive strike in the escalating feud between the two nations. Banks are shutting down across the nation in order to prevent panicked withdrawals and a subsequent collapse of the financial system."

He touched his ear and looked down as he listened to something in his earpiece. His eyes slowly widened and his mouth went slack. A second later, he seemed to remember where he was and looked back up at the camera. A lock of hair flopped down into his face and he finger-combed it back across his forehead.

"We have a breaking news update. We have reports that two F-22 Raptors flying over the East China Sea have been shot down. They were said to be flying reconnaissance sorties as a deterrent to further aggression from the Chinese Navy in the region."

He looked offscreen and listened to his earpiece another moment, then turned back to the camera.

"We've just received news that the American aircraft carrier, the Gerald R. Ford, has been attacked in the same area. Missiles that are believed to have been fired from the Chinese mainland hit the carrier strike group disabling multiple ships and sinking the Ford class supercarrier. The White House has just announced the President will make a statement in the next few..."

The remote in Flo's hand clattered to the tile floor. "Oh my God," she whispered.

Bob's mobile rang.

It was Suyin Li's PLB. Did she find out the news somehow and was quitting before World War III got underway?

Whatever the reason for the call, he dug his digital recorder out of his pocket and plugged the phone into it. They recorded all calls because you never knew what Editorial might end up using.

He started recording and then answered the call. "Suyin, this is Bob. Did you hear the news? Are you tapping out?"

An agonizing scream made him jerk the phone away from his ear.

"Suyin?"

Another shriek and then a frantic voice answered. "It's biting me! A bear! It's..."

Another scream.

"Oh my God," Bob said in shock.

The scream wavered and broke. "Help me! It's eating me!"

The line went dead.

40

Oh no.

A Kodiak bear attacking a contestant. Maybe eating her. How long would it take a rescue team to get to her? Thirty minutes? An hour? More?

If it was more than a few minutes, and it would be, then it might be too late.

She'd be dead by the time help arrived.

Bob called the local number he'd been given when they pulled the permit for the show. He quickly relayed the situation and the identifier codes for Suyin's PLB. He was about to launch into a series of questions when the emergency dispatcher interrupted him.

"We'll call you when we have an update."

And then she hung up.

Bob looked up and stared at the ongoing news broadcast, but didn't hear a word. He scanned the room in a daze.

Flo stood behind the counter talking on a landline with someone as her eyes stayed locked to the TV. The two old guys that were as much a part of the diner as the black and white checkered floor were doing the same.

Bob glanced back at his phone.

What more could he do?

He called his assistant, Valerie.

She answered on the first ring. "Hey boss, have you seen the news?"

"Connect me with Suyin's father. We've got an emergency here."

"On it."

A minute later, she returned. "Patching him through."

"Hello?" a unfamiliar voice said.

"Hello, Mr. Li. This is Bob Randy, producer of the show your daughter is—"

"I knew it!" a triumphant voice replied. "She won, didn't she? I knew she—"

"There's been an accident."

The enthusiasm in her father's voice evaporated. "What? What do you mean?"

"I don't have all the details yet, but she's—"

An incoming call beeped and appeared on his screen.

Suyin's PLB again!

He answered and merged the calls.

"Suyin? Are you there?"

"I... I'm... bleeding."

"Su?" her father said.

"Baba?"

"Yes, baby. It's me. What's going on?"

Another agonizing wail.

"Baba, it... it's... eating me."

"What?" her father yelled.

A low grumble mixed with sickening wet sounds sent a shiver up Bob's spine.

"Baby, where are you? What's happening?"

There was no response.

Just more of the tearing, crunching noises that came through all too clearly.

"Honey, you have to get away! You have to run!" Her father's voice pitched several octaves higher and carried a wild, ragged edge.

She didn't reply.

More of the stomach-churning sounds. Like snapping a thick stalk of broccoli in half. Like squeezing an overripe tomato in your hand.

"No! No! No! No! No!" her father chanted like a machine gun on full auto. "Help her! Help her!"

"We've got a rescue team on the way. That's all I know right now."

"Honey! Are you there? Su, please answer me!"

Another minute of those sounds.

Those sounds.

Ripping flesh and bone. Eating it.

Wet and muffled.

The low grumble and whoosh of heavy breathing.

"Oh my God," her father said. "Please, no."

"Baba?" her voice came through weak like a frayed thread.

"Yes, honey. I'm here. I'm so sorry, baby." His voice broke as he wept. "I'm so sorry I sent you there."

A minute passed while her father sobbed uncontrollably. He finally settled enough to speak. "Baby? Are you there?"

"It... it doesn't hurt as much now."

"Please. Please. I'm so sorry." His voice came through punctuated with sobbing, like a sentence with periods after every word.

"S'okay, Baba" Suyin replied. "I... I'm..."

"I'm here, baby. I'm here. Oh my God, I'm so sorry. I'm here."

"Baba, I... I love you."

"I love you, honey. I love you so much."

"I... I'm... be..."

A gurgling exhale and all that remained was the nauseating tearing and rending.

Her father's unhinged wailing soon drowned out everything else.

After a few minutes of nothing more from Su, Bob flopped back in the booth. He glanced down and saw that his digital recorder was still ticking away seconds, recording it all.

He couldn't believe what just happened.

He'd just saved his job!

The corners of his mouth crept upward.

Yeah, it was a tragedy. A disaster no one could've foreseen. One that legal had been careful to ensure wouldn't come back to bite the network.

But the ratings.

Oh my God! The ratings!

Once word got out, this show was going to pull ten, maybe fifteen million viewers. Everyone was going to be talking about it. He hadn't sniffed anywhere close to those numbers since the curtains came down on his last big hit, *Schwartzfeld*.

And that was a different time, back when a single show could capture the nation's imagination. Back when everyone would end up around the water cooler the next day, recounting and opining on what they'd watched the night before.

Bob let the phone call continue, recording the father's grief. He probably didn't need any more, but he wanted

Editorial to have plenty of material. They'd figure out how to best tell the story later. The key was to have plenty of raw material to work with.

He couldn't wait to see his boss's face when he heard the news. As much as Bob hated him, he had to admit the power-grabbing back-stabber knew good TV when he saw it.

And he'd know this was good TV. No, this was great TV. As good as it came. Better.

Bob couldn't wait to hear Malcolm groveling, telling him how wrong he'd been to almost fire him. Maybe that's when Bob would tell him he was quitting to go work for another network. To bring his next big idea to a direct competitor.

Having and using leverage was such sweet, sweet revenge.

He imagined the encounter and how he'd make Malcolm eat crow until he turned black and sprouted feathers. He'd make him beg.

The lurid anticipation was almost enough to make him hard.

Sure, it was sad what happened to the girl, but she knew the risks. They all did. And people died everyday around the world without getting the chance to win a million bucks.

And it wasn't like it was his fault.

He had nothing to do with it.

It was just life. Some people lived and some people died.

The network would, of course, spring for a funeral. They could probably get another few episodes detailing the girl's life and how it ended. Then end with cameras at the funeral recording her father's grief.

It would be tragic, and beautiful.

It would be the best TV anyone had ever seen.

Bob grabbed his cup and took a gulp that burned his

tongue and throat on the way down. He glanced up at the TV on the wall.

The news anchor continued to drone on and Bob couldn't have cared less. All that was too far away to matter.

He looked out the window at the finger-like lake below. A battered old seaplane lifted off the surface. Long ropes of water trailed off behind as it climbed into the air heading toward the diner. As it drew nearer, he saw the belly was a patchwork of faded green paint and bare metal that looked like an unintentional camouflage pattern.

Another minute and it would bank left to head inland or right to head to sea, like they all did.

The sky flashed white.

From nowhere and everywhere at once.

So bright Bob snapped his eyes shut in pain.

He covered them with his hand until the discomfort ebbed and the red glow through his eyelids did the same.

Squinting through shadowed eyelashes, he saw the seaplane with one wing dipped lower than the other and pitched forward, heading straight at the diner like an arrow.

The roar of the engine vibrated the glass window.

Bob sat there, frozen in fear.

It was headed right at him.

So close he could make out the pilot's bushy beard and the arm covering his eyes.

Run!

Get up and run!

But he couldn't move. It was like he was stuck watching his own train wreck.

An image of the blurred prop smashing through the window and slicing him to ribbons turned his insides to ice.

What a gruesome way to go.

After all he'd been through. And just when things were looking up.

The pilot dropped his arm and the two stared into each other's eyes. They both knew what happened next.

The pilot yanked back on the yoke with both hands. His beard parted as he screamed something.

Bob snapped his eyes shut.

He didn't want to see his own death.

The roar of the plane vibrated through his body like standing in front of a speaker at a rock concert. Like when he and his ex-wife had danced together at that Zeppelin concert so long ago.

He saw them there. Drunk and high. Young and happy.

Together.

She took a long drag off a joint and the ember crackled and glowed bright orange. She leaned into him and locked her soft lips to his. Warm smoke filled his lungs. His head swam.

He'd wanted nothing more than to stay in that moment with her.

They'd been good together.

Why did the good times always have to end so soon?

41

FLORENCE BICKLE looked out the diner's front window, wondering what that flash was about. She'd been facing the TV and so it hadn't blinded her like some of the other customers. Several of them staggered out of their booths with arms waving in the air. One guy crawled under his table. The two old timers sat there holding their spiked coffees as if nothing had happened.

She saw Hugo Howey's old DHC-2 Beaver tilted to the side and thundering straight at them.

Seconds away from plowing into the diner.

The diner's latest regular, Bob, sat there with his eyes closed.

What was he doing?

Meditating on death?

She grabbed his arm and yanked him away from the window.

It wouldn't be enough. But she wasn't the type to accept the end just because it was inevitable.

He was heavier than he looked and she wasn't the athlete she once was.

She tripped and he came down on top of her as the plane screamed closer.

Flo looked around Bob's head just as the Beaver jerked upward and Hugo's pale clenched teeth buried in a dark beard blurred by. The pontoons shot over the roof, clearing it by inches.

The vibrations rattled a glass of orange juice off the edge of the table. It hit the tile and sprayed glass shards and cold liquid against her leg.

She forced air into her lungs. Bob was dead weight on top of her, making it difficult to breathe.

The plane's noise faded into the distance outside as Bob opened his eyes. Inches above hers.

He stared at her in silent shock.

Through labored breath, she tried to roll him off. "You're alive." she sputtered.

"Really?"

"Yep, now could you move?"

"Oh, sorry."

Bob rolled to the side and she sucked in a welcome breath. He got to his feet and then helped her up. "Thanks. I... I didn't..."

Flo smacked his shoulder. "You owe me one. Now what's going on?"

Bob nodded as she stepped toward the booth to look out the window. Bits of glass crunched underfoot.

Several cars out on Mill Bay Road were stopped in the middle of the street with doors open. Their owners stood outside looking around. People were starting to wander out of storefronts along both sides of the road.

Flo turned back to the TV and noticed it was off. She looked around.

All the lights were off.

"What happened?" Bob said, his voice tinged with panic.

"I'm not sure." She dug the TV remote out of her smock and tried to turn it on.

No luck.

Maybe the main breaker blew. It happened now and again. This old building combined with her cheapskate boss meant something was always breaking down.

Bob grabbed his phone off the table and started tapping the dark screen. He looked up to say something but she was already headed to the back to check the main panel.

She marched behind the counter, through the kitchen, and to the utility room. After a minute of troubleshooting, she'd flipped the main breaker a few times, did the same to a few individual circuits, and discovered that her limited knowledge of all things electrical had run out of road.

It didn't seem to be a problem with the breakers, which wasn't totally unexpected. The town of Kodiak had infrequent power outages.

The bell strung to the front door tinkled as she stared at the breakers, trying to think of something else to try that might work.

Nothing came up.

Flo returned to the front and noticed a few folks had left. Most everybody that came to the diner was a regular and they knew exactly how much to leave to cover the bill and tip. From a glance at the two vacated tables, she saw they'd each left the usual amounts.

Earl and Jim hadn't moved from their usual booth. Those two owned it as much as her boss did. They sat there all day, everyday. Earl caught her eye and held up his coffee cup. He pointed at it with raised eyebrows and lines in his face that were so deep they looked like dried and cracked mud.

She grabbed the pot as she spoke loud enough so that the few folks there would all be sure to hear. "Hey everybody, the power has cut off. Not sure but it looks like a problem with the town's power. You're welcome to stay, but we're cash only for the rest of the day. IOU's are fine too if you don't have it."

Jim stared up at her through eyebrows that looked like they belonged in that building at zoos that held all the crazy spiders, snakes, and other creepy crawlies. "This ain't no power outage with the town."

She refilled both their empty cups. "Sure looks like it."

The canyons in Earl's face shifted as he spoke. "What about that flash of light?"

She'd never seen anything like it. "Maybe an electrical explosion or something?" Even as she said it, it sounded unconvincing. The fact was that she had no idea what had caused that.

Jim continued, "First the flash, and now we have no power."

Flo set the pot on the table as she considered. "Maybe a blown transformer. Happened last summer when that squirrel chewed through and shorted the wires." The whole town had gone dark for a few days until they'd replaced it.

"That squirrel was a Russian agent," Earl said and Jim nodded.

Flo rolled her eyes. "Not this again."

Jim's eyebrows jumped like they were alive. "It's true! The Russians have trained animals to carry out secret missions since the start of the Cold War. The proof is out there for folks who want to find it. Anyway, that Russian squirrel's got nothing to do with this. The Chinese did this."

Bob approached the table. "What are you talking about?"

Jim gestured at the TV. "They was just talking about it all on the news. Our planes shot down. Our ships sunk. They started a war and that flash was an attempt at finishing it."

Bob's hands trembled as he spoke, "What was that flash?"

Jim and Earl looked at each other, and then both nodded as if accepting some secret knowledge. Jim turned back to Bob. "Son, that was what they call an E-M-P."

"A what?"

Earl joined in. "An electromagnetic pulse. E-M-P. It's a high altitude nuclear strike that causes a cascading ionization that energizes the atmosphere."

Bob shrugged. "So we're still here. We're not melted or turned to ash. What's the point?"

Flo shook her head as Earl's eyes widened in apparent disbelief at the Outsider's ignorance. "Here we go," she muttered.

"That ain't the point at all. An EMP is designed to zap all our modern electronics. Anything that has a microchip inside is liable to get fried. And nowadays, everything's got 'em. If it's powered by electricity and was made in the last thirty years, chances are good it got fried."

Bob's gaze drifted to the TV.

"That for sure is dead."

Flo could see the fear rising in Bob's face. They'd both nearly died in a plane accident seconds before. She was in no mood for conspiracy theories from the two resident experts in the field. "That's enough, Earl. Don't be starting a panic for no reason."

Jim pulled a flask out, unscrewed the metal cap, and poured an unhealthy portion of clear liquid into his steaming coffee.

Earl tapped the lip of his cup and Jim added a similar amount to it before putting the flask away.

The two old dinosaurs each raised their cups and clinked the stained porcelain together.

"Why are you raising a toast?" Bob asked.

Flo agreed with the sentiment. Her son, Rome, had told her about EMPs before. He was big into all things zombie and apocalyptic. She'd talked with him before about having such an unhealthy obsession. Fantasizing about the end of the world wasn't a productive way to live in it.

She didn't recall the details of what he'd said about an EMP, but something about turning us all back into cavemen came to mind. Whatever was happening, it sure wasn't something you raised a toast to.

Earl turned to Bob. "Youngster, the end of the world has arrived."

"And why is that a good thing?" Bob's voice cracked with a barely hidden fear.

Jim smiled. "Nobody said it was a good thing. But it's a powerful reminder to fully appreciate this steaming cup of coffee." He took a sip and savored it before swallowing. "Right down to the last drop."

Earl finished the thought. "Yep, because this right here." He waved his cup around, encompassing the whole of the diner, and perhaps all of the world beyond. "This might be the last cup of coffee we share in this life."

42

DR. GANESH stood behind the technician's shoulder verifying the spike in the power readings on her screen. They didn't make sense. A thousand tera-electron volts? Ten times the theoretical maximum of what could be achieved by the subterranean nuclear reactor that powered the facility and the accelerator ring.

The Large Hadron Collider at CERN had achieved thirteen TeV and Project Hermes had beaten that ten years ago with the thirty TeV test that had opened the first time gate. And with this test designed to operate at forty-three TeV, he was hoping to finally crack the code to both stability and precision.

But a thousand TeV?

How could that be possible?

"Doctor, the comm link to Mr. Hill is down."

Hari looked over his shoulder at the large monitor on the back wall. It was dark. No mysterious bean counter watching and waiting to cut his funding.

Good.

He didn't need the distraction. He turned back to the terminal screen, eyes tracing the readout.

Everything had been going according to plan and well within specs just minutes ago. And now, out of nowhere, the power of the collisions had increased an order of magnitude.

More.

How was that possible?

It wasn't.

It had to be a sensor malfunction.

"That can't be accurate," Hari said.

The technician shook her head. "I thought the same thing. But I've run diagnostics and all sensors appear to be working properly. "

Should he shut the test down?

Now?

When he was so close to what he'd worked tirelessly for ten years to achieve?

No.

He couldn't stop now, not when the end was within reach. Not when he was closer than ever to righting the wrong he'd done so long ago.

The operator monitoring topside conditions interrupted his thoughts from across the room. "Dr. Ganesh! You need to see this."

Hari hurried over to his desk, hoping for some clarity. "What do you have?"

The screen showed a graph which had a line that crawled along the bottom axis until the end where it had a massive spike that went straight up to the top edge of the screen and just as quickly dropped back to the bottom. The operator traced his finger along the bottom. "These are the expected levels of background electromagnetic radiation."

His finger hit the spike and he traced it up. "A few minutes ago, for whatever reason, this happened." He stopped his finger at the top and then traced it back down. "Whatever it was didn't last long. Some kind of powerful pulse."

Hari rubbed the aching bones in his right hand.

The technician answered Hari's question before he asked it.

"And yes, I already ran diagnostics. Twice. Everything came back within parameters." He touched the spike again. "Everything but that pulse."

"What could cause that?"

"A coronal mass ejection or a massive solar sunspot emission. Maybe."

But neither was likely. Per the standard operating procedures, they'd reviewed NASA's report on solar activity and nothing of note had been predicted. Besides, the entire facility had been built to withstand unexpected electromagnetic interference. The depth underground combined with the hardened electrical infrastructure should've prevented it from being a problem.

But the readings on the graph showed a huge spike.

Two desks over, the communications operator spoke. "Dr. Ganesh, I'm getting some strange readings here."

"Could you be more specific? Strange readings don't seem to be all that unusual just now."

"Sorry. It's just that all topside communications appear to have gone quiet. I'm running diagnostics."

A window popped up on the screen as Hari approached the terminal. The results.

EXTERNAL COMMUNICATIONS ARRAYS: ONLINE

The online word appeared in green and flashed off and on.

"Pulling up the log," the technician said before Hari

could request it. There was a reason each and every person in the control room was here. They each had a function and area of responsibility. And they knew what Hari expected and delivered on it every single time.

Aptitude without consistency wasn't much better than blind luck. And while blind luck sometimes played a part in scientific discovery, it was a terrible method to depend on.

A log of entries scrolled vertically on the screen. A time-stamp on the left with a brief description of the communication on the right.

The technician scrolled down until the descriptions abruptly ended. The last timestamp was a few minutes ago. The same time as the recorded pulse.

"So, it's not a problem with our equipment?"

"It doesn't appear to be. But we aren't receiving any external transmissions. Sat links appear to be down. We aren't getting verifications that our transmissions are being received." The technician shrugged. "I don't know what to make of it."

"Dr. Ganesh! Dr. Ganesh!"

Hari hurried over to the tech's console and saw a digital map of the island. He stared at the red blips that dotted the island. There were at least twenty of them.

He stood there, dumbfounded.

"They all appear to be time gates," the tech said.

How could that be possible?

And so spread out over the island?

Hari pointed at one off the coast of the island. "Pull up that one."

The tech's fingers blurred as the map zoomed in and a window of technical data popped up. "It appears to be three hundred feet under water about a mile off the coast."

How could it be so far away?

"And the quantum signature suggests it's huge. Maybe a hundred feet square."

Hari traced his finger down the column of numbers that wouldn't mean anything to anyone outside the control room. "Look at this," he said as he highlighted a particular bit of data. "If this is accurate, this gate could go back several million years."

None of the seven time gates they'd managed to create over the last decade had gone back further than fifteen thousand years.

Millions?

The tech nodded and then pointed out another set of data points. "And this. We've never seen this before."

Hari followed the data and the implications numbed his brain like a powerful anesthetic.

The tech ran a check to verify the readings and they came back the same. "That gate's quantum signature is showing no stochastic variance. Zero. If it's accurate, that gate isn't going anywhere."

Hari knees buckled and he grabbed the edge of the desk to keep from collapsing. It took him a moment to regain conscious thought. And the first one that returned had Zhang at the center. "Do any of the gates match TG1?"

"It'll take a few minutes to check."

"Do it."

Hari watched as the tech zipped through various screens that organized the data in different ways. What would've taken him days to collate and compare took the tech less than five minutes. As the director, he operated at a higher level and this was exactly why he had a team of highly capable and specialized individuals.

"Everyone, I want systems checks across the board!"

Every keyboard in the room started clacking at once.

"Got it," the tech said. "None of the time gates show a matching signature to TG1."

"Another failure," he muttered under his breath. He gritted his teeth. His stomach churned and started to burn like he'd gulped down half a bottle of bourbon.

This whole thing was out of control. Tearing open the fundamental fabric of time and space was a delicate business. And something had knocked this test sideways.

Maintaining a reasonable level of safety was no longer remotely possible. But aborting would mean another eight months minimum before another test could be performed. Probably double that considering the extensive investigation that would be required by the unusual nature of terminating this one.

As much as it turned his stomach, it was the only choice. If the power levels were accurate, there was no telling what kind of damage had been done to the collider ring's equipment. It wasn't made to handle near that much power.

And what about all those open time gates around the island? Who knew what could be going through them right this second.

The whole facility blowing up like the last gasp of a dying star wasn't outside the realm of possibility. Pundits and critics of particle accelerator research had shouted such warnings for years. Maybe they'd finally turn out to be right.

He'd waited ten impossibly long years. He'd have to wait longer.

"Abort all systems checks and initiate the emergency shutdown sequence! Do it now!"

Dr. Ganesh closed his eyes and slipped his bony fingers up under his glasses. He rubbed the sockets causing the liquid within to squish and splutter.

A moment passed while the control room echoed with

the rapid-fire clicking of numerous keyboards carrying out his command.

The clicking slowly faded away to silence.

"Dr. Ganesh?"

"What?" he snapped, poorly controlled irritation evident in his tone.

"It's the shutdown sequence."

"What about it?"

"I've disconnected power from the ring. Transmission lines are reading zero current."

Hari exhaled with relief. At least something was going right today. "Good. You cut the power and the collisions stopped. What's the problem?"

"That's just it, Doctor. I cut the power, but the collisions haven't stopped. The ring's energy levels haven't decreased. Not one volt."

"Are the time gates still open?"

The tech seated next to him exited out of a screen filled with data and returned to the map of the island. A few of the red dots had vanished, but most remained.

"Many of them remain open and stable."

Hari didn't respond. The possible consequences of what they'd done had short-circuited his brain. They'd lost control of the experiment.

And without the necessary control, how could anyone predict what would happen next?

43

EMILY slid her hand up the wooden shaft closer to the axe head. She hefted it into the air, took aim at the log, and then swung down letting the sharp edge sweep through an arc picking up speed as it went.

It hit a little off center, but still split the log along its length.

Her cargo pants slipped off her hips and dropped around her knees. She'd never been especially curvy, not like the pictures of her mother that were all the memories she had. Even so, what roundness she did have when she'd arrived was gone. The fat dissolved to provide calories. The muscles now starting to do the same.

She set the axe down and pulled them back up. She lifted her filthy thermal shirt and cinched her belt a notch tighter. It was the last hole available. Any tighter and she'd have to punch new holes in it.

Her shoulders trembled with exhaustion. She was running on fumes. No, she was running on the memory of fumes.

And even that was fading.

Just as she was.

Thirteen days with almost no food.

Massive calories out and minimal calories in.

She turned to the camera sitting on a nearby log. The little red light flashed on the small screen. She examined herself and noted that her waist was starting to look distubringly thin.

Exactly the look every fashion magazine espoused. Why they pushed half-starved women as the pinnacle of beauty made no sense. It was like they purposefully idolized the exact opposite of what made evolutionary sense.

In days long past, a woman so bereft of calories would have nothing to offer her offspring. And even if she had no children, she wouldn't survive a single winter or unexpected period of resource scarcity.

It made zero sense.

And maybe that was what made it so appealing. It was a direct slap in the face to everything reasonable. It was the ego looking in a mirror and drowning in self-concern. A vain appeal to form over function. A final act of hubris in the victory of humans over their environment.

And aside from the dirt that smudged her face and covered her hands, she had exactly the kind of hollow cheeks and protruding hipbones figure that graced every supermarket checkout aisle in America.

"Ladies, forget the fad diets! Forget the all carbs all the time diet or the no carbs none of the time diet or whatever it is that someone is trying to sell you. I've got the real deal diet. It's called starvation. And it sucks."

She walked over and picked up the camera so her face filled the screen. "Could you do me a favor? Go have a huge slice of pizza. The giant ones that are a whole meal in one slice. One with cheese oozing off the sides. One that's so hot it burns the roof of your mouth." She closed her eyes and smelled the spicy scent of marinara sauce. Her mouth watered in anticipation of something that wasn't coming.

Her stomach pinched so hard she winced.

Food. It was so easy to obtain in normal life.

Grocery stores were filled with unending aisles piled high with food of every imaginable kind. And you could just walk in and buy something. Anything.

And then eat it.

If someone had asked her what heaven was like just then, it would've sounded a whole lot like the local supermarket.

Emily sat down to rest for a minute. She was the exact opposite of the Energizer Bunny. She never had energy. A single minute of exertion left her weak and sometimes dizzy.

She'd struck out in every possible way. Hunting. Fishing. Foraging. Scavenging. Her shelter burned to ash. And a single bony fish, as delicious as it had been, didn't count for much.

It was like the island personally wanted her to fail. Like it wanted to take her out just as it had her father.

Nature didn't hate anyone.

She knew that logically.

But her logic and reason weren't especially strong with her body so weak.

She'd been sleeping in a pile of leaves for the past four days. Even wearing every bit of clothing she had in addition to the black trash bag, the cold was brutal.

Building another proper shelter was impossible. Attempting it would've burned through her last reserves and pushed her over the edge. She'd given up on a real shelter, but she still needed fire wood. The nights were painfully cold without a steady fire going.

As much as she hated to admit it, she was hoping for a miracle at this point.

Like if a Sitka deer walked up and fell over dead. Or if a plane flew over and tossed out a pallet of food strapped to a parachute. Or she walked into a hidden glade and happened upon a secret gathering of fairies at a banquet table brimming with delectables of every imaginable kind.

She could smell the heavy, rich scent of roasted ham. The yeasty warmth of freshly baked bread.

Why did fairies always have the best food?

What did they do to deserve it?

Because nature loved fairies. It gave them whatever they wanted. And it wasn't fair.

Her head swam in the afternoon sun.

Her heart thumped in her ears.

It beat louder and louder. Faster and faster.

Until she knew she was going to pass out.

At least it would be restful.

The thumping grew louder yet, until in surprise, she realized it wasn't her heart but was coming from the outside world.

She glanced up as a helicopter appeared in the distance. It was bright orange with a diagonal white stripe on the tail. The kind the Coast Guard used for search and rescue missions. It raced by heading northwest.

No parachutes with food fell out.

Where was it going?

Was it heading back to base or out to a rescue?

The chopper descended and buzzed over the distant treetops. Must've been out on a mission as it didn't seem like they'd fly that low for no reason. The thump of the whirling blades faded as she half-regretted not trying to flag it down. Maybe she should've held up a sign like those people on street corners did.

~

STARVING. PLEASE HELP.

~

THE THOUGHT of begging for anything didn't sit right. Her grandmother had instilled a sense of self-reliance and pride in working hard to get what you wanted. Grammy would've fallen over dead while working three jobs before she would've spent a single breath asking for help. Maybe it was a bit extreme, but it had served her well and she'd ensured Emily had grown up feeling the same way.

That said, she wouldn't have turned down one of those giant slices of pizza if someone drove up and offered one.

She watched the helicopter shrink in size.

And then something unexpected happened.

In the middle of the day, with the bright sun overhead, the sky flashed hot white.

Not a part of it. The whole thing.

She couldn't tell more than that because she snapped her eyes shut to avoid being blinded.

It was like stepping out of a dark closet and having the brightest flashlight on Earth shoved in your face.

What was that?

The pink faded from her eyelids and she squinted them open. The flash in the sky to the north continued to fade. The dark silhouette of the chopper seemed to punch a hole in the surrounding light before its shape got lost in the trees.

Surely it had continued flying on the other side of a distant ridge.

Then she heard it.

A faint boom. Like a car backfiring a few streets away. A minute later, a pencil-thin column of gray smoke rose into the air.

Flying helicopters didn't cause explosions and smoke.

44

Why had it crashed?

What was that flash about?

Had there been a massive solar flare or something?

Maybe a giant meteorite burned up in the atmosphere?

A nuclear bomb?

The sky to the north was still brighter than it should've been, but there was no enormous mushroom cloud. No blast wave that melted her flesh or fried her to ash. Nothing that she could see or feel, at least.

She pushed the question to the background.

What mattered right now was that there had been an accident. And if anyone survived, they'd need help sooner rather than later.

Emily paused for an instant, wondering if she should just let someone else handle it. She realized with a start that the camera was still in her hand. She started to shut it down and then noticed it was already off.

Had she turned it off?

A few button taps later and she gave up trying to turn it

back on. The battery must've died. Whatever. The entertainment of the folks at home no longer mattered.

Surely, the pilot would've radioed in the emergency before going down. But what if there wasn't time?

Emily hurried over to her daypack and grabbed the PLB. She could call in the accident. Even if no one got a signal from the chopper, they could use her position to find it.

She pressed the button on the side to bring it out of sleep mode.

The display remained blank.

Her brows scrunched together as she mashed the button again and again.

"What the..." she muttered.

Then she remembered. It wasn't ever totally blank. It usually showed the time and had a few icons along the top left edge indicating something or other.

Another dead battery?

That wasn't supposed to happen.

What was the point of a personal locator beacon with integrated SAT phone if the stupid thing didn't work? It was nothing more than an expensive brick of silicon and plastic.

She wouldn't be able to call in the emergency. And if the pilot hadn't been able to do it either, then what?

Then it was up to her to help.

To do something.

The world was full of people that saw a problem and then waited around for someone else to do something about it.

She wasn't like most people.

Emily grabbed her pack, verified she had a full canteen of water, kicked dirt over the smoldering fire, and then took a last look around her campsite.

The tendrils of smoke given off by the dying fire. The

scorched black earth where her shelter used to be. The log that she used for a seat. The small pile of stacked firewood. It was home. Not one that had done a great deal to sustain her, but still.

She wasn't going to make it back tonight and the thought of spending a night out in the cold at some unknown destination sure made the few amenities feel bigger and more valuable.

Emily turned her back on it all and faced the black column of smoke on the horizon.

It was hard to judge the distance, but she guessed the chopper had gone down around five miles away. In her condition, she wasn't going to set any speed records, but she figured she could make it there in a few hours.

Hopefully in time to help out if anyone survived.

She set off, moving at a deliberate pace that was neither fast nor slow. Within minutes, her mind settled into the rhythm of the movement and the lethargy that had gripped her began to melt away.

Eyes scanning ahead for a bearing. For predators. For prey.

One foot forward and planted.

The other foot forward and planted.

Aching shoulders from the weight of the daypack, which wasn't all that much, and so was another sign of her depleted condition.

The sun as it slipped down toward the horizon in the west.

The blue sky above as it shifted to indigo.

It was a pattern.

One that pulled her forward as long as she didn't think too much.

Ridges and valleys came and went.

Open fields of long grass gave way to short grass. Short grass gave way to rubble and patches of greenery. A towering forest of moss green Sitka Spruce rose in the distance.

The trees grew taller as she drew nearer.

Something interrupted the pattern.

A burst of electric red shot up through the canopy, flashing like lightning in a cloud bank, before it broke through and arced up into the darkening sky. A duller crimson tail trailed behind.

Then another, chasing after the first.

Emergency flares!

Someone had survived! That was good news. But why were they shooting off flares now?

Had they done it now because the flares would show up brighter against the darkening sky?

Or because the emergency had gone from bad to worse?

Emily picked up the pace as she broke into the tree line. A full moon rose over the horizon, spilling pale light over the landscape. She took one last bearing on the dwindling column of smoke before the canopy swallowed the sky.

A little ways into the forest and the density of the branches above formed a lattice-like roof. Ever-shifting in the slight breeze. The moon spilled small patches of light on the ground where it managed to leak all the way down, like water seeping down through soil.

She'd walked for another half hour before doubt started creeping in. That and the cold. The temperature was dropping fast. Spending the night exposed to the elements would be dangerous. Possibly deadly. The growing sense of being lost gripped her insides. It threatened to run over her tenuous grip on reason and then flee like a terrified animal into the night.

Emily blew out a breath that transformed into a small cloud that quickly dissipated as it expanded.

"Keep it together, Emily," she whispered.

Something flickered a ways off into the trees.

She paused and focused her eyes just to the side of where she wanted to look.

It was a trick of night vision. The inside of the eye had two basic kinds of photoreceptors. Rods and cones. Cones specialized in color vision and had high spatial acuity. They exclusively populated the area directly behind the retina. The surrounding area, like the halo of the moon, was populated by rods, and they specialized in low light reception.

So shifting her gaze a little to the side of where she wanted to focus sent the few light rays to the photoreceptors best able to utilize them.

For a second, she thought she'd imagined it. A trick of her exhausted brain.

Then, the mass of branches shifted and a warm orange light flickered.

A fire of some kind!

She angled to the right about twenty degrees, thankful that she'd caught it. Another few minutes in the direction she'd been going and she would've missed it completely.

A surge of anxious energy tingled in her fingers. She was almost there!

Emily hurried on with the flickering light growing brighter and more constant with every passing minute.

The crash site came into view. In a small clearing, the orange and white chopper lay on its side. The side door open and facing up. The tail had been sheared off and lay a few dozen feet from the cabin. The front glass made opaque by the density of splintered cracks.

A crackling fire blazed on the ground casting a dancing

light into the gaping hole that was the missing rear of the cabin.

Someone had definitely survived! And was in good enough shape to build and start a fire.

A silhouetted figure popped up from the open side door of the cabin.

A flower of flashing light blinded her.

TA TA TA TA TA

TA TA

The staccato crack of automatic gunfire split the air.

She half-dove and half-fell to the ground. Moist dirt and decomposed pine needles punched into her mouth as she face-planted onto the forest floor.

The sound died away as she froze in place, her ears straining for clues, her eyes slowly recovering.

Nothing more happened.

Was she being shot at?

No, the aim had been off to her left.

Was it a bear?

The thought of being out here alone with a bear potentially stalking nearby sent a chill down her spine that settled in her gut.

She had to get to that fire!

Now and not later!

Emily pulled herself up and broke into a jog.

Low-hanging branches slapped her face as she plowed through. She was about to say something to announce her presence when a uniformed man popped up and pointed a rifle at her face. The end of the barrel a dark circle that threatened to swallow her.

"Whoa, lady!" the man shouted. The barrel lifted toward the sky. "I almost blew your head off!"

A thrashing sound from behind made Emily spin

around.

At the edge of the firelight, something large and long rippled by. Something indistinct. Like a section of the forest had turned to water and flowed by like a river.

TA TA TA TA

Emily dropped to the ground as she covered her ringing ears.

"Get in here! Now!" the soldier shouted.

Emily grabbed the lip of the helicopter's open doorway and scrambled over as the soldier scanned the forest behind her. She made it inside as the soldier ducked down next to her.

Their eyes met in the dim light.

The soldier's were wide and unblinking.

Panic or focus?

"What was that?" she asked.

"Don't know. Nothing good."

45

MARCO stalked through the long grass with short, fluid steps, an arrow nocked and ready. The late morning sun cast the landscape in bright relief. And more importantly, the warm rays drew ptarmigan out of hiding. After making it through the chill of the night, they wanted to warm up just like he did.

A gentle breeze from the northeast made the knee-high stalks sway in shifting patterns as far as the eye could see. A soft rustling sound combined with a twitch of stalks that went against the surrounding motion showed him where Oscar crept through the undergrowth.

In their short time together, they'd become formidable hunting partners. Oscar would flush out the game, if not kill it directly, and Marco would use the bow to finish the job. A few days ago, the fierce little weasel had taken down a Snowshoe hare nearly three times its size all by himself.

With the finished bow and a quiver full of arrows, taking down prey wasn't the problem. Finding it was usually another issue entirely.

But this shallow valley an hour's walk east of camp was

proving to be an unexpected bounty. They'd already bagged two birds and had only been at it for a couple of hours. In survival in the bush terms, that was a jackpot level of return and easily worth additional investment.

So as much as he wanted to jog back to camp and cook up the birds strung to his daypack, he wanted to remain on the hunt even more. It was like mining gold. When you happened upon a rich vein, you didn't close up shop and head off somewhere else looking for more. You stayed on the vein and kept digging to see how far your luck held.

He crept through the grass, scanning left and right looking for a patch of white or gray in the field of green.

They were here.

Somewhere.

He and Oscar just had to find them.

Which was no easy task. They were expert at staying hidden and still. He'd probably walked by several already without realizing it.

The phantom smell of cooked meat made his stomach grumble and his mouth water. Focusing on the hunting and not on the eating was half the battle. With the hare from a few days ago, a ptarmigan last night, and the two over his shoulder today, life was getting better.

For the first time in over a week, Marco felt some optimism for his ability to stay on the island and keep going. Sure, the first few days had been filled with optimism as the beginning of every big adventure was. But then the hunger and exposure began wearing him down. Like water spilling over ice.

Thirteen days out here so far.

Lucky number thirteen, as far as he was concerned because things were looking great.

Shelter. Water. Food. No encounters with bears since that last one had nearly killed him.

He knocked the bow with his knuckle for luck.

No more confrontations with bears would be a wonderful pattern to continue.

He'd come close to tapping out after that close encounter. Things could've easily gone the other way. He owed Oscar his life, and he wasn't the type to let a debt like that slide.

A chirp and the sound of crunching potato chips in the grass brought a smile to his face. Grasshoppers were nature's potato chips and apparently Oscar had found one.

Things were going well. Maybe he was finally reaching cruising speed.

Don't get a big head.

A positive mental attitude was a key survival trait. Many thought it was *the* key survival trait. But overconfidence was the exact opposite. Not only was being overly confident likely to make you overlook something vital, it also seemed to encourage nature, or the gods, or Mother Earth, or whatever it was that dealt in cosmic consequence to throw down a giant palm and squash you flatter than a mosquito.

No, things had gone better lately. But that was no guarantee, implied or expressed, that they would continue that way. The trick was to enjoy it while it lasted, while at the same time not counting on it going forward.

Minutes passed as Marco silently crept through the grass, generally tracking the slight rustle of Oscar's movement.

A screech and buffeting sounds.

A ptarmigan shot up out of the grass.

Oscar leapt up above the grass and missed it by inches before falling back to the ground.

In one fluid motion, Marco raised and drew the bow, tracked the bird's flight, and let loose.

The string twanged and the arrow blurred through the air before hitting the rising bird dead center.

The bird and arrow dropped like a stone.

"Yes!" Marco whooped and leapt through the grass to claim his kill. He hurried partly from excitement and partly to recover the bird before Oscar ripped it to shreds.

While the long-tailed weasel was an excellent partner in hunting, his eating habits were where the partnership ended.

Marco loped forward to the spot where the grass shifted back and forth in a frenzy. He found the weasel with its jaws clamped around the bird's throat. He picked them both up. "I think this one's dead, buddy."

Oscar's head shifted and his black marble eyes regarded Marco. The weasel pulled his teeth out of the bird's neck, bared his needle-like fangs, and hissed.

Marco grinned. "Fine, this one's yours. The other two are mine."

Oscar hissed again, apparently not agreeing to the deal.

Marco laughed, and not for the first time, thanked the heavens for his strange little companion.

The weasel grabbed the bird by the neck and wriggled out of Marco's grip. They both dropped to the grass and Oscar started into his meal.

It was messy and so Marco decided now was a good time for a rest. He spotted a rocky outcropping a little ways off and headed over to it.

He took a seat and the surface radiated warmth into his bones. He unstrung the two birds and set them to the side. Close enough that he could swat Oscar away if the little bugger got greedy. He then lay back with the daypack for a more than passable pillow.

The bright blue sky had fewer clouds than usual. The breeze tickled the hair on his face. He'd never been a beard guy, but he had the beginnings of a proper mountain man one going now.

Before he knew it, his eyes drooped and fluttered shut.

Chirping and squeaking woke him up.

He awoke with a start, disoriented and wondering where he was. He turned to the side and saw one of the two birds was now a mangled mess of feathers and shredded meat.

Oscar chirped again and Marco twisted around to find the little thief a few feet away, standing on his hind legs and staring into the distance.

Marco followed his gaze and didn't see anything of note.

A few seconds later, the faint sounds of an approaching helicopter caught his attention. The chopper lifted above a distant ridge a minute later. One of those orange and white ones the Coast Guard used in search and rescue missions. It banked to the right and headed north.

Had one of the other contestants had an accident?

Marco watched it shrink into the distance.

And then the sky flashed white.

46

The intensity of the light burned his eyes. He pinched them shut and turned away until the pain receded.

When he opened them again, he saw what looked like the helicopter descending into the ocean of green trees. Not long after, a column of dark smoke rose into the blue sky.

"Oh, no," he whispered.

How far away had it gone down?

Ten miles? Fifteen? More?

And what was that flash in the sky?

Surely help would be on the way. A rescue mission for the rescue mission. But, it wouldn't hurt to call it in to make sure people back in Kodiak knew about it.

Marco reached behind him and unclipped the PLB from his pack. He mashed the button to bring up the call menu.

Nothing happened.

What the... ?

He punched it several more times, this time using his index finger as his large thumb probably didn't hit it right. His oversized hands were better at carving wood into usable tools than typing on a keyboard to send a Facebook update.

Part of it was a matter of interest, but part of it was also logistics.

He'd never learned to touch type. And his fingertips were bigger than individual keys. Every time he tried to press one, he also accidentally pressed another nearby one. He made certain this time to press the button on the side.

Still nothing.

There wasn't even the default screen that showed the time and other information along the top.

He hadn't looked at it in days. It represented surrender and that wasn't an option. So, he'd chosen to ignore it.

Had the battery died at some point?

So calling in the emergency wasn't possible.

His mind was made up almost before he considered the options.

Odds were that a distress call went out before the chopper went down. Odds were he wouldn't get halfway there before another helicopter thumped by en route to the accident.

Those were the odds.

But what about the flash?

And his PLB dead?

Something didn't feel right.

Something that made the odds feel like a losing bet.

Marco recovered the sole surviving bird and strung it onto his pack. He glared at Oscar. "I don't care if you saved my life. This one's mine."

The weasel hissed bloody murder. Bloody because his muzzle was covered in crimson. Murder because he looked very much like he was about to attempt it on Marco for swiping a potential feast.

"Come on. We have to go. Now."

Oscar jumped over to Marco's leg and scrambled up

onto the top of his pack. He nipped at the back of Marco's neck and then curled up and nestled into the warm hollow there.

Marco ensured everything was squared away, took a deep breath knowing the task ahead, and then took off in the direction of the thin column of smoke on the horizon.

His long, smooth strides began to chew up the distance. Like so many long hikes he'd done on his own land back home.

Hikes with Justine.

Justine, his ex.

He realized with surprise that the thought of her didn't make his stomach churn or his jaws tighten.

Hours passed as the landscape slid by. He sipped from his canteen and nibbled on some of the smoked hare that he'd saved.

Oscar demanded a bite each time, but got nothing. The two ptarmigan he'd already scarfed down had his belly bulging like he was nine months pregnant.

The sun dipped below the western horizon as they went along. Oscar happily slept while Marco did all the work.

Marco didn't blame him. If his belly was as distended as the weasel's, he wouldn't want to do anything but lay around and let it digest.

Night fell and a full moon rose as Marco continued on at a steady, deliberate pace. He moved with the effortless grace of a shark in water. His powerful legs bounded over small obstructions, launching into the next stride like a coiled spring unleashing its energy.

He'd been going for hours when he saw a flare launch out of the shadowed forest ahead and race up into the dark sky. The crimson star arced through a parabolic curve back to earth. A few seconds later, another followed.

Someone had survived and they were in trouble.

Marco quickened his pace. He continued on as the darker band in the distance grew into a towering forest of Sitka Spruce. Smaller trees grew along the edge like a splatter of future potential. Beyond them, a dark wall rose high overhead. So thick it seemed to swallow the pale light.

He was passing under the outlying trees when the faint sounds of gunfire peppered the air. Like firecrackers but he knew better.

He preferred primitive weapons. Ones carved and formed with his own hands. Ones that humans like him had been using for tens of thousands of years. That said, he knew his way around a rifle. Firearms were as common as cars in Montana.

More common.

Oscar crawled up with his front legs perched on top of Marco's head. Like a hunting dog pointing, but without being helpful.

Marco batted him back to the top of the pack and got a bite on the finger for his efforts. He unstrapped his bow and smoothly strung it while scanning the darkness ahead. Huge tree trunks, low-hanging branches, and patches of midnight between. There wasn't much to see.

Another short burst of gunfire and he set off into the woods at a trot.

Whoever was firing those shots was in trouble. And it wasn't hard to imagine from what.

A Kodiak bear following the scent of blood from the crash site. They could smell a carcass upwind from twenty miles away.

Branches scratched his forehead and cheeks as he bounded over fallen branches and exposed roots as thick as his waist. The ground felt springy like a gymnastics floor. A thick layer of fallen pine needles absorbed his weight and then provided added spring as he lifted off.

He continued on, his eyes now adjusted to the darker interior of the forest. A ghostly glow illuminated patches here and there where the moonlight somehow managed to find its way through.

One of the patches looked different than the others.

Warmer.

Marco angled toward it, not slowing down. The bow held low with an arrow nocked and ready. He'd once taken down an adult elk with his favorite bow back home. That stag had weighed over seven hundred pounds. But Kodiak bears were known to grow over twice that. And as formidable as a set of adult elk antlers could be, they were not in the same league as the claws, teeth and killer instinct of a top-of-the-food-chain predator.

A rifle wouldn't have been a bad thing just then.

The spot of warmer light got brighter as he went. He dodged around a thick trunk and spotted a fire.

And the downed helicopter on its side next to it!

The fire flickered light into the gaping hole where the tail had ripped off.

Something large moved in the trees to his left.

Oscar leapt off his shoulder and darted away.

Branches snapped and something heavy scraped over the forest floor.

Marco spun toward the sound with his bow up and string drawn taut. He sighted along the arrow shaft and moved the aim with his eyes as he scanned the area.

His heart thumped in his chest. Echoed in his ears.

The sharp tingle of adrenaline spiking in his veins. Every pore seemed to open and orient toward the source. Like tiny radars.

Listening.

Alert.

Ready.

His shoulder burned from holding the bow fully drawn.

He scanned back and forth.

Nothing.

A mass of branches snapped in unison as something blurred toward him.

From right where he'd been looking.

Like a long swath of the forest had come alive.

Marco let loose and the arrow twanged forward.

It punched into something twenty feet away and stuck.

The blur raced forward with the arrow waving back and forth before a low branch snapped it off.

The survival equation running in Marco's mind computed the new variable in an instant. Flight was the recomputed solution and he followed it almost before it was solved.

He bounded toward the small clearing and the downed chopper.

A crashing avalanche followed.

Marco's muscles strained as adrenaline flooded his system. He broke into the clearing with the fire and helicopter forty feet beyond.

The ground trembled with the pounding pursuit behind.

Two figures popped up out of the cabin.

One with a rifle pointed right at him.

The thing behind was so close that wind buffeted his backside.

"Don't shoot," Marco shouted as he sprinted the final distance and then launched through the air. He flew over the lip and dropped down through the open cabin door.

Something smashed into the chopper's underbelly, shoving the wreckage several feet and denting it like a skyscraper suicide dropped onto the hood of a car.

Marco landed hard on his shoulder and rolled over onto his back.

A girl peered down at him with wide eyes. Her cheekbones stuck out more than he remembered. Dark smudges covered her face almost like camouflage, but he still recognized it.

"Emily?" he said.

"Marco?"

TA TA TA TA TA TA

The interior of the cabin strobed as the soldier next to her fired his rifle over the edge of the cabin.

Marco spoke in grave voice. "That was no Kodiak bear."

"What was your first clue, Sherlock?" the soldier said as his eyes scanned the area outside.

47

BOB let the crowd steer him through the glass front doors of the Afognak Center. What little room there was in the parking lot funneled down to shoulder to shoulder at the entrance to the building. He struggled to maintain personal space as the press of bodies jostled forward. He especially tried to keep his distance from the fat teenage kid who was smacking gum like it was his last meal.

The crowd shifted and the kid stumbled. His enormous bulk fell over onto Bob squeezing the breath out of him. He tried to shove back but there wasn't enough room to get his arms up in defense.

Bob groaned and strained, trying to breathe as well as push back against the boy who was about to kill him.

They stayed like that for an instant, the weight of the boy's body crushing him. The only thing keeping them both standing was the mass of bodies on Bob's other side.

The press of flesh shifted and the kid was pushed upright. He turned with an apologetic look on his face. A look that died when Bob snarled in anger.

"Watch where you're going, fatty."

His fleshy face hardened. Or maybe it didn't because it couldn't. But his eyes did. "You suck, mister."

"You suck, kid. Too many shakes by the looks of it."

Anger flashed in the kid's eyes as he pulled his cap down tighter on his head. The front of it had a picture of a female that appeared to be half cave woman and half zombie. She was all curves, crazed eyes, tangled hair, tattered clothes and red lips. She made it look pretty appealing. Above it said Delta Luvr!

What was a Delta anyway?

Bob wondered if he had it in him to do something more than look pathetic. He didn't get a chance to find out as the crowd surged forward and the kid drifted away on the shifting current.

Bob wondered if he could've taken him if it had come to that. Sure, the kid was probably about as dangerous as a potato, but Bob wasn't in the prime of health either. Age and decades of poor living... okay, downright terrible living, had taken the bloom off his rose.

He could've kicked him in the balls or something. Maybe jabbed his eyes. A throat chop might've worked except it would've run into two chins worth of defensive padding.

That and Bob wasn't exactly sure how to do a throat chop.

Did you go straight in with your finger tensed like a spear?

Or did you come at it from the side like a Kung Fu move?

Twenty years ago, it wouldn't have mattered. That was back when his body still hadn't succumbed to the consequences of the lifestyle it had been subjected to.

Youth was wasted on the young.

Like that fat kid. What was he? Seventeen? He should've

been out getting drunk and getting laid. Or at least getting drunk and getting rejected in his attempts to get laid. And what was he probably doing instead? Eating Cheetos and going for the all-time high score in DeathMatch Six Thousand?

He was blowing his prime years. The good years. You were supposed to live them up so you had something nostalgic to remember in your old age. Some memory to distract from the horror of becoming a decrepit old fart that couldn't even get the satisfaction of rubbing out a good jerk session.

Getting older sucked.

Sure, it was better than the alternative.

But that was just choosing a crap sandwich over a crappier sandwich.

Anyone who told you otherwise was just trying to sell you something. Probably a medication that you were supposed to ask your doctor about.

One that would fix a limp libido but that might cause a heart attack, had a fifty-fifty chance of causing kidney failure, and would definitely give you ulcers.

At least he'd lived it up back in his youth.

At least he had the satisfaction of fondly, if vaguely, remembering that three way with his ex-wife and that aspiring starlet that had gone on to a mediocre porn career when Hollywood didn't work out.

That had been good.

From what he could remember.

The jostling bodies packed into the space behind the large central area filled with rows of chairs. The chairs were already filled and so he, like hundreds of others, was forced to remain standing at the back.

In front of the section of chairs, a small stage held a

number of seated figures. A short, plain woman with gray
hair and glasses that were too big for her face stood at a
podium watching the crowd file in. She remained quiet but
a nervous tension exuded from her stiff posture and darting
eyes. A man in a uniform walked onto the stage and whispered something into her ear.

She nodded. "Ladies and gentleman, Fire Chief Woods
wants me to remind everyone that the number of people
here is far beyond its legal capacity. Due to the unique
nature of this meeting, I'm not going to ask him or Police
Chief Stuckey to clear the room. However, we do require,"
she gestured with her arms extended, "that we keep the
aisles clear on each side."

The crowd grumbled as uniformed officers went about
forcing people out of those areas and into the center, further
compressing the middle.

"Thank you for your cooperation," the woman said.

"Get to the point, Mayor" a voice shouted above the hum
of a hundred conversations. It was a middle-aged man with
a bushy auburn beard and a matching tangle of wild hair.
His frame was big, but his belly was bigger.

A fleeting look of irritation crossed the mayor's face
before a manufactured smile returned. "Yes, Red. My
thoughts exactly."

"What happened yesterday?" someone else shouted.

"When's the power coming back on?" yelled another
voice.

The mayor tried to speak but a continuing barrage of
voices drowned her out.

"Does this have anything to do with that secret government project going on?" shouted a voice.

"Yeah! Why have we never heard exactly what they're
up to?"

The mayor continued trying to gain control but with little effect.

A man with broad shoulders like a linebacker stood up from one of the chairs on stage. A blue-black uniform with a gold badge over his chest marked him as the aforementioned Police Chief Stuckey. He walked over next to the mayor and shouted. "Hey! Quiet! Give Mayor Okpik your attention. Anyone that insists on being disruptive will be thrown out of the building."

"Thank you, Chief Stuckey, but I don't think that will be necessary."

The chief glared out at the crowd like he was disappointed.

"You can sit back down," Mayor Okpik said when the chief didn't move, waiting and seemingly hoping someone would start shouting again.

He shrugged and returned to his seat.

"I'd like to start tonight's discussion by reminding everyone that we are a proud community here in Kodiak. We will stand together to solve whatever problems come our way. We've overcome many challenges in the past to get where we are today. And we'll continue doing exactly that."

"Blah, blah, blah. What about what happened to the McKinley kids last night? Out by Buskin Lake. Must've been a brownie that got 'em. Blood and bodies everywhere. Anything done about that yet? Cuz I got kids, too. Lots of us do."

The crowd murmured agreement.

Chief Stuckey's eyes narrowed and he was about to stand when the mayor waved him down.

"Red, we're all concerned and Chief Stuckey has officers looking into it. It's a tragedy and we're all devastated by what happened. We're doing everything possible to ensure it doesn't happen again. Now," she looked away from the man and over the assemblage, "I want to fill you all in on the event that occurred yesterday."

The rise and fall of whispered voices fell away. The room went dead quiet.

"Like you have already discovered, whatever it was yesterday caused a power outage throughout Kodiak. It also seems to have destroyed all of our usual channels of communication. Be that satellite links, radio towers, mobile phones, walkie-talkies. We are, at this point, cut off from the outside world. We're currently looking for anyone that may have an older model short wave radio."

"Why older model?" someone shouted.

"We have reason to believe it may work whereas the newer model at the station, like everything else we've tried, does not."

"What caused everything to break down?" someone yelled.

The mayor twisted her mouth to the side. "We're investigating that. At this time, we don't know—"

"Don't lie to us! It was an EMP!" Red shouted. "Kim Joon Wong attacked us! It's war!"

48

The crowd broke into a riot of noise. Shouting and wailing and cries of dismay. The mayor stood with her hands raised trying to regain control before things completely went off the rails.

Police Chief Stuckey jumped up and marched to the edge of the stage. His face flushed crimson. "Shut up! Everyone! Shut your mouths! Now!"

Bob hadn't been talking in the first place. He was still trying to remember what those two old guys at the diner yesterday had said. Something about a nuclear bomb that destroys electronics. But he hadn't seen a giant mushroom cloud in the sky. Just that bright flash.

Even though the chief wasn't yelling at him, the fury on the chief's face made his mouth shut tighter and his body lean back a little.

Chief Stuckey looked like he could knock down a tree. Crush boulders in his hands like overripe tomatoes. Plus, he had a large gun on his hip.

The crowd quieted.

The chief pointed at Red. "Red, open your mouth again and I'll personally shove my fist into it!"

Bob looked back and forth, like everyone else, watching the two square off. Red was bigger than most, and looked like he'd seen more than a few fights in his time. Even so, he snarled and his eyes shouted what his mouth didn't. He crossed his arms over his belly and flopped down into his chair.

Those two had a history. One that no doubt had a future.

"You can't do that! You're a public servant!" someone else shouted.

Bob searched for the owner of the voice, but couldn't identify it. Probably someone hiding behind someone else.

"Yeah! You don't own us!" someone else shouted.

Several more people joined in and the shouting and yelling reached a new peak. It wasn't long before everyone, including the people lucky enough to score a seat, was on their feet.

Yelling. Pushing. Screaming. Shoving.

Bob did his best to keep the flailing arms and lurching bodies at bay. He looked around, not liking what he saw.

"That's it!" shouted the chief from the stage. "Everybody out!" He gestured to the officers standing on each side of the stage. "Get them all out! Now!"

A dozen officers formed a line and moved toward the crowd.

Shrieks of fear and shouts of rage punctured the air.

Bob lurched backward as the crush of bodies moved back toward the entrance. Those at the back were already hurrying for the exit.

And he did everything in his power to join them.

The crowd squeezed down through the bottleneck of the glass doors and then spilled loosely into the parking lot beyond. It was like the sands of an hourglass shoving through the narrow neck.

Bob broke through and stuttered to a stop on the sidewalk.

People streamed down Alimaq Drive toward the bridge that crossed over to downtown Kodiak. A few old trucks fired up. Their tires squealed as they got out ahead of those on foot.

How did they work when so many others didn't?

Someone shoved him from behind and he stumbled off the curb and nearly bit it before recovering. He spun around. "Why don't you watch..."

His anger twisted into fear as he looked up into a snarling face and smoldering eyes.

Red glared at him. "What'd you say?"

"Nothing." Bob raised his hands like an olive branch. "Nothing at all."

Red spat on Bob's loafers. "Standing like a post right where people are trying to get out. You're lucky I don't knock your teeth out."

Bob took a step back. He had no doubt this man could send him to the hospital with very little effort. "I'm sorry. I didn't mean—"

"Stay outta my way, Outsider," Red said as a thick arm shoved him aside and he stalked away.

Bob watched as the jerk stalked over to an enormous old truck, climbed up, and got in. The beater was more brown from rust than red from faded paint. It towered on enormous tires as tall as Bob's chest.

It was such a perfect match, Bob almost laughed. But he was scared Red might notice and return to beat the snot out of him.

The jalopy roared and the tires screeched as Red and his ridiculous redneck ride took off.

People leaped left and right to clear a path for the monster. It rumbled away. Like a river around a boulder, the crowd merged together in its wake.

Bob watched the bulk of the crowd head over the bridge. He stood there in silence until only he and a few others remained.

What was going on?

This was insane.

And why did he have to be here in the first place?

On any normal day, he'd be at lunch right now at a posh restaurant in Beverly Hills or West Hollywood. He'd be looking forward to an afternoon latte from Veronica to keep his engine going for the rest of the day.

Instead he was in BFE. No, worse. Bone-Freaking-Egypt at least had delicious shawarma sandwiches and hot hookers that understood the value of the American dollar.

This place had six streets that all led to nowhere. It stank of fish when the wind came through. And worst of all, he hadn't seen his assistant's curvy backside in over two weeks.

"Hey," someone said from behind.

Bob turned around, still in a daze.

Police Chief Stuckey stared down at him. "You okay, buddy?"

Bob blinked. "Uh, yeah. Yes." He nodded. "I'm fine, thanks."

"You staying in town somewhere?"

"Yep, The Weary Traveler."

A spasm of disgust fleeted across the chief's face. "Well, better than a hole in the ground. Maybe. Anyway, you should get back there. And I'd recommend staying put until things quiet down."

"Yes. Okay. I'll do that."

Stuckey stared at him a moment longer.

Bob tossed up his hands. "Okay, I'll head there now."

"You do that."

Bob turned and started toward the bridge.

He was supposed to stay put in his room. Stay put in that disgusting hovel.

What was he supposed to do all day?

Find and kill cockroaches?

Yeah, that could take a while.

Bob continued over the bridge, thinking about his situation.

And then he froze.

If he was going to stay in his room for however long, what was he going to eat?

49

The local Safeway was packed with people. And not packed like at the Hollywood Trader Joe's at five on a Friday. That was stuffed with a different kind of people. A lot of them delicious MILFs wearing tight yoga pants that accentuated their surgically lifted and toned parts. Others wearing sleek pant suits and high heels that communicated power and position while also accentuating legs that were miles long and promised to wrap around your waist.

This wasn't packed like that.

Bob waited at the very back of a line that never seemed to move. It should've been simple.

Need some food.

Get some food.

That's how it had worked every single time he'd ever done it.

But not this time.

Apparently, everyone else in town had had the same idea, only before he did. Because by the time he got here, the shelves were nearly picked clean. It was eerie. Almost un-American. It was like a grocery store might've looked in Siberia after the fall of the Soviet Union.

He glanced at his quarter-full shopping cart. It was all that was left over that had seemed remotely useful. A blue beach towel with a sea stars pattern, a brown bottle of hydrogen peroxide, a potato he'd found half-hidden under a display shelf, a couple cans of corn hominy. Other random stuff.

Corn hominy.

Lord. He prayed it didn't come to that.

He'd try dog food before opening a can of that lumpy, pale goo. He'd probably vomit. But then he'd try another mouthful before moving on to the hominy.

Bob stood on his tiptoes and cursed under his breath at the twenty or so shopping carts ahead of him. The store had all four checkout lines going, but each one had people stacked all the way to the back of the store where he was. The reliance on pencil and paper to total up each cart meant it would be days before he finally got to the front.

Most of the carts ahead of him were filled with things he wanted. Everything from canned peaches to Pepto-Bismol to toilet paper. Made sense. A direct chain of action and reaction. Mounds of stuff so high above the rectangular rims that things constantly slid off and fell to the floor. The fallen items were hurriedly retrieved as everyone yelled at the people in front to hurry up.

The register workers looked like condemned prisoners standing in front of a firing squad.

It was madness.

Mayhem.

Bob felt like he was in a movie, which had the vague feeling of being pathetic. Like in modern society, any time something unexpected happened, the only way for our brains to process it was to think of it in the context of a movie.

What was happening?

Life had been normal a little over two weeks ago. Terrible, but normal. And then he'd ended up on this God-forsaken island. And if that wasn't bad enough, now everyone was going crazy. And he had no way of getting ahold of anyone back home.

No way of getting home himself.

A box of Cheesy Macaroni slid off the mound of the cart ahead of his. The temporary owner of the cart stood in front of it with one hand on it and his other hand on another cart in front. And he wasn't the only jerk doubling up, taking everything before Bob could get a chance.

The jerk didn't notice the rattling of the hard noodles jostling inside the box when it hit the floor. All the yelling and chattering voices drowned it out.

Bob slid along the side of his cart and stopped near the front. He kept his top half still while he reached out with a toe, tapped it on the box, and slowly slid it backward. When it was within reach, he leaned down and swiped it off the floor. He tossed it in his cart with a triumphant exhale.

Maybe he could score a few more things before he checked out.

Maybe he could help a few things slide off.

Mr. Jerk glanced back, noticed Bob was not where he was a minute ago. That he was within arm's reach of his second cart. His eyes narrowed as they met Bob's. "Outsider, you try to steal any of my stuff and I'll beat you bloody."

Bob's stomach went queasy. "Just waiting my turn. Just like you." He edged back and then behind his cart.

Mr. Jerk cast a warning look and then turned back to yell at the people up front.

Bob exhaled and leaned on the handle like he'd just run a hundred miles. That had been close. And the idiot in front of him didn't look like the type that made idle threats.

He glanced down at the box of Cheesy Macaroni that now resided in his cart.

He smiled.

It was a million times better than corn hominy.

With one hand down by his side and further concealed by the plastic mesh sides of the cart, Bob made a fist, rotated it, and extended his middle finger at the guy.

The thrill of the act soon faded though because he hadn't made forward progress in the last ten minutes. He'd seen at least one person pay and leave in that time, but still the line hadn't moved.

Were people sneaking in somewhere along the way?

Was he ever going to get out of here?

The line shifted forward a few paces further up, and like an inchworm, the line moved forward segment by segment until Mr. Jerk pulled his two carts forward a few feet. As he came to a stop, a bag of cashews slid off the nearest cart and hit the floor.

Bob's heart jumped.

Cashews. Now that would be a score.

He pushed his cart forward until it almost touched the handle of the cart ahead. He slid along the side to the front of his cart, darting his eyes at the bag of nuts on the floor. He barely had to extend his foot to get at it, and then dragged it within reach. He stood up to drop it in his cart with a smile that reached from ear to ear.

Until he saw that Mr. Jerk was watching him the whole time.

The smile evaporated like morning dew in the Sahara desert.

"I'm gonna make you bloody, old man!" He scooted around his cart toward Bob.

Bob panicked. He shoved his cart forward and the jostling impact shook the mountain of groceries in Mr. Jerk's cart. The precarious equilibrium of tension between stacked and irregular items was shattered.

An avalanche of goods fell to the floor.

"You're dead!" the man yelled.

The confrontation grabbed the attention of several people further up and they all stared at the cans of vegetables rolling along the floor, at the boxes of cake mix tumbling down, at the bottles of vitamins bouncing everywhere.

Mr. Jerk thought about going after Bob but then changed his mind as he scrambled to regain his fallen supplies. "Nobody touch it! Any of it! I'm warning you!"

Bob yanked his cart back and spun around the end of the aisle. He knew exactly what was going to happen after the guy gathered up all his stuff.

He hurried along the aisle that ran along the back of the store. The dank smell of the meat department lingered but not a single cut remained.

There was no way out. And if he hung around at the back waiting his turn like a good citizen, that jerk was going to run into him sooner or later. Maybe wait for him outside.

No, Bob had to get out now.

He guesstimated the total of the stuff in his cart, dug through his wallet and yanked out three twenty dollar bills.

Sixty was about right.

He jogged his cart to the far side aisle and passed empty shelves where vegetables and fruit had once been. He made it to the front and scanned the area.

The security guard was at the far register dealing with something.

As he passed the nearest register, he flung the three bills at the worker. "This will cover it!"

"Hey, you can't do that!" the worker replied. Other voices shouted similar sentiments, but with more cursing.

Bob didn't answer.

Or he did, but with action instead of words.

He raced out the entrance and his chest swelled with victory. Finally, a good turn of fortune came his way.

It was about time.

And then a shopping cart appeared from behind a car and he slammed into it. His cart knocked the other one over and a mountain of groceries and supplies spilled out onto the pavement.

Bob's cart rebounded and knocked him backwards onto the ground. He looked up while trying to breathe through the gut punch.

A man leaned over him.

A man with a shaggy auburn beard and a matching tangle of wild hair. "You again, huh," Red said as an evil grin festered on his wide face.

The first kick smashed into Bob's ribs making the last bit of air in his lungs shoot out.

The second kick caught him in the temple and sent tiny flashes of white popping and swirling in his vision.

The third kick... well, they started blending together after that.

His head lolled to the side as something warm trickled into his ear.

A woman was running across the parking lot, waving her hands in the air, yelling something Bob couldn't hear over the high-pitched whine in his ears.

50

FLO saw it all go down. Bob, the Outsider who had become a regular at the diner over the last two weeks, crashed his cart into another cart sending them both flying.

The other one belonged to the one man, well there was more than one in this little Norman Rockwell facade of a town, that you didn't want to mess with.

Alexei Volkov. But everyone called him Red for obvious reasons. He claimed to be descended from the Kashevaroff family, arguably the most prominent family in the history of Kodiak. He swore that Artamon Kashevaroff was his great-great-great-great something or other.

There were no longer any Kashevaroffs around to deny the claim, but nobody believed him anyway.

Red was a cheapskate, a drunk and a bully all wrapped up in one. Like if you picked the worst trait of three different horrible people and combined them into one superhero level horrible person. Not that he was a serial killer or anything.

Not that she knew of... not that he couldn't be.

Nah. He wasn't the type you heard about *after*.

After the dots showed a connecting line.

After all the neighbors swore he was a quiet boy who never did anybody any harm.

After the decaying bodies were found.

After the national news described every horrid murder in excruciating detail.

After everyone realized that he was, in fact, a ticking bomb that, in retrospect, was inevitably going to explode.

After the truth came out.

Nah. Red wasn't that complicated. Or ambitious.

But that didn't mean he wasn't dangerous. He was the kind of person who knew what morals were. They were those giant paintings on buildings that gay artists did while claiming unemployment to pay for their smoking dope addiction.

That was the kind of idiot conversation you were guaranteed to have if Red cornered you at the bar.

Flo had a general dislike of the guy, as well as a specific one. She'd banned him from coming into the diner years ago when he'd come in stumbling drunk, ordered enough food for four, ate half of it, threw the other half on the floor, and then staggered out without paying the tab while she was in the back getting a broom and a dustpan to clean up the mess.

Related to the Kashevaroff family, her bony butt.

Red slammed his boot into Bob's side and then delivered another kick to the poor man's head as Flo arrived.

She ended her run with a stiff shoulder into Red's back. It was like hitting a tree. Her head bounced off an instant after her shoulder did. She rebounded, wobbling as she blinked the cobwebs away.

Red spun around with froth splattered on his beard. "Who the... " He trailed off as he recognized her. "You'll

mind your own business if yuh know what's good for yuh."
He started to turn around as if that had decided it.

Flo grabbed his shoulder and did her best to yank him
back. "Stop it! Stop it right now!"

Red turned back around with an evil grin distorting his
broad face. His breath washed across her, stinging her eyes.

"Jesus, Red! You drunk on gasoline?"

His hands raised toward her. "I told you to go away. Now,
you're gonna—"

Flo's knees wobbled before she locked them tight again.
"No, you didn't."

His eyes narrowed. "What?"

She crossed her arms, doing her best not to appear terrified, and also to hide her trembling hands. "You didn't
say that."

His face twisted as the muscles in his jaw flickered.

"You said I would mind my own business if I knew what
was good for me."

He grabbed her shoulder and his fingers tightened like
they were made of steel.

She clenched her teeth to avoid crying out. "Take your
hand off me." She took another tense breath. "Or we'll get
Chief Stuckey down here to take it off for you."

Red blinked. Literally. The grip loosened as his lips
curled up. "You best leave before there is an accident."

Now that Flo could breathe, she circled around and
stood next to Bob's inert body on the pavement. "Red, you'd
better leave if you know what's good for you."

Red towered over her, probably trying to weigh the odds
in his dulled mind.

"Now," she said. "I bet Stuck would enjoy throwing you
in jail for a few days. I heard he's already looking to talk to
you for what happened at the town meeting this afternoon."

Uncertainty washed across his idiot face. He took a step back and then stumbled a few more. "This ain't over, Flo." He spat her name out like it was a rat turd. "Not over one bit. See you around."

The last part sizzled with threatened violence. His eyes flashed a crazed light, like he was imagining all the horrible things he was going to enjoy doing to her.

Maybe he was a serial killer. Or maybe just a killer.

He staggered away without remembering to pick up the groceries scattered everywhere.

Flo watched him go until she was confident he wasn't coming back. Not confident. Hopeful. She turned both shopping carts upright and then knelt down next to Bob. She gently squeezed his shoulder.

His face was a mess of blood and swelling skin.

"Bob, are you okay?"

"Do I look okay?" The words came out mumbled and barely understandable. He half-grinned, leaned his head to the side and spat. Along with a spatter of blood, a dull white tooth flew out and bounced across the pavement.

"Can you get up? We need to leave."

Red might come back and decide a night in jail was worth finishing the job. And maybe starting a new one on Flo.

She put her arms under his shoulders and pulled. "Bob! Come on!"

Bob moaned in agony, but he did his part in getting up.

She leaned him onto the cart. "Can you hold there a minute?"

He nodded and she decided to take the chance because they really had to get out of there. But not before gathering up the fallen groceries. She darted around sweeping up boxes of bandaids, a glass bottle of scotch that had miraculously remained intact, and a hundred other things that were now hers.

Or mostly hers.

Some of it was Bob's.

They could sort it out later.

Now that the altercation was over, the small crowd that had gathered had already started snatching up things so it was a race to recover as much as possible. She picked up a plastic bottle of olive oil and dropped it in the cart. She raced around recovering things until she dropped the last can of corn hominy into Bob's cart.

Who ate that garbage?

Still, they had two carts that were nearly full.

It was an unexpected bounty. And it was free.

Or was it technically stealing?

Maybe it was just putting to use some stuff you found. Not letting it go to waste. It was admirable, when you thought about it like that.

"Alright, put your arm over my shoulder. My car's over there."

Bob groaned as she lifted his arm into place. Blood dripped like a leaky faucet from the tip of his nose. He was busted up good.

She arrived at the car and wrenched open the door with a horrible squeak.

Did one of Bob's eyebrows raise?

"What? You have a problem with the Pinto Bean?"

He laughed. Or maybe choked. Did something that expelled air from his mouth along with a splatter of blood.

"I'm taking you to my place. We'll get you cleaned up and then see if you need to go to the hospital."

51

Spruce Landing apartments weren't what they'd been thirty years ago when Flo had first moved in. Thirty years of wear and tear could do that.

She was an unnecessary testimonial to that fact.

Hair that grew where it shouldn't. Hair she still plucked because she wasn't ready for anything resembling a mustache or for her nipples to have gray hairs sprouting like weeds in an untended garden.

Not that her garden had been tilled in... God. It had been too long to remember. Better not to.

Her crotch was like a corner in the attic. One that held nothing that nobody ever wanted and subsequently where nobody ever went. The cobwebs would be thick as fog.

Bob lay on the green floral quilt her step-mother had given her as a wedding present to her ex-husband. He'd been the one she'd waited forever for.

Until he'd decided Kodiak was too small for his big life and so took off before Rome's first birthday.

The hand-stitched creation was amazing. The memory

of her ex was not. And so it got assigned any job too dirty for things she actually cared about.

She gently patted a blood-soaked cloth on Bob's face and then dipped it into a bowl of water next to the bed. Red tendrils dissipated into the water turning it pink.

Most of his face was cleaned up and it wasn't as bad as she'd first thought. Though the splotches of yellow, darker browns and blues were beginning to blossom. She dabbed at the cut on his temple.

Bob winced.

"That one's going to need help staying closed."

"Great," he mumbled and took another awkward sip of scotch. He winced again but took another sip after that.

Flo glanced at the old wall clock that looked like it had been in fashion thirty years ago, then again five years ago, and now again looked dated and sad.

"I'll take care of it. It's better than having to go to the hospital at this hour."

"Call 911," Bob said.

"How? The landline doesn't work. My mobile doesn't work. None of it works."

Bob didn't have an answer.

"Besides, that little thing isn't worth an ER visit. I can close it up for you."

Bob's eyes opened wide. "No way! You're not stitching it up! You're a waitress for Christ sake!"

Flo bit down on her lower lip and breathed long and slow. Smacking an already battered old man wouldn't accomplish much.

But it would make her feel better, which was something.

"Sorry," Bob said. "I mean, thanks for everything you did. But, you're not a doctor."

"No," she said with a frown. "But I've fixed up enough

cuts, scrapes, and bruises to know whether an ER visit is needed."

She looked at the clock again.

9 PM.

Where was her son?

He should've been home hours ago. He'd better get home soon and get home safe.

A splinter of worry stabbed her chest.

He was all she cared about in the world. She needed him as much as he needed her. More.

Why wasn't he home already?

She turned to Bob. "A little super glue will close that right up. Being on the head, it's a bleeder, but it's not deep and it split open pretty cleanly."

"You wanna super glue my head together?" Bob said.

Flo reached over to the tray of bandages, gauze, cotton swabs, and other medical supplies. Tools of her motherly trade, unfortunately.

As much as she tried, she hadn't been able to protect her son. It simply wasn't possible. She couldn't be with him every second of the day. And he'd pushed her away when she'd first tried. And then came the excuses.

He'd tripped on a curb.

Someone had accidentally opened a door in his face.

He fell off his bike.

It was always something. A month, sometimes two, would go by and she'd think it was over. That whoever the bullies at his high school were had moved on to other prey. Then another "accident" and her demands to know who'd done it would go nowhere.

Nowhere but drive a wedge between them.

And he was the one man in her life she would never give up on. Never quit on.

A dagger of guilt joined the splinter of worry in her gut. How much of his situation was her fault? She hadn't been the best mother. But she'd done the best she could considering the circumstances.

She grabbed the small tube of super glue and then pinched the cut together with her other hand.

Bob raised his hands in terror, but she shoved them away with her elbows. "Hold still! And stop being such a pansy."

That shut him up, except for quick inhales when a particular pain must've peaked above the ambient misery.

Flo squirted the super glue along the pinched skin, making certain the edges of the flesh lined up nicely and so wouldn't leave a big scar. She finished and then continued to hold it together while the glue dried.

"Owwwwwww," Bob said with as much breath as voice. "Why do you know how to do this?"

The sound of the front door opening echoed through the two bedroom apartment.

"Rome?" she called.

"Who else?" he replied.

"My room. Pronto."

Now that he was safe, the anger was displacing all the worry. And there had been a lot of worry.

She let go of the wound now that the glue had hardened enough to keep it closed.

"What?" Footsteps followed words and then he appeared in the doorway.

Her heart squeezed in her chest. He was home. Safe. Although she didn't like that hat. Something about making a wild zombie girl look super sexy didn't sit well with her. The words splashed above the girl's head didn't make it better. Delta Luvr! It was from some series he'd binge watched online. The Darwin something or other. She'd offered to buy him a different hat, but he hadn't gone for it.

His eyes narrowed as he saw the man lying on her bed. "What is that buttnugget doing here?"

"Romero Andrew Bickle! You will mind your mouth or I will wash it out with soap. So help me, you know I will! You're not too old!"

Her son gulped. "Sorry. What is that idiot doing here?"

Why was he acting this way? Embarrassing her. Treating a guest like that. It wasn't how she'd raised him. "What is your problem, Rome?"

He crossed his arms over his chest. "Why don't you ask him? We met this afternoon. At the town meeting before Stuck kicked everyone out."

Flo looked back and forth between them.

Bob had a haunted look on his face. Wide eyes. Mouth parted and silent.

What was going on here?

She turned back to her son. "Would you mind telling me exactly what it is that you're talking about?"

He told her what happened.

Rage coursed through her veins like burning gasoline. She almost slapped Bob's temple to pop the wound back open. Let the jerk bleed. She turned back to him. "Is this true?"

She knew it was. Bob didn't seem like a terrible person. She'd kind of liked him, if she were being honest. But her son didn't lie.

Well, not any more than any teenager did and definitely wasn't about this.

Bob held his hands apart. "It was a misunderstanding. A mistake."

Flo was about to explain what a mistake helping him had been when gun shots split the air.

Loud.

From outside and not far away.

She jumped up, raced to the front door, locked it, then retrieved an old Beretta M9 from a shoe box in the hall closet. She inched the slide back to verify a round was chambered.

It was.

She wasn't expecting someone to knock down the door and attack them, but then she hadn't expected to hear gunshots outside her window either.

If anyone did try to break in, she knew how to aim and fire. More than that, she knew she would fire if it came to that.

Flo returned to her bedroom carrying the firearm.

Bob whimpered when he saw it. "Please! I didn't mean it! Don't do this!"

"Shut up," Flo replied with venom in her voice. "I'm not going to kill you. But I am going to move you to the couch." This jerk wasn't going to spend another second in her bed.

How could she have been so stupid?

Thinking he was decent.

Thinking that just because he tipped well and didn't make a mess that meant he had a good heart.

Thinking maybe there was something more.

She was an idiot, which was no big surprise. Her judgement in men had a long history of disastrous outcomes.

"Get up!" she shouted, consciously keeping the gun pointed at the ground even though her arm wanted to raise it.

"Okay! Okay." Bob said as he struggled to his feet. He staggered into the living room and sat on the couch.

She followed him in and launched the quilt at him.

He managed to block it, to her disappointment.

"You messed up, Bob. Now, I don't trust you. And trust is going to be more precious than gold in the coming days."

"Jerk," her son muttered soft enough that he thought she didn't hear.

She heard, but she didn't correct him this time.

Because he was right.

52

EMILY grabbed her canteen and climbed into the cockpit of the downed chopper. Being on its side, everything was in the wrong place and what little light made it in from the fire made it like walking on a lake covered with ice. Every step a test, alert for something to move or give way. Something that would throw her off balance and send her sprawling.

She made it without incident and, making certain not to put weight onto the collapsed portion of the console, worked into a stable position with one foot anchored to the side of the pilot's seat and her back against the controls.

Below her was Chief Petty Officer Flores. Her seat twisted to the side and her legs pinned under the console. They'd tried to pry her out yesterday, but between not getting anywhere and causing her to pass out from pain, twice, they'd decided to stop.

Waiting for rescue was better.

It was the only chance Flores had. Even if they somehow managed to get her out without killing her, she wasn't going to be walking anywhere in that condition.

They'd done what they could in the tight space,

bandaging her up, stopping the flow of blood, giving her water, keeping her company. But looking at her now, Emily knew that it wouldn't be enough.

Her face was pale and even the bruises seemed to have faded. Her eyes were closed. She'd been mostly out of it all day. It looked like she was resting. Or unconscious. Or dead.

Emily unscrewed the canteen's cap and took a sip.

Half-empty and all they had left.

Alton Brewster, the soldier who'd nearly blown her head off when she'd arrived the night before, poked his head into the cockpit. He hissed a whisper. "I told you not to waste it on her! Those of us who have a chance at living need it!" He reached out to grab the canteen.

And she pulled it out of reach.

"Give it to me!" he said, this time with a snarl and definitely not whispered.

"No. It's not yours. It's mine, and I'm sharing it with everyone. Your pilot included."

"Thanks," a faint voice said.

Emily looked down and Flores grimaced. "Hey, you thirsty?"

Flores swallowed hard and nodded.

Emily flashed a look at Brewster before leaning down and tipping some water into the pilot's open mouth. She tipped a little more after Flores swallowed. A fleeting smile stole over her face before she winced again.

Brewster cursed under his breath as he ducked back out of the cockpit.

Emily watched him return to the back of the chopper and slump down next to Marco. Beyond them, a gaping hole where the tail should've been had a crackling fire on the ground just outside.

The fire offered warmth and protection.

Warmth because the night air made your fingers numb in minutes. And protection because that thing, whatever it was, was still out there.

Beyond the glow of the fire, the night quickly faded into darkness. The moon wasn't high enough yet to offer any appreciable light.

The wrecked chopper had two possible points of egress. The cabin door faced upward as the chopper had come to rest on its side. The tracks had bent and it had taken hours of effort that day to wrench it shut. The last few inches had turned out to be impossible, but it was reasonably secure against attack. The giant hole at the back was another matter entirely. The tail end lay thirty feet away, but was too heavy to drag back into place.

They knew because she, Marco, and Brewster had tried that afternoon. But all three together didn't so much as budge it.

"He's a piece of work, huh?"

Emily turned back to the pilot and nodded. "Yep, where'd you get hooked up with him?"

"Not my choice, trust me. He's not a Coastie. We were tasked with ferrying him out to Terror Lake when we had to divert for a rescue operation." She closed her eyes and Emily wondered if she'd drifted away.

They opened again. "Some poor girl got attacked by a Brownie. And we didn't get there to help." She said it like it was her personal fault. "Too late now."

Poor girl?

"What was her name?" Emily asked.

"Hadn't gotten to that yet when we crashed."

This was the most she'd spoken since Emily had arrived at the crash site the night before. Maybe she was getting stronger. Strong enough to survive until rescue arrived.

"I saw the crash," Emily said. One minute, you were flying fine, then the flash, and then you went down. What happened?"

Flores shook her head and then sucked in a breath as the movement caused agony.

"Where does it hurt?"

"Everywhere... except my legs."

That wasn't a good sign.

She stared up through Emily, to the memory.

"I don't know why she went down. Never seen anything like it. One second everything was a-okay, the next she went crazy. All systems dead. The stabilizer went and I had a hard time keeping us from landing on our heads."

Her eyes refocused. The direction didn't change, but, like a camera lens, the depth did. "How is Lawson?"

Emily's lips pressed into a line as she shook her head.

Her co-pilot had died that afternoon. Internal bleeding. Punctured lungs. Whatever it was, they hadn't been able to help. Lawson's body, along with the three others that had died on impact were now shoulder to shoulder under a tarp outside the chopper.

They'd kept them inside the cabin at first, but the increasingly suffocating smell had forced a change of plans.

Emily had another question about the rescue operation, and was about to ask it when she noticed the pilot's eyes had shut again and her head canted to the side. She licked her finger and held it under the woman's nose.

The barely perceptible movement of air cooled her damp skin.

Flores was still alive.

For now.

53

Was not leaving someone who needed help different than waiting for that person to die?

Emily wasn't the type to leave someone behind. But she also wasn't the type to waste time pursuing the impossible.

And so her thoughts ate at her belly like an ulcer as she climbed out of the cockpit and made her way to the rear to join Marco and Brewster.

Oscar, the strange little weasel that Marco treated like a dog, was nowhere to be seen. Out hunting maybe.

"...not coming." Brewster finished whatever he was saying.

"What isn't coming?" she asked as she took a seat beside Marco.

Brewster stroked the scope on his rifle as he answered. "Rescue. That's what."

"How do you know?"

"Because nothing works! Comms are down. We couldn't radio in our location. You saw the beacon. It's dead. And if we don't get moving, we'll end up the same way!"

Emily and Marco didn't have an answer.

"Look here," Brewster said, "the longer we sit here waiting for her to die, the less chance we have of making it out ourselves. Less food. Less water. Less energy. Not to mention whatever that thing was last night!"

Hot anger blossomed in Emily's chest. She was about to stand when Marco laid a hand on her shoulder and gently squeezed. She settled for a reply. "Maybe you should leave."

"If I leave, you and nature boy here would be dead in no time. You should be thanking me for hanging around keeping you alive."

She was about to hurl an insult relating to his outsized ego when Marco intervened again.

"None of us want to be here," Marco said. He lowered his voice. "But we can't leave Flores to die."

Brewster gritted his teeth as he shook his head in disgust.

Something rustled out in the dark beyond the warm glow of the firelight.

Brewster's rifle leapt up to his shoulder as his eyes and the muzzle scanned the darkness beyond the firelight.

Marco grabbed a rifle that he'd recovered from one of the dead. He dropped to a knee next to Brewster and the two pointed their weapons out into the darkness.

Brewster shot him a look. "Thought you preferred bow and arrows."

Marco answered without taking his eye off the front sight. "I do, but I'm not stupid."

Emily stood behind them, a holstered Sig Saur P229 DAK at her hip. The .40 caliber Smith and Wesson rounds packed a punch, but nothing like the rifles the other two carried. It had been Lawson's sidearm, but wherever he was now, he no longer needed it.

Nothing outside moved.

Nothing beyond the bending branches and rustling leaves responding to the infrequent breeze.

She looked up through the glass of the closed side door. On the edge of the clearing, high up near the top of the trees, the sky glowed pale white. The full moon had nearly made it above the trees.

More light would be a good thing. With only the yellow flickering of the fire for light, there were plenty of shadows for something to hide in.

Plenty of darkness ready to swallow them whole.

A sudden movement outside and a blast of wind sent a tornado of orange embers swirling into the cabin.

Emily shielded her eyes as choking smoke filled the interior.

A massive crash into the underbelly of the chopper made the cabin lurch, knocking her down. She landed hard, with a corner of a seat punching her in the gut, stealing her breath.

She rolled onto her back trying not to panic. Trying to breathe.

And not succeeding at either.

Thunder exploded inside the cabin as Brewster fired his rifle and Marco followed an instant later. The interior strobed with blinding speed that left her blinking and dazed.

The firing ceased and the interior again dropped into the flickering orange glow of firelight. Emily lay on the floor as small sips of hot air seeped into her already burning lungs.

"Did you see it?" Brewster said in a tight voice.

"What?" Marco said. "Jesus, my ears are ringing."

"Did you see it?" Brewster yelled.

"Oh. I think so."

"It looked like the forest. What was it?"

"I... I don't know."

The air was coming easier now, and the screaming in her brain getting quieter. Unfortunately, the ringing in her ears more than made up for it. She pulled herself up as Marco glanced back.

"You okay?"

She crouched to stay low as a thick layer of smoke hugged the roof. It swirled in little eddies and sucked out of the gap in the door above.

Reading his lips as much as hearing him, she replied, "Yeah, just got the wind knocked out of me."

The sound of shattering glass sent a shock up her spine. She glanced up thinking the thing had broken through the glass in the side door and was about to crash down on top of her.

The glass was cracked from the initial crash, but still intact, just as it had been since she'd arrived.

More glass shattered and gunfire again ripped through cabin.

Emily spun around and saw the cockpit flashing from light to dark. She launched forward and saw everything blink in and out of time.

Massive reptilian jaws lined with huge teeth jutted through the shattered front windshield.

Not a bear.

A much longer muzzle. Larger. Hairless leather skin. And patterned. Irregular swathes of brown and green like camouflage. A smaller patch on the muzzle turning pale.

The mouth lunged forward and knocked the gun out of Flores' hand as it snapped down on her arm.

Flores screamed as her bones crunched.

The mouth yanked back, dragging Flores forward, slamming her head into the metal frame.

Emily drew her gun and fired.

The thing was only a few feet away.

The mouth twitched to the side and took off Flores' arm just above the elbow. More of the bumpy skin shifted paler, like the ink had leaked away. The mouth jerked back ripping more glass away as it disappeared.

Emily crept closer, aiming her gun at the jagged hole in the canopy, waiting, knowing the jaws would return.

Something hot and wet splashed across her face.

She turned to Flores and saw eyes wide with shock.

Eyes staring in silent horror at what was left of her arm.

"Flores! Oh my God!" Emily yelled as she tried to keep one eye on the dark hole in the front window and also searching the shadows for something to help Flores.

Some kind of tourniquet.

The seatbelts.

She holstered the gun and grabbed the kukri from the small of her back. In no time, she had a good length cut free. She couldn't wrap it and keep an eye on the window at the same time.

Flores was going to bleed out if she didn't get this under control. She was certain of that.

And that monster was going to attack while her back was turned. Snap her spine in half with those massive, terrible jaws. She was equally certain of that.

Emily turned her back on the hole to focus on Flores. She cinched the seatbelt tight around Flores' upper arm. The hunk of exposed meat on the end still bled, but at least it wasn't shooting out blood with every beat of Flores' heart.

"What happened?"

Emily glanced up and saw Marco leaning into the

cockpit holding a small torch from the fire.

"That thing came through the windshield. Almost dragged Flores out."

The wavering light caught the stump that was the pilot's right arm.

"Jesus," he said. "I'll get the med kit."

He disappeared back into the cabin as Brewster popped his head in. "She's a goner."

"Go away, Brewster," Emily said as she turned to Flores. "It's going to be okay. Just hang on, okay?"

Flores' wide eyes didn't move from her arm. From what used to be her arm.

A rush of movement outside and something slammed into the chopper sending Emily tumbling. She got to her feet and saw Marco standing at the gaping hole looking out beyond the fire.

"Oh my God," he said.

Emily joined him as Brewster did the same.

Beyond the fire, at the edge of the light, a scene from a nightmare unfolded.

An enormous lizard, it looked like a lizard but was over twenty feet long, was tearing apart one of the bodies of the recently dead. It ripped the body in half and then choked down what clearly used to be someone's chest and head. It continued with the lower half and legs dangled out over its jaws before another few gulps swallowed them whole.

Marco fired an instant before Brewster and Emily did. All three weapons unloaded on the monster.

And then, in a blur or a flash or like a magic trick, it seemed to become the forest and disappeared.

Brewster slammed a fresh magazine into his rifle and racked the slide. "If we somehow survive tonight, I'm leaving at sunrise. You all can stay here and die."

54

MARCO soared through the sky with the wind whipping through his hair. The air slipped over him like water over a dolphin.

The rush of total freedom.

The warm sun above made the bare skin on his back tingle. Like when he was a kid out for a day hike on his family's lands. The endless hills and valleys below with the limitless blue sky above.

A gauzy cloud drifted below. He dove and then flew just above it, running one foot through, carving an expanding wake behind.

The cloud dissipated and the ground again appeared far below.

Something pulled at him.

Not like hands around his ankles.

More like gravity tugging every atom.

He started to descend, slow at first, but then faster.

He tried to pull up, but kept dropping.

He gritted his teeth and strained for the heavens.

The descent slowed, but didn't stop. Still, it dragged him down. Relentless. Inevitable.

Something watched from below. Something that made the little hairs on the back of his neck prickle.

He reached up for the sky. Every muscle in his body contracted in total exertion.

The sun fell upon his face. In his eyes.

Marco blinked them open and squinted as golden rays of sunlight lit his face like a mask.

Where am I?

His mind spun like a slot machine until the result locked into place.

Right. Inside the chopper.

And still alive!

And with a full belly after the last day and a half of chowing on the emergency rations found in the wreck. Meals, Ready-to-Eat. That was what they called them. But due to their generally disgusting nature, a number of more apt nicknames had been devised.

Meals, Rejected by Everyone.

Meals, Rarely Edible.

But while they often tasted about as good as dog food, they delivered plenty of calories.

He lay on his side on the floor covered by a blanket they'd found in a backpack in aft hatch. The pack was now Emily's but the blanket was shared. The air was cold enough to see when he blew out a deep breath.

Oscar was curled into a tight ball in a fold of the blanket. The heat radiating from his tiny body helped.

But what helped more was Emily. Her warm body molded against him. They hadn't gone to sleep spooning. And he wasn't sure if it was okay that they woke up like that.

Emily made a sound and then shifted slightly back into him.

Oscar grumbled in his sleep.

Marco shivered, and not from the morning chill.

She was gorgeous. No doubt about that. Strong jaw and button nose. Light brown eyes that glowed like sunlight through amber. Too skinny from starving for the last two weeks. A small silver heart pendant hung from a thin silver chain around her neck. The slender elegance contrasted with the crusted line of dirt ringing her neck. It was the only sentimental thing about her. It had to mean something important.

Part of him wanted to lean down and kiss her lips.

And another part of him thought about how creepy that would be and how she'd probably punch him in the face.

Then again, maybe she'd wrap her arms around him and pull him down on top of her.

Nah, she'd punch him.

Marco looked around. Where was Brewster?

He'd taken the last watch and was supposed to wake them at dawn.

Had he taken off without even waking them?

A muffled noise came from the cockpit.

A shuffling.

Marco eased up out of their makeshift sleeping space, making sure not to wake Emily or Oscar. It had been a rough night, even considering the beast hadn't returned.

Another noise from the cockpit.

Flores might need something.

He crept through the cabin and leaned into the cockpit.

Brewster was there standing over and covering Flores.

"Hey," Marco said.

Brewster whirled around as one hand went to his holstered pistol.

"Whoa!" Marco shouted. "Easy."

Brewster's hand stopped, but didn't move away from his hip. His narrowed eyes watched.

Something was off.

"What are you doing in here?" Marco looked past him at Flores lying in the corner. The bandage wrapped around her stump was stained dark red. "How is she?"

"She's dead."

"What?" Marco pushed him aside and climbed down to the pilot. He touched her cheek. "Flores. Hey." He pulled up her eyelid and it slid back down. "Flores! Flores!" he yelled as he shook her shoulder. He checked her neck for a pulse and found none.

He whirled back to Brewster. "She was alive at the end of my shift! Three hours ago! She was alive! What happened?"

Brewster shrugged like he was a bad student being asked about another missed homework assignment. "She died. What do you think happened?" The hand floating next to his holster twitched.

Had he killed her?

It wasn't an accusation he wanted to throw out. One, because as much as he didn't like the guy, that didn't make him a murderer. Besides, she'd been bad off yesterday, and that was before getting half her arm ripped off. And two, he was unarmed. And if Brewster had killed Flores, Marco wasn't going to bring him to justice by getting shot to death himself.

"Okay," Marco said with a nod.

Emily peeked into the cabin. "Hey, what's going on?"

Marco's mouth twisted to the side. "Flores didn't make it."

"Are you sure?"

Marco nodded. "I'm sure."

"We need to get moving. Now," Brewster said.

Marco and Emily turned to him at the same time.

"What? Nothing we can do for her now. Let's go."

Emily's gaze hardened. "We're not leaving her like this to get eaten by that monster."

"Well, we sure don't have time to bury her," Brewster replied. He looked at what was once Flores. "She's dead. That corpse is meat. Meat doesn't care what happens to it."

Marco's body tensed as he lined up a right cross that would knock the bastard's teeth out.

SLAP.

Emily's palm hit Brewster's cheek before he could blink.

"You're an idiot." She spun around and disappeared back into the cabin. "We're going to burn them. So get up and help me gather some wood."

55

The heat from the flames lingered on Marco's face as they continued through the forest. He'd stood too close and chapped the skin. Like lying in the sun for too long without sunscreen.

It had been a few hours since they'd left the bonfire that was the final resting place of Flores and the others. They'd siphoned fuel from the chopper and soaked a small pyre with the bodies laid next to each other.

Four bodies.

Four people who had families.

Husbands and wives that didn't know when their partner would come home.

Sons and daughters that would never see mommy or daddy again. Fathers and mothers that would never see their child again.

Four families that no longer had four people.

And didn't even know what happened to them.

They had to make it out if only for that. The families deserved to know what happened to their loved ones.

Marco understood the absolute importance of that. The

closure. The anguish. He understood because he'd lived through it himself. It wasn't healing. It was scarring.

But even that was better than open wounds.

Another couple of hours and they expected to hit the coast. That's what the map they'd found in the chopper indicated. At least, that's what they thought it indicated. The utility of a map was somewhat diminished when you didn't know exactly where you were on it.

If their estimate was right, their northward trajectory would eventually take them to the coast. And if they followed that, they would have to run into civilization at some point.

That was the plan anyway.

Emily sidled up next to him.

Marco was glad Oscar was snoozing in his usual spot in the pocket between Marco's pack and his neck. The little weasel seemed to get grumpier than usual when Emily was nearby. Or maybe he was imagining it.

Brewster was twenty yards ahead on point. With his rifle held low, he moved over the terrain with practiced ease. He hadn't said it, but he didn't have to. He'd been in the military before his latest private contractor job with Project Hermes.

"Hey," Emily said as she kept pace.

"Hey. How are you doing?"

Emily pulled a lock of bangs to the side and slipped it behind her ear. "Been better. A lot better. But I've been worse, too."

She'd known suffering.

What exactly, Marco didn't know. But twenty-year-olds didn't act like she did. Not unless they'd suffered through and survived a nightmare. Or nightmares. There was a seriousness to her that was out of step with the overriding concerns of your typical twenty-year-old.

The hot guy you kissed from the party.

The pic that totally caught him with his hand cupping another girl's butt.

The drama and revenge.

The heels that made your legs look model thin and miles long and would totally make him regret what he did.

Marco chuckled, despite the somber events of the morning. Or maybe because of them.

"What?" Emily asked.

"Nothing. Just thinking of alternate worlds."

She cast him a sidelong glance, maybe wondering if he was starting to lose it. "What happened this morning?"

"What do you mean?" She'd been there right next to him.

"I mean when you woke up."

His face flushed, and he was thankful the skin was already red from the fire.

"Uhh."

Well, what was he supposed to say? We were spooning tighter than a sock on a foot? Any which way he tried to explain it was going to sound stupid.

"Umm."

Emily glanced at him. "You can't remember? Because I certainly do. To say it was a shock would be an understatement."

Marco's face felt like the flames were again just feet away. He hadn't felt like this big of an idiot since he'd been a freshman in high school and asked Michelle Young (a senior AND the captain of the cheerleading squad) to the senior prom.

She could've just said no and left him with his dignity intact.

But that wasn't how high school worked.

Marco swallowed hard. "It just happened. Uh, I wasn't planning on it. Uh."

Emily looked at him like he was crazy. "What are you talking about?"

"I'm just explaining... you know, about... what are you talking about?"

"About what Brewster and you were doing in the cockpit this morning."

"Oh! Yeah! Me too."

"Are you okay? Do you need to stop and rest?"

"No, I'm fine. Anyway, I woke up and heard a noise from the cockpit. A groan or something. I climbed in and there's Brewster standing over Flores. His back was to me so I couldn't see what he was doing. He heard me and spun around and nearly drew his pistol on me."

"Think he did something to her?"

"I don't know. He looked off, shifty, you know. But then again he always looks like that."

"What if he killed her?"

"We can't prove it."

Emily studied the ground as they walked, long strides that chewed up the distance. His longer than hers. "No, but we can keep a close eye on him. I don't trust him."

"Agreed."

Brewster looked over his shoulder. He'd pulled ahead as they spoke. He yelled back, "You two are dragging. Let's go!"

As much as neither of them trusted him, they also knew he wanted to get back to civilization just as much as they did. They had so many questions and none of them were going to get answered by ending up dead out here.

Marco went quiet as he focused on the movement. One foot forward and then the other. Over a fallen branch. Next to a loose rock.

Hours went by.

They made it to the coast and found nothing and no one, and so continued on following the shore, cutting up into the forest when the ground turned to marsh, and then back down again when it looked passable.

Sweat soaked through his shirt and pooled in his boots making his socks soggy. Prime blister conditions. They'd stopped for a few minutes after midday to inhale an MRE and down some filtered water they'd refilled from a stream they'd crossed. Marco's MRE had been beef lasagna.

Beef Lasagna should've been in quotes or had an asterisk after it. The cold mush he'd forced down tasted only remotely edible, much less like Italian food.

The only thing that indicated it had been something resembling lasagna was the marinara burps that burned his throat. He burped again and then forced a swallow. He took a sip of water from his canteen to wash it back down.

His feet complained as he walked. There was the general ache and also a localized pulsing stinging. Like a scorpion was zapping his right foot on the outside of the pinkie toe.

They'd done their best to tape up hot spots on their feet, but there was no getting around the punishment of the hike. A fresh pair of socks would've done wonders, but he didn't have any and neither did the others. Before they'd soaked the bodies with fuel, he'd considered pulling the socks off one, but couldn't bring himself to do it.

It had felt wrong. Disrespectful of the dead, somehow.

He regretted that decision now.

The sun dipped below the horizon as they walked. The sky went from blue to orange to purple. They'd have to stop soon. They were all exhausted, but no one wanted to spend another night outside.

Especially now that they weren't protected by a metal shelter.

"Hey!" Brewster shouted from up ahead. "Look!" He pointed with his rifle. Further up the coast to the left, the sky was brighter than the surrounding area. "Must be a town further up along the coast!" He took off with renewed vigor and Marco and Emily hustled to keep up.

She marched along ahead of him, always keeping pace, never complaining. How she was doing it, Marco wasn't sure. She had to take a step and a half for every one of his. She carried a pack the same weight as he did. She'd insisted on it that morning.

She was tough. That was all there was to it.

They continued along, doing their best to follow the water. After another hour, they emerged from the trees and made their way down to a narrow beach covered with huge piles of driftwood.

The glow in the sky was much brighter now.

They stopped at the water, staring across a midnight expanse at the orange light on the other side.

"That must be Port Lions," Emily said. "We came up on the wrong side of the inlet."

"Doesn't look like it mattered anyway," Marco replied.

"No."

Brewster didn't say a word. He just stared across the open water of the bay. A couple of miles away, a bright orange glow engulfed the tiny town.

Port Lions was burning.

And there was nothing they could do to help.

And it also meant they'd be spending another night outdoors with no shelter, no protection.

And probably no chance of making it to morning.

56

BOB couldn't wait to get out of Flo's apartment. He'd had just about all the crow he could eat for one lifetime. It was a wonder he didn't have bits of feathers stuck between his teeth.

In retrospect, he probably shouldn't have called her son a fatty. How was he supposed to know that the kid she always talked about at the diner was the very same one that nearly ended up squashing him at the town meeting?

He considered himself a decent guy all around and never would've insulted the kid had he known Flo was his mother. Especially not after Flo had stopped that hillbilly from stomping his brains out in the grocery store parking lot.

What a pitiful obituary that would've been.

Pathetic producer of forgotten hit series died in a Safeway parking lot. A redneck kicked him to death.

He wanted to go out in a blaze of glory. Maybe a heart attack after an all-nighter fueled by coke and hookers. Three hookers.

Sure, that fantasy used to feature a whole harem. Five

beds full of naked and squirming bodies. But he wasn't twenty any more. And three ladies were maybe two more than he'd have any use for.

The ticker would sputter out and he'd collapse into a pile of splayed limbs.

Now that would be a worthy obituary.

Then he remembered.

Would there even be obituaries any more?

"Are you gonna just sit there looking stupid?"

Bob glanced up across the small table that straddled the kitchen and living room in Flo's apartment. Rome nibbled on a cracker and stared at the Monopoly board between them. Bob gathered up the dice and tossed them across the board.

Snake eyes.

Two ones.

Pathetic.

Just like his life for longer than he cared to recall.

He moved his metal shoe piece two spaces forward. He'd have preferred the car, but Rome grabbed it and the only other piece they had was the wheelbarrow. A wheelbarrow was like a promise of being blue collar forever. Like his father before he'd keeled over. Like his mother clung to even after he'd made it big in Hollywood and suggested she retire.

Nope. Not a chance.

Worked until the day she died. She'd had a terrible obituary. He knew because he'd written it.

What?

Was he supposed to make up stuff like she helped poor kids stay in school or she rescued puppies from being put to sleep?

She'd worked and drank and drank and worked until one or the both of them killed her.

"That'll be $832. Pay up!"

Bob suppressed a returned insult and instead started counting out the money. It *was* three houses on St. James after all.

Rome snatched the bills and made a show of counting them to verify the total. "You shorted me two dollars."

Bob grimaced and wished he could fling the stupid board onto the floor. Now that he was about to lose, he didn't care about this stupid game. And he would've done exactly that, except Flo was seated on the sofa knitting or quilting or whatever it was that old ladies did. "Are you kidding?"

"You gave me $830." He fanned the bills. "See? No ones."

Bob shook his head as he sifted through his thin pile of money. "I don't have ones."

"Get them from the bank."

Bob's head nearly twisted off. "It's two dollars! You just screwed me with the three houses and you're haggling over two dollars?"

"I want my two dollars. And I'm not haggling."

"What?"

"I'm not haggling. We aren't doing a deal. You owe me two dollars. Give me my two dollars."

It was everything Bob could do to keep from going ballistic on the little punk. Well, big punk. "Fine." He ripped a ten out of his stack and handed it over to the bank, which was Rome.

He should've been the bank.

Lesson one in Monopoly and life. You never let someone else control the money. His ex-wife had taught him that expensive lesson.

Rome accepted the ten with a grin that made Bob want to slap him. "Would you like ten ones or five ones and a five?"

The pounding in Bob's head got louder and louder. Or was it his heart? When was the last time he'd taken a glycerine pill? Supposed to be once a day.

The room swayed and the edges of his vision darkened.

He grabbed the arm of his chair to steady himself.

"Bob," Flo said from across the room. "Bob, are you feeling okay?"

His chest felt tight. The cut on his face burned.

Flo jumped up and grabbed him under the arm. "Come lay down on the couch. You need rest."

He let her lead him over and help him lie down.

She lifted his head and pushed a pillow into place.

She was a good woman. Taking care of him after he'd insulted her only child. Yeah, she'd slapped him so hard the cut opened up. But after that, she'd gone back to taking care of him. Sure, the bedside manner was noticeably colder than before, but still. If someone had insulted his kid like that, he wouldn't have peed on them if they'd been on fire.

She was something else.

"I win. You suck." Rome said as he placed his metal race car back in the box. Yeah, race car. He got to be the bank and grabbed the race car leaving Bob with either the wheelbarrow or the shoe. Where was the top hat or the cannon or the battleship?

"Rome, please," Flo said in a tone that every mother had mastered since the beginning of time. His own mother had earned a Ph.D. in *the tone*.

"Sorry, mom," he said and then mouthed *Screw you* to Bob after his mother looked away.

"I think I should turn in early. You're right. I could use the extra rest."

Flo nodded. "Fine." She stood and turned to her son. "Come on, Rome. I challenge you to a game. And I'm the race car!"

Bob closed his eyes as the two gathered their things and shuffled into her bedroom. He reached up and twisted the blinds shut to block out the setting sun. He took a slow breath and could feel the tension ease. His chest expanded and the hammering in his ears quieted.

He had to get out of here.

One person that openly hated him and one that was kind enough to not express it. For the most part.

Flo wanted him out. She hadn't said it in so many words. But she did. He felt it. The chill. The anger. Just under the surface.

He needed to do them all a favor and shove off.

His eyes flickered as he considered the how and the when.

Then they shut.

When they flickered again, he blinked several times thinking maybe he was still dreaming.

Everything was dark.

His eyes slowly adjusted and he saw the table across the room. The Playstation, controllers, and rat's nest of cables piled next to the TV. None of it worth anything since the EMP two and a half days ago.

How long had he been out?

He glanced at his watch but couldn't see anything. He pushed up and swung his feet around and onto the floor.

The apartment was quiet.

He stood up with a groan and shuffled over to Flo's door. He knocked softly.

No answer.

He eased the door open and the flame on a squat, pink candle fluttered. The candle sat on a dinner plate on top of her dresser. The frail light seemed ready to surrender to the surrounding darkness.

Bob looked at Flo sleeping in bed.

The warm light hit her face at an angle, deepening the wrinkles and lines. There was a sweetness to her that didn't come through any particular part, but only altogether. As a whole.

She had a good heart.

Something glinted on the nightstand next to the bed.

Bob shifted his gaze and saw the shadowed shape of her pistol.

Lying there.

It was the kind of thing that could come in handy with times being what they were. With that psycho Red liable to be around any and every corner.

Without thinking, without needing to, he tip-toed over and picked it up. It was heavier than it looked. And cold. He fitted it into his hand and aimed it at the wall.

Yes. This could be very handy.

He grabbed the candle with his other hand and backed out of the room. He found a bag in the kitchen and hurriedly packed a few groceries that they'd surely not miss.

With everything ready and a gun in his hand, Bob opened the front door and stepped out. He paused at the threshold, one foot in and one foot out.

"Thanks for everything."

He closed the door, left it unlocked because he didn't have a key, and took off.

57

The Weary Traveler motel was a little over a mile down Mill Bay Road. He didn't know if the distance or the fact that it was pitch black outside was worse. A mile wasn't a distance he'd voluntarily walked in over a decade. Longer, probably. He wasn't philosophically opposed to exercise. It undeniably had benefits for those foolish enough to engage in it with regularity. It was that last part that didn't work for him.

Regularity.

Exercise was basically pointless if you only did it when you felt like it. And he rarely felt like it. Then, on those infrequent days when the inspiration to break a sweat did strike, he'd remember how pointless it was because he hadn't done it in weeks and likely wouldn't again for many weeks after.

If only they could come up with a routine that really worked for all the people like him that were totally committed to doing it once a month.

But there'd still be all the sweating and feeling horrible.

And if that was the case, he wouldn't have guaranteed once a month. Not without getting some measurable results.

Anyway, he regretted the lack of regular exercise now.

After only two blocks, he was sucking wind like a vacuum. He clutched the bag holding the gun and groceries to his chest. Sweat beaded on his sparsely populated hairline and slid down his forehead. He leaned against a brick building and took a minute to catch his breath.

The hands on his analog watch said it was just after eleven at night. Curfew had begun four hours ago. Where there would normally be cars moving up and down the street, there were none. None moving, anyway. Quite a few cars littered the street, but they hadn't moved since the EMP hit.

There was still no official confirmation of what had happened, but then again there wasn't official confirmation of anything after the town meeting the other day fell into chaos. He only knew about the curfew because there were hand-drawn signs posted up at every street corner.

A single dim light spilled out of a doorway a few buildings down. The door opened and out stepped Police Chief Stuckey with a long flashlight in his hand. The kind that could just as easily light your path as bash someone's skull. That would be the police station. He remembered passing by it a few times since he'd arrived in Kodiak.

Stuckey looked up the street in Bob's direction and Bob froze. The flashlight clicked on and a scallop of light on the sidewalk raced toward him.

He ducked around a corner and into the shadow between two buildings. Even with the full moon rising in the east, the town was still dark.

Scary dark.

Dark like this didn't make sense for a town, even a backwater burg like this one.

The beam of light swept across the nearby building and Bob ducked back just before it painted his face.

His heart pounded in his chest. He looked over his shoulder looking for an escape if the chief walked up this way to investigate. The alley behind was pitch black.

Like a fish tank full of ink.

He couldn't see more than a few feet into it. Not knowing what might be back there sent a chill through his limbs that nearly made him drop the bag.

He peeked around the corner and the chief was gone.

As much as he didn't want to get caught out after curfew, the not knowing what was in the darkness behind him set his feet in motion. He crept out of the alley and along the buildings, praying a blinding beam of light didn't flick on out of nowhere and spotlight him like a prisoner trying to escape.

If he did get caught, he'd spend the night in jail. As much as he hated the thought of enduring another minute at Flo's apartment, with the floors being more eggshells than cheap linoleum and threadbare carpet, a night in jail sounded worse.

He almost laughed out loud as he crossed the street to avoid the puddle of dim light spilling out of the police station. It had the warm orange hue of propane or gas lanterns, not the harsher white of lightbulbs.

To think, he was almost looking forward to sleeping in his own bed at The Weary Traveler. That dilapidated roach motel!

What had gone wrong to bring him to this point?

Where in his life had the turning point passed without his recognizing it?

What was the point of continuing on?

The only thing he had to look forward to was the fifth of vodka that was in the tiny fridge that didn't work even when the electricity did.

The bottle was only half-empty.

Or half-full, if he was looking at it optimistically.

Nah. It was half-empty. And it was going to be a lot more empty before morning.

Bob passed Queen's Diner on the right. One of the big windows in the front was smashed out. Looted maybe. It was too dark inside to tell. Not his problem. He kept moving, passing Lilly Lake and other buildings as he made his way toward downtown.

With a sigh of relief that nearly made his bowels empty, he finally made it to his room. A little bit of pride swelled in his chest.

Why not?

He'd made it safely back all on his own.

He shoved a hand in his pocket to grab the key and then froze when his fingertips hit the bottom without encountering anything.

Where was his key?

A carousel of images blurred through his brain.

Where was the last place he'd seen it?

He had no clue.

A scraping noise behind him made him freeze. With fingers numb with fear, he eased his hand into the bag and found the pistol.

The shuffling, scraping noise again.

Someone approaching.

He yanked the pistol out and whirled around to face the unknown threat. Rather, he tried to whirl around, but his cheek slammed into the large and unforgiving muzzle of a double barrel shotgun.

The man holding it had thin, stringy hair that looked about as clean as an old mop. "I'll blow your brains out!"

It was the owner/manager/front desk person that did absolutely nothing anytime Bob asked for something.

"Easy!" Bob said with a whimper. The twin metal circles burned like a brand into his cheek. "This is my room. I'm staying here."

"Whatch you doin' creepin' round my place?"

"I'm not creeping around. I'm going to my room."

"After curfew, huh? How about I report you to Stuck? He's fond of making examples to show folks he means business."

Bob lifted his hands to signal peace. The gun in one hand came along for the ride.

"Whoa!" and the shotgun barrels banged through his skin into his teeth. "This trigger's a quarter-inch away from painting your brains on that door!"

"Sorry! I'm not here to cause trouble. I just want to get back to my room."

"Give me that pistol."

"Why?"

"Give it over! Now!"

Bob let the gun be taken from his extended hand.

"This'll pay for me not reportin' you tonight."

"Are you kidding me? That gun is worth way more than you keeping your idiot mouth shut." Acid burned in Bob's stomach. He wanted to take a swing at this lowlife. And he would've if he'd had any confidence that doing so would've been anything other than the fastest way to die.

"You best go inside before I change my mind."

Bob gritted his teeth. The urge to scream obscenities barely under control. "I don't have my key."

"You lost it?"

"No," he bit off. "I just don't have it right now."

"That's lost. And it'll be an extra charge." The owner

tucked Bob's pistol into his waistband and then flipped through the ring of keys attached to his belt. "Move over, and don't do anything that'll get you shot."

Bob stepped to the side, being sure to move slow.

The owner opened the door and stepped back with the shotgun barrels conspicuously occupying the space between them. "Oh yeah, you ain't paid for tomorrow."

"What?"

"You paid a week ago and that's through today."

"Fine. Put another week on my card."

"Don't take cards no more. Cash only. Or maybe if you have another gun or something valuable."

Bob had nothing worth trading for more time. He stepped through the door and slammed it as hard as he could.

The owner's voice came through the cheap wood door as clear as if it hadn't been there at all. "If you can't pay, check-out's at ten. And trust me, fella. You don't want me to have to kick you out."

Bob slumped down onto the bed. Tears would've sprung from his eyes if he could've remembered how to cry.

How had it come to this?

He'd be kicked out of this dive tomorrow and then what? Where would he go?

What was the point of it all anymore?

58

FLO rolled over and her eyes blinked open at exactly 4:40 in the morning. She stared at the silhouette of the digital clock on her nightstand, wondering why red glowing block numbers weren't verifying the unerring pattern of her daily schedule. Over twenty years of the opening shift at the diner had made her internal clock so accurate and dependable that a Swiss watchmaker could've learned a thing or two.

Had the plug fallen out of the wall?

She had to bend the prongs wider every few months to keep it lodged in place.

Wait.

No.

The events of the last two and a half days clicked into place like her brain was a Rubik's cube. The last rotation that made every side a plane of uniform color.

The clock was dark because there was no power. There was no power because an EMP, or whatever it had been as there had yet to be any official report from the mayor or police chief, had taken out the grid, everything connected to the grid, and just about everything else, too.

Through the cracks in the blinds, she could see it was still dark outside. She reached for where she remembered leaving the mini flashlight on the nightstand.

Nothing.

Her fingers splayed as she glided over the surface, thinking she was just tired and not thinking clearly.

Still nothing.

Maybe it had fallen onto the floor, or Rome had grabbed it thinking it was his.

Flo rolled onto her back and stared into the darkness.

No power, no diner. No diner, no work.

She had no reason to get up this morning. But not having a reason didn't suddenly make her body forget so many years of training. After a few failed attempts at closing her eyes and relaxing, she gave up.

Lying in bed getting annoyed at not being able to sleep was pointless. Worse than pointless. She sat up and put her feet on the cold carpet. She'd needed a new pair of slippers for ages. Dull aching radiated from both of her knees. It was worse when it was cold.

And it was cold.

The heater didn't work. Not a surprise but unwelcome all the same. It must've been fifty degrees inside the apartment. And this was late May, approaching the relative heat of summer. If this wasn't all figured out come winter, there were going to be a lot of folks in big trouble.

Flo massaged her knees, trying to convince them that they could put in another day's shift. A high school and part of a college career in track and field had left her body with reminders that the glory days were long gone.

These were the payback days. The days when her body paid her back for how hard she'd pushed it back in the day. She'd been good. Gotten a scholarship for running hurdles and throwing javelins. In practice one time, she'd thrown one for sixty-five meters, just seven short of the current women's world record.

But her knees could take only so many blowouts.

Whether it was genetics, fate, or bad luck, her career had ended abruptly with a complete ACL tear in her left knee.

It took a few more minutes of massaging, but her knees finally came around.

She pushed off the bed and ran fingers through her hair and made sure her sweatshirt and pants were presentable. She tip-toed into the living room to check on Bob.

He'd seemed like such a nice guy. Sure, a typical know-it-all Outsider type but spending most of every day of the last two weeks with him at the diner had showed her that he could be thoughtful, too. And wickedly funny.

And experience had taught her that a great sense of humor meant a lot more than having a nice butt or strong jaw.

Besides, she'd caught him staring at her backside on more than a few occasions. It felt good to have the eyes of a man stroking her, imagining the skin below the clothes. He should've been too old and too mainland for her tastes, but something about him had her thinking thoughts that hadn't circled her brain in years.

That was until he'd insulted her son.

Now, she'd just as soon he exit stage left and let her get back to being lonely and okay with it. Fine. Not being okay with it but doing it anyway because what other choice was there? To do that though, she had to get him well enough to kick him out the door.

It was ironic, no doubt.

Caring for him with the explicit goal of never caring for him again. But she was a good person, if not necessarily a good Christian like her mother had been. Religious or not, she wasn't the type to turn a blind eye to someone in need.

It was the right thing to do. And the protective fury she felt at him for her son would have to hold off long enough to get him well enough to get walking.

In the darkness, Flo stared at the couch and the blanket covering it. She tip-toed closer.

Something was off.

As her eyes adjusted, she realized with a start that he was gone.

In the bathroom?

She shuffled back to the hallway and to the open bathroom door. Not there either.

A light clicked on and swept over the couch.

She turned and Rome stood sweeping his mini flashlight over the empty couch. "Where's the butthead?"

"Romero Andrew Bickle! Language!"

"Sorry, I meant buttface."

"Not better," she said as she turned back to the couch. "And I have no idea."

Rome swept the flashlight across the living room and over to the kitchen.

The pantry cabinet doors were open. An empty bag of Doritos. Scattered piles of orange crumbs were all that remained. A noticeable gap in the supplies evidence that there was less now than when they'd gone to bed.

'He stole our food and took off," Flo said with a voice tinged with shock.

Who would do that?

After she'd saved him from a beating. Well, cut it short, at least. And then invited him into her home and taken care of him.

What else might he have stolen?

A cold shiver slid down her back.

She snatched her son's flashlight and hurried back to her room. She saw it at once. Rather, she didn't see it at once. The Beretta on the nightstand was gone.

Her jaw dropped open. Slack and unbelieving.

Rome looked over her shoulder.

A smoldering anger ignited in her belly. She was going to kick the cuts on his face back open. She should've let Red beat him to death! But since he hadn't, she was going to finish the job!

"That heartless thief stole my Beretta," she said in a low voice full of menace. She went to her dresser and began pulling out clothes.

"What're you doing?"

"I'm going to get my gun back."

"I'm going, too."

"No. Absolutely not. You're staying put."

He crossed his arms and blocked the door. "You're not going without me. We go together or not at all."

Flo bit down on her lower lip until she tasted blood. She could threaten to ground him, but what would that help? The Playstation, the laptop, his phone. None of them worked and so held no power, neither the electrical kind nor the grounding kind.

He seemed so grown up all of a sudden. A part of her fought it, but another part won out. He was sixteen. Not an adult, but not a child either. He would be a man someday. And that didn't happen overnight or automatically. It required time and experience.

She nodded to herself as much as to him. "Get dressed. I know where he's staying."

59

Bundled up and ready to go just after five, Flo waited by the door for her son. She noticed the deadbolt was unlocked and they didn't have a lock on the knob.

Unlocked.

Ever since that thief had snuck out.

Leaving her and her son vulnerable.

Kodiak wasn't ordinarily the kind of place where one necessarily had to worry about home invasions or big city crimes like that.

But these weren't ordinary times.

Logically, she knew Bob didn't have a key and so couldn't have locked it even if he'd wanted to. Whatever. He'd still done it.

Rome came out of his room looking like a bear wearing a jacket. He was huge, not just overweight. Although she knew he was that, too. He was tall like his father. Taller than her by a foot. And broad-shouldered like him, too.

He was beautiful. The cherub-faced little boy still recognizable in the man he was becoming.

If only he didn't have to carry such a burden.

Was it a thyroid problem?

Was she a bad mother?

Was he too addicted to video games and TV?

She didn't have the answer, and that was the worst part. Parents were always supposed to have the answer. Even if it wasn't a good one.

For the millionth, no, trillionth, time, Flo cursed whatever it was that caused her baby such suffering.

"Ready," he said with a grin as he showed her a short metal baton.

"What's that?"

He whipped his wrist and it extended to a few feet long. He swung it through the air making whooshing sounds. "In case we need it."

"Where did you get that?"

"Online. It's tempered steel and can smash a brick in half without breaking. I saw it in a video."

"No."

"No?"

"No, you may not take it. Go put it away."

"Mom," he said with that agonized whining sound that every child mastered by age three.

"Mom, nothing. No."

The smile faded from his face. His shoulders slumped. "We need–"

"No."

He returned to his room and came back empty handed.

"Thank you," she said. "I'm letting you come along because, you're right, you're old enough. But that doesn't mean I'm putting my own son into danger. We're going there to have a discussion. Not to kill him or have a showdown at high noon."

"Fine. Let's go."

They could've driven the Pinto Bean but she decided against it. It was one of relatively few cars still working in town and she'd noticed while driving home from Safeway the other night that she'd gotten a lot of strange looks.

Some of them curious.

Some of them innocent.

And some of them not.

It was safer to walk.

Curfew had ended at five and so they left not worrying about being harassed by Stuck or any of his deputies. That wasn't to say they didn't worry at all. The streets were strangely empty. Not empty. The same cars were in the same positions on the street since the event.

But empty of people.

The few people that were out at that hour kept to themselves and disappeared around corners as they approached.

They passed the diner and saw that one of the large front windows was gone. A border of razor-sharp shards all that remained. Looters maybe. Or idiots causing damage for the fun of it. She didn't know which was worse.

A part of her wanted to go inside to check it out, but a bigger part of her was furious at Bob and couldn't wait to confront him. Besides, she wanted that pistol back. The food he could keep. He probably deserved more than he'd taken considering how much she'd gotten from Red's upturned shopping cart.

They arrived at The Weary Traveler as the sky shifted from orange to gold in the east.

Flo's first thought was how much of a dump the place was. It made their apartment complex look modern and perfectly maintained in comparison. At least Spruce Landing had been nice when it was new. This place looked like it had always been a garbage heap.

It was a small parking lot edged by rooms on three sides. Single story. Faded blue paint peeling in more places than not. The doors mismatched and obviously replaced with whatever was available at the time. Windows missing screens. What screens there were had large frayed holes that served no other purpose than adding to the feeling of decay. A shopping cart by the door of whoever had stolen it from the grocery store. A few potted plants that were overgrown with weeds.

She'd passed this place a thousand times in her life, and yet this was the first time she'd ever really noticed it.

It faded even as she looked at it. The kind of place that your eyes naturally passed over.

They stopped outside the entrance of a building that had a sign hanging by one screw. Sloping down to the right, it said Office. She didn't know what room Bob was in so this was the first stop.

"Wait out here," she told her son.

"What? No."

"For the love of God, Rome. Please don't make this harder than it already is!"

He twitched like she'd zapped him with a taser. He took a step back and turned to face sideways to her.

Flo exhaled and opened the door and stepped into a dim, cramped space. The filthy windows on either side of the door didn't let in much light. You had to wash them once a decade for that to happen.

A man leaned back in a chair with his feet up on the counter. His hair was stringy and greasy like it had last been cleaned about the same time as the rest of the property. He snored in stuttering fits and starts. Sitting in his lap was a pistol.

Her Beretta!

60

She could see the custom wood grip.

She rapped on the counter. "Hello. Hello!"

The man jerked awake and grabbed for the pistol. His hand knocked it to the floor and he scrambled for it. He managed to grab it and then stood with it held by his side.

Aimed at the ground, but still in his hand.

"Good morning," she said, trying to keep it cordial.

"No credit cards. No checks. Cash only. Or trade if you got something good."

"I'm not looking to stay." A grimace echoed across her face as she considered the horror. "I noticed that pistol in your hand."

He looked down at it. "Yeah. So?"

"When did you get it?"

His eyes narrowed. "Why do you care?"

Flo had no intention of getting killed, but she also had no intention of leaving without her gun. "I care because that is my Beretta which was stolen from me last night."

"It's mine. Had it for years. Now, get out!"

Flo didn't move. "I wonder if Chief Stuckey would agree

with your claim? And I especially wonder what he would do when he finds out it's a lie!"

The man slammed a fist on the counter. "I'm not going to ask you again!" The hand holding the pistol started to raise.

Fear squirmed in Flo's belly. She wasn't so sure all of a sudden that she'd played this one right.

"Get out!" he screamed with eyes filled with hate.

A shadow moved behind him and a whoosh of air followed. A metal baton smashed the man's wrist and the gun dropped to the floor.

The man screamed at the way his hand hung limply to the side with the pinkie touching his forearm.

Rome picked up the fallen pistol and passed it over the counter. "Here you go, mom."

Like he was passing the mashed potatoes at dinner.

She accepted it, verifying the safety was engaged and that the muzzle always pointed down and in a safe direction. The idea was to get her gun back, not shoot someone.

Flo stared at the pistol. She had what they'd come for... but it was somehow not enough. She'd pictured confronting Bob and extracting an apology or at least an explanation. She looked back at the man cradling his broken wrist and shouting obscenities. "What room is Bob Randy in?"

The man's eyes went wide. "Him!" He spat out the word like it tasted like dung. "He gave the gun to me! Gave it to pay for the room!"

She didn't have the time or inclination to listen to this lowlife blather. "Rome," she said and nodded toward the man. It was a threat display. Hopefully, her son understood that and didn't bash the guy's brains out.

Rome lifted the baton.

"Five! Room five, okay! Don't hit me again!"

"Give me the key," Flo said. She wasn't about to go bang on the door to confront him and have that coward hide behind a locked door.

They got the key and proceeded toward the room across the parking lot. A white number five painted on the door. Drip lines evidence of how little care had been taken in applying it.

"You were supposed to wait outside," she said to her son.

"Lucky I didn't though, right?"

It had worked out, but that didn't mean that was the only way it could've gone.

They stopped at the door and she knocked. She was going to give him a chance to be a man. Not that she expected him to take it, but that wasn't the point. "Bob! Open the door! Bob!"

She pounded again.

No answer.

Of course.

Coward.

She unlocked the door and kicked it open. The smell made her stomach churn and twist. Dank, metallic, heavy. Wrong. The hot anger in her chest snuffed out in an instant.

An empty bottle of vodka lay on its side on the night-stand next to the twin bed. The room looked like a bomb had gone off. Clothes were scattered everywhere, on the floor, hanging over the lamp, wadded in a corner. The sink in the far corner had running water spilling over the lip onto the patchy carpet. There were several fist-sized holes in the walls. The glass TV screen was cracked with a large triangular piece missing from the middle.

"Whoa," Rome whispered from behind her shoulder.

There was one more reason it looked like a bomb had gone off. The biggest reason.

The blood.

Everywhere. Splattered on the wall by the bed. Covering the bedsheets and down the sides onto the floor.

"Oh Jesus," Flo muttered as she hurried to the bed.

Bob lay on it with his arms spread wide like they were nailed to a cross. His skin a pale gray color. He was naked but for the crimson soaked sheet twisted over his waist. His eyes were open and ghostly white, all but a sliver of the irises rolled up into his head.

And his wrists.

Jagged wounds from which blood still oozed.

"Help me!" she screamed at her son. She grabbed a shirt off the floor and wrapped it around one of Bob's slashed wrists, making sure the knot held it tight. "Go get that shopping cart that's outside!"

Rome stood in the doorway, the morning sunshine sneaking in around his broad shoulders.

"Now!"

He lurched into action as she wrapped Bob's other wrist with more improvised bandages. She pressed two fingers into the fold of his neck and waited. There was a pulse. Ever so faint.

If she wasn't imagining it.

In the narrow space between the bed and the wall, she spotted something on the ground. She picked it up. The missing piece of triangular glass from the TV. Light streaming in from the doorway shown through it, casting a red glow on the wall.

A stained glass window.

Stained with Bob's blood.

Rome crashed into the room pushing the shopping cart in front.

"Help me lift him into it!"

Rome looked at her in confusion but didn't say anything.

With Rome carrying most of the weight, they managed to get Bob on his back in the shopping cart. His wrinkled legs hung out over the front.

She struggled to turn the cart around.

Rome helped out and got it facing the door. "What are we doing?"

"We're taking him to the hospital!"

Rome's brows scrunched up. "Why?"

Why? It was a good question.

It wasn't because she loved Bob. She didn't even like him. More to the point, she hated him. Hated that she'd started to like him. Hated that she'd started to imagine sharing a beer over dinner.

Just the two of them kind of dinner.

Hated even more that she'd started to trust him.

And that he'd betrayed that trust. Hurting her baby? Stealing from them? Taking off in the middle of the night like a criminal?

No.

She was doing it for a different reason. Doing it because it was the right thing to do. Simple as that.

Flo shoved the cart toward the door. "Because the kind of people we choose to be doesn't depend on the choices other people make."

61

EMILY drew a deep breath into her aching lungs. The pass hadn't looked that high from the beach. But it was high enough to make her lightheaded if she went too fast. She'd had ample calories from MREs and filtered water from streams they'd come across.

She looked over her shoulder at the coast far below and the smoking ruin of Port Lions across the bay. They'd camped on the beach last night, watching the flames light up the sky, wondering what tragedy had befallen the small town.

Also wondering if the beast that took Flores' arm would return.

But the night had passed without incident. They'd either lost the monster back at the chopper or it had chosen easier prey to pursue.

They were now following a route they'd picked out after consulting Brewster's topo map. It showed a seam between two mountains heading southeast which joined a central plain that, like a star, had other valleys extending from the center. One branched northeast and looked like it might take them to Kodiak Station. From there, the airport was a short distance east and then Kodiak not far to the north.

The map made it look so simple.

It wasn't.

Emily glanced ahead along the trail and Brewster was already peeling away, apparently unconcerned about how the rest of the group was doing. She gritted her teeth and got moving. There was no chance she was going to be the weakest link. She'd march until her feet fell off if she had to. And then she'd keep going until her ankles wore down to the knees if that's what it took.

She muttered profanity in Brewster's general direction. A descriptive word her grandmother would've scolded her for using.

Grammy.

How was she doing?

She was sick. By herself. A world away.

They had to get back to Kodiak. Back to civilization. Surely, they'd get some answers and help there. What would happen to the contest? To the million dollars?

Was it off? Or paused?

If it was off, what would happen to her grandmother? She didn't want to think about it.

A shout pulled her out of the dark thoughts swirling in her head.

Brewster. Up ahead and calling to her, pointing at a dark spot further down in the valley they were descending into.

"What's he going on about?" A voice from behind her said. Marco appeared beside her on the narrow trail.

The annoying weasel on his shoulder hissed at Emily, and then crawled around to his far shoulder. It leaned out around his head and hissed at her again in case she'd forgotten the first one.

What was that thing's problem?

Marco shushed him and then nodded toward Brewster. "What'd he say?"

"No idea. I guess we have to go talk to him to find out."

"Do we have to?"

Emily laughed and it came out only partially forced.

"Should we knock him off the trail and keep his rifle?" He peered down the steep slope. "Wouldn't be hard to slip and fall to your doom."

Emily stared at him trying to figure out if he was kidding. The words made it come off like a joke, but the flat delivery gave it a more serious edge. "Are you serious?"

Marco cocked a brow at her and grinned. "I'm not sure yet. Ask me in a few more hours."

The two finally arrived next to Brewster as he was staring through his scope at something in the distance, where the descending trail met the valley floor.

"What is it?" Emily asked.

"A person. I think."

"Let me take a look," she said as she held her hand out.

Brewster's eyes narrowed as he saw she wanted his weapon. He held it tight to his chest.

"Oh for the love of God! What? I'm going to take your rifle and shoot you with it? Stop being an idiot and let me take a look."

Brewster chewed his lower lip as he handed it over.

Emily brought the scope to her eye and sighted on the dark spot. The image jumped across the screen and disappeared. She fine-tuned the adjustment this time and brought it into focus.

It was still too far away to be entirely clear. But it did look like a man kneeling next to a large carcass. He seemed to be covered in ragged clothes. She steadied the rifle, held her breath to lock it in, and looked closer. Not clothes, animals skins, like a French-Canadian trapper from the 1700s. She'd heard stories about old school types that lived on the land and had little contact with the outside world.

The fabled Alaska mountain man.

Had they run into one?

And would he help? Or shoot them for intruding on his territory?

"It's a person, right?" Brewster said with growing excitement.

"Looks like it," Marco said as he stared through the scope of his own rifle. "A real backwoods type from the looks of it."

Brewster yanked his rifle back. "Give it here! I'll signal him!" He pointed the rifle at the sky and fired three measured shots.

Emily uncovered her ears and shouted. "Why did you do that?"

"Distress signal. Three shots with five seconds between each shot. We don't want him to leave while we're making our way down."

Emily watched as the dark spot moved away from the carcass. "What's he doing?"

The dot moved away.

Brewster stared through his scope. "He's running away! Why is he running away?"

Marco growled under his breath. "Probably thinks you shot at him!" He slung his rifle over his shoulder and shoved by Brewster before heading off down the trail.

Emily followed right behind, though she suddenly didn't love the idea of Brewster with a rifle at her back.

Another hour at a quick pace and they arrived on the valley floor and the carcass they'd spotted from above.

Oscar leapt off of Marco's shoulder onto the dead animal. He sniffed around looking for something.

Its abdomen was sliced open from top to bottom. The innards lie in a pile to the side. The skin had been cut away from the ribs. The man had been butchering it before Brewster's shots scared him away.

Emily circled around to the front to where Marco knelt examining the head.

He pulled its mouth open revealing four broad curved teeth protruding from the upper and lower jaws. Each one six or seven inches long. "Looks like a giant beaver. Only I've never seen one anywhere close to this size."

"No way that's a beaver," Brewster said with a laugh. "They grow 'em big in Alaska, but not that big."

The carcass was seven feet long and weighed in the neighborhood of three hundred pounds.

"Well, genius," Marco said to Brewster, "then what is it?"

A thought tingled at the back of Emily's mind. A memory of looking through a book with her father long ago. A picture with an animal just like this one.

"It's a Castoroides," she said. "It went extinct around ten thousand years ago."

Brewster looked at her like she was crazy. She didn't disagree. "Uh, this one looks a lot fresher than that."

Marco let the mouth close and looked up at her. "How do you know that?"

"My father... it's a long story."

And not one she wanted to get into.

62

The fire threw off heat and light, but not enough of either for her tastes. Emily wrapped her arms around her middle and rocked back and forth trying not to think about the biting cold or the pinching in her bladder. She had to pee so bad. She squeezed her thighs together and that helped, but not enough. She stood up and walked in a small circle, working feeling back into her toes.

On the ground next to the fire lay the sleeping forms of Marco and Brewster. Each lay bundled in the few blankets they'd recovered from the chopper.

They'd made camp near a stream in a wide valley covered in lush green grass. Green by day when the sun was shining. A void of inky shadows now. A mosaic of blurred emptiness. An impenetrable layer of clouds hid the full moon above. A chill wind rustled over the gentle contours of the land and spiked the hairs on her arms. It caught the fire now and again, whipping the flames and sucking away the heat.

It was her turn to stay awake. And between being exhausted and having to pee, the two hour shift had already felt like two days. She dug into her coat pocket and pulled out the mints tin. She popped open the lid and checked the time. Her bandless G-Shock watch glowed and delivered the bad news that she had another ten minutes before it was Marco's turn. She tucked it away and gritted her teeth in frustration.

It felt like her bladder was about to explode, but she held it because the discomfort helped her stay awake.

And there was no way she was going to nod off and be the reason they all got killed.

The reptilian beast hadn't returned since the attack at the chopper. That was good news. But with her back to the fire, staring out into the dark, it felt like the chill prickling her arms and legs wasn't due to the temperature of the air alone.

As she watched, at the limits of what she could discern, a section of shadowed grass seemed to swim. She peered harder, trying to force her eyes to gather more light or make her brain better interpret the little data it was receiving.

The breeze rustled the grass in irregular waves.

Emily shook her head. No. She was imagining things. Exhausted. Stressed. Probably delirious from her brain floating in pee. She would've relieved herself already but the only thing worse than peeing her pants would've been to fall asleep on her shift.

She wasn't going to let that happen.

But the thought of soaking her pants in pee wasn't all that appealing either. Sure, it would be warm and nice for a minute. But then it would turn freezing cold and she'd be wet and miserable, not to mention smelly, until she could find a change of clothes. Whenever that turned out to be.

In the wilderness at night, needing to pee and actually doing it were two different things.

She went back and forth and finally decided to get it over with before her body made the decision for her. She picked up Marco's rifle and slipped the sling over her head. She rotated it around until the rifle hugged her back.

With a last look at the fire and the two sleeping forms beside it, she stepped a dozen feet away and decided that was plenty far. She stared out into the shadows, trying not to imagine a hundred horrible things ending her life in a million monstrous ways.

No way she was going any further.

None.

She glanced over her shoulder and both men were still sound asleep.

What if one of them woke up while she was mid-stream?

Whatever.

It was biology, and it was calling.

Emily got her pants down around her ankles and stamped around before she squatted so the grass wouldn't tickle in an unwelcome way. And then she went.

Or tried to, but didn't because she'd been holding it for so long, now she couldn't.

She muttered a curse and tried to relax. The chill breeze stung her exposed skin. Grass rustled out in the darkness making her flinch for an instant.

Not exactly a calming situation.

Emily closed her eyes.

Just relax.

It worked.

"What are you doing?"

Her eyes popped open and she looked over her shoulder, turning enough to pee on her boot in the process. "Marco!" she said as she corrected course. "I'm peeing! Can you give me a minute of privacy?"

The words came out lashing like a whip. A result of her exhaustion and discomfort.

"Oh, sorry! It's hard to see anything. You were squatting there. Then I heard the gushing sound. Makes sense now that—"

"Stop talking!"

"Sorry," he said as she heard his sleeping bag unzip.

Emily finished up with a quick shake, stood, and yanked her pants up. She was about to consider apologizing for snapping his head off when the words died on her lips.

The grass shifted and rustled in a discordant way.

She reached for the rifle at her back when the grass a few feet away parted, like a rip in the fabric of reality, and huge teeth appeared.

The creature lunged at her and she barely got the rifle around in time as the gaping mouth smashed into her. It knocked her down like a hurricane force wind.

She screamed. At least, she thought she did. Maybe it was Marco yelling.

It was a blur.

Both the thing and what happened.

She tried to get the rifle loose but the monster's jaws were clamped tight around it.

She couldn't breathe.

It jerked her around like a rag doll. Its crushing weight made her ribs creak.

Gunshots and flashes as someone fired at it a few times.

The beast jerked and spun around. In seconds, it crawled away from the fire dragging her along between its legs.

She tried to squirm free but the sling around her back held her fast.

Its powerful body moved with surprising speed. It breathed hot, dank air over her that made her want to vomit.

Under its belly, she caught a glimpse of Marco's and Brewster's silhouettes against the orange light of the fire.

How far away they seemed already.

Bouncing and jerking around under the creature, she managed to grab one of the sling's attachment clips and tried to wrench it free.

And then her head bounced off the beast's leathery chest.

It rebounded as all things did. Cause and effect. Action and reaction.

The back of her head arced backward and slammed into the ground.

Everything went dark.

63

MARCO awoke in confusion, knowing something had pulled him up out of sleep, but not knowing what. His sense of place shifted through scenarios like twisting the knob on an old radio—the stations faded in and out.

He stared up at the overcast sky that shrouded the land in darkness.

Was he on his land? Another night under the stars. Or under the clouds that were under the stars.

No.

He was somewhere else.

Alaska.

Was he at his camp? That didn't seem right.

Then the dial found the right station and the broadcast came through.

Out with Emily and Brewster. Heading toward Kodiak to find out what was going on with everything.

But what woke him up?

A noise.

Something moved under the blanket and it took him a panicked instant to remember that Oscar was curled up in the crook of his arm. The cute little weasel was snuffling in his sleep.

Marco scanned the area and saw the dark shape of Emily at the edge of the ring of firelight. She was squatting.

Was she okay?

He pushed the blanket down a little and propped up on an elbow to get a better look. "What are you doing?"

She flinched and he heard a gushing, splattering sound.

"Marco! I'm peeing! Can you give me a minute of privacy?"

The words came out barbed and stinging like a scorpion.

"Oh, sorry! It's hard to see anything. You were squatting there. Then I heard the gushing sound. Makes sense now that—"

"Stop talking!"

"Sorry."

Oscar wriggled out of the bag and his body went rigid as he stared in Emily's direction. He chirped and hissed as the wind rustled the grass beyond.

Marco saw a blur of movement just before the thing attacked Emily. He didn't waste time shouting a warning.

It was too late for that.

The monster rushed her and knocked her down like a speeding car. The orange firelight reflected off the black-green pattern of the wrinkled skin covering its back and sides. The pattern looked painted, like an expressionist version of the surrounding landscape.

Closer now than when he'd seen it at the downed chopper, it still made no sense.

It was impossibly long, over twenty feet from snout to tail. A thick body perched a few feet off the ground by front and back legs ending in huge splayed fingers with glistening claws. A paler underbelly showed beneath.

The thing latched onto Emily and flung her around like she weighed nothing.

Marco scrambled out of his bag, pulling out the pistol he'd traded Emily as he got free. He fired several times at its back half to be certain that he wouldn't accidentally hit Emily.

The beast jerked and spun around with lightning speed and then took off with an odd wagging gait.

Like a Komodo Dragon.

That was how it looked and moved. Only much bigger. And with a skin color and pattern that blended into the surrounding land.

Marco leapt to his feet but it was already gone. He ran to the edge of the firelight and noticed that the thick grass was flattened where it had retreated. It would be easy to track in terrain like this. He holstered the pistol, raced back to his spot by the fire and shoved his feet into unlaced boots. "We have to go after them!"

Brewster was on a knee with his rifle raised and covering the darkness. "No point."

Marco spun around in confusion, certain he hadn't heard right. "We have to go! Now!"

On his sleeping bag, Oscar chirped in agreement.

Brewster snarled at the weasel and then looked at Marco, shaking his head. "No point. She's already dead. You saw that thing. It could bite her in half without trying. We go after her and we all end up dead."

Marco's brain seemed to expand inside the fixed volume of his skull. The outward pressure painful. "What? Get up! We can save her!"

Brewster frowned and shook his head. "Nope. Not gonna do it. That's not a rescue mission. It's a suicide mission, and I'm not throwing my life away for nothing."

Marco couldn't believe it. The pressure in his head exploded. He grabbed Brewster's jacket by the collar and yanked him up to his feet. He leaned down so their eyes were inches apart. "We are going after them! Now!"

Something hard jabbed into his side. Hard enough to hurt.

He glanced down and saw the muzzle of the rifle and more, saw the finger curled around the trigger. He looked back up to meet Brewster's gaze.

The eyes were cold. No emotion. Dead. Deadly.

"Get your hands off me," Brewster said in a whisper, "or I'll blow a hole through your gut."

Marco considered going for the holstered Sig at his hip.

No.

This wasn't *Buffalo Bill's Wild West Show* and he definitely wasn't the fastest draw in the West.

He let go and slowly raised both hands. Hands that wanted to curl around this coward's neck and squeeze until the fingertips met in the middle.

But the look in Brewster's eyes stopped him. Something sinister about them. An eager anticipation.

"Easy there," Marco said. "Fine. You stay. I'll go."

The pressure in his side eased and Brewster stepped back, pointing the gun down at an angle. Though it would still be a small adjustment to move it up to point at his chest.

Marco continued backward, widening the space between them, keeping his movements slow and measured.

Oscar leaped onto Marco's leg and scurried up onto his shoulder. His soft tail wrapped around Marco's neck for balance.

Marco paused at the edge of the firelight. He needed to turn around and get going but the thought of turning his back wasn't an appealing one.

Brewster stood by the fire shaking his head, the rifle still noticeably occupying the space between the two men. "You're gonna die just like she did! This is one of those evolutionary choices, man! Weeding out the genes of the stupid!"

Stupid or not, Marco wasn't going to give her up without a fight.

He spun around and took off, gliding over the flattened grass like a hawk in flight.

64

The trail of flattened grass continued on, angling now and again as if the animal had a particular destination in mind and was correcting course to stay on track. With so little light, keeping on the trail tested Marco's tracking skills. He'd veered off one time but Oscar had thrown a hissy fit of chirping and squeaking until he'd followed the weasel's pointed and sniffing nose back to the trail.

The little guardian angel on his shoulder.

Marco moved at a jog. He longed to go faster. His brain urged him to RUN! To hurry before it was too late! But after leaving camp at a sprint, he hadn't gone twenty yards before his toe caught a jutting rock and he'd Superman'd into the ground. The short flight ended with a busted lip and a face that felt like he'd gone a round with Mohammed Ali in his prime. After that, he'd settled for a jog. And the slower pace helped with staying on the trail, as well.

But the slower pace made the pursuit take too long. Every minute that passed might be Emily's last. And forty of them, more or less, had already slipped by.

He felt the ground rising beneath his feet. The dim

silhouette of a low ridge appeared as he drew near. He crested the spine and stuttered to a stop as he saw a scene unfolding in the valley below.

A hundred and fifty yards away and a little below his position, he spotted the beast.

But that wasn't all.

It was in the center of a group of over a dozen people. They surrounded it carrying blazing torches and long spears. The orange flickering glow surrounded it on all sides, revealing in starker clarity than before just how massive the thing was. Twenty-five feet long. Maybe two thousand pounds. The beast's body seemed to shift from black to orange as torches drew closer.

Whenever it turned its head to bite at one side of the circle, that side fell back while the other side darted in for quick stabs with the spears.

Why weren't they using guns?

He was all for creating and using primitive weapons. It was his thing. He preferred a trusty bow when hunting game. But he'd never hunted an animal that size nor one as lethal.

Marco watched from above as the beast jerked its head toward one side of the circle. A figure moved in, grabbed a dark shape on the ground near the beast, and dragged it back out of the circle.

Emily!

Not moving that he could see from this distance.

He broke into a sprint with Oscar digging his claws into his coat to avoid getting thrown off. He kept the pistol pointed at the ground as he chewed up the distance between and soon arrived a little ways from the circle. He veered toward the figure kneeling over Emily.

As he got within twenty feet, the already strange scene got stranger yet.

All of the people were men wearing thick furs. Their faces covered in equally thick beards. So much so that it was hard to tell where the beards ended and the furs began. They were all shorter than him but wider.

Marco was big enough that most men unconsciously stepped to the side when their paths crossed on sidewalks or in the grocery store. But these guys had shoulders that looked like you could build a house on them. Arms that looked like they could rip a door off the hinges as easily as open it.

The three in the circle nearest him turned with their spears now aimed at him.

Marco skidded to a stop. He kept the gun pointed down and raised his other hand as a show of peace. "How is the girl?"

Most of the circle kept their attention on the giant lizard while the three facing him broke off and advanced toward him. The circle closed ranks behind as the three spread out as they approached.

"I don't want anyone to get hurt! I'm here for the girl!"

The lizard roared as one of the hunters buried his spear in its underbelly, just behind its front leg.

Marco pointed at Emily with his free hand. "How is she?"

None of them spoke.

Not a sound.

In the flickering light, their broad flat faces showed no response of any kind.

Another hunter in the circle darted in and thrust his spear into the beast's neck. It roared again and stumbled.

Faster than seemed possible, the circle collapsed and many spears drove into its body at once.

The three approaching Marco were now arced around him in the exact same way as they'd surrounded the lizard. Their spears were ten feet long and as thick as small trees. The points ending with sharpened stones as large as his hand. The tip of the nearest one in the middle less than fifteen feet away.

They were preparing for the kill.

Marco raised the pistol and pointed it at the man in the middle.

Was it a man?

It was. But different.

"Stop! Don't come any closer or I'll shoot!"

The three paused.

Stared and waited.

Marco started moving toward Emily and the man kneeling above her, trying to remove the rifle slung around her back. Her head and limbs were slack. He got it free and peered at it, turning it end over end.

God. Please let her be alive.

Please.

Without a word, the three smoothly pivoted their half-circle and the man in the middle cut off Marco's path.

"Get out of the way," Marco shouted as he aimed the pistol at the man's chest. "Move! Now!"

The men on each side of him rushed in at the same instant. Their spears forward and aiming to skewer him.

Marco pulled the trigger as he leapt forward.

BANG. BANG. BANG. BANG. BANG.

The man collapsed in a heap.

Marco leapt over the body and ran toward Emily. He

launched through the air with his arm and shoulder locked and hit the man kneeling over her in the back.

A jolt of pain ignited in Marco's shoulder. Almost like he'd gotten the worst of it.

The two rolled end over end and the man was up on his feet in the blink of an eye. He held a spear cocked back and ready to throw at Marco.

Oscar darted up the man's leg and under the enormous volume of layered animal skins. Chirps and screeches followed the weasel.

The man's eyes went wide. He dropped the spear and frantically tried to dig inside the skins covering him.

Marco rolled to his side, brought both hands together to steady the pistol and fired two shots into his face.

The man's head snapped back and he collapsed.

Marco scrambled over to Emily and shook her shoulder. "Emily! Emily!"

She didn't respond. She didn't move at all.

Several of the hunters surrounding the dying beast broke off and charged him with raised spears.

Marco lunged for the fallen rifle, rolled and brought it up firing in a single, fluid motion.

The closest man fell.

Marco pivoted and fired another burst of shots.

Another hunter fell.

The others cut off the attack and retreated a few paces.

Marco pointed the rifle at the next closest hunter and he staggered back a few steps like he'd already been shot. "Stay back! I'll kill every last one of you!"

It worked. They maintained their distance.

Marco squatted and struggled to lift Emily over his shoulder while also keeping the rifle free and covering the assailants. He maneuvered her into place and then stood up with a grunt.

Tickling scratches on his pants as Oscar scurried up and perched on top of Emily. He stared back at the hunters with his jaws open and hissing.

Moving the rifle back and forth to keep them all covered, Marco backed away. He got fifty feet away when half of the group started toward him at the same time.

They spread out as they came.

Crouching low, limbs flowing like cougars.

Not good.

He'd been bluffing earlier. He didn't have enough ammo to kill them all.

Marco fired off a few rounds to get their attention, then spun around and took off.

65

___

MARCO spotted the approaching tree line with a breath of relief. He'd be able to lose them once he got into the forest. He glanced over his left shoulder, the one not carrying Emily, and saw the pinpoints of flickering orange light bobbing and weaving down the valley.

The torches grew brighter as he watched.

They were fast.

And persistent, too.

He'd taken the risk of running as fast as he could for the last half hour and still hadn't managed to lose them completely. The wide open landscape didn't help.

The forest though, that would do it.

He turned back and charged forward. In another few minutes, he darted into the thickening trees and the deeper darkness of the heart of the old growth forest.

Running was no longer an option. Although the way was relatively free of dense thickets and smaller brush, there were too many exposed roots and fallen branches. The larger roots were like pipes bringing water to the skyscrapers above. Other roots were slender and almost invisible, like trip lines for the unwary traveler.

There was too little light to move with any speed.

And so the going was slow. Too slow. But at least his pursuers wouldn't be running either.

Marco picked his way forward, his ankles absorbing the torque as his feet landed at awkward angles on unseen hazards.

After a while, he started to get used to the pace and the environment. He was starting to feel confident when he dodged below a low-hanging branch and leaned a little too far to the right in doing so. With Emily over that shoulder, his balance began to slip.

Oscar leapt to the ground as Marco staggered to the side, grunting and straining to keep from going over.

It should've worked.

Would've worked if not for the exposed root that caught his boot.

He went flying, doing his best to roll under Emily and so absorb as much of the impact as possible.

It was hard to know if it worked, but Emily's weight smashing into him from above doubled the force of the root that punched into his kidney from below. An electric jolt zipped through his teeth as his jaws slammed together.

Emily bounced off him and rolled to a stop.

She moaned.

He wished he had a flashlight. Any light. The full moon would've worked. The sun would've been even better, as long as he was wishing for things he had no control over. He flipped over and crawled to her side. "Are you okay?"

"What? Where? Marco?" Each word trailed off as if she'd forgotten the question before another question arose. She blinked her eyes open.

"Yes," he tried to keep his voice calm, but doubted it came out that way. "Emily, we have to get moving."

"What happened? The lizard thing. And my head hit the ground." She reached behind her head and then squeezed her eyes shut. "Oww, God that hurts."

Marco slipped his arm under her. "Can you stand?"

"Maybe."

He helped her up and then braced her to keep her from collapsing. "The hunters are chasing us. We have to get moving."

From a few feet away, Oscar chirped and squeaked. Presumably agreeing.

"Hunters?"

"I tracked the lizard and ran into them. They killed it and tried to kill me when I arrived." He glanced back through the forest.

Were his eyes playing tricks?

No.

Blinking on and off as they went behind trees and then appeared again, he saw flickering orange points of light.

They were coming.

"Can you walk?"

"I think so."

"Try."

He kept his arm around her for support as she made a few tentative tries. Her strength and certainty grew with every step. They walked together for thirty feet.

She nodded. "Yeah, I can do it."

"Okay. Keep moving that way," he said as he knifed his hand a little to the right. "I think Kodiak Station is somewhere in that general direction." He hovered nearby as she went along, ready to grab her arm or waist if she set a foot wrong.

Oscar bounded over the forest floor easily keeping pace.

The quality of the light in the forest ahead slowly changed, like the darkness bled away, step by step.

He didn't realize it at first, but after a few minutes, the change hit his conscious brain. A sound filtered through the trees.

Something.

A rumbling.

Growing louder, closer, and then receding.

Could it be...

No.

Was he hallucinating?

Probably.

The two kept going until the trees opened up and they climbed up an embankment to...

Pavement!

A road!

Two lane. Narrow. No yellow center line. Towering trees encroaching on both sides.

But a road!

Marco helped Emily up and the two looked around. He remembered the map and the wandering line that started at Kodiak Station and cut across the interior to the northwest. "This must be Anton Larson Bay Road."

They both oriented in the same direction at the same time.

"That should be east," Marco said.

"Agreed. Should eventually take us to Kodiak Station."

Hopefully. If they were anywhere near where they thought they were.

Emily turned sharply back toward the forest from which they'd emerged. "Look!"

He followed her gaze and saw them.

The burning torches. The strange men carrying them.

They were close. Maybe a couple hundred feet in the trees.

How did they make up so much ground so fast?

The side of Emily's face flickered with a pale light.

Marco turned to look down the road and...

Yes!

In the distance.

Headlights!

Coming this way.

Thank God!

The two broke into a jog toward the light. Another minute and the lights wound through the curving road, drawing nearer. They were higher than expected. Must be a truck. A pretty huge truck. Not quite monster truck size, but in the same family.

"Stay beside the road," Marco said. "I don't want both of us dying if they don't see us in time. Here, take this." He handed her the Sig Saur before slinging the rifle around his back. He didn't want to scare off the rescuer by waving a gun around.

Emily nodded and shuffled over to the far side. She was putting up a brave front, but anyone could see she was hurting.

She was amazing. Tough as nails. Tougher. The rock that bent nails in half.

The engine roared as the truck approached. The curve in the road swung the headlights onto Marco.

Too close for comfort, but Marco wasn't going to lose this chance. Perhaps their last. He waved his arms like he was a Christmas snow angel. There wasn't any snow, but their guardian angel had arrived.

The tires squealed and skidded. The rear-end fishtailed

out before the driver got it under control. A trailer carrying two quad wheelers slid out to the side as the truck came to a stop some twenty feet away.

Wow. It was huge.

Way beyond what was actually useful.

Marco was a country boy. Grew up his entire life on the vast lands surrounding Baker, Montana. He understood the utility of a big truck.

But this was different.

This was an expression of ego.

Marco stayed put in the pool of light with his arms raised. He shouted to be heard over the rumbling engine. "Please! We need help! There are..."

His words trailed off into silence.

A man with tangled hair and a matching beard leaned out of the driver's side window and shouted. "Get out of the way!"

That wasn't why Marco went quiet.

The pistol the driver pointed at him was the reason.

66

EMILY stared in shock at what was happening. They weren't bandits and this wasn't a war-torn third world country. What kind of imbecile would point a gun at a person that clearly needed help?

"Last warning! Move it or else!"

The engine roared and the truck lurched forward as the driver eased off the brakes.

Marco held his ground. "Please! There are people coming! They're going to kill us! Please help us!"

"I'm going to kill you if you don't get outta my way!" The driver paused and looked around. "What do you mean *us*?"

Emily was already moving. She climbed up the passenger side and smashed the butt of her pistol against the glass. It shattered and fell away.

The man tried to reorient his gun at her but he was too late.

Three feet away. Finger tense on the trigger. One squeeze and this guy would have a very bad day. She wasn't the carjacker type, but this cretin had threatened to kill Marco. He was lucky he wasn't already dead.

"Put it in park."

The idiot didn't move.

"Now!"

The man's beard parted an inch to reveal stained teeth clenched together. "You're making a big—"

They didn't have time for macho posturing.

She angled the muzzle at the triangular side window to his right and fired.

BANG.

The sound in the cab was deafening. The glass window blew out. The acrid stink of burned powder filled the space.

"You're crazy!"

"Do it or you get the next one!"

He slammed the shifter up into place as his face turned six shades of red and purple.

An instant later, Marco was outside the door. He reached in and grabbed the driver's gun with both hands.

The man thought about fighting back, but his eyes met Emily's and he wisely changed his mind.

She opened the passenger door and slid in, keeping the gun aimed and ready.

Marco ran around and climbed in beside her. Oscar climbed up and settled onto his shoulder. He slammed the door shut. "Drive! They're here!"

Emily looked out the windshield and saw men wearing animal skins walk up onto the road ahead. Broad-shouldered with thick beards and wild hair. Not totally unlike the man sitting next to her.

And exactly like the hunter at the Castoroides carcass earlier.

The driver leaned forward as he stared ahead, and then did as ordered. He jerked the shifter down into drive and slammed a foot on the gas.

The engine roared, huge tires squealed, and they launched forward. More like a rocket than a truck.

Several of the strange men split apart and retreated to each side of the road as the truck picked up speed. One did not.

He stood his ground in the middle of the road as the distance between them disappeared. He tossed his torch to the side and gripped the long spear with both hands.

What was he doing?

Was he going to jab the engine as the front bumper turned him into red jelly?

Emily realized she didn't much care. She was about to yell at the driver to run the hunter over, but it was unnecessary.

The truck never slowed.

The headlights lit up the man like a spotlight.

He had a broad, flat face. Ruddy skin with deep set eyes. Eyes that showed no fear. Knees bent and body crouched with the spear held forward.

He was about to learn a very valuable, and terminal, lesson. Giant trucks weren't like hunting elk, or bears, or whatever this guy was used to hunting.

Emily stared in horrified fascination as the man remained frozen in place. Now fifty feet away.

Twenty.

Ten.

She flinched, expecting the crunching sound of metal on bones. The wet slap of blood on everything.

The hunter leapt to the side with a blurred speed that seemed impossible. He thrust the spear forward as the truck flew by.

A hollow explosion rocked the truck. The front left corner dropped and it swerved out of control.

The cabin shook like an earthquake as the truck careened first to the left, and then when the driver yanked the wheel to the right, back right across the road.

The driver tried again to correct, but it was too much this time.

They shot off the road and down the embankment. A second later, they slammed into a massive tree trunk.

Emily's head whipped forward and smacked into the console. She bounced back and blinked in confusion.

Her chest hurt like she'd been stabbed. A high-pitched ringing in her ears slowly faded to the truck's horn wailing on without end. She turned and saw Marco leaning against the passenger door. A huge cut across his forehead poured blood into his eyes. He mumbled something as one shaking hand lifted and wiped at his eyes.

Where was the weasel?

She looked the other way and winced as a sharp pain shot through her neck.

The driver slumped over the wheel.

A cloud of steam hissed out from under the crumpled hood. She looked in the rearview mirror and saw the flickering torches approaching.

"Marco! We have to get out!"

He mumbled something unintelligible and scraped at the blood spilling into his eyes. He wasn't going to be running anywhere. And she couldn't throw him over her shoulder and hope to do anything other than fall over.

What then?

She found her pistol on the floorboard and then climbed over Marco and out the window. Holding onto the door, she fired a couple rounds at the approaching men. Neither hit but it did make them all pause.

That's when she saw another option.

A chance.

She dropped to the ground and groaned when the impact of her boots on the ground sent a sharp stab up into her head. She lumbered back to the overturned trailer that had broken away and come to a stop a dozen feet back. Both quad-wheelers had fallen off the trailer during the crash. One lay upside down. The other lay on its side. She leaned against that one and put all the power of her legs into it.

With a slow creak and then a sudden shift, it fell over onto its tires.

She swung a leg over and found the ignition and chirped with glee to also find the key sticking out.

Please let this work.

She twisted it and the ATV grumbled and spit and threatened to die. She gave it a little gas to keep it alive and then kicked it into gear. It jumped forward with a jerk that nearly sent her flying off the back.

She brought it to a stop next to the truck's open passenger door and found neutral. She glanced back and saw the torches advancing again.

She fired a few more rounds and the slide locked back.

Empty magazine.

The torches and the shadowed men carrying them continued forward.

Emily got the door open and found Oscar in Marco's lap, hissing at her. She ignored it and pulled Marco toward her.

He slumped into her arms nearly bringing them both down. She managed to direct the fall onto the ATV and Marco landed with a groan of agony.

Light as a feather, the weasel landed on his chest and stared up at Emily like she was the one that had caused all this.

She swatted Oscar aside and then pushed and pulled

and got Marco seated in back. She jumped on and glanced over her shoulder.

A squirm of terror rattled her spine.

With torches and spears held high, the men were running at her!

Emily wrapped Marco's arms around her waist. "Hold on!"

The crunch of approaching feet was close behind.

The spears ready to punch holes in their backs.

She cranked the gas and the knobby tires spun on the shoulder, shooting out dirt like a fireworks fountain.

They rocketed forward and she steered left back up onto the road, spun it around, and gave it some gas.

Chill wind lashed her cheeks and buffeted her squinted eyes.

Soon, they left the hunters behind. And the driver, too.

If he wasn't already dead, she had a feeling he soon would be.

The eastern horizon began to brighten as they followed the road southeast. With any luck, it would take them to Kodiak Station and Kodiak beyond that.

And most importantly, it would take them to the hospital on the north side of town.

As beat up as she was, Marco was worse.

She had to get him to the ER.

Fast.

67

It took an hour to get to the southern edge of town. Probably should've taken half that but Marco kept moving around slipping in and out of consciousness, and so she worried about him falling off the ATV. Kodiak Station had turned out to be no help. Every house and building was closed up and quiet. That wasn't a total surprise as it was just after sunrise.

The orange gold glow that ringed the horizon showed a deep blue above with the clouds of the previous day and night dissipating.

Emily clamped one arm over Marco's arm wrapped around her stomach. She squeezed as hard as she could to keep him from falling over. "Marco!" she shouted into the wind. "Wake up! Come on! Stay awake!"

No response.

Not good.

She wound the nimble four-wheeler through an obstacle course of vehicles seemingly forgotten on the road. All along East Rezanof Drive, they sat silent and abandoned.

Like the people decided to throw it into park and then commit to a monogamous future with bicycles.

Which was ridiculous. This wasn't Berkeley.

So what was it then?

The rapture? The Second Coming? The puffy white cloud coming down to spirit away the good eggs and leave the bad ones to fry?

Nah.

There would've been way more accidents if the drivers had suddenly vanished.

They passed the marina on the right and then cut left onto Mill Bay Road. Providence Medical Center was a block east of Lilly Lake. The number of stationary cars clogging the road increased which required her to slow down even further.

The upcoming intersection had a knot of stationary traffic blocking both lanes so she steered the quad up onto the curb, around, and then bumped back down onto the road on the other side.

After so long in the wilderness, being back in town was surreal. Like a weird dream that you were sure was real. And that was before all the creepy unmoving cars and lack of people bustling in and out of Monk's Rock Coffee House. She slowed down to read the sign hanging in the front window as they passed.

CLOSED UNTIL FURTHER NOTICE. **Stay safe!**

STAY SAFE?

It was like driving through the stage of an elaborate play or big budget Hollywood movie. Everything looked real enough, but it felt like if you opened one of the front doors, you'd find the wood framing keeping it upright on the other side.

Where was everyone?

Emily wove through another dense area and again made it through to a sparser stretch. She saw Lilly Lake up ahead to the left, and Queen's Diner beyond that.

Since entering town, her head had been on a swivel. At first, to keep from running over anyone and later in hopes of running into someone.

Anyone.

She briefly slowed again as they passed the diner. No one was there and it was dark inside. One of the large front windows was busted out.

What was going on?

Flashbacks of her last day there raced through her mind. The two old men with their casually patronizing tone and breath scented with booze. Local flavor, she thought with a smile that didn't quite make it to her mouth.

How long had it been?

The last several days had been a blur, and she didn't have the focus required to sort through it, but it was definitely over three weeks since she'd been dropped off on that beach.

Alone.

Full of enthusiasm. Optimism. Confidence. All of it together a belief. A belief that she was going to win and bring the million dollars home to Grammy.

Looking back, she felt like an idiot for thinking it would be so inevitable. The only thing inevitable about the experience had been the suffering.

She'd understood that going in.

Intellectually. Academically. As an idea.

Now she understood it experientially. In her bones. Bones that were still showing far more than was healthy, even after filling up on MREs.

No!

She'd missed the turn thinking about everything and not thinking about what mattered. She cranked the handle-bars to the left and started the turn.

The arm around her waist slipped as she took it faster than she meant to.

Marco's body slipped against hers. His arms started to pull free as the weight of his body shifted.

Emily kicked off with her left foot, spun around and wrapped her arms around him as he fell over. She torqued her body just before they hit the pavement.

The ATV kept going and smashed through the glass front door of a pizza shop. The painting of a pizza exploded into a thousand shards tinkling to the ground.

Marco landed on top of her, knocking the wind out of her in the process.

She gently rolled him to the side and laid his head back while at the same time grunting at the aching burn in her chest.

The weasel stood next to Marco hissing like crazy at her. There was no question in its mind who was at fault.

An upside down face appeared above hers. "Hey, are you okay?"

He had shoulders like mountains and a bright gold badge was pinned to his dark blue shirt. He spun around so they weren't looking upside down at each other. He glanced at Marco and then at the ATV stuck in the door frame and still rumbling. His eyes narrowed before he returned his gaze to her. "Can you hear me?"

Cool morning air was returning to her lungs, slowly quenching the fire there. She nodded.

"Do you know what just happened?"

She nodded and was finally able to speak. "We crashed. Marco." She turned to him. "He needs a doctor."

"Okay. What about you?" he asked.

Emily groaned, but shook her head. With his help, she sat up. "I'll make it. Please, call an ambulance."

"I'm afraid that's not an option at the moment. But we can get him to the hospital. It's just around the corner."

Emily cursed herself for missing the turn.

The officer nodded at Oscar, who was still hissing and screeching at both of them now. "This your friend?"

"I wouldn't say we're friends."

He nodded. "I can see that. Can you walk?"

"I think so," she said and extended her hand.

He helped her up and she felt stable, more or less. He stared at her a second waiting to see if he could let go or not.

She released his hand and nodded at Marco. "How are we going to get him there?"

"Be right back." He ran across the road and into the police station. A minute later, a rumbling truck roared around from the backside of the building. An old F150 with more rust than paint.

Did everyone own a truck here?

It spun around and backed up next to them.

The officer hopped out and dropped the gate. He lifted Marco's inert form.

Oscar did not like that. What had been hissing and carrying on before turned up twice as loud.

Emily started to help, either with Marco or by smacking Oscar, but the officer shook his head.

"I got it. Besides, you don't look much better." He gently

laid Marco in the bed, watched in surprise as the weasel joined him an instant later, and then secured the gate. He ran around to the passenger door and opened it. "Hop in!"

Emily hobbled over and climbed in.

They were off a moment later.

The officer glanced at her as he took a left.

There was the hospital a block away!

Thank God!

"You're not from around here."

"No."

"I'm Police Chief Stuckey."

"I'm Emily and that's Marco in the back."

"What about the weasel?"

"That's Oscar."

"You mean like the grouch on Sesame Street?"

Marco had told her the reason for the name. She agreed completely.

"Yeah."

They pulled into the parking lot and headed toward the ER entrance.

"Emily, were you aware that the ATV you just crashed was reported stolen yesterday?"

68

FLO stood by the hospital bed in room fourteen and changed her mind again, for the hundredth time. And that was a reasonable estimate, not an exaggeration for effect. Her mouth tasted foul and her stomach churned.

Fifty-fifty odds she was either going to vomit or pass out.

Hospitals weren't her thing. Not after what she'd gone through after Rome's father took off. The depths she'd allowed herself to sink to. She'd considered quite a few different endings all those years ago. And she'd been the width of a razor's edge from choosing one a couple of times.

But one thing, and one thing only, had pulled her back from the abyss.

Rome shuffled into the room and went straight to the floor-to-ceiling window opposite the door. "Nice view. Almost worth dying for."

She joined him at the window, taking in the sweeping beauty of the shore and deep blue ocean beyond. She took his hand and squeezed.

He was the reason she was alive.

Yeah, there was begging to God and making grand

promises and desperate deals that would've made a used car salesman proud. But none of that had done anything more than perpetuate a cycle of endless wallowing in self-pity.

Rome had brought her back into the world. He'd forced her to come back. A one-year-old baby wasn't going to raise himself.

"Mom, why are we here?"

She didn't know how to answer because she wasn't certain herself.

Yesterday morning, they'd rushed Bob to the hospital in a shopping cart. He'd looked so pale she'd thought he was already dead.

But he'd survived.

The doctors said they saved his life. Another hour alone in the hotel room would've sealed the job. They'd done more than most people would've in the same situation. That should've been enough. So why had she insisted they come back today to check on him?

She didn't owe Bob anything. In fact, it was quite the opposite. But she understood his perspective. The bleak reality of seeing death as the only answer. The only way to end the suffering. She knew too well how the black unknown could be more attractive than the suffocating weight of the world.

Flo connected with that suffering because she'd lived through it herself. And she'd been lucky enough to have someone that pulled her through. Bob had no one here. And that isolation tugged at something deep inside her that wanted to help, wanted to heal.

Rome didn't know about any of that. She'd never told him about it.

Flo cast a sidewards glance at Rome. "I don't know. Just

wanted to see if he was doing okay." Another part of her wondered how Bob would feel about being saved.

Maybe life wasn't the outcome he wanted.

Who was she to make that decision for him?

A whispered voice came from the hospital bed. "Thank you."

Flo and Rome turned around and saw Bob was awake. He still looked mostly dead. A tube carrying oxygen was attached under his nostrils and was connected to a tank next to the bed.

"I woke up for a few minutes last night. One of the doctors told me what you did."

Now that he was awake, the part inside Flo that hated him began to overpower the part that had saved him and then brought her here today. "Next time you want to off yourself, don't steal any of my stuff beforehand."

Bob adjusted the part of the oxygen tube hooked behind his ears. "Did you get your gun back?"

Rome grinned. "Yep! And we scared the crap out of the owner!"

"Rome! Language!"

"Sorry, Mom," he said as he looked sorry for half a second and then grinned again. "I swear he took a dump in his pants. I smelled something horrible!"

Bob started to laugh and then groaned like his entire body hurt.

Probably did. Attempted suicide was a horrible way of taking care of yourself.

"Man, you shoulda seen you when we busted into your room. It looked like a zombie had chewed on you! Wrists ripped up and blood everywhere! I'm talking everywhere! The sheets. The bed. The floor."

Bob flinched and turned toward the window.

"Well, good luck with your life," Flo said as she started for the door.

"Wait!" Bob tried to raise his voice but it came out like a ragged whisper. "Let me make it up to you. Please."

Flo's eyebrows arched in disbelief. "I think I've had enough of your company for one life. Goodbye." She started again for the door when a chorus of shouts echoed down the hall.

CRACK.

She halted and instinctively held her arm in front of Rome.

A crazed voice followed the gunshot. "Drop your gun! Drop it now!"

Another voice followed. This one deeper but just as unstable. "You heard him! Do it or the next one's gonna blow a big ole hole in your head!"

69

EMILY poked the straw through the lid into the plastic cup of water and then extended it to Marco's lips. "Here you go."

He arched an eyebrow at her and grabbed it out of her hand. "I'm not an invalid."

"No, but you are touchy," she replied with a smirk.

He set the cup on the table next to the hospital bed. The tiny curled ball under the sheet shifted and made an annoyed chirp.

"And so is he." She looked at the cup in his hand. "Nurse Ratched said you're supposed to drink that."

He lowered the railing on one side of the bed and then threw off the thin hospital sheets. "My bladder's gonna explode if I drink any more without peeing first."

Emily jumped up and circled around the bed to help.

Marco waved her off as he stood. He notably kept one hand on the bed as he tested his balance. "I don't need help."

"I know. I know. You're not an invalid. But you are pretty beat up."

He shrugged. "I'll be fine." He let go of the bed and shuffled toward the bathroom door a dozen paces away. He made it halfway there when the standard issue smock with the split in the back billowed open.

His sculpted butt cheeks peeked through, alternating up and down as he stepped. His muscular thighs rippled.

She looked away, then back again, and tried to suppress the grin bubbling up. "You're uhh... wide open at the back."

He moved through the open bathroom door. "I know. Too sore to reach around to fix it." He stood in front of the toilet and then turned to catch her staring.

She hadn't meant to stare. It obviously wasn't the right thing to do.

"Could you go over by the window or something? I'd prefer to shut the door, but it'd be pitch black and my aim is a little unsteady right now."

Emily hurried over to the window and stared out at the lush green landscaping and the deep blue water beyond. Several cars were in the parking lot to the left. From this angle, everything looked normal.

But things weren't normal.

She couldn't remember the last time things were normal. Not since a giant, invisible lizard nearly killed her. Not since she got dropped off in the wilderness over three weeks ago. Not since her grandmother got diagnosed. Not since her entire life, for that matter.

May you live in interesting times.

Most people thought it was an old Chinese proverb that suggested interesting was better than disinteresting. And that rang true on the face of it. However, the proverb was actually more of an ironic curse because folks in ancient China understood the reality of too much interest.

Pain and suffering were a type of interest. They held the attention like little else. And yet, no one wished such things on others as a blessing.

And by any standard, Emily's soul was like the pocked surface of the moon. It bore the scars of every single meteoric impact.

Marco finished up and shuffled out. "Thanks. I sometimes have a shy bladder." He joined her by the window. "It's gorgeous, isn't it?"

"Yep. But I prefer it from here."

"Yeah. Do you know what that gigantic lizard thing we ran into was?"

Emily nodded. "I think it was a Megalania."

"Never heard of it."

"Not surprising. It's been extinct for forty thousand years."

"What about that beaver thing. What did you call it?"

"Castoroides. It's extinct, too."

"Extinct doesn't seem to mean what it used to. How do you know all this?"

Emily touched the silver heart pendant hanging on a thin chain around her neck. The one her father had given her mother so many years ago. The one she'd inherited after her mother had been shot dead.

She'd had a family once.

A long time ago.

Most times, it left a hollow ache in her chest.

But sometimes, it hurt like it just happened.

"My dad was a paleontologist who specialized in the Pleistocene epoch. When other girls were playing with dolls, I was building dioramas with clay figurines of extinct animals."

"That's seriously nerdy."

"Yeah."

"Did you notice how Mega-whatever shifted colors to match the surroundings? Did you know it could do that?"

Emily shook her head. The memory of how the forest had blurred into huge jaws and teeth made her tremble. "Megalania. And no, the fossil record doesn't show things like that. It looked like some kind of active camouflage. Like how an octopus can instantly shift colors and patterns to match its surroundings."

"Terrifying is what it looked like."

Emily nodded, still trying to think about anything other than how the lizard had snapped off the pilot's arm and then swallowed one of the dead bodies whole.

"So why are these extinct animals suddenly showing up everywhere?"

Emily shook her head as she stared out over the water. "I have no idea."

Marco turned to her and she met his gaze. His eyes went soft as he took her hand and squeezed. "Thank you for saving my life."

"We're even," she said, a little colder than intended.

His face imperceptibly hardened.

She wasn't good with the touchy-feely stuff. Keep it all at a safe distance. As much as possible. It was how she'd survived the curse of such an interesting life.

"And you're welcome," she added with a squeeze in return.

He nodded and they both turned to stare out into the endless blue.

Still hand in hand.

After a moment of silence, his lips popped as he spoke. "Do you think—"

CRACK.

They both flinched at the sharp sound.

Through the closed door of room fifteen, muffled voices screamed. Voices that had a desperate edge to them.

She and Marco stared at each in confusion while Oscar burrowed out of the sheets and then stood motionless, except for his nose sniffing the air.

"That was a gunshot, right?" she said.

"I think so."

They hurried to the door and Emily cracked it open.

Two men in gray hoodies and blue jeans were down the hall behind the nurse's station. Their hoods were up and those Scream Halloween masks covered their faces.

They carried pistols and waved them at the three women on duty. The taller man grabbed the nearest nurse and shoved a gun against her forehead. He screamed and spit pelted her face. "Now! Do it now or you die!"

The woman's eyes were white with terror. She tried to answer but her quaking mouth couldn't form words.

The shorter man yelled. "I know they got Oxycontin! Ricky got prescribed some last week!"

His partner, the taller one with the deeper voice, spun around and punched him in the chest. "You just connected us with him!"

"Sorry, Otis! I didn't mean to!"

The taller man whipped his gun over and smashed the shorter man against the head sending him stumbling. "You just said my name, Junior! My name! Are you high or just a complete idiot?"

The shorter man recovered his balance and held his head with his free hand. "Owww! Don't hit me! Mama said you can't hit me no more!"

"Drop your weapons!"

In the hall beyond the station, an officer appeared. Local

police because his uniform was the same as Chief Stuckey's. He had his pistol zeroed on the two would-be robbers.

They both raised their guns and fired at the officer.

The shorter man got hit in the chest. He spun around and crumpled to the floor. Blood geysered out of his chest splattering the wall.

The officer must've gotten hit because he staggered back and then fell through a doorway.

The taller man faced his partner and ripped off his mask. "Oh God!"

The shorter man held his chest as it turned glistening crimson. He opened his mouth to speak, but all that came out was bubbling blood. He reached up with one blood-soaked shaking hand.

"I'm sorry, Junior!" The taller man whirled around and the three nurses all ducked behind the counter. "You take care of him! You hear me!"

The head of the officer leaned out and his weapon followed. He slumped down along the doorframe as he fired.

CRACK. CRACK.

The man jumped and sprinted down the hall toward Emily and Marco.

Emily quickly eased the door shut and they both stepped to the side. She kept both hands on the handle, holding on as tight as she could.

The pounding got louder and then receded as the man ran by and headed for the exit.

They waited another minute to be sure he was gone and then stepped out into the hallway.

A woman walked out of the room next door. She turned and Emily recognized her at once.

"Flo!"

"Emily and Marco?"

70

The clouds in the sky burned with an incandescent orange. The sun had to be close to the opposite horizon but the large windows in room fourteen only offered a view to the east.

A stunning view though.

A view that would sell a postcard in a gift shop.

A view Emily would never forget.

But it was only part of the picture.

The rest of the world waited beyond the rectangular metal frame.

After the crazed rampage earlier that day, they'd all been instructed to stay put until Chief Stuckey or another officer arrived to take statements. That had been hours ago and the chief had finally arrived five minutes ago. He was talking with Flo in a nearby room.

Presumably getting her perspective of what happened. He'd already told the rest of them not to speak further about it until he had a chance to have one-on-one interviews.

Emily admired his adherence to proper protocol on the one hand, but the other hand held a big bag full of WTFs.

As in, WTF? The idiots said each other's names. As in, WTF? The nurses already knew the men were two of the three McClendon brothers. Now, two brothers.

How did Emily know?

Because they'd told her and presumably told the same thing to the chief.

As in, WTF? She didn't feel like answering questions when she had so many of her own.

Speaking of getting some answers, she turned to Marco who was back in his hospital bed, staring at the same sunset. "I'm going to talk to Bob."

Marco twisted his lips to the side. "Nurse Ratched already told you to leave him alone."

Emily smiled. He had a point. That lady did not take kindly to not following her instructions.

"Can you believe he tried to off himself?"

Emily shrugged. "At this point, I'm open to believing just about anything. And I'm sick of waiting for answers." She started for the door.

"Hold your horses," Marco said. He groaned and pushed up out of bed. "I'm going with you." He curled the sheets around the sleeping weasel and then turned to join her.

"Didn't Nurse Ratched warn you about getting up for anything other than a bathroom break?"

"She did. But she's too busy to notice now that the police are here."

Emily cracked open the door and peeked down the hall toward the nurse's station.

An officer was kneeling next to the body of the man that had been shot and subsequently bled out. A part of Emily wondered whether his death had been unavoidable or if the medical attention he'd needed from the people he'd threatened to kill perhaps wasn't delivered with the usual enthusiasm and speed.

A bigger part of her didn't care.

Another officer stood behind the counter talking to the nurse that inspired both respect and a little fear in everyone she came across. Another couple of officers were walking over the crime scene and doing whatever it was that homicide detectives did.

The violence from earlier played across her eyes and the scene beyond. Like two images blurring through each other. The man's blood splattering on the white wall and pooling on the floor.

A mural of his dying breath.

Emily blinked to clear the memory. She'd seen too much death. Too much her entire life. Sure, the ones from long ago faded as time passed. But they never went away. No. Suffering wasn't like that.

It was a physical wound that scarred over but always ached when you gave it the least bit of attention.

"Go," Marco whispered, "quick!"

They both hurried out and barged into the room next door. Emily swept it shut behind them and turned to see Flo's son, Rome, sitting in a chair facing the bed.

She did a double take as she noticed what his hands were doing.

He had both elbows resting on the arms of the chair and both hands curled into fists with the middle fingers extended.

Bob lay in the bed and his eyes met hers as she glanced over. "Rome thinks his mother should've let me die."

"That's right."

Emily and Marco hadn't gotten the backstory as to how Bob and the other two ended up together here at the hospital, aside from him trying to commit suicide. They hadn't gotten much information whatsoever, for that matter.

But clearly they were missing something big.

And whatever it was, it wasn't her problem.

She had enough problems already. Too many to go looking to take on more.

Rome could flip off Bob until his hands cramped and his fingernails turned blue.

Whatever.

Bob looked at Marco with appraising eyes. "Shouldn't you be lying down?"

"I'll live."

Emily stepped beside the bed. "I need answers and, so far, nobody has had time to give them. I need them now."

Bob nodded. "Okay. Ask away."

"What was that four days ago?"

Rome jumped in. "It was an EMP. Definitely. Anyone with half a brain knows."

Bob cut back in, as if correcting a willful student. "He means to say that while there has been no official word, it does appear that our country has been attacked with an EMP nuclear device."

Another voice continued from the doorway behind.

Emily hadn't heard the door open.

"It's official. We've confirmed it over shortwave radio." Chief Stuckey gestured Flo to enter and then followed her into the room. He glanced at Rome's flying birds but didn't say anything.

Flo walked over and pushed her son's hands down into his lap. "Please," she whispered. She circled around to the back of his chair and cast an equally baleful glare at Bob.

With his hands in his lap, Rome resumed flipping Bob off.

Grounded birds.

But flying nonetheless.

"We've got another town meeting scheduled for tomorrow at noon. Folks need to know what we're facing here."

Flo slipped her hands over her son's shoulders. "What are we facing?"

The chief bit his lip and stared at his mud-caked black boots. He looked up and at each of them in turn, measuring each against what he was about to say. "I'm not gonna lie to you. It's bad. From the information we've gathered so far, I think it's fair to say that World War III has arrived."

Silence.

What could anyone say to that?

Or maybe, what was the first thing to say?

"Who attacked us?" Marco said.

"They think it was the Chinese. Nothing one hundred percent confirmed yet, but it appears they hit us with high altitude nuclear EMP strikes across the country and ground level strikes in several major cities."

"Jesus," Bob said. "Did we return fire?"

"Yes, but to what extent hasn't been verified yet. There isn't much communication coming from the feds at this point. Some chatter from a few shortwave operators around the country, but it's hard to know what to believe."

Grammy!

The realization pierced Emily's chest like a dagger.

Was she alive?

Had Oakland or the Bay area been hit?

And then another thought struck her.

This time like a spear thrown by Goliath.

The agony made the room swim and tilt.

Emily lurched for Marco's hand to keep from falling down.

He took it and held her steady.

Emily stared into his face and saw the same question in his eyes.

Even if home still existed, how were they going to get there?

71

DR. GANESH squeezed the spray bottle, gently misting the precious orchid. Spherical droplets beaded on the pale green leaves. Some stayed put while others broke free and ran in tiny rivulets down to the tips where they dripped off in a sprinkling of wasted opportunity.

Would it ever bloom again?

There was a chance it would.

Not like so many other orchids in the world. They would wilt and die after global weather patterns eventually distributed radioactive fallout over the entire planet.

It was such a delicate creature.

The plant and the planet.

And humanity had finally fallen into the abyss created by its own ambition.

Four days after what they now knew had been the beginning and end of World War III, and Hari still hadn't decided what to do next. The sleepless nights didn't help his lack of clarity. The complex had been on lock down since before the latest collider test and, by his order, it remained so.

No one in and no one out.

Tensions around the facility were growing and the custodian Bert had told him yesterday that there was talk among the staff that their director was no longer fit to lead. That maybe someone else should forcibly assume command.

Hari didn't disagree.

But what was he supposed to do?

He'd never been trained for this. None of the manuals included what to do in the event of a global nuclear holocaust. From what the communications team had gathered, the simmering tensions between the United States and China had finally boiled over. The conflict had gone nuclear.

There was no confirmation of who had fired first.

Not that it mattered.

Numerous high altitude strikes over the continental United States had released massive electromagnetic pulses which had devastated the nation's electrical infrastructure. One of those strikes had caused the malfunction in the collider test.

Though where exactly the extra nine hundred plus tera-electron volts of power came from, they still didn't know. Not only did they not know where the power was coming from, they still didn't know how to shut it off.

And that wasn't the worst news.

There were reports on shortwave frequencies that numerous cities had been hit with ground level strikes. If they were true, Washington DC, New York City, San Francisco, Los Angeles, Chicago and several other major urban cities were now craters of smoking ruin. Tens of millions vaporized, turned to ash in an instant. Tens of millions more burned and poisoned with radiation. The death toll would only climb in the coming days and weeks.

And China must've gotten hit even harder from our side. Beijing, Shanghai, and other population centers were likely rubble where not a single soul survived.

How did humanity let it come to this?

Was there any hope of surviving such devastation?

Hari's mobile buzzed in his pocket. "Yes?"

"Dr. Ganesh, we have a small bit of good news."

Good news?

What could possibly qualify as that?

"As you directed, we've continued adjusting the ring's targeting coils in an attempt to tweak the quantum signatures of the remaining time gates. As you know, we've had no success."

How was more failure considered good news?

"Well, that may have changed."

"What do you mean?"

"The nearest time gate is topside less than two hundred yards from the emergency back entrance. It's showing a shifting signature."

"Is it controlled?"

"It appears to be."

Dr. Ganesh dropped the water bottle and hurried down the path toward the distant elevators. "Does it match TG1?"

"Not yet, but it's getting closer. And there is another thing."

"Yes?"

"It appears shifting the signature has destabilized the quantum entanglement. We're reading increasing stochastic variance. If it continues like this, the gate will collapse."

The ache in Hari's knees and back vanished as he jogged through the vast gardens. "Get an excursion team together! Security, medical and diagnostics. I'll meet them at the blast doors in twenty minutes!"

"Are you certain that would be wise?"

"Do it! Now!"

72

The six ton blast doors swung open without a creak. In perfect operating condition. Hari appreciated the attention to detail. The emergency exit was never normally used. It was simply insurance that the facility wouldn't become an inescapable tomb in the event the main entrance blast doors experienced catastrophic failure.

The doors opened to reveal the carved out interior of a narrow corridor. Having travelled through it a few times over the years, he knew that the right sequence and direction of turns would lead to a cave that exited onto a wide valley.

He also knew that the original builders had encountered numerous natural fissures and they hadn't taken the time to adequately seal all of them. And so getting lost in the dark would've been more likely than not for anyone who didn't know the way.

"Ferguson, take point," Sergeant Yamada said as he chopped his free hand toward the front.

"On it, Sarge," Ferguson said as he hustled into the dimly lit passage. White-blue lights in the carved roof illuminated the space to a degree, but their wide spacing and relatively small size kept everything in as much light as shadow.

"Gonzales, you're on our six."

"Copy that," another soldier said as he shifted behind the small group exiting into the corridor. Two medical doctors carried white cases with red crosses on them. Three diagnostics techs carried shiny metal cases full of sensors and other gear. The sergeant and two soldiers all carrying military rifles set the pace.

"We have to hurry!" Dr. Ganesh said as he nipped at the heels of the soldier in front.

"Dr. Ganesh, the topside sensor array in this quadrant is mostly cooked," Yamada said. "We have no idea what's in here or what's out there. We move quickly, but safely."

It took every ounce of Hari's immense willpower to keep from shoving the lead soldier aside and taking off without the rest of the group. His next inclination was to remind the sergeant who was director of the project and who was its head of security. But he opted for diplomacy. There wasn't time for a peeing contest or battle of wills. "Sergeant Yamada, if we don't get there in time, then this potentially dangerous excursion will have had no purpose and no point. Let's ensure the risk is worth the effort."

Yamada nodded. "Understood. Ferguson, double time. Everyone, keep up! Gonzales, anyone lags and you'll answer to me!"

"Affirmative, Sarge!"

The lead soldier picked up the pace and the rest of the team followed suit. The sound of heavy breathing and out of shape intellectuals echoed through the cramped corridor.

They followed the path of lights, passing by numerous dark fissures that led who knew where. Eventually, the ambient light started to get brighter and warmer. They made another turn and entered a wide cave.

The orange glow of the sunset outside spilled into the space. A low valley carpeted in deep green stretched into the distance.

"Hold here a second and stay sharp!" Yamada shouted as they arrived at the mouth of the cave. He and Ferguson scanned the land for threats. Their rifles followed their eyes.

"There it is!" Ferguson shouted.

Dr. Ganesh followed his pointed hand and saw it.

Two hundred yards away and lower down in the valley. Like water rippling in the air. A kaleidoscope of shifting colors. Double the size of any of the time gates they'd created in previous tests.

"Let's go! Let's go!" Dr. Ganesh yelled as he pushed Yamada in the back.

The sergeant flashed an irritated look and then complied. "Keep it tight! That means you, Gonzales!"

"Stuck on your backside like a wad of used toilet paper, Sarge!"

The phone in Hari's pocket buzzed. He fished it out as they jogged toward the gate. "What?" His breath came in short, quick gulps.

"Dr. Ganesh, the gate's signature is showing a perfect match to TG1!"

Yes!

Zhang was within reach!

"But it's also showing increasing instability. The variance is already well beyond acceptable parameters. It could collapse at any second."

No. No. No!

He couldn't let this happen!

"Faster!" Hari shouted as adrenaline sizzled in his veins.

The whole group picked up the pace and they soon arrived at the shimmering gate.

A chill wind blasted out, whipping snowflakes through the air in curling gusts. One landed on his forehead and the warm skin melted it. A large snow drift spilled out in an arc of white covering the green grass.

Hari peered into the rippling window.

73

A wide valley with towering mountains beyond. A massive glacier filled much of the valley. In the center, a deep crevasse of white-blue ice sparkled like diamonds under a bright sun. The impossible portrait had an electric quality to it. Iridescent currents raced through the undulating surface. A patch several feet above Hari's head crackled and vanished.

The glowing orange sunset showed through.

"The gate is collapsing!" one of the diagnostic techs shouted. "No one touch it!"

Hari sucked in a deep breath. His heart hammered in his head.

He hadn't come so far to stop here.

He stepped forward and extended a hand.

His fingertips disappeared into the curtain. An electric current buzzed in his hand. Strange, but not unpleasant. The sensation inched up his arm as he pushed through.

Fear fought to throw him back. An almost physical force resisting his progress.

With a final push, Hari plunged forward and the gate

swallowed him. He gasped as the tingling shot through him like being struck by lightning. It was almost painful, but not quite.

The wind shifted bringing a new scent. Sharp and heavy. Smoke.

He turned and saw a faint trail of smoke rising behind a small snow-covered hill to the right.

And then his heart almost stopped in his chest.

There!

Walking toward the smoke!

Zhang!

Trudging through the deep snow with his lab coat pulled tightly around him.

"Zhang!" Hari shouted, but the distance and the howling wind drowned him out.

Something crackled behind him and he spun around to see another patch in the electric fabric vanish, showing the snow-covered field beyond.

They had no time!

He took off toward Zhang, fighting forward as the snow swallowed each step to his knees.

Zhang stopped on a ridge, staring down at something.

Ten years of heartache and guilt drove Hari like lashes to his flanks. He staggered on, closing the distance between them.

As he drew nearer, he noticed a man coming up the ridge from the other side. A man, but different. He wore layers of tattered animal skins. His face was so dirty and beard so unkempt that it was hard to see where he ended and the skins began. He carried an enormous branch with a crackling fire burning at the end.

"Zhang!" Hari shouted again.

Zhang turned and his eyes opened wide with surprise.

Hari couldn't believe it. He looked just like he did all those years ago. Bleeding and hurt. But Zhang. Like ten seconds had passed, not ten years.

"Come! Now! The time gate is collapsing!"

Zhang must've heard because he forgot about the strange man less than a dozen feet in front of him and spun around. He lurched back through the snow toward Hari.

Hari continued forward as it was obvious that Zhang was injured and the depth of the snow was making his progress too slow.

A minute later, Hari grabbed his arm and pulled it over his shoulder.

Zhang looked dazed.

Tears welled in Hari's eyes as he touched a face he thought he'd never see again.

A face that he'd sentenced to death years ago, and yet minutes ago for Zhang, and yet again thousands of years ago in time.

Hari touched their foreheads together as his tears spilled onto Zhang's face. "I'm so sorry. I sent you in to copy the project files. The world deserved to see our work. It's my fault you're here. I'm so sorry."

A deep growl made the hairs on the back of Hari's neck stand on end.

He turned around and his knees went weak.

A bear larger than any he'd ever seen stood on its hind legs not forty feet away. It towered above them at over twice their height. Its paws were the size of car tires.

Hari squeezed Zhang's shoulder. "I love you. You are the son I never had. My son." He shoved Zhang to the side, toward the fading gate in the distance. "Go! Run! The world needs you! Now more than ever!"

Zhang stared at him in confusion.

To Zhang, he would've looked ten years older. More from the added wear of stress and guilt.

"Run!" Hari shouted and his breath billowed into a cloud around Zhang's head.

"I love you, my father," Zhang said and then left.

Hari turned to the bear and watched in horror as its head tracked Zhang's movement.

Hari screamed and ran straight at it.

The bear turned its attention back to Hari. It paused as if confused by such a small animal charging it. The confusion didn't last. It dropped to all fours and broke into a loping trot.

It slammed into Hari like a train, knocking him head over heels backwards into the snow.

Hari lifted his head as pain engulfed his body.

The bear appeared above him. It roared and its breath stank of blood and carnage. Huge teeth larger than his fingers hovered several feet above.

Hari looked to the side and saw Zhang at the collapsing gate.

It was already much smaller than minutes before. The perimeter a patchwork of remnant rainbows.

Zhang looked back and their eyes met.

"Go!" Hari shouted as Zhang disappeared through the gate.

The electric fabric dissolved and the snow and land beyond was all that remained.

Hari closed his eyes. "Thank you, Brahma, Vishnu, Shiva."

The beast lunged at him and tore out his throat with a single bite.

Hari's warm blood splattered onto the white snow.

A weak smile creased his face.

His last thought was one of optimism.

Not for himself.

But for mankind.

Zhang would understand. He would show them.

The time gates were our last hope.

Our sole refuge.

THE END OF BOOK 1

Sole Chaos, book 2 in the *Extinction Crisis* series, is coming soon!

Turn the page for a preview of *The Last Day*, book 1 in the *Edge of Survival* series. Preview only available for ebook format.

WANT BOOKS FOR FREE?

Join the Readers Group to get a free copy of The Last Day, Sole Prey, and The Plunge. One novel, one novella and one short story, all for free. You'll also receive exclusive discounts on new releases, other freebies, and lots more.

Go to WWW.WILLIAMODAY.COM to find out more.

OTHER WORKS

Extinction Crisis series
SOLE CONNECTION, a Short Story
SOLE PREY, a Prequel Novella
SOLE SURVIVOR, Book 1
SOLE CHAOS, Book 2
THE TANK MAN, a Short Story
THE PLUNGE, a Short Story

Edge of Survival series
THE LAST DAY, Book 1
THE FINAL COLLAPSE, Book 2
THE FRAGILE HOPE, Book 3
THE DESPERATE FIGHT, Book 4

The Best Adventures series
THE SLITHERING GOLIATH
THE BEEPOCALYPSE
THE PHARAOH'S CURSE

Short Stories
THE GENDER LOTTERY
SAINT JOHN
SHE'S GONE

QUESTIONS OR COMMENTS?

Have any questions or comments? I'd love to hear from you! Seriously. Voices coming from outside my head are such a relief.

Give me a shout at william@williamoday.com.

All the best,
Will

THE GOAL

I have a simple storytelling goal that can be wildly difficult to achieve. I want to entertain you with little black marks arranged on a white background. Read the marks and join me on a grand adventure. If all goes well, you'll slip under the spell and so walk alongside heroes and villains. You'll feel what they feel. You'll understand the world as they do.

My writing and your reading is a kind of mechanical telepathy. I translate my thoughts and emotions through characters and conflict in a written story. If the transmission works, your heart will pound, your heart will break, and you will care. At the very least, hopefully you'll escape your world and live in mine for a little while.

I hope to see you there!
Will

MY LIFE THUS FAR

I grew up in the red dirt of the Midwest, the center of the states. I later meandered out to the West Coast and have remained off-center ever since. Living in Los Angeles, I achieved my Career 1.0 dream by working on big-budget movies for over a decade. If you've seen a Will Smith or Tom Cruise blockbuster action movie, you've likely seen my work.

The work was challenging and fulfilling... until I got tired of telling other people's stories. I longed to tell my own. So, now I'm pursuing my Career 2.0 dream—a dream I've had since youth—to write stories that pull a reader in and make the everyday world fade away.

I've since moved to a more rural setting north of San Francisco with my lovely wife, vibrant children, and a dog that has discovered the secret to infinite energy. His name is Trip and he fits the name in four unique ways.

WILLIAMODAY.COM

Printed in Great Britain
by Amazon

72319870R00241